Praise for *In Another Time*

"*In Another Time* returns readers to the place for which Jillian Cantor is known and adored: the heroism and heartbreak of the Second World War. . . . With her bracing prose and unflinching eye, Cantor catches us up in the sweep of history and reminds us of the interminable power of the human bond and the moments that can last a lifetime."

—Pam Jenoff, *New York Times* bestselling author of *The Orphan's Tale*

"Jillian Cantor's *In Another Time* is a love song to the most powerful of all human emotions: hope. It is the story of Max and Hanna, two star-crossed lovers fighting to stay together during an impossible moment in history. It is gripping, mysterious, romantic, and altogether unique. I was enchanted by this beautiful, heartbreaking novel."

—Ariel Lawhon, author of *I Was Anastasia*

"*In Another Time* is a stunning testament to the power of books, music, and love, and how they can endure, and ultimately prevail, during calamitous times."

—Fiona Davis, national bestselling author of *The Masterpiece*

"*In Another Time* is a spellbinding story about the power of love and the strength of the human spirit. . . . A stunning, transporting novel."

—Chanel Cleeton, author of *Next Year in Havana*

"*In Another Time* is a beautifully written, utterly romantic story about a love that transcends time. The sort of book you wish could never end."

—*PopSugar*

"Cantor elevates love as a powerful force . . . and shows how music speaks to even the cruelest hearts. [*In Another Time* is] a powerful story that exalts the strength of the human spirit."

—*Kirkus Reviews*

Praise for *The Lost Letter*

"A total page-turner."   —*New York Magazine*

"[A]t the center of the novel are two beautiful love stories involving two seemingly star-crossed couples, whose love overcomes all obstacles. . . . Getting it right is an art, and Cantor is an artist. She got me from that first page, and I stayed hooked throughout. It's not just that Cantor kept me interested—she got me involved emotionally with the story."   —*Jerusalem Post*

Praise for *Margot*

"Inventive. . . . Cantor's what-if story combines historical fiction with mounting suspense and romance, but above all, it is an ode to the adoration and competition between sisters."

—*O, the Oprah Magazine*

"A convincing, engaging might-have-been. Francophiles will want to dig in."   —*People*

"Intriguing . . . with compelling sensitivity."   —*USA Today*

"A page-turner. . . . A wishful, thought-provoking love story."

—*Bust* magazine

"A thoughtful speculation about postwar life."

—*Kansas City Star*

"If *Huffington Post* Books gave a star rating system for books, *Margot* deserves five bold stars." —*HuffPost*

Praise for *The Hours Count*

"[A] down-to-the-wire thriller." —*New York Times Book Review*

"We kind of love historical novels, and Cantor's is quickly climbing to the top of our all-time faves list. . . . You won't be able to put it down." —*Glamour*

"Cantor mixes fact with fiction to create a moving portrait of two of the most vilified figures in modern history." —*Cosmopolitan*

Half Life

HALF
LIFE

A Novel

JILLIAN CANTOR

HARPER

An Imprint of HarperCollinsPublishers

HARPER ● PERENNIAL

HarperCollins books may be purchased for educational, business, or sales promotional use. For information, please email the Special Markets Department at SPsales@harpercollins.com.

P.S.™ is a registered trademark of HarperCollins Publishers.

Designed by Jamie Lynn Kerner
Title page image © Lamio/stock.adobe.com

FIRST EDITION

Library of Congress Cataloging-in-Publication Data has been applied for.

ISBN 978-0-06-296988-0 (pbk.)
ISBN 978-0-06-296987-3 (library edition)

21 22 23 24 25   LSC   10 9 8 7 6 5 4 3 2 1

For Gregg, my love in any timeline

She died   a famous woman   denying
her wounds
denying
her wounds   came   from the same source as her power

—ADRIENNE RICH

MARIE

⚜

France, 1934

In the end, my world is dark. My bones are tired, my marrow failing. I have given my whole life to my work, but now, science brings me no comfort.

My two Nobel medals aren't here, keeping me warm, holding my hand. My *Petites Curies* cannot drive me into a heaven that I do not even believe exists, nor fix my bones the way I used them to help fix soldiers in the war. I can no longer really make out the glow of the radium tube on my nightstand. I know it is here, but that does not make me feel better. My eyesight has failed me enough that everything is almost blackness.

I am sixty-six years old, and I convalesce, my bones no longer able to carry the weight of me out of this bed. Nearly all day I sleep, but still I dream. Pierre comes back to me most of all, though it has been so long since I've seen him. And yet, when I close my eyes it could still be yesterday, and all the pain catches in my chest, and I stop breathing for a moment. Then I awaken, and I start again. I am not dead just yet.

Ève is here, though. She calls my name out in the darkness.

Maman, is there anything you need?

I can see the shape of her when I open my eyes again, more a shadow than my youngest daughter. *The girl with the radium eyes.* I wish I'd learned to understand her piano music more when I'd had the chance. *There is more than science,* I want to tell her now. *Play all the concert halls you dream of, find a man who is your equal and love each other.* But the words don't quite come out.

Of course, I will play you a song, she says.

Maybe that is what I have asked of her instead. Because then there is the tinkling of piano keys, like raindrops on the metal roof of our laboratory that last morning with Pierre.

So much has happened since then; it is strange to be thinking about that rainy day again, that moment, now. I do not believe in the afterlife, or in God. I do not believe that Pierre will be waiting for me, somewhere, after all of this. My body, my bones, will be interred in the ground, and eventually turn to dust. And what will any of that matter anyway, once my heart stops, my brain deprived of oxygen, my mind completely gone? My mind. *That* is who I am, and who I was. Irène and Fred will carry on my work at the Institute, and everything I have done will not be lost. That should be enough now. I know that it should. But somehow it is not; my mind is still craving one last scientific problem, one more quandary before I go.

MAMAN. ÈVE'S VOICE AGAIN.

Hours have passed, or maybe just minutes? Or has it been days? My beautiful daughter, she is a shadow, hovering again. No, there are two shadows now. I wish for the second one to be Irène, my eldest daughter, my heart, my companion, my confidante. But the shadow is much too large, much taller than Ève.

Someone came to see you, Ève says. *He says you were friends long ago, back in Poland.*

He?

The shape becomes a memory, and my sense of smell has not left me yet. I inhale: peppermint and pipe smoke. And then the icy river in Szczuki; the pine cones and fir trees lining the road where we walked together.

Marya, he says my given name now, a shock after some forty years of being called Marie. Or maybe I am remembering it the way he said my name back then, when he asked me to marry him, once, by the river.

We were so young then, we had nothing but the way we felt about each other. Until we didn't even have that and I left Szczuki heartbroken. Kazimierz Zorawski is from another life.

Marya, he says again now. He must've sat down in a chair by my bed, because when I open my eyes again, his shadow is smaller, closer to me. I feel the weight of a hand on mine, and I know. I just know. It is *his* hand, and it still feels the same after all these years, all this time. I am twenty-two again, skating on the river, dizzy and laughing. Which is ridiculous, scientifically impossible. My bones are nearly dust. I cannot move out of this bed.

Why are you here? I think I say. Or maybe I don't say anything at all.

The biggest mistake of my life, Kazimierz says, *was ever letting you go. I should've married you.*

But is it the biggest mistake of mine? What would a life with Kazimierz have been like? How different would everything have been?

I close my eyes, and I imagine it.

MARYA

⚜

Poland, 1891

I packed my things in such a haste, barely even seeing my clothing through my haze of tears and anger. My valise lay open on my bed, and I pulled what little I owned from the corner chest, stuffing it inside, wiping away at the tears on my cheeks with the backs of my hands. It didn't matter that my dresses would wrinkle. They were threadbare, and anyway, who would see them now except for Papa and Hela when I returned to them in Warsaw? *Penniless. Worthless.* Abandoned.

That was the feeling that hurt most, sent a physical pain shooting into my stomach. Mama and Zofia had already abandoned me years earlier, but not by choice, by getting sick and dying. And though I was so very sad that I'd become listless then, I was not angry, too, the way I was now. Kazimierz was not dying. He was very much alive, and he claimed he loved me. I *knew* he loved me. And yet he had left me anyway.

It is not my choice, you see, Marya, he had said to me hours earlier. *My parents will not allow us to marry.* We had walked along the path toward the river, away from his parents' manor house in Szczuki, my younger charges, his younger siblings, taking their afternoon rests. Kazimierz held on to my hand, the way he always did when we walked together in the afternoons, but now that he was delivering terrible news, terrible words I did not want to hear, he gripped me tightly. My wrist began to ache, and I pulled out of his grasp. *I have no choice*, he said again, when I pulled away. *Marya, please.*

"You have a choice," I'd told him. "There is always a choice." That very idea was what had gotten me through months and months of being a governess for the Zorawskis before Kazimierz had arrived. I did not want to care for children. I did not even enjoy them the way my sister Hela did. My mind ached to learn. I'd dedicated every evening to self-study since I'd been in Szczuki, and though I'd arrived here equally enamored with literature, sociology, and science, in the past few years I'd decided that science was what I wanted to study at university. But to do so I would need to earn enough money to move out of Russian Poland, where women were not allowed to be or do anything of import, and most definitely not allowed to attend university.

I had planned to move to Paris to be with my older sister, Bronia, before I'd fallen in love with Kazimierz. We'd even had a deal, Bronia and I—I would work and send her money while she earned her medical degree, and then I would move to Paris, and she would work as a doctor and help put me through university. I had made my own choice: act as a governess for just a few years until I could afford to do what I really wanted. Here Kazimierz was, *a man*, and an intelligent one at that, and he was claiming *he had no choice.*

"What would you have me do, Marya?" he'd asked me, grabbing my hand again, lowering to his knees as if he were begging me to understand him, to forgive him, which, of course, I wouldn't. "If I disobey my parents they would disown me, and then . . ."

"And then, what?" I'd snapped, pulling away again. "We would be penniless together? Or, what is it you said your mother said about me, I am *worthless*? I'll never amount to anything?"

"I do love you," he'd said softly.

"Do you?" I'd asked him, and then when he didn't say anything else, I'd turned and run back to the house alone.

I'd spent the rest of the afternoon crying in my bed, not even bothering to tend to the children when they woke from their naps. How could I continue to be their governess now, knowing what Pani Zorawska truly thought of me? Now knowing that Kazimierz agreed with her, that he and I could not be together.

I threw everything into my valise, and after the house grew dark, the night quiet, I snuck out without so much as even a goodbye to my employers. I put my bag on my shoulder and walked into town to hire a carriage to drive me through the beet sugar plantations that seemed to stretch for an eternity—it was a five-hour carriage ride to the closest train station. But I would use all the rubles I had left to pay the carriage man, then the train back to Warsaw, back to Papa and Hela. And I would arrive home, truly penniless.

BACK IN WARSAW, I STAYED IN BED, AND WHAT MUST PAPA and Hela have thought? *Poor Marya, too thin, too fragile, and destined to be unloved forever.* Hela was my closest sister in age— she was just one year older than me, and I had always been so advanced in school that we'd been placed in the same grade at the female gymnasium as girls. We had been something like twins, and she was the one I'd written to about Kazimierz the past few years. I'd even told her the secret I'd told no one else, that we'd been engaged. But all I would tell her when I first returned home was that it was over, and that I did not wish to talk about it.

"Marya," Hela called for me through my bedroom door, her voice so high and sweet like a songbird. I wanted to go to her, to hold on to her, the way I had as a young girl when our oldest sister, Zofia, had died. But the absence of Kazimierz was a heaviness in my chest, and I could not move. I pretended to be asleep, turning on my side, and squeezing my eyes tightly shut.

Hela opened the door, called my name again into the darkness. I didn't answer her, or move. "You're not the only one," she finally said, before giving up, shutting the door behind her.

And part of me wanted to ask her what she meant; the other part of me wanted to sleep forever.

One afternoon, a few weeks after returning to Warsaw, Papa knocked on my bedroom door, and unlike Hela, he walked right in, without waiting for my answer. "It's time to get up, get ready," he said.

My mind felt dull, my body listless. I was weak from hunger, or disappointment, but I had no desire to get up and eat or live my life. "I have nothing to get ready for," I moaned. Eventually, I supposed I would have to get out of bed and try to secure another governess position, but I could not face that prospect yet. Bronia was just about finished with her degree, and she said I could move in with her and her new husband in Paris, but I would need enough money to register for classes and pay my fees, and I had nothing to my name. *Penniless.*

"You are leaving for Paris soon," Papa said, brightly. He

walked to my window and threw open the curtains. "There is much to be done."

"Paris?" I sat up in my bed, squinting my eyes to adjust to the sunlight streaming in. "I cannot afford Paris yet. I quit the Zorawskis, remember?"

"I have some money saved that will help cover your first year of tuition at the Sorbonne. You can begin classes in November."

"But Papa . . . I can't let you do that. You can't possibly have enough money for that."

The Sorbonne. Even the very idea of it felt like a confection for my mind, and my body hummed, alive again, in a way it hadn't since I'd left Kazimierz in the woods, weeks earlier.

"Helena and I will get by. You need to go and get your university education," Papa said. "You are brilliant, Marya. And you have worked so hard, for so many years. You deserve this."

Who was right—Papa or Pani Zorawska? Was I brilliant or worthless? But Papa was going to help me get to Paris. That was enough to get me out of bed.

I stood up and kissed his cheek. "Thank you," I said to him.

He embraced me, kissed the top of my head. "You will thank me by earning your degree at the Sorbonne."

That night I did not dream about Kazimierz or the way his kisses had left the feel of sunshine upon my skin as we'd traversed the woods, hand in hand. Instead I dreamed about the beautiful laboratories that surely awaited me now. The fantasy lingered in my mind in the moments after waking the next morning, leaving a sweetness in my mouth like I'd just eaten a *kolachke*, the jam still on my tongue. Paris was waiting for me, only two train rides away now: everything I'd ever wanted.

Well, almost everything.

THE MORNING I WAS TO LEAVE, PAPA OFFERED TO WALK WITH me to the train station to help me with my things. Hela hugged me goodbye at our apartment door, saying it would be too hard, too emotional to say goodbye at the train. She was right. I already felt teary-eyed as Papa and I walked the short distance, mostly in silence.

I was not bringing much, and did not truly need Papa's help, but I was glad for his quiet company all the same. I had only a folding chair to sit on—my fourth-class ticket did not come with a seat—and one suitcase of belongings. My suitcase was heavy, as it contained more books for the long ride than clothing. I only owned a few dresses, and I had sent the rest of my things ahead by freight.

"You take care of yourself," Papa was saying now. "And remember to eat." Papa was always saying I was too thin, and truth be told I did have a habit of forgetting food when my mind was otherwise engaged. Whether it was Kazimierz or my studies.

"Don't worry, Papa. Bronia will keep me fed." If Hela was my sister-twin, Bronia was my sister-mother. She was the oldest, and most responsible, and when we were younger, after our mother died, she was the one who'd stepped into the mothering role in our household. Even all these years later, even living so far away, her worry for me and Hela came through in her letters.

"And you have all your papers in order?" Papa asked, though he had already asked before we'd left the apartment. He was nervous about the Russian officers examining me too closely on the checkpoints out of Poland, a woman traveling alone and with the *Sklodowska* last name. Years ago, before I was born, Papa had been involved in the January uprising against the Russian army—it was how we'd lost our family's money and property and become poor in the first place. But in the years since, the Russians had many others to worry about. The Sklodowskis kept out of their way. And Bronia had traveled this route herself several times with no trouble.

"You know I do, Papa," I reassured him. "You worry too much."

"I can't help it. I worry because I love you, my dear sweet Marya," he said as we arrived at the station.

We both stopped walking, and I grabbed Papa in a tight embrace. I couldn't hold back tears any longer, and for just a moment, I buried my wet cheek into the stale wool of his jacket. I'd already been away from him and Hela for years in Szczuki, but this felt different. Paris was so far—forty hours by train. And Papa was placing all his money, all his trust, in me to succeed at the Sorbonne, something we'd long thought out of reach for me, growing up both poor and female in Warsaw.

In the distance, we could hear the whistle of the train approaching. I let go of the embrace, picked up my things, and stepped closer to the tracks. The city of Warsaw, majestic and gray and stifling, would be behind me now. And suddenly, I felt lighter, dizzy with excitement at what lay ahead of me.

As the train pulled into the station, I thought I heard my name in the distance, from somewhere across the street. I ignored it, sure I was imagining it, because it sounded just like Kazimierz's voice.

But then I heard it again: "Marya, wait!"

I turned around, and there he was, running across the street, waving his arms. Kazimierz was tall and lovely, with a long face and deep-brown brooding eyes. Now he was red-faced, and sweating, out of breath from running. The fall air was crisp, and it suddenly chilled me. All of my skin turned to ice. My own voice froze inside my throat, and I could not respond.

Papa turned toward Kazimierz and frowned. "What is happening?" he asked, turning back to me. He knew about Kazimierz, but only in a general way. Kaz was the man who'd broken his daughter's heart, who did not believe she would ever be good enough to marry him.

"What are you doing here?" I put my suitcase down, put my hands on my hips, and demanded an explanation of my own.

He stood in front of me, his breath jagged. "You can't go," he said, glancing behind me at the train, which had begun to board. "Wherever it is you are going, you . . . you can't. Stay here. Stay with me." His voice broke, making him sound desperate in a way I hadn't heard before. My love for him ran through my body, a shiver.

"How did you even find me?" I asked. The question slipped out, but what I truly meant to ask was *why?* Why was he here? His parents disapproved of us; he would never disappoint his parents or risk them disowning him, making him penniless, just like me. That's what he'd told me, wasn't it?

"I went to your apartment first. Helena told me maybe I could still catch you, before it was too late."

"Too late?" I asked.

Papa stepped from behind me and put his hand on Kazimierz's shoulder. "I think it's best you leave." Papa spoke calmly, but forcefully. He was not a menacing man—Kazimierz was several inches taller, but Papa seemed to grow in that moment, and Kazimierz took a step back.

"I love her," he said to Papa now, not me. "I want her to be my wife."

"But your parents," I said.

"I don't care about my parents. There is no one in all of Poland, no, all of the world, as smart and as beautiful as you, Marya. Remember that last afternoon, skating on the river, what you told me?" I had told him that he steadied me, that my entire life had been one giant river of ice before him: I kept falling and falling and falling, being so poor and often prone to bouts of emotional darkness. But holding on to him, I knew I wouldn't fall any longer. "Well, it is the same for me," he was saying now. "I have been falling these last weeks without you."

"Marya is on her way to Paris," Papa said, bringing me back, here.

"Paris," Kazimierz exhaled, and his face fell. He knew about my deal with Bronia, but after we had gotten engaged, we had agreed that I would stay in Poland instead, that I could be his wife and teach at a girls' gymnasium, the way Hela did. I wanted to attend university, but I was not going to upend my life over it if I had love, if I had him, here in Poland.

"You can write letters," Papa was saying now.

Friends wrote each other letters; siblings wrote each other letters. Husbands and wives did not live half a continent apart.

Kazimierz turned back to me, grabbed my hands. Not squeezing them hard, but gently now, and I warmed again at his touch. "Please, Marya. Stay here with me. Marry me. Our love means more to you than university. You said so. And if Paris is really that important to you, we can go there together, someday, after I get my degree here."

I had told him that, too, skating on the ice-covered river in Szczuki: *his love meant more to me than university.* But that was when the Sorbonne still felt so far away, perpetually out of my reach. Now, I wasn't so sure.

I looked from Kaz to Papa. Papa was frowning; Kaz was smiling. His smile was infectious. I could not let go of his hand. I wanted to go to Paris, wanted to continue my studies, but I wanted to be with the man I loved, too.

And then I made a choice.

MARYA

Poland, 1891–1892

You have a choice. There is always a choice.

Kazimierz and I chose each other. We were married a month after that day on the train platform. I became Marya Zorawska at a small church in Warsaw with only Papa and Hela in attendance. His parents disowned him, as they'd promised they would, refused to speak to him, or come to our wedding, or give him any money. But I had never had money, and anyway, what was money when we had love? We had each other, and that was everything.

I worried Papa would be disappointed in me, but at my wedding, the only thing I could detect on his face was joy. *My sweet Marya.* He held on to me and kissed my cheeks after the ceremony. *All I want is for you to be happy.*

I am very happy, I assured him. And I was. I really was. The periods of my life where I had felt sadness weighing me down, darkening my every thought, felt behind me. Being with Kazimierz filled me with an all-consuming sort of joy and contentment that I could never remember feeling in my life before. At least not since Mama had died of tuberculosis when I was ten. Being with him made me feel permanently steady.

Hela told me she envied me, and she admitted that she had been in love with a man in Warsaw when I was in Szczuki. Josef had told her he couldn't marry her because she was poor. *You're not the only one*, she'd said into my darkness.

"You did the right thing," Hela said to me, just after my wedding. And with the reassurance of my sister-twin, I felt even more certain, even happier.

Only Bronia, who could not make it back to Poland for the wedding, expressed her doubts in a letter. *We had an arrangement*, she wrote. *I want you to come to Paris and get your education. I owe you for all the help you gave me in achieving my degree*. Bronia, our sister-mother, always wanted everything to be fair. *And besides, you cannot pass up your chance for an education*.

I wrote her back and told her not to worry about old promises, or owing me anything. I told her I still could come to Paris in time, but there wasn't any rush. Education would be there, whenever we could afford it. And besides, she must understand how I was feeling—she had recently found love herself, married a doctor, also named Kazimierz. Papa now had a running joke that if only we could find a third Kazimierz, Hela would finally be happy, too.

Then Bronia found out she was carrying a child, and it was joyous news, and she had more to worry about than her little sister. Her letters came less frequently, and when they arrived they were filled with details of her condition.

And I did not need her to worry about me anymore. Now I had a husband for that.

WE WERE POOR, BUT WE WOULDN'T BE FOREVER, WE PROMISED each other that. Kazimierz had a brilliant mind for mathematics. He'd almost completed his doctoral studies in analytical geometry, and he was able to secure a teaching position at a secondary school in Loksow, a small city about an hour train ride from Warsaw. He had been accepted into a program at Jagiellonian University in Krakow, to obtain his complete doctorate in mathematics. But without his parents' support, we could not afford for him to enroll or for us to live in the beautiful and cultural city of Krakow, in Austrian Poland. Kazimierz said it didn't matter, that we would save up, and we could move, he could enroll in another year or two.

"And Paris," I reminded him, each time Bronia's letters arrived. Eventually we would go to Paris, and I would do my coursework at the Sorbonne.

"Yes, of course, my darling." Kazimierz kissed the top of my head. "Someday, Paris."

But for now, Kazimierz had a job in Poland, and after our wedding, we moved from Warsaw to Loksow. We rented a tiny one-room apartment above a bakery for seven rubles a month, and all the day long the smells of bread drifted up into our one-room, taunting us. We did not have money for enough food, or enough coal to heat our room regularly in winter. But never mind that. We had each other.

In bed at night, Kazimierz wrapped his large arms around me, pulled me in close to his body, holding on to me while he slept. His breath matched my breath. *Steady*. And we fit together perfectly. I slept enveloped in a cocoon of love and happiness, and I was plenty warm and plenty full.

In Warsaw, in the years before I became a governess, I had taken classes at the Flying University. In Russian Poland it was illegal for women to obtain a university education, and the Flying University classes were taught in secret, the locations ever changing to avoid detection. I'd learned about chemistry and physics and literature. In Loksow, though, there was nothing of the sort. And after we had been living there for three months, I announced to Kazimierz over a dinner that I was going to start a Flying University myself.

"What, *kochanie?*" He was distracted, grading student exams at the table while we ate. He did not mean to ignore me, but it was the best time of evening and best place in our apartment to get any light, as the late spring sun had not yet set and our only window framed our tiny table.

"Flying University," I said again. "I want to start one here, in Loksow. Women here need a university. *I* need a university." I made circles with my spoon in the dinner I'd made, a clear broth that I had tried (and failed) to make more interesting by adding an aging potato.

During the day while Kazimiez taught, I worked as a governess for twin boys. The Kaminskis were a family Kazimierz had known from his other, wealthier life, and they were not put off by the fact that his parents had disowned him, since I was cheap labor for them. But at night I longed for more. I read Kazimierz's books, but that wasn't enough. I wanted stimulating conversation and experiments and problem solving, and most of all, a community. My entire life, other than in Szczuki, I'd had people to learn alongside: first banned Polish books as bedtime stories and discussions with Papa and my sisters, later the Flying University classes I attended with Bronia in Warsaw.

Kazimierz finally put down the exam he'd been focusing on and looked up. His eyes were dark brown, nearly black, and I had stared at them enough times now to understand the subtle differences in his expression between desire and anger, worry and hunger. Now, his eyes were filled only with worry. "I'll teach you maths at night if you want to learn something."

"Oh, Kaz," I said. "You're already exhausted from teaching all day. And besides, I want to find other women like me to interact with." I'd done years of self-study in Szczuki; I was ready for so much more. And as much as I loved my husband, it was lonely here in Loksow with no family, no friends, and no learning opportunities outside our apartment.

"But a secret university? That sounds much too dangerous, Marya. If you were caught, you could be arrested, jailed."

"I won't be caught." I did not want to be arrested, but maybe there were worse things. My mind felt numb, soft, restless. I itched to exercise it among new people and new studies.

"I don't like the idea," Kazimierz said. He covered my hand with his. "I couldn't bear the thought of anything ever happening to you, my beautiful sweet Marya."

"But it won't," I promised him. "Bronia and I attended classes in Warsaw before I met you and everything was fine." Truth be told, there had been a scare or two, a raid from time to time. A woman I'd actually known in my chemistry class, Petra, had disappeared, rumored to have been arrested. But there'd also been another rumor circulating about an illicit affair, a baby, and though I never saw her again, all the danger had felt muted, far away. I let myself believe she had moved somewhere else, out in the countryside, with a family perhaps. "I will start something small," I promised Kazimierz. "For a few women. We will only meet once a week. I need this," I said again.

Kazimierz sighed. He knew me well enough to know that nothing he might say now, no worry he might have was going to change my mind. He squeezed my hand. "Just promise me you'll be careful," he finally said.

"Of course, darling." I leaned across the table and kissed him once softly on the lips to mollify him. I sat back down and began to chart it in my head, how I could begin this university, where I would even start.

Kazimierz was still staring at me, and he put the exam down again, reached his hands up to hold on to my shoulders and pull me closer to him. He kissed me, more forcefully than before, as if to remind me that he was here, that he was the most important thing. And he was.

But we were going to get to Paris, I was going to go to a real university eventually. And in the meantime, I had to prepare as much as I could, so I would be ready.

MARIE

❧

Paris, France, 1891

You have a choice. There is always a choice.

I get on the train to Paris, leaving Kazimierz still standing at the station, looking as though I had trampled upon his heart. But my own heart feels free, bursting with so much possibility for my future. The heavy sinking cloud that had crushed my thoughts and my hopes, working so many dull years as a governess, begins to lift as the train pulls away from Warsaw. My university education is finally within my grasp, after all these years. Maybe my *love* for Kazimierz had not been love at all, as now the prospect of giving up university, *for him*, does not feel even remotely right to me the way it had only months earlier, skating in Szczuki.

Forty long and uncomfortable hours later, Bronia is waiting for me at the station in Paris. She completed her course of study in obstetrics and is a married woman now—having fallen in love with another doctor, a Polish man, a political dissident exiled from Russian Poland.

It is wonderful to see her again, and my heart swells further. She looks so beautiful, so happy and so grown up and . . . it can't be! I rest my hand gently on the round bulge of her belly, before I even give her a hug. "You are having a baby?" I ask, stunned that my sister is about to be a real mother to her own child, not just a sister-mother to me and Hela. And, that she has kept this last bit of news from me until now.

"Yes." She laughs a little and holds me tightly to her, kissing the top of my head. She smoothes back the wisps of my blond hair that have come loose from my bun on the very long journey. "You are going to be a *tante*." She quickly corrects herself in Polish: "*Ciotka*, I mean."

"*Tante*," I repeat back, the French word both foreign and delightful on my tongue.

BRONIA AND HER HUSBAND LIVE IN A SMALL APARTMENT IN La Villete, on rue d'Allemagne, an hour and two horse-drawn omnibus rides away from the Sorbonne.

I take a few days to unpack my things and settle in, and then Bronia draws me out a map. I manage to navigate the omnibuses into the city for the first time alone, without getting lost. And as I walk the rue Saint-Jacques to go and register for my classes, I've never felt such a lightness, such a happiness before. In Poland, a woman cannot simply walk into a university, pay the fees, and register. But in Paris—anything is possible!

I do not feel at all like that same girl, that same woman, who had been skating through life as a lovesick penniless governess, not too long ago, in Szczuki. And when I sign my registration card, instead of Marya, I write *Marie*. The French version of my name seems more suitable for my new life here, as a student, as a scientist. In Paris *Marie* can be anything or anyone. And I vow to leave that sad and listless Marya behind.

"ARE YOU AWAKE?" BRONIA'S VOICE CUTS THROUGH THE DARK-
ness of my bedroom.

"Yes," I say. "Sorry, did I wake you, Bron?" It is November
third, the morning I am officially to become a student of the Faculty of Science at the Sorbonne, and I've been awake since the
middle of the night, unable to get back to sleep, my mind and
body restless, eager and excited.

"No," Bronia says, lifting the curtain a bit now, only to reveal
darkness. "I heard you rustling around in here. But it was the
baby who woke me." Bronia sighs. "Should I make some coffee?"
she asks. "I'm not falling back to sleep."

"Neither am I," I admit. "Will we wake up Mier?"

"He'll be fine," Bronia says dismissively. I feel a little bad for
my brother-in-law, who is kind, but also quiet—no match for the
two independently minded sisters who now inhabit his apartment. Mier is short for Kazimierz, and every time Bron has said
his name these past few weeks I couldn't help but think about
my own Kazimierz standing on the train platform in Warsaw.
But I do not regret my choice. And besides, my brother-in-law
is nothing like him. Mier's love and adoration for Bronia are so
clear on his face each time he glances at her, and he agrees to
everything Bronia asks of him, anything to make her happy and
fulfilled. He would never ask her to choose him over medicine,
and that alone makes me quite fond of him.

Bronia leaves to start our coffee, and I rise and dress in the
darkness. I don't have many dresses to choose from, and I pull
one blindly out of the wardrobe, not caring which one it is. I
spent all of Papa's rubles on my tuition and registration fees,

with none left for new clothing or anything else now. I'm relying on Bronia for food and shelter. And anyway, I don't care about how I look. As long as it covers me, any dress will do. I wrap my blond hair back into a tight bun and then walk into the dining room to share a coffee with my sister.

"Are you nervous?" Bronia asks, handing me a cup.

"Nervous? What is there to be nervous about?" I laugh, the sound coming out higher than normal, and I realize, yes, perhaps I am a bit nervous.

"You will most likely be the only woman in your physics classes today," Bronia says matter-of-factly. "And the men will not take kindly to you doing better than them." From the slightly bitter edge to her voice, I'm certain Bronia exr̲   ̲nced something similar when she began her medi̲ ̲ ̲ourse a few years earlier. Though the letters she ha̲d̲ ̲ ̲ ̲ten to me had conveyed nothing of the sort—they ̲ ̲ ̲ ̲ been filled only with how much she'd been learning, the joy she found in all the medical knowledge and practice.

I shake my head. Who cares about the men? If I'm nervous about anything, it's that deep down, Pani Zorawska might be right about me. That I'm not good enough, that I will never amount to anything. Perhaps the courses will be too hard or I'll run out of money before I earn my degree. I can't imagine how I would feel to return to Poland both penniless and also a failure.

Outside the apartment window, the sun begins to rise, and the sky glows orange and purple. I finish my coffee and take a deep breath. Nervous or not, I am more than ready. My years of self-study have taken me as far as I will ever get on my own. Now I need brilliant professors, access to laboratories. "I should leave," I tell Bronia. "I want to arrive early."

Bronia reaches across the table, grabs my hand and squeezes it. "Good luck, *ma petite soeur.*" *My little sister.*

I've been practicing my French these past few weeks: *"Merci, ma grande soeur,"* I answer back.

THE SORBONNE IS UNDERGOING A RENOVATION, WHICH IS only partway done, and as a result, the noise of men with shovels and hammers echoes off rue Saint-Jacques, and my first lecture has been relocated to an old house alongside the street. I arrive an hour before class begins, and take the chair closest to the front. The rest of the students file in after me and sit behind me inside the dusty parlor.

The professor stands directly in front of me—an older, balding man with a long white beard, dressed in a black jacket with tails, a long white tie. He looks more like he's dressed for a dinner party than a laboratory, other than the chalk dust marking up his sleeves. His clothing is another reminder of how important, how much bigger, this class is compared to any other I've ever taken before. I swallow back the nervous swell in my chest, the coffee washing back up, burning the back of my throat.

He begins to call out the names of the students one by one, and when he says *Marie*, then terribly mispronounces my last name—*Sokol—ow—ska*—I don't respond at first, not realizing he's talking to me. A man behind me taps me on the shoulder. All eyes are upon me now, and my cheeks redden with embarrassment. Of course, everyone else knows whose name the professor is calling. Looking around, I am, as Bronia had predicted, the only woman in the room.

"Oui, présente," I call out quickly, feeling the hotness from my face creep to my neck as I raise my hand. Professor Appel

checks me off and moves on, calling out the names of the remaining men.

Someone whispers loud enough for me to hear: *Who is that foreign woman with the beautiful hair?* Foreign woman? Beautiful hair?

Another man says: *A pretty little thing like her in the physics course? Is she lost?*

There are snickers, but Professor ignores them, continuing to call the roll.

So I am allowed in, unlike in Poland, and yet, none of these men will take me seriously? *Pretty little thing.* Is that all anyone will see me as here?

My embarrassment is quickly replaced by annoyance. Bronia told me this would happen, and I'm determined now not to let it bother me, ruin my first morning of classes. I stare straight ahead, eyes eagerly trained on Professor Appel in his elegant tails, pretending there is nothing else, no one else, in this room but his voice.

Anyway, I am not here to make friends. I am here to learn, to be the best in physics. I will show them all.

MARYA

❧

Loksow, Poland, 1893

My Flying University of Loksow did indeed start small, as I had promised Kazimierz it would. It was, at first, just me and one other woman, Agata, who worked with me, cooking and cleaning for the Kaminskis. Our little university met each Wednesday night at one of our apartments, and we took turns teaching one another things we knew. Agata's father had been a doctor before he died when she was a teenager, and she knew many things about the ways and structures of the body, while I shared with her the chemistry I had been taught at Flying University back in Warsaw. After only a few months, Agata had a friend, Emilia, who wanted to join us, and soon Emilia had a friend, too, and then another, and then by the following year, there were six of us.

Leokadia Jewniewicz was the seventh to join our school, having found us through her cousin, Joanna, and Leokadia was also the only one of us artistically inclined. She was a pianist, already performing private concerts throughout the city, and when she first came to our Wednesday night meeting, at my apartment—

which really wasn't even big enough to fit six people, much less seven—I could tell that she was different from the rest of us. And not just because of the music. Her red dress looked brand new, made with a rich, expensive fabric. And her fingers were so pretty and clean, her nails clear and shiny.

"I don't mean to sound rude," Agata said, her tone sounding perfectly rude. I liked Agata for her bluntness. She spoke this way at work, too, even with Pani Kaminska, and sometimes I was in awe of her sheer ability to speak her mind and not get fired. "But why are you here?" she said to Leokadia now. It wasn't Leokadia's presence that had particularly thrown any of us, but more the deep red chiffon of her dress, the perfect smooth line it made around her ample waist. We were all struggling to survive in ways she clearly was not. If you had money, why wouldn't you leave Poland for a real university?

Leokadia opened her eyes wide in response, but did not answer at first. Her irises were a bright blue, the color of the robin eggs in the nest outside our apartment window, and somehow their color alone softened her, made her seem younger and more delicate than the rest of us.

"Every woman is welcome," I chided Agata with a stern look, though I wasn't sure yet whether Leokadia deserved my defense or not. "As long as she can contribute knowledge and keep our secret."

"I can," Leokadia said quickly, shooting me what appeared to be a grateful smile. She had a heart-shaped face, and when she smiled, she revealed tiny, pearl teeth, with the smallest of gaps between the top two. "And I will," she added. I stared at her, wanting her to go on, explain herself. "I can teach you all about music, piano lessons for anyone who wants to learn. And my father is a mathematician. He does not approve of women getting a higher education and has forbidden me from getting one, but he's away teaching in Russia and I've been teaching myself maths, sneaking his books." That explained why she hadn't sought out an education outside of Poland. *Her father.* "I don't know anything at all about science or literature." Leokadia was still talking. "And I wish I did . . ." Her voice trailed off, and she stared at us all. No one said anything for a moment.

"She plays piano quite beautifully," her cousin, Joanna, finally said, her voice teetering with reluctance. Perhaps she worried now she had made a mistake bringing Leokadia here to begin with. Joanna's pale cheeks flushed scarlet, and I felt all the women turn their eyes to me. I was the one who'd started our Flying University, and they still saw it as mine.

But the truth of it was, it wasn't mine. It was *ours.* Flying University was for every woman who wanted to learn and couldn't. It didn't matter now in Poland whether you were a rich woman or a poor woman, whether you dressed in rags or silk, whether you had enough to eat or you didn't—none of us were allowed to attend university here, and why would we deny Leokadia the knowledge we so hungered for ourselves?

"I would very much like your piano lessons, Leokadia," I finally said, though I had never before desired to play or learn anything about music. To me music was *babka* and science was *kielbasa.* You could live without sweets, but you could not live without sustenance.

Leokadia smiled wider this time. "I would love to teach you, Marya. And please, call me Kadi."

"Welcome, Kadi," I said, and five other voices followed suit, murmuring the same.

There were not enough seats for seven people in my small apartment, and barely even enough floor space, but I pushed our tiny table up all the way to the coal stove, and then there was just enough room for us all to sit on the bare wood floor in between the table and our bed.

The June air was heavy, stifling, and even with the window cracked, and it being nighttime, it was much too hot for so many people, sitting shoulder to shoulder. Sweat trickled down the back of my neck, from under my bun, and I fanned myself with the paper Emilia had made for us all, to teach us Latin, which she had learned as a child from her older brother.

But we all sat together, repeating Latin words after her into the simmering growing darkness, speaking softly, so as not to alert the neighbors, or the patrons below in the bakery. And there, just like that, sweaty and crowded among women, it was the happiest I'd felt all week.

JUST AS EMILIA WAS TEACHING US THE LAST PHRASE ON HER paper—*omnium rerum principia parva sunt (the beginnings of all things are small)*—the apartment door swung open. All seven of us reacted the same, a collective jump, shoulders bumping, knees banging together. Then I looked up, let out a sigh. It was only Kaz coming home, not the Russian police coming to arrest us. *Of course it was Kaz.* "This is my husband," I told the other women. "Don't worry. We're fine."

I knew he would be home by eight, and I had planned we would be finished by then, all the women already gone home. But our fascination with Kadi meant we'd started a bit later than we'd intended and I'd lost track of the time. Kaz knew what I'd been doing all along, but only in the abstract, in theory.

Now, for the first time, he was face to face with my little university.

He quickly shut the door, stepped to the side, which was the only space for him left, save for our bed, which sat on the other side of the room and would require climbing through the whole seven of us to get to. His eyes caught mine, and for a second I thought he might laugh. The ridiculousness—an entire group of women, taking up all the floor space in his apartment, all of us sweating and whispering Latin to one another in the almost darkness. But then he frowned instead.

I stood up quickly, accidentally bumping Agata's shoulder with my knee. "Thank you, Emilia. Let's end for tonight."

Kadi stood up next. "This was so wonderful," she gushed. "Thank you for letting me join in, Marya. Next week you'll come to my home. There's more room, and there's a piano. I'll teach."

Everyone else's eyes turned to her now, including my husband's. But mine were only on him. It was too dark in here for me to really understand the look on his face, or what he was thinking as he took in her red silk dress, her pretty blond hair, her invitation to teach piano, of all things. Kadi was everything he'd had once, in his other life: wealth and privilege and destiny. And for a few seconds, I felt something strange bubbling up inside of me, a flicker of doubt.

All the women whispered goodbyes and left, one at a time. Agata left last, and as soon as she shut the door behind her, Kaz came to me. Two strides, and then his arms were around me.

He put his finger to my face, traced the lines of my lips ever so gently, until my doubt and my worry turned into a half smile. *Steady.* "I love you so much, Marya," he said. "What would I do if anything ever happened to you, *kochanie?*"

My dear sweet devoted husband. "Nothing will happen," I promised him.

"But there were too many women here tonight. It's dangerous for you all to meet like this. What if you are caught? Arrested?"

"It was only seven," I said. "Our apartment is just so small, it felt like more. And who's to say we were not here . . . baking together?"

"But you weren't," he snapped, the crease of his frown growing deeper. He sighed, then pulled me tightly against him. He kissed the top of my head. "You are everything to me," he said into my hair. "Everything."

Everything. I felt a crushing weight in my chest, and for a moment, it was hard to breathe.

I still had my family: Papa and Hela were only a short train ride away in Warsaw and I visited with them every few months, and Bronia was still writing me letters from Paris, though more infrequently now, since my niece, Helena (who Bronia wrote they'd nicknamed "Lou") had been born. As far as I knew, he hadn't talked to his parents nor any of his siblings since we'd been married two years earlier. I had my friends in Flying University now, too. But what did Kazimierz have in Loksow? His work, the insufferable young boys he taught, and . . . the inability to further his own education, to light his mind the way he needed.

If only he were able to take up his own studies again, I would no longer be his everything, his only thing. Maths would consume his mind, I knew it would, and I would be able to breathe a little easier and focus on my own studies. That gave me an idea: tomorrow morning I would write Papa and ask if he would send the money he was still saving for me for the Sorbonne so Kaz could use it for his education. Paris now felt like a world away. The only real way for me to get there would be for Kaz to finish his education first, and be sought after enough in his field to secure a job in Paris so we could afford to move there and both be fulfilled.

I liked this new plan of mine, and I knew Papa would want to help. I exhaled and reached my hand up to Kazimierz's face, ran my fingers against his beard. "Come to bed, my love," I said. "You worry too much. Everything will be all right tomorrow, you'll see."

Kazimierz leaned in closer again and kissed me, and then all else fell away: concern, regret, suffocation. For at least this night, he was my everything too.

MARIE

❧

Paris, 1894

My mind has been filled with my studies at the Sorbonne, focused on passing my exams at the top of my class, putting all the other students, the men, to shame, while also having enough money to move to my own room closer to school, and to stay alive, warm, and fed. So I have not thought about Kazimierz Zorawski in years, until the letter arrives from Hela from Warsaw, with a newspaper clipping inside:

> *Julius and Kazimiera Zorawski proudly announce the marriage of their eldest son, Kazimierz Zorawski, to Leokadia Jewniewicz, esteemed concert pianist and daughter of prominent mathematician Hipolit Jewniewicz. Zorawski is completing his doctorate in mathematics at Jagiellonian University . . .*

I put the clipping down, not wanting to read any further, my face already turning hot at the words about his fiancée, Leokadia: *proudly, esteemed, prominent.* All the things his parents never would've said about me, and probably still wouldn't, even now. Never mind that I passed first in my class in my physics examination, or that I was awarded the prestigious Alexandrovitch Scholarship last year that had come with a generous and much needed 600 rubles. But my world is bigger now than the Zorawskis. I do not regret the choice I made to come to Paris, even if it is still a constant struggle to prove myself as a woman. I have opportunity here nonetheless and my freedom to learn, and that is everything. I put the clipping back inside of Hela's envelope, then hide it all inside a chemistry textbook, on the shelf in my lab.

I've already stayed much too long in the lab, and I am running late for a meeting with Professor Kowalski and his wife.

As I walk along the streets of the Latin Quarter to the Kowalskis' hotel, I try to put the newspaper clipping out of my mind. I have other things to worry about. I was recently tasked with doing a study by the Society for the Encouragement of National Industry, researching the magnetic properties of different kinds of steel. And the possible outcomes, the idea of testing, day in and day out, in the lab, an experiment all my own, has been endlessly thrilling. But there isn't enough room in Monsieur Lippman's lab for all the equipment I will need to properly test the different steels, and I'm not exactly sure how I'm going to complete the study.

I'd confided this much to Monsieur Kowalski last night, after I'd attended his lecture. I know him, and his new wife, from back in Poland. They're in Paris right now, both on their honeymoon and for him to give lectures. "Just come to tea tomorrow," Monsieur Kowalski had said when I told him about my concerns last night. "I have an idea for you to fix your lab problem."

Monsieur Kowalski is a prominent physicist in Poland, and it would've been too rude to turn him down. Though I also don't know what he can truly do to help, given that he's based in Poland, and I must stay in Paris for the time being, at least until I complete this study and my examinations. I have been dreading the idea of socializing with him and his wife today, though, as I anticipate so much stilted conversation, so much effort, and it is why I stayed so long in the lab to begin with, why I attended to all my unopened mail before leaving. *Oh, Hela.* Why did she even send that clipping to me?

I climb the stairs up to their suite now and knock on the door. Madame Kowalska answers with a bright smile. She has blond hair, pulled tightly back into a bun, and a pretty face like a cherub. Her cheeks glow pink—perhaps customary for a new bride on her honeymoon, and for the briefest moment, I wonder if this is what *Leokadia* looks like now too?

"Marya, come in." It's strange to hear someone call me *Marya* again, other than my sister. In Bronia's voice it sounds like a pet name, a reminder of our childhood, but in Madame Kowalska's voice, whom I barely know, it sounds all wrong.

"I've been going by Marie," I correct gently.

"Oh yes, of course. That's right. Marie." She shakes her head. "You are very French now, I suppose?"

Perhaps she means to make a compliment, but it comes out sounding like an insult. I want to tell Madame that France is a place for me to learn, that I am still a Pole, just like her, and that I would never abandon our native country altogether, whether I've grown used to my adopted French name or not. But before I can say any of that, I notice a stranger, a man, standing across the room at the window. He leans his elbows on the window ledge, staring, as if entranced by the street below. He's quite tall, and well dressed—his suit looks made of much newer cloth than anything I own, and it fits his lean frame nicely.

"Sugar in your tea?" Madame asks me.

"No, thank you," I say, and when the man hears my voice, he turns, looks at me. His eyes are bright blue, and he immediately smiles, the corners of his mouth turning up just above his beard, making him seem younger than the few gray hairs in his beard might imply.

He walks over, picks up my hand and kisses it, the rough hair of his beard scratching just enough on the back of my hand to make me feel oddly delighted. It is the first time a man's lips have grazed my hand since Kazimierz, and how strange it is to recognize now that it gives me a little thrill. "Pierre Curie," he says.

He's another scientist. We've never met before, but I recognize his name, having heard it come up in conversation in the lab once or twice. "Yes, I've heard of you, Monsieur Curie," I say.

"Pierre, please."

"Pierre . . . You are studying crystallography?" He nods, and his eyes light up, with curiosity, or excitement for his work. "Marie Sklodowska," I say. "I am working with magnetic fields."

"Ah, you have made introductions to each other before I got the chance." Monsieur Kowalski walks in from the other room. "Here he is, Marie, the solution to your problem."

"Solution?" I am genuinely puzzled. I don't need another scientist's help, particularly not one who doesn't even specialize in what I'm preparing to research. And I'm certainly not about to hand *my* study over to a man. Am I going to have to spend the entire evening explaining myself, justifying my capabilities?

The very idea of it is exhausting, and I wonder if I can leave now without appearing rude.

But Madame Kowalska has just poured everyone tea and invites us to sit around the table. I have no choice but to take my place, and thank her for her hospitality. She's not a scientist, and she appears vaguely bored already, stifling a yawn. I take a seat across the table from Pierre, accept my cup of tea and take a sip. I feel Pierre's eyes on me, and I look away, stare into my tea.

"Yes," Monsieur Kowalski finally clarifies as he takes a sip of his own tea and smiles at his bride. Madame Kowalska blushes at the obvious attention. "Pierre, Marie is conducting an experiment and needs more lab space. Marie, Pierre has the extra space. I thought if I introduced you both, you could work on an arrangement." Are they truly trying to help me? Many of the men I have encountered since I've moved to Paris want nothing more than to bring me down. No man likes giving up anything to a woman.

"Tell me about your study," Pierre says. He stares at me, his eyes so attached to my face it is unnerving. Is this some kind of a test? Maybe he *is* like the men in my physics classes. And if that's true, I would not want to share a lab with such an insufferable creature.

"I have the funding, if that's what you're worried about," I say, rather brusquely now. He continues to stare at me; it really is disconcerting.

"No, no." He laughs a little. "I don't care about the money. I am fascinated by your work. What kinds of steels will you be using, and how do you plan to account for the different variables? And I wonder if you might allow me to observe your methodology, so I might learn from you. Your reputation and your

brilliance in the lab precede you, Mademoiselle Sklodowska."
He speaks quickly, breathlessly, his eyes holding on to mine. Perhaps he isn't feigning interest, or testing me at all. Does he already view me as his equal? Does he truly want to learn, from me?

"Marie," I correct him, softening my tone.

"Marie," he repeats, my name turning into a smile on his lips. "Please, go on, tell me about your study."

I feel myself relaxing, and I explain about the different kinds of steel I plan to test, the ways I will measure the magnetic properties using both vector and scalar magnetometers. He nods quickly; his eyes turn from pale blue to a blue green in the weakening light. When I'm done talking, he jumps in, talking about his piezoelectricity work with his brother, Jacques. Our words fly across the table, fast and electric, leaving me breathless. We're two currents, zipping through water, side by side, charging each other to go faster and faster, hotter and brighter.

When I look up again, the room is quite dim. Outside the window the night is black, and only a sliver of moonlight shines through. The Kowalskis had left the table and neither Pierre nor I had noticed nor even thanked our hosts.

"Do you plan to always stay in Paris?" Pierre asks suddenly, out of nowhere.

"Oh goodness no," I answer quickly. "As soon as my study is done and I complete my examinations I'll move back to Poland to be with my family and to teach." Though even as I say the words, words I've repeated many times with the greatest of sincerity since I've moved to Paris, suddenly they feel like a lie.

MARYA

Loksow, Poland, 1894

I was a terrible piano student, but Leokadia was the most patient teacher. Or maybe she didn't care that my fingers could never find the right notes and that my ears could not hear nor understand the melodies. She nodded and offered an encouraging smile, even when I played her back a D scale much too slow and filled with wrong notes. Of all the women in our university, I was the worst one at music lessons. But Leokadia looked at the chemistry equations I tried to teach much the same way I looked at a page of sheet music she handed out in class. And I offered her words of encouragement too. *It isn't so hard once you memorize all the elements, you see.*

And she said, *Ah, just like scales.*

Still, I remained hopeless at playing a scale, and she could not remember the elements, as hard as she might try.

And yet we kept on, week after week, all of us women trying to teach one another what we each knew and loved. By the beginning of the new year, there were ten of us, and we began to break off and meet in smaller groups, because it was hard to find a place where ten women could go, week after week, undetected. Sometimes, Leokadia and I just met alone a second night of the week, too, and though we always tried to teach each other new things, alternating music and science, we also just enjoyed each other's company.

There was an easiness to our friendship, a comfort that I found hard to come by with the other women, even the ones who loved the sciences, like me. I couldn't exactly put my finger on why. Our interests and our knowledge and our lives couldn't be further apart. I spent my day working hard as a governess for the Kaminski twins, and nights with my husband, trying to stay warm and fed, just above water. And she spent her days practicing piano in her parents' well-heated apartment, her nights dressed in glamorous and expensive gowns, giving concerts around the city, to greater and greater acclaim.

Maybe the reason I was so drawn to her was that somewhere inside of me I knew, of any of us, she was going to find a way to follow her dream, to *become* someone. And already, I liked the idea of having touched just one iota of her greatness.

About a year after I first met Kadi, she got invited to play in a special concert in Krakow. Normally she only gave concerts in Loksow and in Warsaw. She played for free, in private homes or at small parties, where it was acceptable for the background entertainment to be a woman, as long as she was well dressed, beautiful, and unpaid. When I asked if this bothered her, she told me playing her music for other people was her reward.

"How I would love, though," she would tell me sometimes, her voice sounding far away, the way mine sounded when I spoke of the Sorbonne, somewhere still in my future, "to train with Sibelius in Finland or maybe Debussy in France!"

I lacked the means she had, but I always had the support of my family. I was still eagerly waiting for a response from Papa, hopeful he would send me money to help Kaz further his education—I'd written to him how I felt this was the only way for me to eventually get to Paris, get my own education, and I knew that was Papa's greatest wish for me still. Kadi's father would never approve nor allow her to do what she dreamed of. He wanted her to stay in Poland, marry well, and raise children. But as he was still away in St. Petersburg teaching, he did not know much of what she did these days. Her mother was quietly supportive, she told me. And when she got invited to go to Krakow, I felt it was the very first step ahead for her, the beginning of her way out.

"Perhaps you will be seen in Krakow, then *hired* to perform there next time," I told her. "If you are making your own money, you could save up, go anywhere in the world you want, with or without your father's approval."

She cast her blue eyes to her shiny leather boots. "If only it were that simple, Marya. What would Mama do without me? And Papa would never speak to me again."

I wanted to tell her that she could make that choice, that there was always a choice. But sometimes, when the night was long and dark and freezing, and Kaz and I had not had enough to eat for dinner, and we lay in bed feeling the never-ending emptiness of our own bellies, I wondered if he missed his family, his parents, the manor house in Szczuki with their chef. I wondered how it would feel to give up your past, your history, everything that belonged to you, and whether I would've done the same.

"I have an idea!" Kadi looked back up, her cheeks pink with excitement. "Come with me to Krakow and watch me play." She knew that the Kaminskis were in the Baltic for a monthlong holiday, and that I currently had four glorious weeks off while they were away.

I laughed a little. "I wish I could." And truly I did. The idea of getting out of the gray soot-covered Russian-controlled streets of Loksow, and into the Austrian portion of Poland, Krakow, where art and music were supposedly thriving and luminous, sounded wonderful. But Kaz would never want to come—that vibrant world a reminder of his old life and everything he was missing now. Besides, even if he wanted to, we couldn't afford for him to take the time away from his students unpaid.

"Come on," Kadi said. "Mama told Papa we are going to visit friends, and he got us a large hotel suite. You could stay with us. It would be so much fun."

I hesitated for a moment. The truth was, Kaz wouldn't want me to go alone, without him. It would worry him. If I brought it up we would argue about it, and I would eventually end up giving in to what he wanted, making it easier not to bring it up at all.

But what if I went and didn't tell him? I *had* gone by myself to visit Papa and Hela in Warsaw a few times, and we had already discussed that I might go for a visit in the next few weeks while the Kaminskis were away. Could I do that, and take a night or two away in Krakow, too, and Kaz would never have to know? It felt strange, the idea of lying to my husband, but weirdly freeing too, that I might have something all my own to look forward to. I really did want to watch Kadi play in Krakow. And it would be fun to spend a night or two in a hotel suite, away from the worry and the cold desperate hunger of my everyday life.

I wrote Hela and asked her thoughts, and also whether she would be willing to keep my secret from Kaz the next time she saw him.

Yes! Under one condition, Hela wrote back. *I want to go to Krakow with you.*

HOW WONDERFUL IT WAS TO BE WITH MY SISTER-TWIN AGAIN, just the two of us! We'd bought very inexpensive fourth-class tickets for the train, but it was only a six-hour ride, and we did not mind the floor of the railcar so much, especially as we sat shoulder to shoulder, our arms around each other. I leaned my head against her shoulder and inhaled the scent of her—still the same as when we were girls, lemons and corn poppies.

"You are going to love hearing Kadi," I told her. "Her piano is so very beautiful."

"Marya?" Hela said my name softly, a question.

"What is it?" I asked her.

"I need to tell you something, and I want you to know . . . I never want to upset you."

"What's wrong?" I was alarmed. "Is it Papa? Is he sick?"

She shook her head, inhaled, and then exhaled her confession in one fast breath: "Bronia invited me to come live with them in Paris, to help her out with little Lou and to enroll in some courses at the Sorbonne."

"Oh," I said. I'd never considered that Hela might want to go to Paris. We were almost the same age, but I'd always been the smarter one, ahead in all our studies. Hela had seemed content teaching at the girls' gymnasium in Warsaw. I hadn't expected her to ever desire more than that, and I felt ashamed that I had underestimated her ambitions.

But it all made sense, why Papa had ignored my request to use the Sorbonne money for Kaz, writing only about other things in his letters. Now, I understood. Papa was going to help Hela go to France, use the money to pay her tuition at the Sorbonne instead.

"Why would I be upset?" I finally said, swallowing hard. "I am surprised, yes. But . . . this sounds like a wonderful opportunity for you."

Hela smiled and exhaled. "Yes, I will be very excited to live in France for a little while. To expand my mind."

I didn't ask her what she planned to study, the bitter taste so thick on my tongue that it was hard to speak, much less to breathe. The air on the train suddenly felt stale, suffocating as I tried to imagine both my sisters so far away.

I felt like I was slipping again, my footing uncertain. Bronia and I were the ones who were supposed to get the university education. Hela was the one content with Poland. Bronia and I married Kazimierzs; Hela was still alone, wanting. And what was I even doing here now, on a train to Krakow, wrapped up in a lie to the one person who was still completely mine in Poland?

"And perhaps you and Kaz will join us soon, too, and all three of us sisters can be together again?" Hela said, her songbird voice light and hopeful.

"Perhaps," I said softly, my response swallowed by the noise of the train. Suddenly Paris felt further out of my reach than ever before.

MARIE

❧

Paris, France, 1895

Marry me," Pierre says, out of nowhere, one afternoon in the lab in early March.

We'd been in the middle of a conversation about alloy steel, as I hunch over a piece of it, heating it with a fire iron. I'm wearing my dirty linen smock and a pair of lab glasses much too big for my small face. They're made with a man in mind, and it's dreadfully annoying, how I must continually push them up the bridge of my nose as they slip down, again and again.

This is the third time Pierre has repeated such nonsense since I've returned to Paris after a summer back in Warsaw visiting with Papa and Hela. Papa is doing quite well, and Hela has found a lovely position teaching at a girls' school. She's even recently met a man, a photographer named Stanislaw, whom I suspect she might have feelings for, as she could not stop talking about how beautiful his work is throughout my entire visit. It was hard for me to leave them again, return to Paris, and I even considered staying in Poland for good. But there is much more to be done in the lab—before I left, Pierre and I had stumbled into a fascinating experimentation on paramagnetic properties and temperature variance. Pierre had written me daily while I was away, reminding me of all the work I must return for.

I'd moved my equipment into Pierre's lab a few weeks after we met last spring, and from there Pierre and I quickly became good working partners. He was happy to assist with my study, performing any tasks I asked of him, but also offering his intelligent and unassuming suggestions. I've been doing the same in return with his work on temperatures. Working in the lab with him, I am not a woman and he is not a man—we are just two scientists who respect each other's minds. Which is why his marriage proposals have caught me so much by surprise. And I already told Pierre the last two times he's asked: *I cannot marry you.*

For one thing, he is French; he belongs in France. I am a Pole, I belong in Poland and will eventually move back to work there and be closer to my family. But for another thing, after Kazimierz, I promised myself I would never get engaged again. I am bound to live the life of a scientist now, not of a wife. It doesn't matter how much I respect Pierre, or even enjoy his company, our marriage is an impossibility, any way I look at it.

"Consider it, Marie," he prods again now. "We would be so wondrous together, you and I."

Wondrous. It is so very Pierre to make us sound whimsical, instead of logical, scientific. We are lab partners, not lovers.

"You are like lodestone, and I am your magnet." He's still talking.

Lodestone, the most magnetic of all the materials we have tested. The magnet cannot stay away, even from an almost unexplainable distance. I have to bite my lip to keep from smiling.

"Pierre." I shake my head, without looking up from the fire iron. The silly glasses slide down the bridge of my nose and I push them back up, again. "We've been through this already."

"And nothing you've told me has changed my mind. I still want to marry you."

I glance up from my steel. Pierre has crossed his arms in front of his chest, resting them across the vest of his well-tailored suit. He is such a stubborn, beautiful, brilliant man. For a second, I cannot look away.

"You can be a scientist and my wife," he says. "I fully support you and your work, you know I do. I want us to work together, to continue to be partners in the lab, yes, but everywhere else too."

I enjoy working with him in a way I've never enjoyed working with anyone before. Science burns brighter; my mind feels even more alive. But that doesn't mean we must get married. "We already are lab partners," I say.

"Yes," Pierre says. "But I mean permanently. Forever."

"Don't be ridiculous," I say. "Nothing is forever."

"I beg to differ," Pierre says. "What about atoms?"

It's hard to tell whether he's teasing now, or whether he's hurt that I've refused him yet again. But when I glance at him, the corners of his lips upturn ever so slightly above his beard. This conversation, this *proposal* of his, is far from over in his mind.

"Oh, Pierre," I say, shaking my head. But I am still biting back a smile as I turn my attention to the steel and the fire iron.

ON SATURDAY MORNING, PIERRE AND I TAKE A BIKE RIDE TO the Bois de Vincennes, as we have been doing each weekend the weather is warm enough, riding on old bicycles that belong to him and his brother, Jacques. I pedal ahead of him, my hair coming loose from my bun, blowing back behind my shoulders as the wind whips around my face. I enjoy knowing that he is here, riding with me, but also that I am faster.

"Slow down," Pierre calls from behind me. But he's laughing.

I'm breathless and sweating even though the almost-spring air is cool and crisp. Away from the lab, and science, my mind is a sieve, and time and knowledge slip away, my head gloriously empty for the afternoon. I pedal and pedal like fire ripping through accelerant. Past the gates of the park and the still bare-branched cherry trees.

As we near the water, I finally do slow down, and Pierre catches up. I hop off, lay my bicycle on its side, and sit down by the edge of the lake, resting my sweaty face against the cool edge of my sleeve. Pierre is a moment behind me, and when he stops, he pulls a bouquet of white daisies from his bicycle basket, then holds them out to me, like a prize for reaching the lake first. I take the flowers and our fingertips touch, sending a current of warmth up my hand, my entire arm.

He sits down next to me, close enough so our shoulders touch. "Together," he leans in and says softly, next to my ear. "Inside of the lab and out."

LATER THAT AFTERNOON, I TAKE THE OMNIBUS TO BRONIA'S apartment in La Villette for dinner. I haven't seen her much in the few months since I've been back from Poland, as I've been busy in the lab. And yet I am not thinking about her or my little niece, Lou, as I should be on the way to her home. Instead, the entire carriage ride, my mind is back at the lake, with Pierre, the feel of his whisper on my ear. *Together.* I have to forget about Pierre, and I promise myself I won't even bring him up at dinner.

But the first thing Bronia says when I walk inside her apartment is, "That man loves you. Don't be a *glupi.*"

I am no fool, but I'm caught off guard by my sister's words. "Whatever do you mean?" How does Bron know about Pierre? I have made a point not to mention him, other than as a scientist I share a lab with.

"Monsieur Curie came to visit with us one night last week. Mier invited him for dinner."

"Mier invited him?" What business did my brother-in-law have doing that? It feels a strange invasion of my privacy, like these men, they plucked a secret from my lab, stole it away from me. And now my face burns hot with anger.

"Monsieur Curie wrote us a few times over the summer when you were away, telling us how much he wants to marry you. And he kept writing after you came back. We thought we'd better meet him, so Mier invited him. I made my mushroom soup."

At the mention of Bronia's *grzybowa* my mouth waters, and I'm both jealous and annoyed that I hadn't been invited to this dinner, too. What right did they have to eat without me? To talk about me behind my back?

"Don't be angry." She puts her hand on my shoulder gently. She may be a real mother now, but she is still, also, my sister-mother. "We greatly enjoyed Monsieur Curie's company. The way he went on and on about all your work together in the lab. Well, he sounded just like you." She laughs.

"We work quite well together in the lab," I say. "That is not the same as loving someone."

"Isn't it?" Bronia asks, raising her eyebrows.

I shrug, because it doesn't matter. We both know, as soon as I'm accepted for a teaching position at the university in Krakow, I'll move back to Poland. Pierre has work here, in France. "Pierre is French. I'm a Pole, Bron. I belong in Poland. You know that."

Bronia nods, understanding. Poland is her homeland, her birthright, too. "But you cannot choose your country over all else. It's not healthy," she says.

"Choose? What other choice do I have?"

There is always a choice. But I will not choose a man, a marriage, over my family, over my country.

"You could choose to be happy," Bronia says. She picks little Lou up off the floor, where she'd been playing with spoons, and hugs her daughter close to her chest, kisses the top of her head. Bronia had planned to return to Poland after she got her degree, too, but then she met Mier, who can't go back to Poland without risking arrest due to his dissident status there, and now she has a family and a career. Here. But she is always talking about how much she misses Poland, how much she longs to go back there.

"I will be very happy in Poland," I say. Being back closer to Papa and Hela and the country that feels like home, that is what I want.

Bronia raises her eyebrows, gives me a look over Lou's head.

Anyway, what kind of a choice is that? *To be happy.* What is happiness but something unquantifiable, unmeasurable? It seems a terrible way for a scientist to make a decision about one's life, one's future.

"MARRY ME," PIERRE SAYS AGAIN, EXACTLY ONE WEEK AFTER he'd last asked. We are leaving the lab for the night, and Pierre has turned to lock the door behind us, then stops, turns back to me, and proposes, as if he's forgotten what he's supposed to be doing halfway through. Or as if marrying me now consumes his mind, making him obsessive and forgetful, the way our work on magnetism has been doing to him for months.

I reach my hand up, touch his beard gently with my fingers. Though he is thirty-five years old, his face still has a boyishness to it, a lightness that my own twenty-seven-year-old face is missing. Perhaps that's the product of growing up in France, as opposed to Russian-controlled Poland, of having enough to eat, and the money to pay for education, the freedom to get that education when he was ready for it. Pierre's father is a doctor, and his parents live in a beautiful home on the outskirts of Paris in Sceaux. They are lovely, warm and welcoming to me when I have gone with Pierre to dinner there. He and his older brother, Jacques, grew up never wanting. Pierre and I were born into different worlds, we belong in different worlds, and that is never going to change no matter how much he might wish it to.

Pierre reaches his hand up and catches mine on his face. We stand like that for a moment, outside our unlocked lab, neither one of us speaking or moving. Until finally Pierre says, "Before you say anything, I've been thinking about this quite a lot, and I've decided I'll move to Poland with you."

"What?" His words don't make any sense, and I pull away from his face. Whatever would he do in Poland? He doesn't speak Polish, and he would be unable to work in a laboratory there.

"If that is what it takes for you to be my wife," Pierre says. "I'll give this all up." He gestures to the lab, behind us. "I love science, but I don't need it the way you do. You can be a scientist in Poland, and I will be . . . your husband."

"But what will you *do* in Poland?"

"I don't know . . . I'll teach French," Pierre says. "But it doesn't matter what I do. I don't care. Don't you see that? I just want to be with you, Marie Sklodowska. I love you."

He would give up his career, to marry me? To be with me? I would not do the same for him. But he isn't asking me to. Maybe the reason he wants to be with me is because of my devotion to science, not in spite of it.

Then his words settle: *I love you.*

My fingers twitch, wanting to touch his face again, but I clench them into a fist, holding my hand at my side. Bronia is right. *He loves me.* I suddenly think of the pine trees in Szczuki, running through them, skating on the icy river, holding on to Kaz, him whispering in my hair that he *loves* me, and then how quickly he was willing to give up on us once his parents didn't approve of me. I think of his marriage now, to Leokadia. Are they as happy as we were then? Does he love her as much as he said he loved me? Does it matter?

"Marie?" Pierre says my name as a question, interrupting my thoughts.

He picks up my clenched fist, gently unfurls my fingers, lifts my hand up, kisses the back of it softly, then my palm. He moves my fingers back up to his face. His beard gently scratches my fingertips, and I close my eyes for a moment, inhale. Pierre smells like the lab, like fire and metal. Divine. "Marie?" he says, again, softer. And I suddenly understand this will be the last time he asks.

"Yes," I say, tentatively at first, the word feeling like a surprise and a question on my lips all at once. Then I say it again, louder. "Yes."

MARYA

❧

Loksow, Poland, 1895

Marya." Kaz whispered my name in bed one night in early
March, testing to see if I was still awake. I'd come home
late, after a riveting course in physics, compliments of a textbook
Agata had gotten from her brother. I'd thought Kaz was already
asleep when I'd slipped in between the covers a few minutes earlier. Now, my muscles tensed, and I focused on my breathing,
keeping it even and slow.

I was nowhere near asleep, my mind on fire from two stolen
hours with the physics textbook. And part of me wanted to answer Kaz, to roll over and kiss him, hold on to him, and bury my
face deep into the pine scent of his neck. But lately, in bed, he
only wanted to talk about, and act on, us having a baby. It was
easier to pretend I was asleep than to argue with him.

It was true, we had been married almost four years, and I was
already twenty-seven years old. But I loved my husband, and I was
happy like this, just the two of us. I spent nearly every waking moment caring for Jan and Jedrek Kaminski, and did not enjoy any
of it. What got me through so many mind-numbing moments of

each day was the knowledge I soaked in at night at my classes, and the dream that one day I would still learn so very much more at a real university. And then, that I might toil away in a laboratory, not in a nursery. I could not imagine adding another child, a baby, no less, to my day. Even if it were my own. *Especially if it were my own.* How would I continue to go to classes at nights if I had a baby to care for? And I'd been avoiding Kazimierz as much as I could in bed for months, not ready for a family yet, the way he was.

"Marya," Kaz whispered again now. "I want to ask you about your friend, the pianist."

"Leokadia?" I shifted, opened my eyes, surprised enough by his question that I'd briefly forgotten I'd been pretending to sleep. Kaz knew Kadi and I had become close friends, but he still had no idea about my secret trip to Krakow with Hela to hear Kadi play her beautiful, beautiful piano in a real concert hall. I had returned feeling remorseful and had promised myself I'd never lie to him again. My heart pounded in my chest now, worried he'd somehow found out, and I was sure Kaz could feel my heartbeat pulsing through my skin.

"Her father, he is Hipolit Jewniewicz?" Kaz said.

"What?" It wasn't what I was expecting him to say at all.

"Her father?" Kaz said again. "He's Hipolit Jewniewicz?"

"I don't know? I . . . suppose?" I did not know his first name for certain. All I knew of her father was what she told me about him disapproving of her, disallowing her from living the life she truly wanted. He was still teaching in St. Petersburg, but would be coming back to Loksow for good, this summer. Kadi was dreading his return. I was dreading it on her behalf.

"*The* Hipolit Jewniewicz?" Kaz was saying now.

"I don't know," I said again. My heartbeat calmed. I exhaled. "Darling, why do you ask?"

"Today at work, someone mentioned he'd heard his daughter playing at a party last weekend, and when he mentioned the names, I finally put two and two together. Hipolit is only the most brilliant applied mathematician in all of Poland." Kaz's voice rose in the darkness. How wonderful, to hear him sound excited about mathematics again.

I felt my whole body relax against our mattress, and I rolled over and stroked his shoulder softly with my thumb. "And you want me to see if I can get Kadi to set up a meeting for you, hmm?"

We still could not afford Kaz's university tuition, and he was desperate to further his education in mathematics, to have a more stimulating job than teaching basic maths to young boys, which he described as tediously mind-flattening, and not to mention, poorly paying.

"Yes, a meeting!" Kaz said, interrupting my thoughts. He reached up to hold on to my hand on his shoulder, and he squeezed my fingers between his own. "If I could only talk with him. Maybe he needs a research assistant and would be willing to teach me?"

I FELT STRANGE SAYING SOMETHING TO KADI ABOUT HER FA-ther when I saw her next, Wednesday night. We were together in a bigger group—seven of us had turned out to discuss an English novelist at Emilia's tiny apartment. Kadi's father was a complicated and touchy subject for her, and I did not relish bringing him up. But I had promised Kaz I would, and besides I felt like I owed him, too—this uncomfortable ask my penance for lying to him about going to see Kadi in Krakow.

"My father?" Kadi bit her lip and frowned after I asked. Her blond hair was down today, and her face looked prettier, softer than it did when she wore her hair in a bun.

I explained what Kaz had told me, and why he wanted the meeting. "Please," I said. "If nothing comes of it, you don't need to worry. But it will make him so happy if I can set this up for him."

She sighed. "Papa is always inviting mathematicians over for supper, trying to fix me up to marry." She shook her head, and the waves of her hair hit her shoulders. "Maybe now it is my turn to invite one over? Fix Papa up a bit?"

I laughed at the bizarre notion, that here we were, two Polish women, trying desperately to teach ourselves in secret in the dark of night, setting up two men, two mathematicians.

I thanked her, and then I said, "Well, I am married to a mathematician. Who knows. Maybe one day you will find one you like, too?"

Now it was her turn to laugh. "Silly Marya. I am never getting married. I have my piano." She spoke so matter-of-factly, so sure of herself.

I'd watched her in Krakow on a stage otherwise occupied only by men. When she played piano, she'd sparkled under the lights, her music pouring out of her like a sudden rainstorm. I knew she did not want to get married right now, that she wanted to achieve more as a pianist first, but I hadn't known she believed she would never get married.

I wondered what it would feel like, to be so good at something you loved so much that you believed in it more than anything else. It must be freeing, in a way, to know that you and you alone possessed everything you needed for your own happiness and survival.

TWO MONTHS LATER, KADI CAME THROUGH ON HER PROMISE and invited Kaz to come over for tea one afternoon to meet her father. When I arrived back at our apartment from the Kaminskis that evening, he was already home, waiting for me at the table. He saw me and jumped up, a wide smile across his face. Then he ran to me, hugged me so tightly he lifted my feet from the ground, and spun me. It reminded me of our days together in Szczuki, when we were so young and free and in love, holding on to each other on the ice. *His meeting had gone well.*

"Hipolit agreed to teach me," Kaz said, his voice rising with excitement.

He put me down and I clapped my hands together for him, delighted. "Oh, Kaz, how wonderful."

He wrapped me up in an embrace, kissed the top of my head, and laughed, a bright beautiful deep laugh like the sounds that used to echo off the river in Szczuki in the summer.

"And he says if I am a quick study in applied mathematics, which I will be, he will put in a good word for me, help me find a university position in Poland."

He grabbed my cheeks in between his hands, pulled my head toward him, and kissed me on the lips. It was thrilling to feel him so excited about his work again, to know that he would have the chance now to learn and be what he wanted. His mother had been wrong. I hadn't ruined his life by marrying him. And the possibilities now! We might have more money soon, and be able to live in a nicer place and have whatever we wanted to eat. And then, Paris. Eventually he could get a job in Paris and I could be near my sisters and I could study, too.

It was so easy to hope in that moment, that when Kaz kept kissing me, pulling at the buttons of my dress, wanting more, I didn't allow myself to think what might come next. I only allowed myself to feel, to remember exactly the way I loved him.

MARIE

❧

Paris, France, 1895

For a few weeks, everything feels perfect. Pierre and I spend long weekdays working together in the lab. As spring turns warmer, the air fragrant with cherry blossoms, we ride Pierre's and Jacques's rickety bicycles together on weekends, stopping by the lake to enjoy the breeze and discuss the finalization of Pierre's dissertation on paramagnetism and temperatures. I insist that his doctoral work be completely finished before we leave Paris, so that once he learns enough Polish, he will be able to work as a scientist in Poland, too, or at the very least, teach science, not just French. And he says he is glad he has me to push him through, push him to the finish.

I feel both strange—outside myself—and wonderful (or, what was the word Pierre used? *Wondrous.*) too. Sometimes, I lie awake in my bed at night, worrying that it is a crazy idea to marry Pierre, to tie myself to a man, any man, even a great one. But then the next morning, I see him again in the lab, and my body feels oddly weightless, my brain more alive. It is easier to move, and breathe, and even think. If Pierre says I push him, then he pushes me, too. Asks questions, demands answers, helping me achieve more, greater work than I might come to on my own. And by the end of each day my mind is full and exhausted.

Maybe this is happiness. And maybe happiness *is* quantifiable.

If so, I imagine happiness has an almost unbearable lightness, giving it the same atomic weight as helium.

In June, the letter I've been waiting for from Poland finally arrives. I applied for a teaching position at the University of Krakow months ago, and I've been eagerly awaiting my acceptance so I can begin to chart out the rest of my life beyond my education. Even more so, now that I know Pierre is readying himself and finishing his studies to come with me.

But I open up the envelope, read the letter once, then twice, blinking back disbelief and tears. I hand it to Pierre without a word, and he reads it, then turns to me, his eyes ablaze with something I have never seen in them before: *anger.*

"What do they mean, they will not offer you a permanent position *because you're a woman?*" He turns the letter over, as if looking for answers on the other side of the paper, which is blank.

"It's Poland," I say, trying to keep calm, though I hear my voice wavering. "It's not France, Pierre." It's why I'd left, after all, why I didn't choose to stay behind even once Kazimierz had asked. I always knew I couldn't get the education I wanted as a woman in Poland. It had been so naïve of me to believe that if only I were the best in Paris, passed first in all my examinations, applied in the more cosmopolitan city of Krakow outside of the Russian partition of Poland, then . . . what? That Poland would welcome me back to work there? That all those insufferable men would not care about being beat out for a university opening by a woman with *pretty hair*? I want to laugh now at how stupid I was. It doesn't matter how smart or good my science is. All that matters, all that will ever matter in my home country, is that I am a woman.

"Marie." Pierre puts the letter down on our worktable and gently grabs ahold of my shoulders. "Marry me here, in France. We'll go to Sceaux and celebrate with my parents. We can wait until your father and Hela can make it here to have the wedding. And then we'll live in Paris and work together in our lab. You're such a brilliant scientist, you cannot return to Poland if you cannot work there."

His words are like fire, burning everything I thought to be true just an hour earlier, turning it all into ash and smoke. *I am a Pole. I belong in Poland.* I blink back tears. The ache of homesickness is palpable, a heaviness in my chest that makes it difficult to breathe.

But Pierre is right. I know, he's right. I will not go back to Poland if I can't work there. Science is the most important thing. Science is everything.

But no. Science is not everything, any longer. There is also Pierre.

Kazimierz was a young love. It felt sweet and pretty and fresh like the poppies that bloomed in Szcuzki in the spring. I'd liked the way Kaz had held me up, on the ice. But with Pierre, I do not need him to hold me up. I hold myself up, and he stands by my side, or, often, content to be behind me. And then what I love about him is his mind. His beautiful, brilliant mind. I could live inside a scientific conversation with him, going on forever and ever. Poland isn't home, I realize by the middle of July, when we are set to get married. *Pierre is home.*

I tell Bronia and Hela this in the hours before my wedding on July 26th, as they help me steam my dress and fix my hair, and Hela gives me a funny look, like she thinks living in Paris these last years has made me mad. She and Papa made the long journey here for my wedding—and Papa has accepted my decision to stay in Paris much better than I might have expected. But Hela is in love with Stanislaw, back in Warsaw. How can she possibly understand? "Maybe someday," she says, wistfully. "Poland will be better for women, and you and Pierre will come back to us."

Bronia smiles and smoothes the wrinkles from the skirt of my dress. "Who would've thought the most logical one of us would also become the most lovesick, hmmm?"

But Bronia is wrong. My love for Pierre is not a sickness at all. It is light and breath and water: now I need it to survive just as much as I need my work.

My wedding attire is a gift from Bronia's mother-in-law, a beautiful blue dress that I chose for both its practicality and its dark and stunning color. I plan to wear it again and again, and the dark color makes it suitable for the lab.

After they help me get dressed, Bronia and Hela leave to go get themselves ready, and I am all alone in my room on rue de Châteaudun, perhaps for the very last time.

I look at myself in the mirror, and am somewhat surprised by the image staring back at me. I am altogether different in a brand-new dress, more feminine. Perhaps it's the beautiful, spotless material, artfully steamed by my sisters, or the form that has been made just for me, that shows off the curves of my bosom and hourglass shape of my waist. But the person staring back at me is no longer a girl, no longer a Pole. I am an educated woman, a scientist, about to be a wife. A French wife, at that. *Madame.*

Someone knocks on the door, and I spin away from the mirror. "Marie," Pierre's voice comes through.

"Come in," I say, brimming with excitement to see him.

He steps inside and smiles brightly. "You look so beautiful, *mon amour.*"

"You like my new dress?" I turn around, so he can see the full effect of it.

"You could wear your lab coat to our wedding and you would still be the most beautiful bride in all of Paris."

I laugh and turn back to face him. He's dressed in a dark suit, the tails hanging at the perfect length for his long legs. "Thank goodness you changed out of your lab coat," I tease him. "You look quite good today yourself. But I think we're not supposed to see each other before the wedding. Bad luck, they say?"

Pierre chuckles. "Luck? And how might we quantify that?" Neither of us believes in luck. Luck is nonsense, nothing scientific about it. I'm only repeating what Hela told me before she'd left, a superstition and a warning. I repeat it now more for Pierre's amusement than for any real belief in such silliness.

He sweeps across the room in only two large steps, wraps me in a hug, and kisses me gently on the mouth. "I couldn't wait another minute to tell you what I'd gotten for us," he says.

"Something for the lab?" Really we could use so much more temperature-measuring equipment, though we haven't the space for it.

"No, *mon amour,* something for us. My cousin sent some money as a wedding gift, and I purchased us two brand new bicycles. They've just arrived."

"Bicycles?" It is so impractical of him, and yet the idea of a brand-new bicycle all my own, not a rickety hand-me-down from his brother, delights me beyond reproach, and I clap my hands together with excitement.

"Yes, and we can take them on our honeymoon. Ride through the entire French countryside."

"Oh, Pierre. What a glorious idea." We'd already planned a few weeks away from the city, but now the idea of bicycling with Pierre, for weeks on end, through the countryside! My chest swells, and I impulsively stand on my toes and kiss his cheek, the hairs of his beard scratching my lips in that delightful way they do. "I cannot wait to be Madame Curie," I exhale.

"Come." He holds out his hand. "Shall we test them out now, ride them to Luxembourg Station, to catch the omnibus to Sceaux?"

"Oh I don't know. Will we ruin our wedding clothes going by bicycle?" A bicycle ride will undo all of Bronia's steaming work on my dress, and probably mess up the curls Hela spent hours putting in my bun.

"Ruin them?" Pierre says. "Make them better, I say."

I smile and take his hand. Though just a few months ago I had chided him for his ridiculous notion of *forever*, now the very idea of it bubbles up inside of me. I am so full and alive and light, that as I leave my room with this man, about to be my husband, I'm almost surprised my feet can touch the ground.

If happiness is helium, then love is hydrogen, light enough to float our bicycles upward, toward the sky.

Marya

Loksow, Poland, 1896

My body was not built to carry a baby.

From the very moment our child began growing within me, I was ill. At first I could not eat any food at all, because even the smell of it was unbearable. Just to prepare it for Kaz for supper—my stomach roiled, and I had to go lie down while he ate at the table alone. And still our apartment was so very tiny that the smells permeated my skin, even in bed. I could not escape them, nor the lingering metallic taste of my own tongue, and I had to constantly fight back the urge to gag.

After a few months, when my dresses began to fit too tight around the middle, I tried to force myself to eat. I knew enough biology to understand that the baby needed food from me to thrive. But as hard as I tried to force it, half the time, I would throw my meals back up again anyway. The nausea overwhelmed all my senses—I could barely hear or see or speak, because every sound, every sight, every word, made me blindingly, dizzily nauseated.

Kazimierz had begun assisting Hipolit around the same

time I found out about the baby. And ever since, Kaz was gone more than he was home with me. Or maybe it was that I could not even see him, feel him, bear the smell of him when he was nearby. He was no longer my steady, because all I could feel was dizzy and ill.

I wanted to know how his studies were going, wanted to feel assured that everything was well, and that after our baby was born, things would get easier, and we could still move to Paris at some point. Hela wrote me that she was finishing a chemistry course there, passing her exams with the highest scores in her class. And Bronia had good work as an obstetrical doctor. She had two children now, her daughter Lou and her son Jakub, and she employed the help of a governess to look after them while she practiced medicine and Hela took classes full time.

I could still see Paris, like a white blinding light at the end of a long, dark passageway. If only I had the strength, if only I could stop feeling so ill, I might just keep pushing toward it. I might eventually get there.

I CONTINUED GOING TO WORK EACH MORNING AT THE KA-minskis, simply because I did not have the option not to. We needed my salary to afford our apartment and food, and I could not expect Kaz to work any harder when already he was teaching during the day and then learning with Hipolit, too. After dark he came home with a stack of exams to grade and a pile of mathematics books and papers from Hipolit to read.

Hela returned to Warsaw for a monthlong break in April, and both she and Papa begged me to come home and spend some time resting there with them. But I could not afford *not* to go to work, and as much as I longed for the warmth of Papa and my sister and Warsaw, I wrote them and told them only a half-truth: Kaz could not survive alone in Loksow without me.

The whole truth was, I often lay in bed at night, alone, while he worked by candlelight at our table. I could hear the pages turning, turning beneath his eager fingers, the noise of it magnified, heightened, the way all my senses were with this growing baby inside of me.

Some nights I wanted to stand up and yell at him to stop. I wanted to beg him to come to bed, to hold on to me and steady my belly with his warm hands, to take some of the brunt of this discomfort onto himself. Or to do something, anything, to make me feel better. But I never did that. There was nothing real he could do for me anyway, and I bit back the urge to yell. To act upset with him. To demand something from him. What could he possibly give me that would take this awful sickness away?

And then there was the strangest thing of all: though I had not desired a baby, and though I constantly felt ill, I already felt this burgeoning love for my own child that grew and grew inside of me day by day, in between moments of sickness: delicate and ephemeral, like a bubble.

WHEN I WAS ABOUT SIX MONTHS ALONG, KAZ CAME HOME early one evening. It was the first time I'd seen him before dark in weeks, and his sudden presence both surprised and annoyed me. It was a Wednesday, and I was trying to force down some broth before I left to go to Agata's for class. I had spent most of the day lying on the floor of the Kaminskis' nursery, allowing Jan and Jedrek to climb on me at will. My body was sore and heavy, and my mind longed for both the stimulation of class tonight and to be with my friends, especially Joanna who was also expecting a baby. As soon as Kaz walked in, I knew he was going to ask me not to go, and that I was going to have to muster up all my energy to argue with him.

"You're home early," I said, forcing a smile. I hoisted my heavy body out of the chair and stepped toward him for a quick kiss. He tasted strangely of vodka, and the mere hint of it turned my stomach. I inhaled, then exhaled slowly, hoping the little bit of broth I'd managed would stay down.

"Kadi told me she has been worried about you the last few Wednesday nights. You aren't well enough right now to be traipsing around the city, and for illegal classes no less," Kaz said, his words slightly slurred.

I wondered how much vodka he'd drunk and who with. But I didn't ask because there were so many things that bothered me in what he'd just said, it was too much to also worry about how he'd said it. I closed my eyes, breathed deeply again, trying to calm myself down before I responded. I knew he might see Kadi from time to time, as he spent so much time now with her father, but the very idea of the two of them *discussing me*, behind my back—that is what bothered me most. Thinking they knew what was best for me, that they had talked about it even. It was infuriating. Kadi was supposed to be my friend. She was supposed to have secrets with me, not with Kaz.

I went back to the table and choked down another few spoonfuls of broth, as if to emphasize my point. I forced myself to swallow, pushing back the reflex to gag. My stomach churned, and it would be so easy to do what he wanted. Stay here, with him. But once the baby was born it would be harder to attend classes. Maybe impossible. I needed to go while I still could. "I am perfectly well," I said, defiantly.

"Kadi said you would say that." I didn't like the way he said her name, like she belonged to him, not to me. But then he sighed, walked over, and kissed the top of my head. "At least let me walk you there and home tonight, all right, *kochanie?* You know I worry about you."

I softened at the feel of his warm lips on my head and the sweet notion in his voice that he only wanted to care for me, only wanted what was best for me. He didn't wish to hold me back, he only wished to keep me well and whole and safe. And besides, I hadn't really seen him now in weeks. The very idea of a walk with my husband, on a warm spring evening—for a few moments, the swell of nausea abated.

"Yes," I told him, feeling more agreeable than I had in a long time. "I would like that very much."

AGATA LIVED ONLY THREE BLOCKS AWAY, BUT KAZ AND I TOOK our time. He held on to my hand, and for the beginning of our walk, my body felt lighter again, my mind freer. I was just a girl ambling on the cobblestone streets of Loksow, hopelessly in love with this beautiful mathematician. I entwined arms with him so we were walking elbow to elbow, hip to hip. The warm fresh air was good for my sickness, and as Kaz told me about the equations he was working on with Hipolit and how Hipolit was trying to help him secure a place at the university, I felt a sense of calm come over me that I hadn't felt in a while.

"Maybe by the time the baby comes, I will have a job there, and we will have more money," Kaz said. "You could stop working for the Kaminskis."

It had felt a small torture these past few months chasing after those two ill-behaved boys while feeling so ill, and all I could think about each day was that I longed for the baby inside of me to be a girl and to be nothing like those raucous twins. The Kaminskis had offered that I could bring my baby to work and care for all three children. But now the idea that I might be able to stay at home and care just for my baby, and oh my, I could read and study and think all day long too? I stopped walking, stood up on my tiptoes and kissed Kaz softly on the mouth.

All at once, there was a sharp pain in my stomach, and I let go of Kaz, doubled over, and put my hands to my belly.

"Marya?" The pain was so blinding, I couldn't see him any longer. His voice was far away, like it was traveling through water, bending and breaking and garbled. "Marya," he said again.

My belly throbbed and pulled, and I clutched it, wanting the pain to stop. And then from somewhere very far away, I heard his voice again: "You're bleeding."

I blinked and tried to focus my eyes, but everything was black and dizzying, and the pain was so bad, I could not stand up, and maybe I crumpled to the ground, or maybe I didn't, but the next sensation I understood was Kaz picking me up, carrying me, running with me back toward our apartment.

I told him, *Go to Agata's instead.* She knew about the body, studying as much as she could. In another life, another country, she would've trained to be a doctor, like Bronia in Paris. *Oh, Bronia.* I suddenly wished for my sister, for the comfort of her hug and the warmth of her medical knowledge.

But maybe I didn't tell Kaz anything. Or maybe he didn't listen. Because he was breathing so hard, carrying me up the flight of stairs past the bakery, to our tiny apartment. And then for a moment the pain lessened, and I thought, if only I could go to sleep, everything would be okay again when I awoke.

WHEN I OPENED MY EYES AGAIN IT WAS MORNING, OR, DAYtime. Sunlight streamed through our apartment window, making the table a yellow, glowing circle.

"Marya." A man's voice. But not Kaz. I was keenly aware it was not my husband, but I didn't know who could possibly be saying my name. I blinked to focus on his face. He was older, Papa's age, balding with a sparse gray beard. I didn't recognize him.

Then I heard another voice, a woman: "She's coming out of it," the woman said, and the familiarity of her tone struck me, colder than the river in winter in Szczuki. *My mother-in-law, Pani Zorawska.* I had not spoken to her since that day I'd run away from my job caring for Kaz's younger brothers and sisters, years earlier. If she were here now, I must be dying. She must've come here to take back her eldest son.

"No, he's mine now," I tried to say, but the words would not come out. My tongue was thick, too hot. Everything was fire. And pain. There was a knife in my belly, tugging me apart.

"Marya." *The unfamiliar man again.* Then he explained: he was a doctor. The Zorawskis' family doctor. Had Kaz been so worried about me, he'd asked his family for help?

"Kaz." I finally found my voice. "Kazimierz?"

"I'm here," he said, and it was only then that I saw him, sitting by the bed. He reached out and stroked my hair.

"What's wrong?" I said. "Tell me."

"*Kochanie,*" he said. "The doctor says there is a problem with your body, and that the baby might not be okay." He choked on the last words, so that it sounded like he was gasping for air.

The baby might not be okay?

"If only you had come to me sooner," the doctor said now, his tone accusing. *Come to him?* Kaz and I did not have the money for a private doctor. Women had been having babies since the beginning of time on their own, with midwives and female friends to help them. And I hated this man, this doctor, for blaming me for whatever was happening now, and worse, making Kaz believe it too.

"This isn't my fault," I whispered, but the words came out sounding meek, defensive, useless even to me.

Kazimierz turned and exchanged a look with someone, maybe his mother, but I couldn't see her, only hear her sigh from somewhere across the room.

"All you can do now," the doctor said, "is stay in this bed and rest until the baby comes. And pray to our Lord that He forgives you. That He lets you have this baby."

I DID NOT BELIEVE IN GOD. I HAD NOT EVER SINCE MAMA DIED of tuberculosis when I was ten, and just before her, my eldest sister, Zofia, of typhus. It was then that I decided I would put any faith I had into science, not into religion. Science, medicine, could have saved them. God had not. Bronia had felt the same as me. It was why she'd gone to Paris to become a doctor.

But then it was only me and my bed each day, and this baby inside of me. Every time I felt a kick, the small angle of an elbow, I closed my eyes and silently thanked this God that the doctor, and my husband, and probably all the rest of Poland, thought I should believe in.

For an entire week I lay there, my mind numb and blank, my body a useless and terrible vessel. Every kick, I tried so hard to believe.

But then the kicking stopped. My stomach grew hard and still and tight.

And later that night, Kaz summoned the doctor again, and the baby came. She was too early. Everything was wrong.

She left my body still and quiet, her skin icy cold and blue.

MARIE

Paris, 1897

My body is not built to carry a baby.

I am ill and tired, nauseated for months on end, and suddenly instead of my haven, the lab becomes my purgatory. The smells of the fire and metal I used to love incite my nausea so that I often have to run outside and vomit out back.

It had been Pierre's idea to start our family in the first place. *Imagine how beautiful and brilliant our child would be!* Pierre had traced a line on my bare shoulder with his finger, and in an instant I had seen it, too, this imaginary, luminescent child of ours. That had been enough to believe I wanted what he wanted. Besides, Bronia has two children now, and she is still practicing medicine. Pregnancy had agreed with her, too. A few years ago, she'd even helped me move into my first room alone in Paris: eight months along and she was pushing a handcart of my things down rue Flatters. I'm angry with my condition, with my own body for its betrayal, for its inability to succeed at its most base biological function.

"*Mon amour,* you need a break," Pierre insists, but I am not about to give up my work, my research. Then Papa writes that he is returning to France on vacation, and Pierre says it would upset Papa were I to not go see him for a few weeks. Deep down I know the two of them have perhaps conspired on this plan to take care of me: *poor, mad Marie, refusing to take some time for herself.* But I am so tired, and I truly do need a break, so I go off to Port-Blanc without much argument.

Papa and I spend most of July at the Hotel of the Grey Rocks. The sunshine and the sea are glorious and rejuvenating. As I breathe the country air and take my meals with Papa in the hotel dining room, my nausea subsides more than it has in months.

"You are getting color in your cheeks," Papa says, with a slow smile. He is older than I picture him in my head; his voice is gravelly and his hands shake a little as he cuts up his meat. I feel both guilt at not living near him in Poland, and a moment of gratefulness to have this time with him, that being so ill forced me here, now. And maybe it is the sunshine, or being with Papa, or maybe it is that away from the lab and the city, my body understands how to perform its biological functions, but I do actually feel better.

Pierre stays behind in Paris, as his mother, Sophie-Claire, is very ill with incurable cancer of the breast, and we'd both agreed before I left that he could not leave her. But this is the first time I've been away from him for more than a few hours since we got married, and I am shocked by how desperately I miss him. We write each other daily, but it is not the same as being together, and when after three whole weeks apart, he shows up one morning at the hotel, surprises me, I cannot contain my glee. I reach up and touch his beautiful face, trailing my fingers softly through his beard.

"*Mon amour*, the sea air agrees with you," he tells me. "Your eyes have light again."

He's right. I feel so happy, so much like my old self, that I suggest a bicycle ride. Pierre worries it will be too much for me, but I push away his concern. I feel so much better here. We borrow two bicycles from the hotel, and go out and ride all afternoon. I forget it all: feeling ill and about the baby coming so soon. And there is nothing but the wind in my hair and my husband pedaling behind me. I am too fast for him, even with the weight of pregnancy. He still cannot catch me, or perhaps he is letting me ride ahead to make me feel good again. His laughter trails in my dust, and he calls out that our baby might be born riding.

When we get back to the hotel that night, I get off the bicycle, and suddenly I am unsteady, shaky and weak. The nausea hits me, worse than before. I lean over the side of the bicycle, heaving.

"Marie?" Pierre's voice is alarmed, and I look up, wipe my mouth with the back of my hand. He points to my shoe. I look down, and it is dotted with red. "Are you bleeding?"

IN THE DEEPEST, HOTTEST HOUR OF AUGUST, I LIE IN MY BED back in our apartment on rue de la Glacière, heavy and restless. Pierre and I rushed back to Paris, those drops of blood on my shoe enough to turn me cold with terror. Pierre had summoned his father, Dr. Curie, who'd examined me, ordered me to stay in bed for the remainder of my pregnancy, stay as still as I possibly can. He has been checking on me and the baby twice a day, looking for more signs of overexertion or distress. But so far, there have been none. And now that I have lain here for two whole weeks, I believe I will either have this baby soon or I will die of boredom and despair.

Pierre brings me breakfast of toast and tea this morning before leaving for the lab.

"Pierre, I can't." I push the plate away, and he sets it gingerly on my night table.

"You need to eat, *mon amour.*" He bends down, brushes his lips gently across my forehead. "It is simple science. The baby needs nutrients from you."

"I'm not hungry," I say. Then the baby kicks inside of me, as if in protest. My stomach swells again with more nausea.

Pierre rests his hand gently on my belly, then on my forehead. He strokes his thumb softly across my temple. "If I could trade places with you, you know I would."

He's said this so many times these past few weeks, I actually believe him. But biology, science, prevents this, of course, and it is the angriest I have ever felt at something so scientific. "I will have the toast in a bit," I relent. "Go, get to the lab. Go ahead. I'll be fine."

Pierre hesitates before standing, following my directions. He walks out of our bedroom, and I bite back tears as I imagine him walking the short path to our lab without me.

I'm glad he can continue our work, in spite of my miserable condition. I can't imagine how much worse I'd feel if I did not have Pierre now, if all progress had to stop while I am forced to lie here. It just seems so endlessly unfair, the inequity that comes to the woman when a married couple decides to have a child. That isn't Pierre's fault of course.

The baby kicks again, and I take the toast from the plate on the nightstand, where Pierre left it, forcing myself to nibble lightly on the edges, swallow it down, and take a sip of tea.

I put my hand across my stomach, stroke it lightly, hoping to calm both my nausea and the baby's kicks. "You will come out soon," I say to no one, to the empty room, to the being inside of me who does not yet have a fully developed sense of intellect. Rationally I know all this, but spending days on end with nothing to stimulate the mind but books and articles is turning me mad. "You will come out soon," I say. "And your papa will teach you all there is to know about science."

Once this child is outside of me, it will be Pierre's turn to carry him or her. I plan to return to the lab as soon as I give birth.

FINALLY, I AWAKE IN THE MIDDLE OF THE NIGHT ON SEPTEMber 12th, my stomach clenched with labor pains, the bedsheet wet beneath me. I wake Pierre, tell him to send for his father. It is time. *It is finally time!*

"Are you all right, *mon amour?*" The nervousness in his voice cuts through the darkness.

"Yes," I lie. "The pains aren't that bad." They're worse than any pain I have ever felt, hitting every nerve of my body. But they are such a relief, too. I welcome them. These long sick months, these endless days in bed, they will be over soon.

Bronia had told me to remember to breathe in and out slowly to manage the contractions. But breathing doesn't help at all, and each time the pain grips me, I begin equations in my head, focusing on calculating the kinetic energy I might be expending, with a variety of integers. I hold my focus on the numbers, on the mathematical probability. And then the pain subsides, and I leave off the equation and think, *soon the baby will be outside of me*, my life and my body my own again. Everything back the way it was. Tomorrow, or certainly the next day, I'll get out of bed and I'll walk to the lab again, and life and science will resume. I cling to that thought now as I push, as I push again.

Just one last push, Dr. Curie finally says. I look at the window and night has fallen, again. Through the haze of pain, the equations of my contractions, I have lost an entire day.

Pierre squeezes my hand, and I do as Dr. Curie says, muster up all my strength, push again. The pressure in my abdomen eases, and then with a gush, the baby is outside of me. I wait for it, the flood of relief I've been expecting, wanting, for months now. But my chest is tight. My legs are numb, and it is hard to breathe.

"It's a girl," Dr. Curie cries. He whisks her away, wraps her in a towel, and rubs her skin until she lets out a small cry, then a long wail. And suddenly, Pierre's shoulders shake and tears flood his face. "She's so small," he cries out. "I did not think she would be this small."

Dr. Curie hands me the baby, still wrapped in the towel, and I examine her: she is perfectly the right size for a newborn. She has ten fingers and ten toes, Pierre's eyes, and my nose, a symmetrical face, and the softest flesh I've ever felt. This baby that Pierre and I have created, that my body grew and nourished and tortured me with over months and months, she is more perfect than anything we've ever done together in the lab.

I FINALLY DO GET OUT OF THE BED THE NEXT MORNING, BUT not to go to the lab. All that time spent in bed and it had never occurred to me how much the baby would need *me* once she came. Irène cries for me and then suckles me endlessly, leaving my body more tired, more sore, more nauseated than ever before. I go through weeks in a daze, my mind too numb and exhausted to even think in equations. Or about what I'm missing in the lab.

Irène begins to lose weight, and then all I do is worry over her. My mind is so consumed that I don't even notice Pierre is gone all day or wonder about the work he is doing without me. He comes and goes with a kiss to me and Irène, and I say to him, "Should we call your father to examine her again? Maybe she's sick?"

My love and worry for her is like nothing I can explain through any logical reasoning. It is an orchid, delicate and fragile. Beautiful and breakable. If anything happens to Irène, it will be my undoing.

Pierre summons his father, three evenings in a row. Irène cries and cries, and she is much too thin.

"Perhaps you should try a bottle instead," Dr. Curie finally suggests gently, with the detachment of a doctor, not the attachment of a *grand-père*, who leans down to kiss Irène's hollowing cheek after he examines her. "She is healthy, Marie, but I don't believe she's getting enough milk from you."

As soon as I switch her to the bottle to feed, she begins to grow again, plumping up in days. Apparently, my body is not made for motherhood, the way it was not made for pregnancy. Once I accept this, a fact, the worry lifts, hovers above me, like lithium on water. My mind is open again.

"What a shame," Bronia says, when she comes by to visit her niece and check up on us. "Feeding by breast is so much more convenient."

But my breasts are also a tether, and once Irène only requires a bottle, which can be given just as easily by *Grand-Père* or *Papa* as by *Maman*, I begin to feel it so strongly: my deep and abiding love for science.

Then, when I awake each morning at dawn, it is the lab calling to me again—its cries now louder, more pressing than Irène's.

MARYA

Zoppot, Poland, 1897

In early February the Baltic was sparkling and cold: a cerulean gem. I stared at it from the upstairs guest bedroom window in the Zorawskis' resort house, mesmerized by its breadth and depth and color, the deception of its beauty. Just before Kaz and I had arrived last week, a man drowned in the tug of the undercurrent. Or maybe it was that he froze to death—the water much too cold for swimming this time of year. Pani Zorawska had recounted it all to us with sheer horror and excitement upon our arrival, but I was exhausted from the long train ride, and I hadn't really been listening. Her words buzzed above my head like flies, the way so much had these past few months.

It was remarkable the way my body returned to normal in such short time. Seven months had passed, and now my baby girl, my *Zosia* as I had named her in my own mind, had been deceased longer than she had been alive inside of me. My stomach was concave, empty. To look at me, one would never know that I'd carried a baby in my womb, then lost her. To look at me one would not see the emptiness I felt, nor the way, now, my body was a shell and I was a fragment of a real woman. Or that I could not stand any longer for my husband to touch me.

Pani Zorawska had disappeared again from our lives for a few months after my loss, and Kazimierz and I had gone back to at least the appearance of what we had been before. He returned to his studies with Hipolit, and if it was possible, was home even less than before. I returned to work at the Kaminskis and my Wednesday evening classes as a student, though I had not been able to teach again yet, which both Agata and Leokadia remarked on with concern. I told them I just needed time; I just needed to heal. But now months had passed; everything appeared to be as it once was. It was only inside that I felt the constant hollow, that I felt my friends' and my husband's voices buzzing around me all the time like flies, the conversations too hard to follow, too much to understand.

Then, Pani Zorawska had sent a letter: the Zorawski family would be going on a retreat to the Baltic for a week in February, when Kaz's younger brothers and sisters had a break from school and university, and would we like to join them?

This is exactly what we need, Kaz had said. His eyes had lit up, and he'd clutched his mother's letter to his chest. He'd kissed the top of my head. *The sea air! Reuniting with my family at last, kochanie.*

I smiled at him, but inwardly worried about why she had invited us now, when we were broken. But Kaz had not been with his family in so long. I could not deny him that. I bit back my doubts and agreed with him out loud: Yes, *this is exactly what we need.*

AND SO, HERE WE WERE. ZOPPOT. THE BALTIC SEA VILLAGE ON the northern tip of Poland was a playground of the wealthy and

Russian royalty. I had never been to such an opulent place in all my life. The Zorawskis' beach house was twice the size of their manor house in Szczuki, a world away from our small life in Loksow. But even here, especially here, I was as cold and empty as I was at home. Kaz, though—he was full again, alive: his cheeks reddened with excitement as he spoke to his siblings about his work at the supper table.

I heard the words, *Hipolit, analytical geometry,* buzzing around my head. I forced a smile and took a sip of the cold water Pani Zorawska had placed in front of me at the table. The voices of Kaz and his siblings rose and grew dim. I cut my meat in tiny pieces, but I did not eat them—I pushed them around on my plate with my fork, and I looked around the table.

My, had all the children grown since I had been their governess. Even little Maryshna who I had rocked to sleep many nights, a babe in my arms—she was nearly as tall as I was now. She must be ten, or was it eleven? Practically all grown. It was what children did, I supposed, grew up. *Except for mine,* born too early, born blue.

"Marya." Pani Zorawska was saying my name, and I shook my head. If she'd been talking to me, I hadn't heard what she'd said. She put her hand on my shoulder. "Let's you and I go out to the porch and talk, shall we?"

I glanced at Kaz. His cheeks were pink, his eyes beaming, and he was laughing now at something his brother, Stanislaw, was telling him. I rose, and he noticed me again, just briefly. He squeezed my hand, and I squeezed back, then let my fingers trail away. I followed his mother behind the dining room, out onto the covered porch, which had an entire wall of windows that overlooked the cold, reckless sea.

"It's so beautiful to look at it, isn't it? It could almost deceive you." Pani Zorawska pointed toward the bright blue water, but she stared directly at me, raising her eyebrows. I nodded, uneasy here all alone with her for the first time in so many years. She sighed and patted a rocking chair, gesturing for me to sit down. I did, and then she sat in one next to me. We rocked for a little while, staring at the wild expanse of sea, saying nothing at all.

Once, I had admired her, back in Szczuki, when I had cared for her younger children for years and she had treated me with kindness. And when Kaz and I first secretly got engaged, I imagined she might come to treat me as a daughter, that I might have a mother again. But that was before I knew what she really thought of me, that I was not worthy of her son. And here I was all these years later, having not yet achieved my university degree, having failed my husband and myself and my baby girl. It bothered me that perhaps she had not been completely wrong.

"These past years have been unkind to you, haven't they, Marya?" She spoke matter-of-factly now, without sympathy or derision.

"I don't know," I said, feeling a deep need to defend myself, my choices. "I wouldn't say that." I had been sad and empty now for months, but somewhere, hovering just behind all that, there had been joy, hadn't there? Even if I couldn't quite remember the sweetness of it now—it had been there. She did not know about my Flying University in Loksow, about the way love could supersede hunger, longing, as Kaz and I lay in bed together, holding on to each other so many nights.

"Wouldn't you?" She tsked softly with her tongue. "You and my son live like beggars, neither one of you educated as you could be."

I wanted to say that she could've accepted that her son loved me many years ago, that I loved him, too. She could've accepted us, helped him with his tuition at Jagiellonian. Surely, he would've finished his course of study by now, and we could've moved to Paris. Kaz might've taught at the Sorbonne and I could've gone to university myself. But I bit my tongue, said none of that to her. "Why did you invite us here?" I asked instead. Surely, there had been many family trips without us in the last five years. So she had summoned a doctor last summer when I'd needed one, when Kaz had begged for her help, but then she had disappeared again without so much as even a letter expressing sorrow for our loss. So what did she really want with us now?

"Is it so wrong that I would want to see my oldest son? That I would want all my children to be together in one house, after all this time?"

"Of course not," I said, feeling just the slightest twinge of compassion for her. Kaz had missed his family, and they had missed him too. I wrote weekly letters to my sisters and Papa, and though I could not see any of them as often as I would like, we stayed in close touch.

She looked away from me, off toward the Baltic again. Neither one of us spoke for a few more moments. And then she cleared her throat and said it, what she had brought me here to say all along: "Kazimierz is young still. It is not too late for him to be happy."

I nodded, agreeing with that much. Kaz would finish his education, eventually. He would get a better job and we would move into a nicer apartment, and even if my body continued to betray me, my mind never would, and I would continue to learn any way and as much as I was able.

"My husband knows a priest who would be willing to annul your marriage, given what . . . happened last summer."

The distant buzzing finally stopped; her words were sharp and perfectly clear. I felt a stabbing pain in my stomach, a phantom pain, the ache of my empty womb, my beautiful blue Zosia. *Annul the marriage?*

"In exchange, we would be willing to give you the money you need to move to Paris, attend university like you've always dreamed. Or, you don't even have to attend university—you can take the tuition money and do whatever you wish with it. You could start over, too, close to your sisters." She was still talking.

I stared at her, unable to speak. I loved Kaz. I would always love Kaz. But could another woman, a woman his mother approved of, give him everything I couldn't? He could have the education he desired, along with his family's love, his family's money, and perhaps, most of all, his own child.

And Paris. Pursuing my education there had been my dream for so very long. But I put my hand on my empty stomach now and wondered if that was really what I still desired most.

"*Matka!*" Kaz's voice pierced the room, and I jumped. I turned around, and there he stood at the doorway, his face now bright red with distress, not joy. I wondered how much he had heard. I guessed, everything.

I moved to stand, to go to him, but Pani Zorawska was quicker than me. She got to him first, put her wrinkled hand to his cheek. "I just want what's best for you, *kochanie*. That is all. That is all I've ever wanted."

He reached up, removed her hand from his cheek, and walked to me swiftly, in two large strides. "Marya," he said. "I think it is time for us to go home."

"But you just got here," Pani Zorawska cried out.

LATER, ON THE TRAIN BACK TO LOKSOW, KAZ RESTED HIS face against the window, watching the devious blue Baltic drift away behind us. His expression was stony, resolute, and I could not tell if he was sad or angry. I reached for his hand, and when he took my hand, covered it with his own, squeezed gently, I felt myself exhale for the first time. I leaned my head back against the seat and closed my eyes. The lull of the train, the warmth of my husband, made me feel so very tired.

"What were you going to say, *kochanie?*" he said softly.

"Hmmm?" I murmured, on the brink of sleep.

"To Matka. When she offered you that money to leave me?"

I sat up and opened my eyes. Suddenly the rocking of the train made me feel nauseated, not relaxed. "I was going to say no, of course," I said quickly. I moved my hand up to Kaz's face, traced his jawline with my finger. "I love you. You know that."

His expression relaxed, and he put his arm around me, pulled me closer to him, kissed the top of my head. I leaned my head against his shoulder, closed my eyes again.

I did love him, but deep down I worried that Pani Zorawska was right. That she had always been right. And the truth was, I wasn't sure what I really would have said to her, had he not walked out onto the sun porch when he had.

MARIE

⁂

Paris, France, 1898

I am so focused on the pitchblende that I have not even heard Pierre walk into our lab, and when he says my name, I jump, nearly hitting my head on the wooden grocery crates we'd used to construct our ionization chamber a few weeks ago.

In the past weeks, I have decided to look further into Henri Becquerel's research on uranium compounds, and Pierre and I acquired a large ore sample, pitchblende from Bohemia, and built our own little rickety ionization chamber for testing. At present, I am so caught up in the peculiar readings coming out of the chamber that Pierre's voice barely even registers with me.

"Marie," he says again, a little louder.

"This can't be right," I say to him, no time for pleasantries, or to ask where he has been or what he wants of me now. I put the pitchblende back into the chamber. It is heavy and has a terrible dirty smell, and I am sweating, breathing hard. But I must test it again. My reading shows the radioactivity is so much greater than in uranium alone. But if it *is* right . . . then I have discovered something new. Something different. Something no scientist before me has found, and at that thought, my hands begin to tremble.

Pierre reaches out to steady them in his own. "Deep breath, *mon amour,*" he says, his voice softening, his face arched into a deep frown. Then, "I need to tell you something."

I turn my attention fully to him finally, alarmed. "Is it Irène? Is she sick?"

"No, no. It's not Irène at all. I've just received word . . . I didn't get the professorship at the Sorbonne."

Pierre had applied for a vacancy in the science department, and he had gotten the highest recommendation from the esteemed Monsieur Friedel, a brilliant chemist who'd mentored him and his brother, Jacques, with some of their earliest experiments. Jacques had gone on to become a professor of mineralogy in Montpellier on his recommendation. We'd felt certain Pierre would get the position here, and with it would come a higher-paying salary and better lab space, which would allow me to focus on my doctoral studies.

"What do you mean, you didn't get it?" The words erupt from me in disbelief. I'm still sweating from the exertion of my experiment, my breath ragged in my chest. "No one else who applied is more qualified than you."

"They gave it to Monsieur Perrin," Pierre says quietly. He has already taken a moment to digest the news before sharing it with me; he's already accepted it.

I shake my head. *Of course they did.* Jean Perrin is younger, but with a fancier degree, from one of the *grandes écoles.*

"Oh darling." I reach up and touch his cheek, stroke his beard softly. My fingers are filthy from the pitchblende, but it's not something Pierre will notice, nor care about. I'll have to remind him to wash it away later. "Everything will turn out all right. You'll see."

Pierre sighs; he's not sure he believes me. His mother passed away just two weeks after Irène was born, and he has been swimming slowly through his grief ever since. I have left Pierre's father in charge of looking after Irène, and that has helped Dr. Curie immensely. It brings him such joy to care for her, and for me, so little worry. I can fully concentrate on my work again. But Pierre is struggling, having trouble focusing, even asking me to attend séances with him, of all things.

I see it in his eyes sometimes still now, months later, that vacant look he gets as he stares off into the distance or loses his train of thought, midsentence. Pierre has always been absentminded in his brilliance, but lately he has been almost beyond distraction. I had truly believed he would get this job and it would bring him out of his darkness, bring him completely back to science and the world again.

"Well, who cares about them," I finally say. "I'm going to need your help with my pitchblende anyway."

He laughs a little, shakes his head. "What could you possibly need my help for? You have it all under control here, *mon amour.*"

And then I tell him about my peculiar readings of the degrees of radiation this morning, and that, if I can duplicate it, if it was not wrong, there is so much more to Becquerel's research and the pitchblende itself than any of us had ever dreamed, even me. That I might have just discovered an entirely new element, inside our tiny, rickety laboratory and our grocery carton ionization chamber. That I may be onto something so new, so very exciting.

Pierre cuts me off. "You are on the brink of something brilliant. I can feel it." His voice is wild. "Maybe you will need me, to be your assistant, help rush your findings out to the Academy."

"Yes, darling, I will need you for all of that. But first we have to replicate my results with the pitchblende. Make sure I haven't simply made a mistake."

"You? Make a mistake?" He laughs and shakes his head. His eyes finally brim with something other than loss, the excitement I feel too, the excitement that shakes my entire being. And then, buoyed by his belief in me, I stand up on my toes and kiss him softly.

IT ALL HAPPENS QUITE FAST, AND IN A MATTER OF DAYS, I AM certain there are *two* new elements in the pitchblende based on the levels of radioactivity in my testing. I name the first element *polonium* after my native Poland, the second *radium*, for its greater radioactivity. We are in a frenzied rush to write up the paper, because once we understand what we have found, we worry someone else will write it up first. We get the paper to the French Academy of Sciences, trusting Monsieur Lippman to present it on our behalf, as the Academy will not accept Pierre nor I as members yet. And when the Academy responds, they remark with interest, but they say we do not have enough evidence. To truly prove this, we will have to actually *isolate* these elements from the pitchblende.

"Impossible," Pierre says, shaking his head. "It would take years and . . . a ton of pitchblende."

"Difficult, yes." I agree. "But not impossible." We will do it ourselves, I tell him. We will chemically wash away at the rock, little by little, piece by piece, grueling and disgusting work. But we will do it and we will isolate the new elements, if only to prove them all wrong. If only to prove that we can. If only to earn our own place in the Academy.

"You look quite tired," Bronia says to me, a month later. She and Lou have come over on Sunday to teach me how to make jam. I've spent the entire last week in the lab, using chemicals on the pitchblende. My fingertips are raw, my nail beds ugly and scabbed. "Are you ill?" Bronia asks, putting her hand on my forehead. It doesn't matter that I am a mother myself, an accomplished scientist. She will always be my sister-mother. "Pregnant again?" she asks.

I shake my head. The truth is, I feel more exhausted than I've felt in my entire life, worse even than in my terrible condition with Irène. It is grueling and tedious work we are doing in the lab now. And though today it is Sunday, my day of rest, I cannot shake the tiredness, the ache of the work. Pierre, similarly exhausted, has decided to spend the entire day in bed. My fingers ache, my eyes burn. But I'd extended this invitation to Bronia weeks ago, and she has brought little Lou over, and I cannot disappoint them.

"Where's Irène?" Bronia asks now, looking around the kitchen.

"Dr. Curie took her to the park," I say.

Bronia frowns, but Irène is too young to understand jam making yet, and I am too tired to keep her from making a mess. When Dr. Curie offered the park, I'd gratefully accepted.

Bronia is an expert at jam making, having learned from our mother before she died. It is her reward for being older than me, more time with Mama. And I envy her ease now. I wish I could be more wifely, more motherly, like my sister, but it does not come naturally to me the way it does to her. Bronia can somehow manage to be all things: mother, wife, sister, doctor, and still never look tired. I imagine if I can just master jam making, I will master everything else as well.

"All right then, eight pounds of gooseberries," Bronia says now, recording her recipe in my household journal in her neat and perfect script as she speaks. "And an equal amount of crystalized sugar."

There it is, like an equation. And making jam, being wifely, cannot be so hard if you treat it just like this, just like science, can it? My kitchen is my laboratory, the gooseberries my minerals. I squash them beneath my fingertips, the warm juices running down my aching fingers.

Lou mashes the berries with me, and the sound of her little girl giggle, the feeling of the fruit on my fingers is relaxing, and I close my eyes and let the process soothe me. Perhaps when Irène is a little older, we will do this together, too. And I understand now why Bronia enjoys this. For a moment I almost don't realize Bronia is still talking to me. ". . . back to Poland," she says.

"What?" I open my eyes, remove my hands from the berries. My fingers are stained red, as if I'm bleeding.

"Zakopane," she says. "Mier and I are building a sanatorium there to live and work at, and when it's finished next year, we will finally return back to Poland." Her face has softened, her smile is wider than I've seen it in recent memory. Zakopane is a small country town at the base of the Tatras, in Austrian Poland, out of the Russian Empire, so Mier will be safe from prosecution. But Bronia will be back in Poland, only hours on the train from Warsaw, not days.

"Oh, Bron," I say. "How wonderful for you."

And something curls up in my chest: I'm not exactly sure what. It is jealousy mixed with a little bit of sadness, or, maybe it is pride, that my sister-mother has achieved her dream of becoming a doctor, and now she will go back to our homeland and help people there. Maybe one day, once we complete our research here, Pierre and Irène and I will be able to follow her.

MARYA

Poland, 1901

Papa was sixty-eight years old, and his letters to me were getting noticeably shorter, the time between each one noticeably longer. The gap widened from one to two weeks, then three. When it had been an entire month without one, I got worried and told Kaz I was taking the train to Warsaw the following day to check on him. "Do you want to come?" I asked him, knowing full well that he couldn't.

"I wish I could, *kochanie*," he said. And I nodded. I understood. I did. He had his work with Hipolit—he was assisting him with new research on elasticity, and Hipolit, too, was getting older. Kaz told me he felt like a vital part of Hipolit's research, recording notes when Hipolit forgot, making sure all the data was in order in the way the older man could not keep up with. And now instead of simply mentoring him, Hipolit was paying Kaz to be his research assistant. Kaz made twice as much money as he used to, which was a relief and a joy to him—to be paid to study mathematics!

The Kaminksi twins had gone away to boarding school in

Krakow last fall, so I was no longer needed in my full-time position there. In the time since, I'd learned how to *breathe* again, and I began to focus on teaching, my university. In the past few months, free from my governess duties, I realized if I made my Flying University into something real, something a little larger, the women who'd first started in it with me could all teach new women just joining, younger than us. We could begin to charge a small tuition fee to pay those of us who taught. If I were able to pay myself a salary that way, I would not ever need to get another governess job. And besides, I would be growing education for women in Loksow, and that would be a wonderful thing. A thing that filled me with enormous pride.

"But I hate for you to travel alone . . . I wish . . ." Kaz was still talking about my trip now. I knew exactly what he wished. That I would wait, at least until Sunday when he would be able to accompany me on the train ride, but I knew he would not ask me that now either, not when I was so worried about Papa's well-being, and today was only Monday. He began to speak, then hesitated.

"Kaz, I am a grown woman. I have made the trip many times before. I'll be fine."

"But that was . . . before."

Three weeks ago, there had been a pounding on our door during a Wednesday night class—two military police claiming they had gotten word of *illegal activity* here. Luckily I'd only had a few women in attendance that night—two hid under the bed, one in the closet, and then Leokadia and I had hastily wrapped ourselves in aprons before answering the door. Leokadia had thought fast, had used her moneyed charm to regale the policemen with a story about the preserves we were trying to can, a disaster that had happened with the fruit, and how we were trying so hard to learn, to please our husbands. Luckily they had not asked to actually *see* our nonexistent preserves. Her explanation, and her charm, had satisfied the policemen enough for them to leave. I had not recounted the incident to Kaz, and if he knew about it now, it would only be because Leokadia had told him while he was at work. *Had she?*

He stared at me now, his eyes wide, concerned, and I wondered if he was envisioning the Russian police pulling me off the train. "Kaz, really, I'll be just fine."

"What if you take Leokadia with you?" he suggested. "Then you wouldn't have to go alone."

"I'm sure she has better things to do."

Kaz shook his head. "No, she was just telling me how she would like to get out of the house more, have an adventure." Leokadia still played piano all around the Russian Empire of Poland, but she had not been invited back to Krakow in years and had told me how she longed to move away, somewhere freer, somewhere she could be paid to play and free to study at a real conservatory. So why did it bother me that she had told Kaz much the same?

I had this strange creeping sensation on the back of my neck, and I reached my hand up to try and rub it away. "Going to Papa's with me in Warsaw is not much of an adventure," I finally said.

"Please," Kaz begged me. "Just ask her if she'll ride the train with you. I'll come and check in on you both on the weekend."

I relented. Because the truth was I was worried what I would find at Papa's, and going there with a friend, not having to face it alone, actually didn't sound like the worst idea.

LEOKADIA AND I DIDN'T SPEAK MUCH ON THE TRAIN RIDE. WE left early in the morning, and we were both tired, but something else was nagging at me too. Kaz thought he knew so much about what she wanted, and it was something I wanted to be angry with her for. But then, what right did I have? She and her father had done nothing but help Kaz, and by extension, me, and I should feel grateful. And so I pressed my lips tightly together, saying nothing at all.

Leokadia mistook my silence for worry about Papa, and as the train arrived in Warsaw, she patted my arm and said, "Marya, I'm sure everything is fine, and maybe he has just been busy?"

I nodded, but Papa was never too busy to write his daughters, and Bronia had mentioned in her latest letter to me that she hadn't heard much from him either, that she was also beginning to worry. Besides, Papa loved to keep me updated on all the many good things happening with my sisters, bragging about them in a way they would not want to do about themselves. Hela was doing so well in her exams, at the top of her class in applied sciences, and she was dating a French scientist named Jacques—both *very kind* and *very handsome*. Bronia and her Kazimierz longed to return to Poland, but they wanted Hela to finish her schooling in Paris first, as no one wanted to leave her there all alone. I longed for them to return to Poland, too, to be closer to me again, but I also wanted them to stay in Paris. The idea of their return felt like the closing of a door, the final ending of my own dream of Paris.

LEOKADIA AND I WALKED THE FEW SHORT BLOCKS FROM THE train station, up the stairs to Papa's front door. I knocked, once softly, then harder. "Papa, it's Marya. I've come for a visit," I called out. He didn't respond, and then my heart shook against the walls of my chest, and I put my hand to my breast, an attempt to steady it.

"It's still early in the morning," Leokadia said. "Perhaps he's still asleep?" Papa awoke each day with the sun, and went to bed early, soon after the sun set. It would not be like him to still be asleep.

I used my key and let us in. The apartment was dark, all the curtains drawn. I ran my finger across his credenza, his dining table—there was a fine layer of dust covering everything, coating my fingertip. What if he had been here all alone, died in his bed, and no one had known for weeks? "Papa," I called out again, my voice breaking a little.

Leokadia reached for my hand, squeezed my fingers with her own, and in that moment I loved her for coming with me and loved Kaz for suggesting it.

We walked together back toward his bedroom. I knocked on the door. "Papa," I called out. "It's me, Marya." For a moment, he did not respond, and I did not dare to open his door, and then I heard a noise, slow footsteps from the other side, and I exhaled. I realized tears were rolling down my cheeks, and I pulled away from Leokadia and wiped furiously at my face, not wanting Papa to see me cry.

He opened the door. "Marya? What are you doing here?" He looked older than when I'd seen him last, six months ago, and now he stood stooped, in his dressing gown.

"I got worried about you when I hadn't gotten a letter in four weeks. Are you ill?" I asked him. He didn't answer, just kept staring at me, and I kept talking. "Have you been eating? Remembering to drink water, Papa?"

He tilted his head to the side, like he was considering my

questions, or he wasn't sure. He put his hand on his stomach. "I haven't been too hungry," he finally said. He wobbled a little, then grabbed on to the door to steady himself.

"Why don't you help him into bed?" Leokadia said softly. "I'll find him some food to eat."

I took his arm, and he leaned on me. Only then did I realize just how thin he'd gotten, how frail he was. "Papa," I admonished him. "Why didn't you write that you weren't feeling well? I would've come sooner."

"You have a husband to worry about, a life in Loksow. And your sisters are so busy in Paris. I didn't want to be a bother to anyone."

I remembered that morning, ten years ago, when Papa had come into my room, thrown the curtains open, and pulled me out of my darkness. He had offered me hope: money and Paris and an education, and then he had loved me all the same when I'd chosen a life with Kaz instead.

I got him back into bed, felt his forehead with the back of my hand. He felt hot; I worried he had a fever. "I'll call the doctor," I told him.

He closed his eyes, then opened them again. "My sweet Marya," he said, his lips turning into a slow smile. "The doctor just left. There is nothing more he can do for me, other than surgery, and I'm not going to have that."

"Papa, don't say that."

"Just sit here with me," he said.

I pulled the chair from the side of the room, pushed it toward his bed, my eyes welling with tears. I bit my lip to keep them at bay. I sat and took his hand in my own, running my fingers softly over his wrinkled flesh. Papa closed his eyes again, his breathing evened, and I thought he'd fallen back to sleep, but then he said, "Marya, my youngest, my dearest. I always thought you would . . ." His voice trailed off.

"Thought I would, what . . . Papa?"

But then he really was asleep. His chest rattled with a soft snore, and he didn't answer.

I FOUND LEOKADIA KNITTING IN THE PARLOR A LITTLE WHILE later. Her fingers turned, twisting the long needles, moving the way they did when she played piano, swiftly, deftly. She looked up when she heard me walk in, but her fingers kept going—Leokadia's fingers were always moving. "How is he?" she asked.

"Not well," I said. From what I'd learned of biology in my classes, I guessed his liver wasn't functioning fully: his pallor was gray, his eyes tinged with yellow. I wondered how long he'd known he needed surgery, and whether now it might already be too late. I sighed and I took a sheet of paper from Papa's desk, knowing I needed to write out a telegram to send to Bronia and Hela right away. They needed to come from Paris. Papa looked terrible. Thank goodness I'd come here when I did.

"You're quite lucky, you know," Leokadia said. Her knitting needles clicked and clicked, a fast and steady rhythm. "You have two men who both adore and respect you."

I had told her before about Papa's desire to teach my sisters and me as we were growing up. About how he read us banned books as bedtime stories, how he wanted us to leave Poland to get a real university education, and how he believed that as intelligent women, we were just as capable, if not more so, to grow our minds as any man. But there was something in her voice that made me uneasy now, something about what she was saying about Kaz, too, and it was the same thing I felt when I realized she might have told him about our encounter with the police, that they had some sort of relationship outside of me.

But I was grateful for her friendship, too, and that she had come here with me, so all I said to her instead was, "I'm not ready for him to go, Kadi. Maybe I am greedy? I want more time with him."

She put the needles in her lap, reached out both her hands for mine. "How good that he has you, that we are here," she said. We sat like that for a few moments, and then I went back to the stationery, to compose a telegram for Bronia and Hela, to tell them to come on the train from Paris at once, before it was too late.

LATER, WHEN IT WAS VERY DARK, THE MIDDLE OF THE NIGHT, I could not sleep, and I got up and sat by Papa's bed again, held on to him. His hand was cool and dry, the skin around his fingers loose and wrinkled. I stroked his fingers softly with my thumbs and hummed the melody of a long-forgotten lullaby, "Śpij Laleczko," that came back to me only now. Mama had sung it to me and Hela and Bronia and Zosia once, when we were very young, and all ill, before Zosia succumbed to her sickness.

I sat there holding on to him until morning, until he opened his eyes, saw me there, smiled. "Papa," I asked him. "What did you mean yesterday . . . you started to say you always thought I would . . . what did you mean?"

"Marya, my youngest, my brightest." He spoke slowly, his voice trembling with the effort it took him to form the words. "I always thought you would be the one to change the world."

"And I have disappointed you," I said quietly.

"Disappointed me . . . no, not at all. Look at you, still learning, teaching young women in Poland. Education changes everything, does it not?"

"You taught me that," I said. Papa had been a teacher himself, before the Russians took over Poland, and he'd always told us our entire lives how important education was. I squeezed his hands softly between my own.

"I wanted to teach you more," he said, breathless.

"You taught me everything," I told him.

TWO DAYS LATER HE TOOK HIS LAST BREATH, WITH ME SITting by his bed, holding his hand. I was not ready to let him go, but he was ready to leave, and so I had no choice.

Bronia and Hela arrived on the train from Paris, three days too late.

MARIE

Paris & Warsaw, 1902

"Mon amour," Pierre says into the darkness of Irène's bed-room, waking me with a gentle shake of my shoulder. Irène likes me to sit with her while she falls asleep each night, and perhaps she is insecure because she barely sees me during the day. Tonight I must've fallen asleep myself in here. "Come with me," Pierre says softly in my ear.

I peer out Irène's window toward our garden. It is the dark-est of nights, not even a sliver of moon. "Pierre, what time is it?"

"Just about nine." Only nine? I stretch and my body aches. I fell asleep in a strange position in the rocking chair, and I have been so tired as of late, the work we've undertaken so hard, so painstaking, that often I even dream about my own exhaustion. Pierre, too—sometimes he awakens me in the middle of the night, half-asleep, crying out in agony over the pains in his legs. But tonight his voice is soft, happy. Different.

"Come," Pierre says. "Get your coat and come with me to the lab. I have a surprise for you."

I rise, suddenly feeling dizzy, and Pierre puts his arm around me to steady me. We've been working so hard and so long with the pitchblende, and finally, finally, we've extracted enough radium and will be able to present it to the Academy. They asked for us to isolate the element to prove ourselves worthy, perhaps believing we never would. And at long last, we have. But these have been long, grueling, exhausting years, so many days when we are not feeling well in body or in spirit.

Yet in spite of the work and all the illness that has befallen us, Pierre always finds a way to look for the best in everything, and he brings me to see it too. Though it is late, I trust in his surprise, and I get my coat.

We tiptoe out to the front door, not wanting to wake Irène, or Dr. Curie, who is asleep in his own room down the hall. Pierre races out to boulevard Kellerman, forgetting for the moment all the pains in his legs, and I follow, suddenly giddy, or maybe I am just overtired, delirious.

We hold on to each other and proceed to walk, arm in arm. The night air is cool, and the darkness feels dangerous, but I cling to my husband, happy for a moment to feel free, of the science, of our household obligations, even of Irène's little shouts for me each night as she tries to fall asleep.

When we reach the lab, Pierre unlocks the door and says, "*Mon amour*, don't light the lamp."

"But it's very dark, we won't be able to see what we're doing." We walk inside, and I reach for the lamp in spite of his words.

He gently tugs me away. "No, Marie, look."

He points to our worktable, where, since I left, hours ago, he has lined up all our samples of extracted radium inside glass. They line the table now in rows, and in the absolute blackness of this night, they glow, making our dark, small shed of a lab alive with an ethereal light. I gasp, put my hand to my mouth.

How many days in the lab had I said to him that it felt we

were working so hard for nothing tangible, that if only radium were beautiful, striking in its color, I might feel more encouraged.

And now here it is, right in front of my very eyes: our radium. Glowing so brightly it feels alive. Or otherworldly. As if Pierre has reached up into the sky, grabbed starlight, and put it in glass for me in our little lab. "Oh, Pierre," I say. "Look what you have done!"

He climbs up onto the worktable to sit within the glow. His face illuminates green and gold. I go to him and he embraces me. "Look what *we* have done, *mon amour*. All this work, all these years."

"It's the most beautiful thing I've ever seen," I tell him. And it is.

THE GLOW OF OUR RADIUM BURNS BRIGHTER THAN THE DIFFI-culty of the work, the years of aches and pains in our bodies. It is *everything*. It is worth the higher-paying jobs we turned down in Geneva so that we could stay here in Paris and not interrupt our research by moving. It is worth the time and the distance away from my family, and from my country, and the long hours away from our daughter.

But then, only weeks later, an urgent telegram arrives from Warsaw from Hela, and suddenly the glow of the radium dims. Papa has been ill, has recently had surgery for gallstones. In her last letter Hela told me all was well, he was recovering nicely from the surgery, on the mend. But then her urgent telegram: all at once, he is dying. And I must get to Warsaw as soon as I can.

I am wrapped inside my own panic, my disbelief. *This can't be real. This can't be happening.* Not when I am so far away.

I throw a few dresses into a valise, and Pierre hovers, saying he wants to go to Warsaw with me. But someone has to stay here, look after the lab and the household and Irène. "No," I tell him, resolutely. "I will go to Poland alone."

"At least let me get you to the train," Pierre says. And I agree to that much.

A few hours later, I offer him and Irène a quick kiss goodbye before I board the train. "Send a telegram with any news," Pierre calls after me, a worried look on his face. I can see him standing there, looking gloomy through my window, even after I take my seat on the train. I reach my hand up to the glass, partly to wave goodbye, partly to try and hang on to this moment, where my life is still whole.

THE LAST TIME I WENT BACK TO POLAND, IT WAS THREE YEARS ago, and our exhaustion from the work had only just begun to set in. Bronia and Mier and Lou and Jakub moved to Zakopane in 1899, opened their sanatorium, and a few months later my whole family reunited there for a holiday. Hela and Stanislaw, their daughter Hanna (just about the same age as Irène), and Papa all came together from Warsaw. Pierre and Irène and I came from France, and for a few glorious weeks we were all together. It was Pierre's first time in Poland, and how he had enjoyed it so. *I see why you love your country so much,* he'd said to me as we'd taken a hike together on a mountain trail in the sunshine of the Tatras. And I had felt a glimmer of joy, of hope. One day my whole family could be together again in Poland. Pierre would love it enough, just like the rest of us.

When we returned to Paris, I got caught up in our work. Everything else felt so far away, that now, on the train, it is hard to believe it has been years since I've last seen Papa and my sisters, not weeks or months. And I spend the long hours on the train from Paris to Berlin praying to a God that I don't believe in that Papa will hang on longer, that he will make a miraculous recovery. Perhaps now that Pierre and I have extracted our radium we will have more time, and we can make more frequent visits to Poland.

But when I change trains in Germany there is an emergency telegram from Hela, waiting for me at the station. It is too late. *I am too late.* Papa died in the middle of the night.

THE TRAIN ROLLS ON FROM BERLIN TO WARSAW. SO MANY hours and hours and hours. They are excruciating. Guilt curls into my chest like a lion, roaring and hurting, but I am too stunned for tears. My body is cold and numb, from grief, or the shock. Papa was doing fine just last week. How has this all happened so fast?

When the train arrives in Warsaw at last, I have not eaten nor slept for days, and yet I do not feel tired or hungry. I am only angry now. Why didn't Hela write sooner? Why did she wait until the very end? I storm from the train, rehearsing my tirade, and practically run the entire way to Papa's apartment.

"How could you?" I say to Hela, when she opens the door and tries to wrap me in a teary-eyed hug.

Bronia stands behind her. Of course, she made it first, the journey from Zakopane so much shorter than the one from France. Her face is white as snow, her eyes bloodshot from her own tears. "Marya, you are so thin," Bronia says, reaching for me, too, but I pull away from them both. "Are you feeling well?" Bronia asks. Always my sister-mother. Her worry enrages me even more, perhaps unjustly so. But it's not fair; they got to say goodbye.

"I need to see him," I demand, ignoring her questions about my health.

"He's gone," Hela says softly.

And though I am a scientist and I understand what happens in death, I cannot let it go. "I demand to see him," I say again. Tears roll down Hela's face, and maybe they are tears of my doing and I should feel her pain as my own, my sister-twin. But I can only feel my own rage.

Bronia sighs and takes my arm. "The casket has already been prepared," she says. "But I will take you to it."

THEN, PAPA IS A WOODEN BOX. BRONIA WAITS OUTSIDE THE mortuary, giving me, she says, a chance to say my goodbyes.

In the last letter Papa wrote to me, he told me how proud he was, how happy he was to know that his daughter, his little *Maryishna Sklodowksa*, born of Warsaw, Poland, had discovered an entirely new element, opened up the world of science in a way no man had yet done. And then, as was his way, he had told me about the weather. Papa was always as interested in the other-worldly as he was the mundane. The day, he wrote, was cool, but still pleasant. Or had he said it was warm? I can't remember exactly now, nor even where I set the letter down. In the lab, somewhere? Or had I been reading it in Irène's room as I'd tucked her into bed?

It is stupid, and it does not matter now, what he wrote about the weather. But I want to remember the last piece of him, and it infuriates me that I can't. *But it does not matter.* What matters is that he is gone. That I'd been so caught up in the glow of our radium, I hadn't taken the time to write him back yet. And now it is too late.

I stare at the large wooden box in front of me. I have so many things to say to him, so many apologies to make, but I cannot believe it, *this box*, is really him.

"Open it," I command the mortuary worker.

He stares at me with large brown eyes and shakes his head. He does not know who I am, what I have done, that I have spent the last four years away from my family, tearing apart rock bit by bit, just to extract the smallest bit of radium, and that I will tear him apart with my hands, too, if he does not do what I say.

"Open it," I shout at him. "I need to see him." He shakes his head again, and then I go to open it myself. But the box is heavier than it looks. The lid too much for me to lift on my own. "I am not leaving until you help me open this box and I see him." My chest heaves from the effort, and my words are part scream, part like a cry from a feral animal. And maybe I have frightened him because he finally relents, opens the lid to the box.

And there he is. *Papa.* I don't think I've quite believed he is gone until I see him lying there, gray and listless. A bit of blood trickles from his nose, and nausea erupts from my stomach to my chest. I heave, but I've eaten nothing for days. There is nothing left in me.

"Papa," I say. "I am sorry. I am so, so sorry. I abandoned Poland. I abandoned you."

I do not stop apologizing until Bronia comes in from outside, until she pulls me away. "He is gone," she says matter-of-factly. "There is nothing you can say or do. He's gone."

Marya

❧

Poland, 1902–1903

I stayed two months in Warsaw after Papa died, living in his house, getting his affairs in order. Kaz came for Papa's funeral, then quickly returned to Loksow with Leokadia, who had to get back to play a concert. And Hela, too, rushed back to Paris just a few days after we buried Papa, as she was preparing to begin work on her doctoral thesis and urgently had to secure space for a lab, which was apparently in high demand. Not to mention she'd received *daily* letters from Jacques while she was in Warsaw, the content of each making her blush.

But I wanted to know more about this lab she desired, about the experiments she hoped to conduct there, wanted to hold Hela close and absorb all she had learned and experienced in France without me. When I asked, she shrugged, told me it wasn't very interesting at all. "Mineralogy," she'd clarified. Which, in truth, didn't sound all that interesting. But still, I imagined my sister-twin inside her laboratory in France, examining rocks with Jacques, and it made me feel hot with wanting, or jealousy.

After she left, Bronia told me Hela was *lovesick*. Hela looked well-fed to me, her color was rosy: she appeared the healthiest and most vibrant I'd ever seen her. Bronia, though, looked very tired, and I didn't think it would be good for her to rush back to Paris the way Hela had. "I could really use your help sorting through Papa's things," I told her. And always my sister-mother, she couldn't resist being needed.

"I miss Poland," she said, running her finger wistfully across Papa's credenza, which I'd dusted and polished in hopes of selling it before we left. "Paris is . . . becoming too much. It's not home. I'm ready to come back for good, Marya."

I nodded, but I thought of the school my niece, Lou, attended in Paris, a real school, where she was getting a real well-rounded education, not a girls' gymnasium like in Poland. "What about Lou's education?" I asked. My younger nephew, Jakub, would be fine, but he would grow up to be a man, and it wouldn't matter as much for him where: Poland or Paris. A man could be a man anywhere.

"We'd go to Austrian Poland, of course," Bronia said. "And we could afford a private tutor for the children." I knew about their dream of opening their very own sanatorium in the peaceful environs of the mountains. But before now I'd envisioned it more like my dream of one day moving to Paris, somewhere hazy, far off. Hearing her speaking of it with such clarity made me understand how much she wanted it, right now.

"Hela would be fine without you in Paris," I reassured her. "And selfishly, I would enjoy having you closer if you do move back." Jakub was now five, and I'd only met him twice. I'd only seen Lou a handful more times. It would be a wonderful thing to be closer to my niece and nephew, for me and for Kaz, who longed for children of our own still.

Bronia smiled a little and squeezed my hand. She closed her

eyes. "If only you could know how tired I am," she said. "Two children and city life and working full-time as a doctor."

"But you have it all," I said, not meaning to sound bitter, though finding it hard to keep the edge from creeping into my voice.

"Hmmm," she murmured. "I suppose I do."

I ARRIVED HOME AGAIN ON A THURSDAY EVENING, AND EV-erything looked different than it had when I left. The dusky sky seemed blacker, the street from the train to our apartment longer. Even our apartment itself felt smaller after having spent months in Papa's more spacious place in Warsaw. But Bronia and I had sold all of his things, split the rubles between us with a share for her to take back for Hela too, and now with them heavy in a purse in my valise, I wondered if we might finally have enough to move into a bigger place in Loksow.

Inside my apartment, I washed my face, took my hair from its bun, and ran a comb through it. And then I began to feel an impatient longing for my husband again, whom I hadn't seen in seven whole weeks. We had written weekly letters while I was away—I knew he was busy with Hipolit's research, doing al-most all the work himself now, which as I'd written to him really made it *his* research, didn't it? Kaz had written back, deferred to Hipolit's brilliance, but I'd told him he needed to give himself the credit he deserved, to which he replied how much he loved me for writing that.

When the door opened at last, and he walked inside, I felt a light inside my body, the memory of what it felt like to skate with him on the pond in Szczuki so many years earlier. So young and alive and free. I felt that again, suddenly.

He smiled widely, when he saw me. *He felt it too.* He came

to me quickly, ran his fingers softly through my long untangled hair, leaned in and pressed his lips tenderly to my forehead. "*Kochanie*, why didn't you send a telegram? I would've met you at the train."

"I didn't want to bother you," I told him. "I know how busy you are with your work."

"Never too busy for you," he whispered into my hair. "Oh, I have missed you so."

We stood like that for a while, holding on to each other in the darkness of our apartment. I clung to him, inhaling his familiar pine scent. I had not cried, not the whole time, since Papa's death. I had moved ahead, making plans, helping my sisters, ordering the disorder in the aftermath of death. But now that Kaz was holding on to me again, *steady*, I could finally let go. And the tears I hadn't even understood I'd needed to cry came quickly, furiously.

Kaz lifted my head up gently, wiped away at my tears with his thumbs. He leaned down and kissed my cheeks softly.

In the years since my baby Zosia had died, I'd pulled away when he reached for me, afraid to be close to him in that way again, afraid of what would happen if there were another pregnancy, another baby growing inside of me. I never forgot the doctor's words, that it was *my fault*, my body to blame.

But now I was overcome by a need to be with him, and when he tugged at the buttons on my nightgown, I leaned in closer, kissed him, found a desperate sort of comfort in his body that I hadn't even realized I'd been longing for.

KAZ AND I USED OUR NEWFOUND RUBLES TO MOVE INTO A two-bedroom apartment on Złota Street, a few blocks closer to

Hipolit and to Kaz's research. Here, on a street named for *gold*, the buildings were a little nicer, the sky strangely less gray, and flowerpots filled with corn poppies lined the steps in front of our new building.

Kaz quit his teaching position and began assisting Hipolit full-time. He was now doing all the research on elasticity on his own, with only guidance from Hipolit, who was mostly bedridden. Hipolit was paying him well to conduct the research, and Kaz promised Hipolit that he would publish the findings, even if it wasn't during his lifetime. I encouraged Kaz to tell him that whatever findings were published, they should have both their names on it. It might've started as Hipolit's idea but now Kaz was the one doing the work.

I put the remainder of the rubles into hiding in the bottom drawer of my chest, promising myself I would use to it to grow and build my university, somehow. It was what Papa would've wanted, what Papa would've been most proud of. And I would not disappoint him. I would continue to teach and help other women learn. I would continue to learn myself.

THE NEW YEAR DAWNED, AND IN THE SPRING, BRONIA SENT A letter telling me it was official: she would be a resident of Poland again by the end of summer. Construction on their sanatorium in Zakopane had begun, and it would be completed by August. Soon they would be only a six-hour train ride away from me.

This was followed in quick succession by a letter from Hela—she was engaged to Jacques! She wanted to hold the wedding in Paris before Bronia moved away, but only if Kaz and I were able to make it there. *Were we?*

"Are we?" I asked Kaz, showing him the letter, later that evening.

We were in a different place, a new apartment, and in the past few months we had reconnected. We had a newfound pleasure in being together again, exploring each other's bodies at night in bed. I felt a way I had not in years, not since the beginning days of our marriage.

"We have to go to your sister's wedding," Kaz said, frowning a little. I could practically see the thoughts going through his head by the long crease in his forehead. It would take days to get to Paris, days to get back, not to mention the time we would spend there for the wedding. And what would Hipolit do without him in that time? How would his research suffer?

"I could go on my own," I told him. "I wouldn't mind." The truth was I would mind a little. But I also understood how important his work was to him.

"Let me see if I can figure it out," Kaz said, rubbing his chin with his fingers. "Can you wait a few days to write Hela back?"

I nodded, and leaned across the table to kiss him. He kissed me back, deeper, harder. I put Hela's letter down, put my sisters out of my mind. Here on Złota Street, in Loksow, it was just me and Kaz. And that felt exactly perfect.

"MARYA," LEOKADIA CALLED OUT TO ME ON WEDNESDAY AFternoon. She'd been teaching a piano class to three young women interested in music who I'd found at the girls' gymnasium in town after befriending the headmistress, a woman my age who desired more for her students. I'd attended Leokadia's class today simply to watch, as it was my first experiment in pulling girls as young as fourteen into our university. Their talent was astounding—even with a few years of my own lessons from Leokadia, I could still barely play a simple song—and Leokadia's teaching was wonderful. She was kind and patient, and she handed all three of them more challenging pieces to practice, saying she would want to see them again next week. The girls left, their faces glowing, and Leokadia called out to me, asking me to stay.

"I've missed you," she said now, with a smile and then a hug. The truth was I'd kept my distance from her since returning from Warsaw. We were busy moving, and then I'd been focusing all my time on figuring out how to build my school and being happy with Kaz again. And now writing to Bronia about her move and Hela about her wedding. But if I were being honest with myself, there was something else, something gnawing at the edges of me, something I'd been pushing back, trying to ignore. That thing she'd said to me in Warsaw as her fingers had moved so deftly with the knitting needles: how *lucky* I was, to have *two* men who adored and respected me.

"I've missed you too," I said, hugging her back. With my arms around her, I noticed she'd lost a little weight, and when I pulled back, examined her more closely, the bones of her face looked more angular, making her expression seem slightly severe; her cheeks were paler than they used to be, too. But it was cold outside still, perhaps it was the lack of sunshine from the winter months. "Can you stay for supper?" she asked me.

"I shouldn't," I said. "I need to get home, prepare something for Kaz."

"No, no." She waved me away with a flick of her wrist, her fingers running easily through the air like they were playing imaginary piano keys. "Kaz is back in Papa's study. I'll go fetch him. You should both stay. How lucky I would be to have the two of you to myself for an entire evening." There it was again, that word: *lucky*.

And finally I nodded, unable to think of another reason to refuse her.

LEOKADIA'S MOTHER WAS AWAY IN WARSAW, VISITING HER sister, and Hipolit was too ill to dine at the table. Leokadia brought him a tray, prepared by their live-in housekeeper, so it was only the three of us at their long, rectangular dining table, certainly built to entertain a party of twenty or more. The three of us sat at one end, Leokadia at the head of the table, Kaz and I across from each other, both staring uneasily into our bowls of beautifully prepared beetroot soup.

Leokadia chattered on about a concert she had played the weekend before, about a man who had told her she played better than any woman he'd ever heard. "He managed to be both flattering and demeaning. You know how that is, Marya."

I nodded into my soup, and then I looked up at the same time as Kaz. Our eyes met across the table, and something flashed across his face: guilt, or remorse, or sadness, and then I knew. *I just knew.*

"DO YOU LOVE HER?" I ASKED HIM LATER, AS WE WALKED BACK to our apartment together. We were not holding hands; we stood farther apart than we had from each other in months, since before Papa died.

Kaz stopped walking, took my shoulders gently in his hands. "I love you, *kochanie*. Only you. Always you."

He tried to kiss me, but I pulled back. I put my hands on

my hips. "But you betrayed me, with her. You both betrayed me." I stared at him, waiting for him to deny it. But he didn't say anything. I turned away from him, furious, and kept on walking, leaving him behind.

He ran a little to catch up with me. "Marya, wait. Stop. Please, let me explain."

Kaz hardly ever called me Marya, preferring instead his term of endearment, *kochanie*. And the sound of my name in his voice startled me enough to make me stop walking. I turned and faced him.

"You pushed me away for so many years, and I just . . . needed someone. I was lonely," he said. "It was . . . my body needed . . . it meant nothing."

I felt as though I'd been struck solidly in my chest, and it was suddenly hard to breathe. Leokadia was my friend, and Kaz was my husband. Part of me wanted to know every detail of what had happened between them and how long this had gone on, and the other part of me wanted to throw up. My physical needs overtook all my senses, and the beetroot soup I'd eaten for supper came back up, violently, right there in the middle of the street.

"Oh, *kochanie*." Kaz rubbed my back. "Breathe," he said gently.

I listened, inhaled and exhaled until the wave of nausea passed. Then I pulled away from him. "I will go to Paris for Hela's wedding alone," I said. "I'll make arrangements to leave in the morning. I'll go now, stay for a little while, help her with the planning, too."

"But you were just gone for all those weeks in Warsaw," he protested.

I gave him a stony look. What right did he have to protest

my absence? He had betrayed me. I could barely stand to look at him right now.

"I'll talk to Hipolit, get the time off. I'll go with you to Paris, as long as you need me."

"I don't need you," I said. My words were sharp, and they cut him. I could see it in the pained look on his face. But I wanted to hurt him. Wanted him to feel pain. And most of all I wanted to finally, finally go to Paris on my own.

MARIE

Paris, 1903

It is a strange thing to be back in Paris, knowing that in Poland, Papa lies rotting in the ground, Hela and Stanislaw and little Hanna exist in their small home in Warsaw without him, and Bronia and Mier and Lou and Jakub are isolated in the beautiful mountains of Zakopane. Even as the new year comes, I cannot shake this feeling of darkness. My constitution dims, I lose weight, as it is hard to make myself eat when I am never hungry. The photograph I have in my mind of Papa, gray and withered inside a box, overtakes all else. The darkness hovers over me, and even my sleep is disturbed—I awake many nights finding myself wandering around in a room in which I did not fall asleep.

Somnambulism, Pierre diagnoses me when I recount the episodes to him. Pierre has been to the doctor for his own nightly ailments, pains in his legs so bad that he often cries out. He's been diagnosed with only a vague sort of rheumatism, and I wonder if his audible discomfort is what draws me out of bed to wander our house in my sleep. Then, in the mornings, I get pains in my legs too—and maybe it is from too much walking all night. Every day my bones are tired, my body aches.

Papa's death is a shadow. It follows me and hovers over me, even as I begin to teach a course at the girls' school in Sèvres. Even as I go back to the lab with Pierre to continue our experiments on radium. Even as I learn, early into the new year, that Pierre and I are going to have another baby.

Pierre is unable to contain his joy when I tell him the news. "A life ends, a life begins." He grabs my cheeks and kisses them softly. "When Mama died, we got Irène. And now this!"

And then over a few weeks, his joy becomes my joy; the shadow slowly lifts. My stomach begins to grow, and I begin sleeping all night in my bed again. In the lab, our radium glows, echoing the way I feel: bright and happy and alive once more.

It is not like before, with Irène. I work through my condition with barely any trouble, barely any bother. I am so very busy and so very tired, but not more than I was before I went back to Poland.

Pierre is convinced that this baby is a boy, and he says we should name him *Władysław*, after Papa, and I suggest that perhaps *Val* would be more fitting, more French, but still with an acknowledgment to Papa.

And that is my first mistake, that I name him. That in my mind, he becomes a real living person, before he truly exists.

It is the summer of 1903 in Paris, and the air is humid, the sun too warm to walk, never mind to bicycle as I am always wont to do in the summer months. We spend evenings out in our garden on boulevard Kellerman, our neighbors also scientists and parents like us, and it is so good to have the company nearby. Jean and Henriette Perrin live next door, and Jeanne and Paul Langevin on the other side. Irène enjoys playing with their children, and they run back and forth from garden to garden, playing hide and seek just after dusk, while the adults spend the evenings outside, discussing work.

Jean Perrin, who once got the job Pierre was passed over for at the Sorbonne, is quite brilliant and also kind, and I forgive him for taking Pierre's job (which is, anyway, not his fault.) His wife, Henriette, is not a scientist but a writer of stories that she regales the children with. All summer long, she mixes me concoctions of waters and fruits designed to help ease the swelling of my condition. Paul Langevin was once a student of Pierre's but now works in a lab at the Sorbonne. He and his wife, Jeanne, are often in an argument—they are the kind of couple who love to complain about each other. And Paul frequents our garden alone. But Jeanne is kind to me, coming to me on her own, baking us bread to make sure, as she says, *you and the baby are well fed.*

Still, it is funny how, that summer, Papa is gone, my sisters are so far away, but my neighbors, my friends, surround me, care for me. I begin to feel I am not without a family nearby at all. Perhaps Pierre is right. Life cycles. Grief fades and becomes lightness again.

In July, a giant bicycle race is coming through the entire country of France, ending in Paris: the *Tour de France*, they're calling it in all the papers. Pierre has been saying for weeks that we should take a day out of the lab, take Irène to see the men bicycling through the city, racing one another.

But when the day comes, Pierre's rheumatisms are particularly bad, and he cannot get himself out of bed. I have already planned this rare day out of the lab, so I decide I'll still take Irène to watch the race on my own. As the two of us walk together hand in hand, the humid air smothers me. It is hard to breathe, and quite suddenly, my stomach begins to ache.

Irène chatters, as she often does now, telling me about the maths and sciences Dr. Curie is teaching her. It is astounding to hear the theories of geometry in her tiny voice, filled with confidence and aplomb. She is brilliant, this child of mine. Perhaps every mother believes that about her child, but with Irène it is scientifically and objectively a fact.

It is so hot. I let go of her hand to wipe my forehead, and the ache in my stomach intensifies. I clutch my stomach, nearly double over from the pain, which is suddenly blindingly bad.

"Maman?" Irène's small bright voice comes through the darkness. "Maman?"

We have not made it far from the house yet, but I suddenly do not know if I have the strength to make it back there on my own. I want to sit down right here in the street, but I know I can't. Irène is only six, and though she's brilliant, I can't fall down and leave her all alone.

I close my eyes and try to breathe. Inhale, exhale. I am the woman who spent four years extracting radium from pitchblende. I will not let a little pain, a little afternoon heat, stop me in the street.

"Maman?" Irène's voice is softer now, or maybe it is harder for me to hear her through my pain.

"Maman isn't feeling well," I tell Irène. "Let's try and make it back to the house. We'll play a game and you can be the leader.

If Maman falls behind, go fetch Papa or Grand-Père to come back for me. Or if you can't find them, go to the Perrins and get one of them."

"A game," Irène giggles, reminding me that she is still a little girl who loves to play. She skips ahead, and I reach out my hand to try and hold on to her, but I'm not fast enough. She's gone.

The pain is so bad that I have no choice but to sit down now. And the next thing I know, Jean Perrin and Dr. Curie are there, saying my name. Dr. Curie is getting older, frail himself, but somehow he is lifting me off the ground, pulling me toward home, shouldering the weight of me along with Jean. Somehow he is saying, "Oh, Marie, no. No."

And I think, *Val is gone.* Though scientifically impossible, it feels as though my sternum is bursting apart, my heart falling through the walls of my chest.

I ONCE MIGHT'VE THOUGHT IT RIDICULOUS TO GRIEVE A PERson who never really existed, who I never even met. But I cannot leave my bed for weeks after Val dies, the darkness hovering over me again, holding on to me so tightly I can barely breathe, much less think about our work.

"We are marked by death," I tell Pierre. "It will ruin us. No matter what else we do. No matter what happens in the lab." And maybe I have been marked by it my whole life beginning with Mama and my sister Zosia. Then Sophie-Claire and Papa gone too soon.

Pierre shakes his head, always so positive, so hopeful, refusing to succumb to my darkness. "No, no. We have each other, *mon amour.* And our beautiful Irène, and Papa. And our friends next door. Your sisters and their families in Poland and Jacques and his family in Montpellier. This was just an accident of science, *mon amour*. These things happen."

But I do not believe in *accidents of science*. That is the opposite of everything I know: science is purposeful and objective, not accidental at all. Pierre is no help, so I write to Bronia, ask for her advice, wanting comfort from my sister-mother, and also her expertise in obstetrics.

I worry your work in the lab has harmful effects on your health, she writes back. *Look at all the pains Pierre has been having, and now this? Perhaps you should leave the lab before you try again . . .*

Her letter goes on to tell me about what is going on with her family. Lou and Jakub have both been ill with terrible coughs as of late, and even the mountain air isn't helping. But I skim over the rest of her words, turning hot with anger.

It fills me with rage that she would blame my work and make it seem like this is my fault for pursuing science as well as motherhood. She has had two healthy children, and she is a practicing physician. That seems more dangerous than working in a lab, as she is exposed to diseases. I tear her letter into pieces, scattering them carelessly all about my bedroom floor. Later, Pierre will come in and pick them up one by one, tiptoeing around the room, believing me to be asleep.

And anyway, Bronia does not know my radium. It is not harmful; it can't be harmful. It is the most beautiful thing I've ever seen, the brightest thing I have left. Bronia knows nothing.

NOT EVEN TWO WEEKS LATER, PIERRE RUSHES INTO OUR BEDroom in the middle of the afternoon with a telegram, his face white as dolomite, his hands shaking. I am still in bed, and Pierre has been telling everyone I've now taken ill with a summer influenza. But here I am, not ill at all, flattened by grief, spending my afternoon staring out the window at all the flowers in our garden. How dare they bloom? How dare the pinks and reds and yellows flare so brightly?

"What is it?" I ask Pierre, his countenance startling me. Pierre is the one who manages to smile still, who wakes each morning kissing my face, promising me that today will be better than yesterday. That tomorrow will be best of all. And though I turn away from him, his words seep through my skin, lighten me, little by little, piece by piece, day by day.

"Terrible," Pierre says. "Terrible, terrible. It can't be."

He's scaring me, and I get out of bed, my legs unsteady. I take a moment to regain my footing, then walk to him, take the telegram from his shaking hands. It's come from Zakopane, from Bronia. I read the words, as disbelieving of them as Pierre is. Our nephew, little Jakub, took ill, and he died suddenly. *Died. Oh Bronia, no.* My anger for her dissipates, just like that. How could this happen? Jakub was just seven years old, nearly the same age as Irène.

Irène.

I haven't seen our daughter in days, or has it been weeks? I have been so distracted by my grief over this baby I never met. And I run out of the bedroom now, calling for my real living breathing child. "Irène! Irène!" I am shouting, crying, but I cannot stop myself. I want to hold on to her, wrap her into my body, keep her forever safe and still and healthy.

We are marked by death.

"Maman?" Irène's small voice comes from the dining room, sounding frightened.

I run in there and she is sitting at the table, working on her

lessons with Dr. Curie. Someone has put her hair into two pig-
tails, and as it wasn't me, they are parted crookedly, so she looks
out of sorts, disheveled.

"Oh, darling." I open my arms and she gets up and runs to
me. I smooth back her uneven hair, kiss the top of her head, inhale the little girl scent of her, rose petals and dirt from the garden, where her *grand-père* must've allowed her to play with the
Perrins this morning while I was still sleeping. "I am never letting
you go," I say into her hair. "I am never letting you go."

MARYA

❧

Paris, 1903

The sun was shining so brightly the first morning I arrived in Paris, streaming in through the glass ceiling of the Gare du Nord, that for a moment it was hard to see, the light blinding me, turning the station and the people and even the exquisite sounds of French yellow and gold and glimmering.

Then I blinked, and there in front of me was my sister-twin, Hela, laughing, grabbing onto me for a hug. We walked outside the station together, and there was the bustle of a vibrant city, a beautiful city, with wholly different architecture than I'd ever seen before in Poland, and even the air smelled different. I inhaled; all around me, the scent of flowers. "Marya, you finally made it!" Hela said.

Yes, I had made it, on a lie and by dipping into Papa's rubles that I was saving for my school. I'd written ahead to my sisters, told them Kaz was *so busy* with his research and he was sending me to Paris alone, knowing how good the time with my sisters would be for me, for all of us. And how excited I was to help Hela plan her wedding and to make up for some lost time with my niece, Lou, and nephew, Jakub, too. Those things were, at least, true. But on the very long, very uncomfortable hours and hours on the train, the ache in my chest over Kaz grew larger and larger, so that when I first breathed in the flowers of Paris, it was already a chasm: giant and gaping and nauseating all over again. I clutched my stomach.

"Are you hungry?" Hela asked. "I can take you to my favorite pâtisserie before we get the omnibus to Bronia's." Hela had moved out of Bronia's home, into an apartment closer to the Sorbonne, but it was just one small room. Bronia had offered me Hela's old room at her home in La Villete for the duration of my stay, but as Hela was closer to the train, and didn't have the constraints of the children, she'd offered to come and fetch me and take me to Bronia's today.

I shook my head. I should be hungry, but I wasn't. I'd fled Poland days earlier, leaving while Kaz was at work, without even a goodbye, and I'd barely eaten anything but some stale bread on the train. Kaz had left a letter for me on the table, and though I'd put it in my bag, had even been tempted on the train to read it, I hadn't opened it yet. I wasn't ready for whatever he'd felt the need to write. Whatever happened between us, whatever would happen between us, now resided in my stomach, a giant nauseating punch.

"All right," Hela said with a shrug, then a laugh. "You know Bronia. She will have prepared a feast for you already."

Hela walked briskly, and I followed after her. My sister-twin had a lightness about her that I'd never seen in her before. Her cheeks glowed pink, her stride was quick, and she bounced a little as she went. I practically had to run to keep up with her.

ONE HOUR AND TWO DIZZYING OMNIBUS RIDES LATER, WE were in La Villette, standing in front of Bronia's home. It was three stories tall and built of red bricks, and it sat on a quaint cobblestone street, reminding me of something from a storybook I might have found in the Kaminskis' nursery once upon a time. But no, this was my sister's real life here in Paris. The life she told me was *too much*, the life she would be *escaping* soon to move to Zakopane. I stood in the street, staring up at her house for a moment before walking inside, stifling a laugh, or maybe a scream. It was hard to believe anyone would want to leave this. It was hard to believe that a woman with a wonderful professional life, two beautiful children, and a very nice husband would ever want for anything different than what she had. Maybe happiness was a bubble, floating by us, something none of us could quite hold in our hands. Not even Bronia.

"Marya," Hela called my name. "You're catching flies."

I shut my gaping mouth and followed her up the front steps and into Bronia's home. The way she skipped up the steps, opened the front door without knocking, she was at ease here. I, on the other hand, stepped carefully, keeping a distance behind her, looking all around me as I walked inside.

Hela had been right, of course. The inside smelled strongly of my favorite Polish food: Bronia's *zupa grzybowa*, and I supposed that here, in Paris, the mushrooms were fresh and affordable, and her broth would be savory and rich. I inhaled, and then my stomach turned again. I was somehow both starving and still overwhelmed with nausea.

"Bron," Hela called out. "I've found our little sister, wandering off a train from Poland, and now I've brought her here and we'll keep her forever." She smiled at me, reached for my hand, and squeezed it. I knew she was joking, but still, I wondered: *Could I stay here forever?* What would Kazimierz do back in Poland without me? What would I do here, on my own? Could

I use the remainder of Papa's rubles to finally pay tuition at the Sorbonne? They would only cover a semester, a year at most. But that could be a start.

Bronia rushed down the stairs, looking uncharacteristically unkempt, her hair askew, wisps tumbling out of her normally neat bun. "Shhh, Hela. The children have finally gotten to sleep."

"Sleep? It's the middle of the afternoon," Hela said.

"Marya, *moja mała siostrzyczka*," Bronia called out to me as her *little sister* affectionately, her tone softening as she noticed me standing there behind Hela. "How was the trip? It's very long, hmmm? You must be exhausted." She didn't give me a chance to answer before she turned back to Hela and kept talking. "Both the children got suddenly ill with a summer flu, and they were up all night coughing. Dr. Curie just came to administer breathing treatments, and now they've both finally fallen asleep."

"Dr. Curie—Jacques's father—is quite good with the children," Hela said to me, beaming.

Bronia frowned, as if the implication was that she wasn't, and maybe she resented Hela for saying this. But then she sighed and hugged Hela's shoulders, and I wondered if perhaps I was misreading their faces. Bronia looked exhausted herself, and I guessed she'd been up all night, tending to the children and their coughing. "I've discussed it with Dr. Curie, and Marya can stay there until the children are better," Bronia said more to Hela than to me. "They have plenty of room for her."

I opened my mouth to object—I had not come all the way to Paris to stay with Jacques's family, strangers. And besides, I needed my sisters now. More than either one of them knew. But before I could get a word in, Hela was already talking over my head. "Oh yes, and the estate in Sceaux is lovely this time of year. Marya will adore the flowers."

"I don't mind the children being sick," I protested. There had been many days I'd gone to the Kaminskis and nursed the twins through one cold or another. I'd caught many of them myself and still returned to the work the following day. "I can—"

"Nonsense," Bronia said, cutting me off before I could finish saying I'd be happy to help her out with them at night. "I'm not going to have you get sick from my children. You are here to help Hela plan her wedding, not to be in bed, coughing for weeks. Come, have some soup before Hela takes you out to Sceaux to settle in." The idea of being taken anywhere else, riding on another horse-drawn carriage or another train or another anything, turned my stomach again, but Bronia left me no room to argue. And anyway, I was too tired to argue now, too tired to think or do anything but accept her delicious soup and then let Hela take me away.

THE CURIES LIVED IN A LARGE ESTATE IN SCEAUX, ON THE outskirts of Paris, but when Hela and I finally arrived it was dark, and I could not really see the grounds. I awoke at dawn the next morning, stretching out in the unfamiliar comfort of the Curies' guest room, the bed softer than any I'd ever felt in my entire life. I stood and went to the window, and I saw what Hela meant about the flowers: golds and reds and pinks, as far as the eye could see. It was so startlingly beautiful, I gasped.

I hadn't actually met the Curies last night when I arrived, as they'd already gone to sleep and the housekeeper had shown me to my room. But Hela had told me a bit of their story on the interminably long omnibus rides from Bronia's.

Jacques's mother died a few years earlier of cancer, and before she got sick, Jacques had been living and working in Montpellier as a professor, where he'd planned to settle. But when she fell ill, neither his father nor his younger brother, Pierre—both highly emotional, Hela clarified—could handle things at the estate. And besides, Jacques wanted to spend time with his mother in her final days, and so he'd taken a leave of his job in Montpellier and picked up a course to teach at the Sorbonne while he was in Paris. Hela was a student in his class, and she said she knew she was in love with him immediately, and he felt the same about her, but they waited until the end of the session before acting upon their feelings. *Of course*, Hela said, blushing a little. And then, *he forgot all about Montpellier*. Now, five years later, Jacques was in Paris for good, and she was about to become his wife.

Jacques no longer lived at the house in Sceaux with his father and brother, but had his own house in the city on boulevard Kellerman, closer to the Sorbonne, which Hela planned to move into after the wedding. His father and his younger brother now inhabited this great big estate in Sceaux all on their own, with plenty of staff, Hela assured me.

I thought about her story again as I got out of bed, stretched, and stared at all those glorious flowers. Who planted them, took care of them? Did they employ a gardener as part of the many staff Hela mentioned? The idea that my Hela was marrying someone *French* with enough money to *employ a gardener* made me laugh out loud. And then, as if someone had been standing out in the hallway, testing to see if I was awake, there came a quick knock on my door, and I put my hand to my mouth to stop my laughter.

"Madame Zorawska?" came a male voice from the other side of the door. It took a second for me to register that it was me he was calling for, as I was thrown by being called *Madame* and the very French-accented way he pronounced my last name.

"*Oui?*" I responded carefully, testing out my poor and rusty French.

"Breakfast is ready in the dining room, if you're hungry." He spoke in French, but slowly enough that I could follow along. At least, I thought I could. It had been years since I'd studied French, and the sound of it now brought back memories of Szczuki, and feelings I had not felt since that summer when I had believed my life would be here.

I swallowed hard and called back that I'd be right there. I quickly dressed in a clean dress from my valise and wrapped my hair in a bun. I opened the door, and to my surprise he was still standing there, in the hallway at the top of the long winding staircase, waiting for me. I had not met Jacques in person yet, but Hela had shown me a photograph, and this man was most certainly the brother Hela had mentioned. He looked an awful lot like Jacques, only a bit younger and with a lighter expression, a broader smile. He stood before me, tall, raven-haired, with a dark thick beard. His deep blue eyes were trained on my face so steadily that I looked away from him, down at my feet.

"Madame Zorawska." He bent down and kissed my hand softly, in a way that was so very French, so very foreign to me. I had to stifle another laugh, but mostly because he made me feel . . . nervous, outside myself. "I'm Pierre Curie," he said.

His hand lingered on mine, and I gently extracted myself from him, folding my hands together in front of me. "Please," I finally said, "we are practically related. Call me Marya."

"Marya," he repeated. His tone was gentle, and he lingered a little too long on the *y*, so my name sounded more French in his voice than I'd ever heard it before, *Maria*.

I was suddenly, finally, very hungry, and I felt my stomach rumble. "You said there was breakfast?" I asked him.

"Yes, of course. My manners. You had a very long journey. You must be famished. Follow me."

He ran down the staircase, taking the steps two at a time like a child, while I followed behind, holding on to the railing, not wanting to miss a step and trip. All around me this house was an expanse of marble and glass and light. Hela was not only marrying someone French, someone who employed a gardener, but someone who came from a wealthy family.

Downstairs in the dining room, there were enough pastries spread out on the long table to feed the Russian army, and the housekeeper again, who handed me a coffee. The distance between my sister-twin and me never felt greater than it did in this very moment.

"I've heard very much about you," Pierre said, sitting down to eat his own breakfast at the head of the table. I nodded as I took my own seat but did not admit that I'd heard very little about him. Only what Hela had mentioned last night. And what had she said about him—that he had been *too emotional* to handle his mother's death? Jacques was the steady one. "Hela says you are building a university to educate the women of Poland." Pierre was still talking. "What a wonderful undertaking."

Is that what Hela had told him? It seemed so much an exaggeration, as if I alone were educating the women of my entire country, not just a tiny little piece of the tiny little city of Loksow. But I took a sip of my steaming coffee and didn't correct him. "It is very French of you to think that it is wonderful," I said instead. "My husband hates it." At the mere mention of Kaz, I remembered the unopened letter from him in my valise, and my chest tightened again.

"Hates it?" Pierre laughed. "I'm sure that's not the case.

What could be better than giving people education? Education is freedom, is it not?"

He sounded just like Papa, and I warmed to him. As he was a French man, born and raised in France, I didn't think he would ever understand just how much the Russians didn't want women to feel free or why Kaz worried for my safety. And now, here, in Paris, I did not desire to explain it to him, so instead I changed the subject. "And what do you do, Pierre?" I asked instead. "Are you a scientist, too?"

He nodded, finishing off a croissant in one large bite. "I'm conducting research in paramagnetism."

I smiled, as if I understood exactly what he meant. And I did, a little, from my own reading about magnetic fields, but if he were to test me on the details or the differences between paramagnetisim and ferromagnetism, I would surely fail.

"Do you like to ride bicycles?" he asked me suddenly, out of nowhere.

"What?" I hadn't ridden a bicycle in many years, not since Szczuki, with the children, around the lake in the summertime. Thinking of that now, I felt that Kaz-shaped chasm in my stomach again, and I put my own croissant down, losing my appetite once more.

"I enjoy a morning ride after breakfast," Pierre said. "And Jacques's old bicycle is still here, if you'd like to come with me today?"

"Oh, I probably shouldn't." I'd promised Hela I'd figure out the omnibus into the city this morning and that I would accompany her to meet the seamstress to discuss her wedding gown. But now the very idea of watching my sister-twin so caught up in love, so doe-eyed and bright, felt exhausting. Really what I desired to do was to get back into that comfortable bed upstairs and sleep for a long while until my head felt clearer.

"Just a short ride," Pierre prodded. I hesitated for another moment, and seeming to notice my hesitation, he took it as an opening and broke into a smile. "I'll have to get into the city to the lab afterward. I'll escort you there to your sister. I promise. Take a short ride with me. Experience Sceaux by bicycle. There is truly nothing like it."

IT WAS SO STRANGE THE WAY MY LEGS REMEMBERED HOW TO ride a bicycle, how my body remembered the pedals and my mind remembered the lightness of the wind in my hair, the sunshine upon my face. I didn't mean to go fast, but once I started pedaling I couldn't stop, and then I was riding out ahead of Pierre, not at all sure where we were going but following the path through the flowers: yellows and golds and pinks spinning and swirling by me in a blur.

"Slow down," Pierre called from behind me. But he was laughing.

I was breathless and sweating. Away from Poland, and Kaz, my mind was a sieve, and time and knowledge slipped away, my head gloriously empty. I pedaled and I pedaled like fire ripping through accelerant.

"Marya, wait for me!" Pierre called out from somewhere behind me.

But I did not stop; I did not even attempt to slow down. I kept pedaling, faster and faster. Completely and utterly free.

MARIE

❧

Paris, 1903

Marie," Pierre calls out for me as he runs into our lab, his voice quivering. He's clutching a telegram in his hands, and he stands in that awkward way he does when his legs are bothering him, almost bowlegged, but not quite. Fear clenches in my chest at the sight of the telegram. *Not again.*

It has been three months since Val and Jakub died all at once, and though I have come back to work, to teaching my students in Sèvres, and to our lab, I have to force myself out of bed each morning. Force myself to dress and, only sometimes, eat, and make it through the day. Summer is long over, and now it is fall, nearly winter, but I barely notice the change in seasons, in weather and vegetation. I am numb, and I am empty. No matter what I do, what I achieve, Jakub and Val will still be dead. Papa is gone.

Bronia and I have been writing letters back and forth each week, consumed by our own private pain, but we write mostly of our daily work because even writing the other things down, admitting our sorrow to each other on paper, seems too much to bear.

Pierre waves the telegram in the air now and breaks into a smile, so it cannot be bad news, can it? He seems . . . happy? "Marie," he says my name again. "You will not believe this."

"What's happened?" I ask him, sighing with relief as I observe his face. *Surprise*, not sadness.

"The most marvelous news in the world has just come for us from Sweden," he says. "They are giving us half of the Nobel Prize in physics, along with Henri Becquerel, for our work on radium. You and I. Both of us, *mon amour. The Nobel Prize.*" He's breathless with excitement, and he stares at me, waiting for my reaction.

His words ring in my ears. *Nobel Prize.* "I can't believe it," I say. And I really can't.

There had been some whispers about a nomination last year, a letter to Pierre from a Swedish mathematician who had learned the committee was considering the nomination, but only Pierre, not me. Pierre had argued in his own letters to the committee that I was as important in the discovery as he. In fact, more so. And I had thought that would be the end of it, that the committee would simply ignore both of us for the award. A woman has never been nominated before, even for part of the prize. Now, the fact that we have both won it, *together*, science's biggest prize, should elicit something more in me than disbelief. I should be thrilled. The *Nobel Prize.* Pierre and I?

"There will be prize money, *seventy thousand francs.*" Pierre is still talking. His voice quivers with excitement as he reads the telegram aloud to me. Then he rereads it again, a second time, as if he didn't quite believe it in his own voice the first time through. His words wash through me and over me. "*Seventy thousand*," he repeats.

Seventy thousand francs is a lot of money. It will go a long way in improving our lab from the small shed we've been using for years. And that alone should make me quiver with the same excitement in Pierre's voice, and I want to. I really do. But I cannot make myself actually *feel* it. Instead I am very tired and my legs ache, and inside I am hollow.

"They want us to go to Sweden to accept, *mon amour*," Pierre says. I look up again, and his blue eyes glimmer in the morning light.

"Sweden? Sweden is much too far," I say quickly.

Pierre opens his mouth as if to protest, then closes it, says nothing for a moment. "The Nobel Prize, *mon amour*," he finally says again, more gently.

But I am still stuck on *Sweden*.

I envision it in my mind: the trip would take at least forty-eight hours, more if we stop along the way. And what about Irène? We would have to leave her here with Dr. Curie, and I cannot bear the idea of letting her out of my sight for so long. Or, risk traveling with her, and to think of all the diseases she might be exposed to on the trains. Besides all that, I can barely get out of bed and make it to the lab these days. How will I ever make it all the way to Sweden?

"We can't go to Sweden," I say again. Pierre folds the telegram, puts it in his jacket pocket, and reaches out to hug me. He clings to me, kisses the top of my head. "I can't. Go without me if you must."

"This prize is for both of us," he says gently. "I will not go without you." He stands back, puts his hand on my cheek, stares into my eyes. "I will write them and tell them you have been ill over the summer and are still not yourself. The journey is too much right now. Perhaps next year we will make it to Sweden, and we can give our acceptance speech then?"

"Perhaps," I murmur back, but I do not fully believe that we might ever make it there. I say it now to placate him more than anything. If only I could take my seventy thousand francs and use it to buy back time, to take us all back before the summer, and somehow, somehow keep mine and Bronia's children safe.

"Next year, *mon amour*," Pierre murmurs. "In 1904 everything will be better for us." Pierre places his hand over his heart. "I can feel it."

What a ridiculous notion. His heart pumps blood, beats to keep his body alive. It does not hold a feeling, a silly premonition.

And still, Pierre is my glimmer of hope. I want so very much to believe he has a magical heart, not a scientific one.

MARYA

❦

Paris, 1903

The summer in Paris was hot, the heat rising off the streets, visible in cloudy waves that trailed behind the horse-drawn omnibuses. But after only a few weeks, my French improved, and with Pierre's help, I learned how to take the omnibuses in and out of Sceaux, and I became comfortable getting places in the city on my own.

Pierre conducted his paramagnetism work in a small back space inside Hela and Jacques's lab. Hela and Jacques had tables and tables lined with rocks, as they were investigating mineral compositions. My sister's cheeks glowed pink as she showed me the rocks she and Jacques were sampling. As she spoke, my eyes wandered toward the back of the lab, toward Pierre, who had lined up sheets of metals so close together that he barely had any room to work among them. But he was quite thin, and he squeezed in and out of the metals, remarking on measurements to himself.

"Marya, are you listening?" Hela asked, following my eyes toward Pierre. She looked at me and frowned, then leaned in and lowered her voice. "Jacques feels sorry for him," she said.

"Why?" I asked.

"He doesn't have the right schooling," she whispered. "He never did well in traditional schools the way Jacques did, and even with many scientific studies, he's had very little in the way of findings. The university won't hire him to teach. If we don't make the space for him in our lab, who will?"

"But he's very kind," I said to her, narrowing my eyes. Perhaps it was all the food he'd continually offered me in Sceaux or the peaceful moments our morning bicycle rides had brought to me, or the way he had delighted in the idea of my women's university in Poland. But I felt defensive of him now.

"Yes, so very kind." Hela smiled at me and shrugged. "But he is lucky to have Jacques, that is all. His head is in the clouds. Who knows where he would be if left on his own."

BRONIA'S CHILDREN WERE FEELING MUCH BETTER BY THE END of June, and so it was time for me to leave Sceaux and go stay with her for the remainder of my time in France. I felt a little sad to leave the expanse of the Curies' house and my morning bicycle rides with Pierre. So much so that when Pierre offered to give me Jacques's bicycle to take to La Villete with me, to have to ride for the rest of my stay, I accepted his offer.

"What in heaven's name is that?" Bronia demanded, when I stepped off the omnibus, holding Jacques's rickety old bicycle. I didn't answer her—of course she knew what it was—and I kept walking toward her house with it. The bicycle was light and freedom, and it gave me the time and space each morning to clear my head, to think. Though it would not be the same as riding through the flowers in Sceaux with Pierre, I hoped to ride it through the cobblestone streets of La Villette while I was here.

Lou and Jakub, however, were delighted to see me with it, and they both begged me to teach them to ride it. "Absolutely not," Bronia said. "You're both still recovering from your coughs."

Truth be told, they looked healthy to me, and aside from an occasional cough I saw no trace of illness in them. "I'll teach you when she's at work," I whispered to Jakub, and his little green eyes lit up, and he squeezed my hand.

"Marya," Bronia said my name sharply, and I turned away from my nephew. Lou's eyes were wide, worried her mother had heard my whispered exchange with her brother and that now we would both be in trouble. But instead she said, "You've gotten fatter living in Sceaux. What were the Curies feeding you?"

She rested her hand across my belly, which perhaps *had* expanded a little. "Let me examine you," Bronia said, moving her hands to feel my stomach.

"Don't be ridiculous," I told her, pulling away. "I am perfectly healthy." I'd been offered, and eaten, more food than I'd ever seen in my life in Sceaux. And somehow all the worry that had followed me around in Poland for so long had lifted, and I was hungry again. My body was blossoming here, free, in Paris.

A NEW LETTER FROM KAZ HAD COME TO BRONIA'S HOUSE THIS past week, as it had every week since I'd arrived. I had yet to open a single one, but had them in a pile at the bottom of my valise. Bronia brought it to me as I unpacked my things in her small guest room. I'd left the bicycle outside, of course, and I didn't have much in my valise, only a few well-worn dresses and undergarments, and I got them put away in the chest in only a few minutes. I shut the last drawer, and Bronia stood there, holding Kaz's new letter out to me. I put it inside my valise with the others, without opening it, and then she frowned.

"What is really going on?" she demanded, a hand on her hip.

"Nothing is *going on*," I lied. The truth bubbled up in my throat, but I couldn't tell my sister-mother what had really happened, that Kaz had betrayed me. That Leokadia had betrayed me. That Sceaux and a rickety old bicycle and Pierre Curie had made me feel alive again these past few weeks and that now I didn't want to read any of Kaz's letters and face my real life at all, extinguish the glimmer of happiness I'd been feeling in Paris. "I'll open it later, when I'm alone. That's all, Bron."

"I really wish you'd let me examine you. If you'd just lie down, I could do it right here." Her hand went back to my stomach, and I abruptly pulled away from her.

"I promise you, I am fine," I snapped at her.

Her frown creased deeper, but she sighed and let it go, and she went down to the kitchen to prepare supper.

A few days before Hela's wedding in July, there was a large bicycle race running all through France, ending in Paris. Pierre asked if I would go to Ville d'Avray to watch the finish with him, and I offered to take the children along with us so Bronia could help Hela with last-minute arrangements.

The day was quite warm, the air humid, and my dress felt much too tight, constricting even my slightest movements. Bronia was right—I'd been eating too well since I'd come to France, and I had put on weight. I hoped the dress Hela had insisted on paying the seamstress to make for me to wear to her wedding this coming weekend would still fit.

At eleven years old Lou already comported herself like a woman, a miniature Bronia, and as we stepped off the omnibus and into the very crowded street of onlookers, she commanded Jakub to hold her hand and stay close by. Jakub, darling seven-year-old gentleman that he was, complied, attached himself to his older sister. I held on to his other hand and with Pierre just a step ahead of us, we made our way through the crowd to wait for the racers.

"Did you know," Pierre crouched down to tell the children, once we could not walk any farther through the crowd, "eighty men entered this race nineteen days ago, and now at the end only twenty-four are still in it. Twenty-five-hundred kilometers these men have bicycled. In nineteen days!"

Lou's eyes widened. "That's over one hundred and thirty kilometers on a bicycle every single day," she said. I smiled, pleased by her quick math skills. "May I take Jakub closer to the front so we can see the bicycles better, *ciotka?*" she asked me.

"Yes," I told her. "Just continue to keep a close watch on him. We'll wait back here."

Lou and Jakub squeezed through the adults and got up closer to the street. My eyes followed them, and I laughed a little watching them squirm through child-size spaces up to the front of the crowd.

"I always thought I would have children of my own," Pierre said, wistfully, and in that way he had of saying whatever it was that came to his mind whether it was entirely appropriate or not. It was one of the reasons why I liked spending time with him. His unadulterated honesty.

It also made me feel I could be completely honest back, and that he would not judge me or blame me, but he would just listen. "I never knew how much I wanted children," I told him. "Until I lost a baby a few years ago."

"Oh," Pierre said, casting his eyes down. "I'm very sorry, Marya. I shouldn't have said anything. I didn't know."

"It's all right. How could you?" I shrugged, and tears that I didn't realize I still had for baby Zosia welled up in my eyes. I blinked them back, willing them not to spill over. I did not wish to make a scene, right here on the street in the middle of this crowd.

Pierre stared at me for a moment, then shifted his eyes away, straining his neck to catch a glimpse of the children up ahead. "I suppose I always imagined I'd be married by now, too," he said. "Jacques was the one who said he'd be content to be a bachelor forever, not me. And look, even he is getting married." Pierre let out a dry laugh.

"And why aren't you married?" I asked him. Surely a man like him: handsome, intelligent, well-off, could marry his pick of women in France, even if his head were in the clouds, as Hela had said.

"I loved a woman once, many years ago. And then she died, and it almost ruined me," he said. "I suppose I never wanted to let myself feel like that again, and for a long while I wouldn't even consider falling in love."

"Well, it's not too late," I told him.

He looked back up, smiled at me. "And for you, too," he said. I supposed he meant it was not too late for me to have a child of my own, but I had this strange feeling he was really saying something else, something more. Something I shouldn't want him to.

"My husband betrayed me," I said, speaking the truth out

loud for the first time. "I sacrificed my dream of an education in Paris for a life with him in Poland, and then he betrayed me. With my closest friend. They both betrayed me." I paused, blinking back those tears that really wanted to roll down my face now. "That's why I've been here for so long, all by myself. I had to figure out how I'm supposed to feel, what I'm supposed to do next."

"And have you?" Pierre asked. "Figured anything out?"

I couldn't hold the tears back any longer, and I felt them rolling down my cheeks, but I didn't move to wipe them away. Through the blur, I saw the racers approach, the bicycles a swirl of green and yellow and blue as they whizzed by us. "I don't know," I finally said. Hela would be married in a few days, and then everyone would expect me to return home to Poland, to return home to Kaz and to my old life. I had thought that time, that distance, would soften the blow of his betrayal. But it hadn't. "I really don't know."

Pierre reached his hand out, grabbed mine, interlaced our fingers and squeezed gently. I squeezed back, and my body turned warmer from the nearness of him. "Your husband is an *imbécile*," he said.

IT WAS NEARLY DARK BY THE TIME WE ARRIVED BACK AT BRO-nia's. Jakub fell asleep on my shoulder on the omnibus, and Pierre lifted him off of me, carried him across his shoulder up to the house. My arm was still numb from the weight of my nephew, and now Lou clung to it as we walked up the steps. I watched Pierre holding on so gently to Jakub, and his tenderness for my nephew made me smile.

Lou let go of me and ran ahead to open the door for Pierre.

I felt an ache in my chest for him, as I watched him carry Jakub up the stairs. He should be someone's father. *Someone's husband.*

"Marya." Bronia's voice startled me, and I turned.

Then another voice, from behind her: "*Kochanie,* is that you?" Kaz stepped out of the dining room. My face flamed red, as if I'd been caught doing something I shouldn't have. I put my hands to my cheeks.

"What are you doing here?"

"I asked him to come," Bronia said. And it didn't make any sense to me. Why would she do that? Had my sister-mother betrayed me too? But how could she, when I hadn't even told her the truth about what had happened between us. "You're in denial about your condition," Bronia said.

"My condition?"

Kaz walked closer, put his hands on my shoulders, then pulled me toward him, embraced me tightly. He kissed the top of my head, and though I didn't want it to, my body relaxed against his. In spite of myself, I had missed him. "I would not miss your sister's wedding," he said gently in my ear, stroking back my disheveled hair with his hands.

I heard the sounds of Pierre's footsteps, coming down the stairs with Lou, two at a time. Lou laughed a little, and I jumped back. Pierre saw Kaz, then met my eyes and frowned.

"Kazimierz," Bronia said. "This is Pierre Curie. Jacques's younger brother."

Kaz stepped forward and they shook hands. Pierre was still frowning; Kaz shook his head a little, seeming confused by Pierre's expression. I bit my tongue.

"Pierre," Bronia said. "It is late and a long way back. You should get going."

"Yes, of course," Pierre murmured, his eyes still on me as

he tipped his hat, walked out. I looked away, my face flaming hot again.

Kaz put his hand on my stomach, flattened his palm against me, holding still. "*Kochanie*," he said again. "A baby?"

A baby? I laughed a little, glanced at Bronia, who stared back at me tight-lipped, serious.

"Marya," she said, her frown creasing deeper. "You have been riding that silly bicycle around La Villette, your head in the clouds. Somebody needs to help you face the truth."

My *head in the clouds*. It was the same way Hela described Pierre. And for a moment I thought about our conversation earlier, about the way his hand had felt holding mine, about the way everything had felt a little easier when it was just between the two of us.

"The truth?" I questioned Bronia, though somewhere inside of me, I felt a new red-hot terror rising through my veins, pooling in my stomach, nausea hitting me quickly again.

BRONIA PUT HER STETHOSCOPE TO MY EARS, UNBUTTONED A button on my dress, and put the cold end against my belly. She implored me to listen to the sounds that she was positive would come through. I heard them, a steady *thump, thump, thump*. But even then, I told her it was not proof of anything. What about the doctor who said my body could not hold on to a baby, deliver it into the world, living?

Kaz took the stethoscope for his own ears. Then, after he heard the sounds too, he exclaimed: "A baby!" His face erupted with a joy I hadn't seen in him since we were very young, and so in love, and I felt it sharply inside my own chest, an ache, a wanting.

I Ie kneeled down on the ground, kissed my belly. I wanted

to continue to be mad at him. I wanted to insist that I had all I needed right here in Paris, on my own. I wanted to stay with my *head in the clouds* and my feet on the bicycle pedals on the cobblestone streets of La Villette. But there was a heartbeat inside of me, and suddenly that was more important than anything I needed or I wanted.

The day after Hela's wedding, Kaz and I took the long journey back to Poland, together.

MARIE

France, 1904

Pierre's magical heart is right. 1904 changes us.

For one thing, from the very start of the year, there is the money. Seventy thousand francs from Sweden, and more from England for the Davy prize. We install a modern bathroom in our house, and I send twenty thousand Austrian crowns to Bronia and Mier to help with their sanatorium in Zakopane, and also gifts to Hela in Warsaw and Jacques in Montpellier.

Bronia writes to thank me for the money, and I suppose it is strange the way neither one of us mentions this cloud that still hangs over us, the darkness that continues to embrace us, or the way that money, *even money*, which we have needed and needed for so very long, does nothing to ease that. Jakub and Val are still dead. It is almost hard to remember a time back in Szczuki and in Warsaw when I believed that, if only I had money, surely happiness and everything else I ever wanted would follow.

Then with our new money comes more money: Pierre is finally admitted into the Academy and hired as a professor at the Sorbonne. So we have not only our prize money but his steady and good salary. And we can, for the first time, afford to hire a research assistant for our lab.

But strangest of all is our new notoriety, our sudden fame. The press clamors on boulevard Kellerman outside our home, snapping photos of us as we leave for the lab in the morning. Jeanne Langevin makes her way through the garden, into my kitchen, to complain how they are waking her baby with their noise and disturbing the entire street. Paul walks in behind her, shushing her, saying, *It is not their fault the press won't leave them alone.*

"Believe me," I tell Jeanne, throwing my hands up in the air in annoyance. "I do not want them here. I cannot make them stop."

We go to work, but then there is another bunch of them waiting for us at the lab, shouting at us to grant them an interview, to answer their questions. I begin receiving fan letters in the mail, and hundreds of requests for autographs. I throw them all away, unanswered. Or else I would spend my entire day wasted, signing my name instead of continuing with my work.

"They are enamored of you," Pierre says with a chuckle, as if it tickles him. "The first woman to win a Nobel Prize."

But it is not me they want exactly, it is *us*. They want to write us a great romantic love story. And when we refuse to grant interviews, they write their stories anyway. I am a genius and great light to my husband, or I am a shackle to my husband's genius and his success, depending on where the story is printed, who has written it. No one cares that it was my idea to extract the radium. No one cares that I was born poor and Polish. One of the dailies calls me *France's Greatest Living Gem*. Another one makes up a quote of me saying that everything I do, it is in deference to my great husband.

"Perhaps we should just grant a few interviews," Pierre says.

"They might realize how dreadfully hard and tedious our work is and leave us alone."

"It would be a waste of our time," I say. "Let them write whatever they like. What do I care?"

Pierre has his classes at the Sorbonne to prepare for now, and I still have my classes to teach at the girls' school in Sèvres. And there is so much more to be done in the lab. We are trying to assess the atomic weight of radium, and in the bustle of everything, we have mistakenly misplaced some materials; we are dreadfully behind. The committee in Sweden gave us only six months to come in person to make our acceptance speech, but Pierre has been struck with his most violent attack of rheumatism yet, and neither one of us can imagine making the journey to Sweden in that time frame.

When spring semester ends, Pierre and I are both aching and exhausted, and who cares that we have money now? Happiness feels so far out of our reach.

But Pierre has an idea. He has found us a secluded little cottage to rent in Saint-Rémy to while away the first month of summer. "The press will never find us there," he tells me, with a satisfied grin. "And we can, at long last, get some rest."

I GO BAREFOOT IN SAINT-RÉMY IN JUNE, OR SOMETIMES I wear sandals when we take the bicycles out and ride through the pastures, to Lac du Peiroou. And then, even though the water is freezing, Pierre insists on a swim, while I am content to dip my toes in at the edge.

Away from the city, Irène wiles away the days with her *grand-père*, and Pierre and I spend the days together, devoid of responsibilities. Pierre's leg pains ease, and without the constant buzz and hum of the reporters, I should be able to breathe a little easier here too. But for some reason, I can't. We have promised each other to clear our minds of work for the few weeks that we are here. We want to revel in the country air and Irène and each other. And it is only then, only after a week away, that I realize the truth of it: the tiredness, my aching body, my nausea, even all the way out here. *I am pregnant again.* For heaven's sakes, how had I missed this in Paris? I count back . . . I must already be a few months along.

The realization should buoy me, but instead it sinks me, like I've dived into the cold waters of the lake and I can barely breathe.

I whisper my revelation to Pierre in the darkness of our bed that night.

He lowers his face to my belly, kisses me softly. I can feel the warmth of his lips, even through the fabric of my nightgown.

"I am terrified," I admit to him. I think about last time, how the baby came much too soon, only five months along. Not a boy at all as Pierre had felt but a girl, perfectly formed, only born before she could breathe.

"No, *mon amour*," Pierre whispers into my belly, his words tickling the fibers of my gown against my skin. "Everything is going to be exactly right this time, I can feel it."

THE NEXT MORNING I AWAKE BEFORE DAWN. PIERRE IS ACTU-ally asleep, snoring softly beside me. His pains and his mind calm enough to rest out here.

I get up and dress in an old smock I'd brought for bike riding, and I go outside to take a walk to the lake. The sun rises, and the sky turns pink and purple. The world feels beautiful here, like a world that will never harm us again, and I inhale, letting the warm country air wash over me.

"Excuse me," a young man calls out to me, and as I do not recognize him, I keep on walking. "Excuse me, Madame," he calls out again, his French racked with a terrible American accent. I stop if only to get him to leave me alone. I need quiet. I need time for my mind to absorb what my body already understands. Six more months of worry and waiting and aching, and then if the world spins exactly as it should, and if there are no more *accidents of science*, another baby. *Another baby.* "I've heard the Curies are staying here for a holiday," the man says. "Have you seen them? I hear they like to ride bicycles along here, and I'd really like to catch them for an interview."

I reach up to touch my hair. It's out of its usual bun, as I haven't taken the time this morning. My feet are bare, and my smock is old and torn and ragged. He has no idea who I am, and somehow that thought gives me strength to remember *exactly* who I am. "I haven't seen them," I say. "You must be mistaken."

I walk back toward the cottage, a smile creeping across my face. Saint-Rémy is otherworldly and strangely magical, and when I find Pierre in the cottage preparing breakfast I tell him that I think if we can just stay here forever everything is going to turn out okay.

His eyes light up, and he embraces me. And for just a moment, I can breathe again.

BUT WE CANNOT STAY IN SAINT-RÉMY. OUR LAB CALLS TO US, and we have classes to teach. In the fall we are back in Paris, but I am so heavy with the baby and exhaustion and worry that I take a short leave from teaching my classes in Sèvres. Still, every day, I am in the lab, working. The months go slowly: four, then five, then six, then seven. Each one like an experiment. I hold my breath to see if I will make it through, if the results will be good.

In the middle of November, Bronia shows up at our door one evening, unannounced. She is paler than I remember her; thinner. Zakopane has not been as kind to her as I would've expected, once. *Not Zakopane, though*. Life. And death.

"*Moja mała siostrzyczka,*" she says, embracing me. Her Polish shocks me. It has been too long since I have heard it regularly, since I have spoken it. "I did not want you to have this baby without me," she says. She puts her hand on my belly, doctor and sister-mother. But maybe Bronia needs a sister-mother too. I wonder if she is here to see for herself that good things can happen to us, too, that children can live still, even once we have seen them die. Or maybe she is here because she is worried it will happen again, and she knows I cannot survive it another time, on my own.

I cling to her, so happy she is here, no matter what her reason. "Everything is terrible," I admit to her in a way I can't admit to Pierre. His leg pains have returned even worse since the summer, and he is busy with his students. And he is worried how much longer we can put off a trip to Sweden, and with writing the Academy to buy us more time. To him the baby will happen, it will come when it is ready, and everything will turn out fine this time. I cannot burden him with my own dread, with my worry. But Bronia. She is a different story. "Everything is darkness," I tell her.

"I knew you needed me," she replies, more to herself than to me.

BY THE BEGINNING OF DECEMBER, THE WEATHER HAS GROWN cool and my body is so heavy, the baby so large, pushing up into my chest, that I can barely breathe. And anyway, I hold my breath still, waiting, waiting, not daring to believe this baby is real. Refusing to name the baby or love it or imagine holding it. Even when the labor pains begin and drag on and on through the night. Even then, I do not allow myself to believe.

It is not until she comes out wailing and Bronia places her on my chest that I understand that she is real, that she is alive. And even then my body is overcome with pain. I'm numb with it, and I can't quite believe. She comes out chubby and with a head of black hair, looking nothing like slender Irène with her pale hair. Is she really mine?

"She's okay?" I say to Pierre when he comes in to see her, more a question than a statement.

She is still wailing, and Pierre lifts her from my chest, holds her close, and kisses her black swath of hair. "She is perfect," Pierre says softly. "Should we name her after your father?"

"No, no," I say. "She needs a new name. A beautiful, fresh French name." I am done with darkness. I am done with death hovering, marking us and taking away our happiness.

"I like Ève," Pierre says after a little while.

"Ève," I repeat. A beginning.

MARYA

❧

Loksow, Poland, 1904

My Klara was a wonderful baby. She came into the world
blond-haired and blue-eyed, bright pink and wailing. And
then, she hardly ever cried, she was a good sleeper, and she was
content to observe everything around her without much fussing,
even when I began taking her with me to my university courses
again in January. I wore her in a wrap across my chest, her heart
beating close to mine, and I swore she was already listening, already learning, already feeling the heartbeats of my chemistry
lessons.

I had returned to our apartment on Złota Street last August and picked up my life again as if I'd never left it all for a
few months away in France. The remainder of my pregnancy felt
long and filled with so much worry, but Klara was born perfect
in November of 1903, and I was filled with a lightness I'd never
known before. My love for my daughter was a different kind of
love than I had ever felt, than I had ever imagined.

Kaz and I did not discuss what had happened between him
and Leokadia, but before we left Paris, I forced myself to read all

the letters he'd sent to me. They were filled with apologies, and promises. He swore he made a mistake, only once. He blamed what had happened on his sadness over losing baby Zosia. And then, how in the ensuing months, he believed I had lost myself. Which made him feel he had lost me too. It was hard to read that part, because the truth of it stung. *I had lost myself, hadn't I?* Yes, I had nearly drowned, but instead of pulling me out, pulling me up, Kaz had turned to my closest friend.

Kaz promised he would never talk to Leokadia again. But by the time I came back to Poland, Leokadia was already gone.

Agata, not Kaz, told me that Leokadia had packed up one day last summer and moved to Berlin to study with a renowned pianist. And even Agata didn't seem to understand why she had left when she had, so suddenly, with her father so ill and so against the move that he refused to give her any money for it.

I shook my head, as if it made no sense to me either. If I pretended whatever had happened between her and Kaz never had, then maybe I could forget it, too. Maybe, in time, it would become hazy enough that I would forgive Kaz, love him the way I used to. "Perhaps she couldn't deny her talent any longer," I suggested to Agata, convincing enough in my lie that I almost believed it myself.

Agata nodded, agreeing that made sense. The irony was, without Leokadia, my life felt much quieter, lonelier. I didn't *want* to miss her, but she had been my closest friend in Loksow for many years.

Sometimes I thought about the life I'd tasted briefly in France, walking through Hela and Jacques's lab, pedaling through the flowers in Sceaux with Pierre, and I felt a little pang of jealousy for Leokadia, learning and living freely in Berlin now.

As a friend I both envied her and felt guilt for my role in making her feel she had to leave. But as Kaz's wife it was a relief to know she was gone, to know that when he went to Hipolit's to work each day, he wouldn't be tempted.

Klara turned six months old at the end of April, and two days later, Kaz came home from work in the middle of the day and sat down at the table where I was feeding Klara lunch. He rested his cheek on the wood of the table and began to cry.

"What is it?" I stood up, alarmed. I had never seen Kaz cry before, not even when baby Zosia died. But it had been hard to see anything then, through the fog of my own tears.

"Hipolit is gone," he said.

"Oh." My heartbeat quickened, and I put my hand to my chest to steady it. The money we lived on now came from the salary that Hipolit paid Kaz to conduct his research. Hipolit had been sick for a while, but somehow in my mind I'd imagined him lingering on and on and on.

"It was just . . . my parents . . . Hipolit treated me . . ." Kaz shook his head, flooded with grief, not able to finish his thought. But I nodded, I understood. Hipolit was his mentor. Hipolit had taught him and cared for him and nurtured his talent even when his own parents had abandoned him.

I felt guilty now that my first reaction to the news had not been sadness, but a new, and familiar, worry about money. "Oh, Kaz," I said gently. No matter that I was still angry with him, I cared for him, too.

Klara had taken the spoon from my hand while I was paying attention to Kaz, and she chose that moment to test it against the wood of the table, banging it, again, and again, and again, while babbling to herself.

Kaz pulled the spoon from her hands, abruptly, and her face turned, her eyes welled up with tears. Poland's happiest baby turned, in an instant, into Poland's saddest baby. Kaz's mouth opened. "No, *moje dziecko*, don't cry. Papa didn't mean to upset you."

He reached for her quickly, held her against his chest, until her tears stopped. Her heartbeat steadied against his heartbeat, and he kissed the top of her head, gently smoothed back her blond curls with his large fingers.

"It's going to be okay," I said to Klara, or Kaz, or to myself. And that was the thing about being a mother, it had made me into a liar. And a good one at that. I forced myself to smile. "Everything is going to be okay."

PANI JEWNIEWICZ PUT OFF THE FUNERAL FOR A WEEK, UNTIL Leokadia could make it back from Berlin. The day was rainy and quite cold for April, and it was the first time I ever left Klara. Agata offered to sit with her at the apartment so Kaz and I could both attend the funeral. And though part of me did not want to go, did not want to see Leokadia, I thought about how she had traveled with me to Warsaw when Papa was dying, and I knew I had to be there.

"Marya." She smiled when she saw me, reached out to hug me, then stopped herself, put her arms at her sides.

As much as I wanted to hate her, wanted to be angry with her still, seeing her again I remembered exactly why I loved her. I'd missed my friend, and now here she was, right in front of me. She wore a black dress, but it did not dim the brightness of her rosy cheeks, her piercing blue eyes, her beautiful blond curls swept back tightly in a bun. "I'm very sorry for your loss," I said. I reached for her, awkwardly patting her shoulders.

She reached up and grabbed my hand, and she squeezed it.

"Marya," she said my name again. "Can we talk later? I have so much to say to you."

I did not want to talk, did not want to hear whatever she had to say. But how could I refuse her at her father's funeral?

"It was only one time," she said to me later that afternoon, repeating what Kaz had written. As if that made it hurt any less.

We had all left the gray and the gloom of the cemetery to return to a lavish feast at the Jewniewiczes' apartment. Kaz had gone to look through the papers Hipolit had left in his study, and Leokadia cornered me and asked if I would join her out on the balcony. The rain had stopped, but the sky was still steel-colored, the air cool and damp. "Just once," Leokadia repeated.

I pressed my lips tightly together, not sure how to respond. What were you supposed to say to a woman who you'd loved as a sister, who had betrayed you? I missed her, and I loved her still. And I hated her.

"I know that doesn't make it any better, what I did," Leokadia said. She walked to the edge of the balcony, leaned on the iron railing, and stared off at the smokestacks, the industry of Loksow, in the distance. "But I wanted you to know," she said. "I made a terrible mistake, a horrible lapse in judgment. And it never happened again. I would never let it happen again."

Part of me wanted to ask her exactly *when* it had happened, wanted to reimagine where I had been at the time and how I might have changed things if I had noticed more, paid attention more. What if I had not lost my own self in my grief? What if I had reached for Kaz when we were both hurting, instead of pulling away from him? The other part of me knew it didn't matter.

Nothing could change or undo what had happened now. There was always a choice, and they had both made one. Choices had consequences.

"Do you love him?" I asked her. I'd asked Kaz the same question once about her, and he'd denied he'd ever loved anyone but me. I still didn't know if I believed him.

"He's your husband," Leokadia said, a nonanswer.

"But what if he wasn't?"

"I don't know what you want me to say, Marya," she said. "I've missed you," she added softly. "I wish I could just . . . take it back."

"You can't," I said, matter-of-factly. She could no more take back her one night with Kaz than I could take back not getting on that train to Paris so many years ago and choosing to marry Kaz instead.

She nodded. "I know. But I would, if I could."

Would I?

Now that I had Klara, I could not imagine any path, any choice, that would not lead me to her. And now that Kadi was in Berlin, living her dream, I wondered if she could truly regret any choice she had made that had led her there. "You are happy in Berlin?" I asked her.

She turned away from the railing, back to face me, her mouth slightly open in surprise. She had been bracing herself, leaning against the iron, girding herself. "Berlin is . . . very nice," she spoke cautiously, still staring at me. I nodded at her to continue. "I have learned so much and have so many opportunities to perform. That part has been quite wonderful," she finally said. "I should've gone years ago." She swallowed hard and looked at her boots, the weight of what was unsaid caught in her throat. Her father had died angry with her, and maybe if she had left years ago, he would've had a chance to get over it. Or she would've come to terms with it herself by now. "I miss Flying University, though," she said now. "All the wonderful women."

I nodded. "Well . . . now that you're gone, we don't have anyone teaching music lessons. No one else has the talent for it, you know."

"I bet my old piano teacher would do it. I'll ask her for you."

"That would be nice," I said softly. "Thank you."

We stared at each other, so much still left unsaid, but neither one of us said anything for another moment. "If I wrote you letters from Berlin, do you think you might write me back?" she finally asked me. "I practice all day, and I barely know anyone still. It gets lonely."

"Klara keeps me very busy," I said quickly.

"*Klara.*" She smiled, and though I supposed she knew I'd had a baby—her mother must've relayed that detail—she hadn't known her name until now. "That's a beautiful name," she said.

"Kaz wanted to call her Kazimiera, but that's his mother's name, and I said absolutely not. I didn't think she should be Marya either. I wanted her to have her own name, be her own person, so Klara seemed a combination of both of us and that too."

"It's perfect." Leokadia smiled, then added, "I will send you letters, and you will write back if you have the time?"

I thought about what she was asking. "I suppose I will write back," I finally said. "If I have the time."

Later that night, after Klara fell asleep, Kaz was restless in our bed, tossing and turning and pulling the sheets off of me. I put my hand on his arm to stop him from rolling, to steady him, and he reached up and grabbed my fingers, held on to me. He stopped moving, and for a few seconds we lay there touching.

"I don't know what I'm going to do now," he said. "He's gone, and he left no money to continue his research."

It was hard to breathe for a moment in the darkness, and then I thought of Klara sleeping in the next room, and I forced myself to. *Inhale, exhale.* I thought about Hela and Jacques in their lab, about Pierre, who Hela said had done many studies with very little results, and how that was what prevented him from being hired. But Kaz had done so much work already, had so many results. Kaz did not have his head in the clouds; he was steady, practical. "You have all the elasticity research," I said. "You're going to publish it, and then you're going to get a job in a lab or at a university. And we are going to be fine. We are going to be just fine."

MARIE

❧❧

We finally make it to Stockholm to give our acceptance speech in June of 1905, and we are both feeling well and happy at last. This city is so beautiful and calm in the summer—no one from the press even realizes we are here! And I cannot have a bad thought about the world, even if I might still be inclined to.

All around us there is the bluest water and quaintest red roofs, and though we have been dreading and worrying about this journey for so long, now that we are here it feels like a holiday. Pierre and I hold hands as we walk along the river path in the beautiful, flowering Djurgården the afternoon before Pierre is to give his speech.

Though we have written the speech together, wanting to focus on the way our discovery, and radium, might be a great help to humanity, only one of us can give the speech, as is customary. Neither one of us enjoys speaking, but we've decided Pierre, as the man, will be better received before the committee. Still, he is nervous about it, and he recites his way through it again as we walk and walk. It is seven pages long but he has memorized it over the course of the very long days of travel coming here. As have I.

"Pierre," I tell him now. "Don't worry any more about the speech. Enjoy the water and the flowers with me now. And oh." I pull a letter from the pocket of my dress. "This was waiting for us at the hotel, from Irène."

At the mention of our daughter's name, he stops reciting his Nobel speech and smiles. "Writing us the moment after we left, was she?" He chuckles. "*Une bonne petite fille.*"

I nod. Irène really is a good child, exceptionally thoughtful and kind, and quite brilliant for an almost eight-year-old. We had left her and Ève in the care of Dr. Curie in Paris, and though I know they will be well taken care of, that we will be back soon, it was still hard to leave them. I unfold her letter and feel a surge of pride at how neat her handwriting is. "She wants to tell us that Ève is already making a mess and stealing her things." I laugh. At only six months, Ève already feels very formed as a person, with a deep curiosity and spirit and a penchant for invoking jealousy in her older sister. "And she wants us to write back immediately to let her know *exactly* how long until we leave for Brittany, in minutes."

Pierre smiles, shakes his head a little. When we return from Sweden, Hela and Hanna are taking the train from Warsaw to Paris so they can travel together with me and the children to Brittany for a holiday. Hela's husband, Stan, has to stay in Poland to work. Pierre will stay in Paris to work at first, but he will join us by the end of July.

It will be Hela's first time seeing the ocean, and Irène's first time spending weeks on end with her seven-year-old cousin, Hanna. I cannot blame Irène for her excitement. I feel it too, anxious to be with my sister-twin again. Life has been tough for them in Poland, the revolution there making money tighter, food scarcer, and I am excited for her to have rest and relaxation by the sea. I send Hela money whenever I can, and I've already sent money for their train tickets, even bought them clothing for the summer and the beach so Hela will not have to worry about a thing.

It is strange and wonderful the way this summer is filled with lightness, after last summer was filled with such darkness. Ève is growing, and Irène is becoming a young woman. We are a family of *four*, with Dr. Curie extending us to five, and our summer will be filled with a little work and more travel and seawater and family time.

"*Mon amour*," Pierre says now, tugging gently on my hand. "Look across the water. Swans."

There they are, swimming toward us, an entire splendid family of them, their beautiful white long necks bobbing into the water. The male and female peck at each other playfully, and then Pierre grabs me and laughs, and he joyfully plants a kiss on my lips.

A few weeks later, the Nobel speech is finally, finally behind us, and it feels like a weight has been taken away, we have been worrying about it for so very long. The journey to Brittany is easy, and the days there are slow and mostly free of work. We go to the beach, and the older girls play, their laughter a balm.

Hela is afraid of the water, terrified by the waves. "I cannot go in," she protests from the edge of the surf as I run into the sea with the older girls, while Hela stays behind with Ève. "I cannot watch," Hela yells after us, covering her eyes and squealing.

Hela looks so much older than I picture her in my head, paler and with new wrinkles framing her eyes. Her blond hair is half gray, and I wonder if she sees the same in me, if I have changed in so many ways I have not noticed, but she can.

I leave Hanna and Irène running into the cold surf, jumping in between waves. I go back for Hela, offer to hold her hand in the waves. But she still refuses.

She dips only her toe into the water, testing, and then she screams. The girls come running, alarmed. "What is it?" I reach for her, worried she's hurt or falling ill.

She reaches down and pulls something from her toes, and there in her hand is a small shell, a hermit crab. I begin to laugh.

"Stop it," she says to me. But she puts the shell in her palm; the crab crawls slowly across her hand and then her fingers. The girls are out of the water now, giddy and anxious, and in awe of this smallest creature, coming out of his shell. Then Hela begins to laugh too.

"Come," I say to the children. "Pierre will be arriving soon and he knows all about hermit crabs. Let's put this one in a basin in the house, and he will study the creature with us when he gets here."

PIERRE ARRIVES THE NEXT MORNING WITH A BAG FULL OF heavy equipment. And I can tell his rheumatism is acting up again because he walks hunched over, slowly, and limping. "This dampness," he laments, eyes toward the sea. But is it more than that? It has been years and years now that his bones have been aching, and no doctor can really tell him why. He has finally been elected into the Academy of Sciences, has a good teaching position at the Sorbonne, and we have been given a larger lab in the negotiations. Professionally, he has everything, but he does not have his health, and it feels tremendously unfair that he suffers so.

"You brought too much with you from Paris," I chide him,

remarking on his bag of heavy equipment. "I thought we were only going to work a little here? On papers?"

"Yes, *mon amour*, but this equipment is not for work. This is for fun. I've hired a carriage to take us all to Mont-Saint-Michel to watch the eclipse this week. And I brought special viewing equipment with me from Paris so we can all get a better look."

"Of course you did." I laugh, shake my head at his foolishness, while also delighting in it. I have never seen an eclipse before, and I am now quite excited about the prospect of viewing it, and though I have chided him, I am actually quite thrilled that he thought to bring the equipment along.

A FEW DAYS LATER, WE ALL PILE INTO THE CARRIAGE: HELA and the older girls, Pierre, Dr. Curie, and then me with Ève on my lap. The ride isn't too long, the driver gentle, and we are there by late morning, enough time to get out and explore the ruins and the castle and prison of Louis XI. As the sky begins to darken, we go to a viewing terrace in the castle. And Pierre explains the science of it all to the older children, who delight in his explanations and explode with their questions. They spent the whole evening last night studying their hermit crab with Pierre, and today it is the sun and the moon and the sky.

The midday sky grows black, and birds flutter around us, restless and confused. Hela puts her arms around me in the darkness. "Remember when Papa used to teach us about the sunsets?" she says softly into my hair.

"Of course I do." It is one of my earliest memories of learning about the world, loving science and feeling that deep and abiding sense of wonder I still feel now each morning in the lab.

"Pierre reminds me of the way he was with us, so good with our children."

In the darkness it is hard to see that Pierre can barely stand. And in the excitement of his voice, it is hard to remember the way he'd been restless all night last night, moaning in his half-sleep about the terrible pains in his bones.

"I'm worried about him," I tell Hela now. "The doctors cannot say what is causing him so much pain. I worry he will never feel good again, that there is something wrong with him that they do not understand yet. He is only forty-six, and you would never know it from the way he walks and cries out in agony all night."

Only two months ago in Sweden, he was seeming better, but now in the damp sea air, he seems so much worse again. It is hard to love him so much and to watch him suffer. I want to help him, want to fix him, and I have no idea how.

"You are a good wife, a good person. A wonderful scientist! Papa would be so proud if he could see you now." Hela kisses my cheek, and I feel her own cheek wet with a tear against mine. I'm not sure why she's crying exactly, but it makes me start to cry too. "*Moja mała siostrzyczka.* You will find a way. You will fix him, take care of him, help him," she says to me. I want to fix his pain more than anything, but I truly don't know how.

"*Mon amour*," he calls out to me now, his voice rich with excitement, and I pull away from Hela. "It's your turn. Come, have a look at the sun."

I tread slowly to him in the darkness, and then I listen to his instructions for viewing in the large scope. I look at the sky through his lens.

The sun has retreated into a nearly impossible darkness, turning its fiery light black and dim.

MARYA

Poland, 1905

By the beginning of 1905, my Flying University had greatly multiplied in size. Eight of the original women who had come together with me to learn, over ten years earlier, now all acted as professors with me. We taught in our own areas of specialty, ranging from sciences to maths to literature and even music, after Leokadia followed through with her promise to connect me with her old teacher. And we had close to sixty young women enrolled in our courses, each paying two rubles (or whatever they could afford) a month to attend. This money went toward paying all of us teachers a salary. And to pay the rent on a one-room apartment where classes took place a few evenings a week. A revolution was rising in Poland, the people wanting to break free of Russian rule. The Russian police were busy with protests, looters. In a way, it gave our burgeoning school a new safety. They had no time for us.

Still, Kaz continued to worry about me breaking the law, and perhaps even more so now that we had Klara. But I felt an odd safety in our numbers, in the fact that we had gone on and on like this for years with hardly a problem. As long as we did not advertise what we were doing, out in the open. As long as we stayed *secret*, I truly believed the police would continue to leave us alone. What did it matter to them, really, if we were educated? There were no jobs for us in Russian Poland, nothing we could do with our education, anyway.

Kaz had gone back to teaching maths at the dreaded boys' school for only half the salary Hipolit had been paying him, and on nights and weekends he worked to get his and Hipolit's research on elasticity written up into a paper, with the goal of publishing it, eventually being able to secure himself a better job in his field. We moved around each other, both busy, barely talking, barely touching each other.

But Kaz loved Klara, so deeply, so obviously. The first thing he did when he walked in each night after work, before poring over his research, was go to her, where she was often playing on the floor, babbling to herself while I prepared dinner. He would walk in, pick her up: "*Kiciuna*, how I missed you today." He'd swoop her into a hug and tickle her belly with kisses until she began to laugh.

Then he would turn to me, smile a little. Ask me if I'd had enough money to buy food for supper, or if I needed anything else for the apartment. He could always tutor a boy or two after school to make some extra money if we needed it. That was Kaz, *steady*. Even when he himself was struggling with his work.

And sometimes, I would stand there at the edge of the kitchen, watching him with Klara. For just a moment I would remember it. Why I loved him. Why I married him.

I STAYED AT HOME IN OUR APARTMENT WITH KLARA DURING the day, almost every day. She took regular and long naps, and I got a lot of reading done, new papers being published in chemistry and physics, which Hela would send to me in big, thick packages once a month, knowing my hunger for them. I continued to learn, to self-teach, so that I could impart this knowledge to my young students on Wednesday nights. I loved Klara and the days we had together, but even with my time for reading, being at home constantly became somewhat mind-numbing. Sometimes I simply longed for intelligent conversations with adults, longed to be learning in an environment with others, not just by myself.

A few times a month, Agata and I went to the girls' gymnasiums in Loksow to work on recruiting the older girls for our courses, and these were days I greatly looked forward to. First there were the long walks, the conversations with Agata, whose little boy Piotr was two, six months older than Klara. And second, there was the joy I felt in talking about our school, remembering again and again what it had become. What *we* had made it. Now that we had a fixed location, we were no longer a *Flying University*, and we gave ourselves a new name, one so bold it could only be said in secret: Women's University of Loksow.

Whenever I spoke to the girls at the gymnasium about what we did, what they could learn, I got a little thrill saying our new name out loud. *Women's University*. Right here in Loksow. I had started this. Agata and I both had.

BY THE SPRING, LOKSOW WAS BURNING WITH RESISTANCE. It was, at first, a dull hum on the streets as I walked to teach my Wednesday night class, a whisper among the younger women I was teaching. And then it erupted into crowds of people blocking the street, making it hard to get around. Kaz's students went on strike, protesting for the right to learn in Polish instead of

Russian, for better pay for all workers, and so Kaz was at home during the day, with me and Klara. He kept to himself, working all day on his research, but our meager savings dwindled, and I worried we'd soon run out of money to eat. My salary was not enough for us to live on, to continue to afford our two bedrooms on Złota Street.

In Paris, Hela and Jacques had made a finding with their minerals and magnetic properties, winning a prize from the French Academy of Sciences and with it a generous sum of francs. Hela wrote me with the good news and mailed us a portion of their prize winnings, offering this gift as her *very small and faraway contribution to the revolution in Poland.*

Kaz did not like it, taking *charity money* from my sister, but I said to him: "What would you have us do instead? Starve?"

I hated the way he looked back at me, both startled and disappointed. "As soon as I publish this research . . ." he mumbled, turning back to his papers.

But we had gone on this way for so many years, I didn't know if I believed there was something more for us any longer, something beyond what we were and what we had now. And though I hoped for Poland to be free, for my university to be allowed out in the open and for our lives to be easier, ever since I gave birth to Klara, none of the rest of it mattered quite as much as it used to. I did not dream of Paris or the Sorbonne any longer.

Instead I dreamed mostly of enough food to eat, a nice place to live, and for Klara to grow up happy and healthy.

"COME WITH US, PANI MARYA," ONE OF MY STUDENTS, A small, bright-eyed girl, Aleksandra, implored me one Wednesday in May. My walk to class had been lined with students her age, both men and women, chanting in the streets, protesting. And when I walked inside our school, my students were all humming about protesting, too, not readying themselves for my lesson.

"What is going on here?" I asked. I had prepared a lesson tonight on the new research about X-rays I'd been reading that Hela had sent to me last week. A paper by Henri Becquerel, a pioneer in the field, and Hela wrote that she had actually met him recently! He had come to their lab, wanting to view their new prizewinning discovery about his Becquerel rays and their minerals. Imagine that.

"We are going to join the revolution tonight," Aleksandra answered, her blue eyes shimmery even in the dim lighting.

"No." I held my hand up. "Everyone put your signs away. You have paid me to teach you. And do you know where the real revolution is?" They all stopped what they were doing and looked at me, their young eyes eager, trained on my face. "Right here." I tapped my forefinger to my head. "If you become educated. If you learn . . . well, that is how you will beat them. How you will win."

It was something Papa had said to me and Bronia and Hela so many times when we were girls, and remembering his last deathbed words to me again, I smiled a little. "Now," I said to the girls. "Should I begin my lesson? There will still be time to protest after."

LEOKADIA KEPT HER PROMISE AND WROTE ME ONCE EVERY few weeks from Berlin to update me on the goings-on in her life. And I kept my promise to her and replied to the letters sometimes, when I had something to say, or when my heart softened toward her again as she mentioned being lonely in Berlin. She was learning so much, being paid to perform in the city, and beginning to be offered new and exciting opportunities all around Europe. But she had no friends in Berlin, no family.

Hela wrote me from Paris and Bronia wrote me from Zakopane weekly too. But the letters I looked forward to most of all? The ones I treasured and kept in a pile inside the top drawer of my chest? The occasional ones that came from Pierre.

As the revolution was overtaking the streets of Loksow, Pierre wrote me about the flowers blooming once again, taking over the gardens surrounding his house in Sceaux.

Sometimes when I am taking my morning bicycle ride, I can't help but think of you, he wrote. *Hoping that you are well,* belle intelligente *Marya. When do you think you might return to Paris?*

MARIE

❧

France, 1906

Easter weekend we go to our cottage in Saint-Rémy, leaving all thoughts of work and the lab and even teaching behind us in Paris. We while away the days soaked in sunshine and lake water and happiness.

Everyone is in high spirits and healthy, and Pierre is feeling well enough to ride bicycles with me again. We go out in the morning, pedaling toward the Alpilles, until they are closer and closer, almost close enough to touch those stunning brown hills. We return to the cottage sweating and a little sunburned on our faces, and ravenous for the eggs Dr. Curie and the girls have cooked fresh from the chickens while we were riding.

In the afternoon, we lie out on the grass in the sun, in front of the cottage. Pierre and I hold hands, watching the girls. Irène dances around, picking flowers. Ève has somehow managed to remove her dress and runs topless in only a pair of knickers, trying to keep up with her sister.

I roll on my side to look at Pierre, and he turns to look at me. His beard is grayer than when we first met, but his eyes just as blue, just as filled with light. The sun streams across his face, turning his features yellow and radiant, reminding me of the phosphorescent radium tube he made for my nightstand at home. "*Mon amour*," he says softly, reaching his other hand up to touch my hair, to stroke my forehead with his thumb. "I love our life together," he says. "How did I ever get so lucky?"

"There is no such thing as luck." I smile at him. But even my scientific mind now understands a little what he means. The strangest way we came together by chance, the way our children, these particular children, came from us, and now they run around before us perfect and healthy and undamaged. The way we have been touched by phosphorescent light and love, professional success, and even money.

"Everything we have," I finally say. "It is because *we* have made it so, together."

"Together," he echoes back.

IN THE CITY THE NEXT WEEK, THE WEATHER TURNS. ON Wednesday, as the children and I return, the winds roll in and the sky grays, and by Thursday morning it is chilly and rainy. I move about that morning, sluggish and out of sorts, trying to dress the children, ready them for the day, when Pierre calls out to me from downstairs that he is leaving for the lab.

"I have that lunch," he calls up. I recall vaguely what he means. A newly formed association of science professors he's been invited to be a part of, and that they have called a lunch meeting today. It is not so long ago that Pierre was not included in such things, and I remember now that they have specifically requested Pierre's presence at the lunch. I smile. They still haven't included me, as a woman, but I don't care. I much prefer the lab to socializing anyway.

"I'll see you in the lab afterward," I yell back. I have errands to run this morning, food to buy for the house after having been away in the country for days, and then in the afternoon I will settle back into the lab myself. I close my eyes and wish I were there now, with Pierre, instead of suffering through the next hours of household duties and errands.

Ève hands me her sweater, interrupting my thoughts. I sigh. She dislikes it and has already pulled it off twice. "You'll be cold without it," I tell her as sternly as I can manage. I put her arms through the tiny sleeves once more.

Irène lets out an exaggerated sigh. "Why must she make everything so difficult, Maman?"

"Why indeed?" I say, as Ève is taking off her sweater again. The day is gray and cold and wet, and I am so sluggish. "Why indeed."

PIERRE NEVER MAKES IT INTO THE LAB AFTER HIS LUNCH, AND I leave early myself, allowing extra time to walk home in the rain. The streets are flooded, and I walk slowly, worrying about Pierre. If he did not come to the lab, his rheumatism must be acting up again. He seemed so good last weekend, so healthy, that it was easy to forget my worries about his health while we were away. But the dampness today must be affecting him. It always does. I long for more sun-filled days in Saint-Rémy. Even the lab hasn't cheered me up today, and by the time I walk inside the front door of our house, I'm soaked and chilled and feeling as gloomy as the weather.

I lay my umbrella out in the foyer, take off my wet boots. "Pierre," I call out, and when he doesn't answer I try again.

"Marie." Dr. Curie walks in from the dining room. He's a tall man, and despite his age, his white hair and beard, his wrinkled skin, I always believe I am seeing him in my mind the way he must've been when he was young. He usually walks gracefully, his voice filled with light. But now from the way he is hunched over, the way he has just said my name . . . His face is pale, expressionless. Something is wrong.

"What's happened?" I ask. "Is it his legs again? Have you called for the doctor?" I hang up my coat and move to walk toward the steps, to check on Pierre in our bedroom.

"Marie." Dr. Curie says my name again, more sharply. He reaches his hand out to catch my arm, to stop me from going upstairs. Dr. Curie has never grabbed me in anything but a hug before. My heart suddenly pounds in my chest. I look back at him and now he is crying. "The gendarmerie are in the dining room. They want to talk with you."

The gendarmerie? In my house? "The children?" I gasp, suddenly panicked.

"They're fine. They're at the Perrins'." Irène is often next door, playing with her little friend when I arrive home, and that in itself is not unusual. It is the way Dr. Curie's voice breaks, the way his eyes cloud with tears.

I pull out of Dr. Curie's grasp and rush into the dining room. There, sitting at my table, are two policemen, along with Professor Appel and Jean Perrin. They all stare at me as I enter, with serious faces, wide eyes.

"What is it?" I demand. *Has Pierre has gotten sicker? Is he in the hospital?*

"There was a dreadful accident," Jean Perrin finally speaks, his voice shaking. "Pierre was run over by a carriage, Marie."

"Run over? By a carriage?" I repeat the words back, and they sound empty, untrue.

"He was always dreaming of something, never paying attention," Dr. Curie murmurs, almost to himself, as if he's in such a state he doesn't realize the rest of us are in the room with him.

"I'm so sorry, Marie," Professor Appel says. "He didn't make it."

Pierre was just here, this morning. Just riding bikes with me in Saint-Rémy last weekend and saying how *lucky* we are. How he loves our life. I shake my head. "That can't be," I say. "It must be some mistake."

"Marie." Jean Perrin stands, comes to me, holds on to my shoulders, as if to hold me up, to keep me standing. I shake him away. I do not need him to carry me. I carry myself, I always carry myself. "It is true," he says gently. "Pierre is dead."

"Pierre is dead." I echo him, the words coming out too loud, hurting my own ears. "Dead? He is absolutely dead?"

No one says a word for a moment. I have frightened them with my logic, or with my lack of tears or with the way shock ripples through me, making my voice loud and angry and so absolute.

"Yes," Jean Perrin says again. "Dead."

"Where is he?" I demand. "I need to see him."

"Madame." One of the gendarmerie rises. "I don't know if that's the best idea. He will not be as you knew him."

"I have to see him," I say again,

The men all look at each other. "His skull was crushed," the other gendarme says, his tone gentle, as if that will soften it.

His brilliant, beautiful mind, *crushed*. Trampled by a carriage. In the street.

"Bring him to me," I say louder, and all around me the men's voices buzz and hum. They are bees in my garden, annoying me.

A FEW HOURS LATER, THEY BRING HIM TO THE HOUSE BY AM-
bulance, carry him in on a stretcher, and lay him out in our living
room. It is dark inside the house, but neither Dr. Curie nor I
have lit the lamps. A gendarme hands me Pierre's things—his
pocket watch, not trampled at all, completely unbroken, still
ticking. It feels impossible, that it continues to keep time. That
time is still moving forward at all.

I clutch the watch in my hand, feeling it ticking against my
palm, and I go to him. His head is wrapped in bandages, but his
face looks exactly like him, when he is sleeping. *My Pierre.* I grab
his hand and it is still warm, still feels responsive to my touch.
Could they be wrong? I put my hand to his neck to feel for his
heartbeat, but there is nothing. Nothing at all.

I sit with him, holding on to his hand with one of my hands.
His watch with the other. I cannot speak, and I have no tears.

Behind me, Dr. Curie stands quietly, watching, waiting for
me to break apart. But morning comes first, and Pierre's brother,
Jacques, arrives at our house from Montpellier.

"Marie," Jacques says, touching my shoulder gently. He
tries to pull me up, pull me away from Pierre, but I refuse to
budge. "Papa says you have been here all night. But they need to
take him away. Prepare his body for the funeral."

Maybe it is that word, *funeral*, that I have not considered
until right now. Or maybe it is the sound of Jacques's voice, an
echo of Pierre's. But quite suddenly my tears come, my body is
racked with sobs that I cannot control, that I cannot stop, even
if I would want to.

MARYA

⁂

Paris, 1906

Klara and I arrived in Paris just before Easter weekend, and enduring the long train rides with a two-and-a-half-year-old, even a usually pleasant one like Klara, was a hellish sort of torture I did not wish to ever repeat. Never mind we planned to return to Poland in only a month's time, and I would have to do it all over again. Stepping out from the Gare du Nord, into the warm, bright Paris morning, I inhaled deeply and tried to put that thought out of my mind.

Our trip to Paris was at once a last-minute decision and the culmination of eight long months of Hela's worried letters to me and Bronia. Truth be told, Bronia was the one Hela longed for in her condition, the one she begged to come to Paris to help her through childbirth. But Bronia was too busy with Jakub and Lou, and her sanatorium was quite busy as well. Bronia could not leave Zakopane for an entire month, and she had written to me, begging me to be the one to go instead. I'd showed her letter to Kaz as proof. *See. Hela cannot survive without me. Even Bronia said so.*

What I did not show Kaz was my correspondence with Pierre. Not because I was doing anything wrong—Pierre had been keeping in more frequent touch to update me on Hela's condition, which he promised he was keeping an eye on for me. But because my letters from him felt private. Something outside of our family or the friends I had in Loksow who Kaz also knew. Before Pierre, Leokadia had been my closest friend, and look what had happened when I'd involved Kaz with her life. No, Pierre was separate. All mine.

I wrote to Pierre last week, to let him know of our upcoming trip, and he wrote back, letting me know he'd taken Jacques's bicycle out again. Fixed a broken spoke, and oiled it, and put air in the tires. *And perhaps*, he wrote, *if she is old enough and wants to learn, you would let me teach your Klara to ride, too?*

THE WEEK BEFORE I LEFT FOR PARIS, I RECEIVED A LETTER from Leokadia. She would be in Paris the week after Easter, too, giving a series of concerts at Montmartre. And she enclosed two tickets for me, should Hela and I wish to attend. She wrote how she would love to see me again, and though I folded the letter and tickets back up, thinking I would never actually *go* to her concert, I had brought them with me all the way to Paris, just in case I changed my mind.

The day of her concert, a Thursday, it was dreadfully dreary and rainy outside. Hela lay in her parlor moaning about her heaviness, her swollen ankles, and the way her mind felt as though it had been stretched and rolled into pastry dough, flat and malleable, *and I can't even concentrate on keeping up with the latest papers*, she complained.

I sliced some bread for Klara and heated some water for

Hela in the kitchen, squeezing a full lemon into it, before taking it to her. "This will help with your swelling," I told her. "I promise."

She frowned, as if to say, who was I? Not her sister-mother. Not her sister-doctor. Not even someone who had obtained a doctorate in science from the Sorbonne. But then she sighed and took the hot water from me. She blew on it before taking a sip. "I'm sorry I've been so difficult," she said. "I just feel so miserable. Tell me it gets easier when the baby gets here, Marya?"

I laughed a little, and lied to her, assured her everything would be easy. Everything *would* be easy, and harder, too. Though Hela, who already employed a servant to cook for her, would probably also be able to afford a wet nurse and a nanny to look after her baby. Perhaps nothing at all would ever be as hard for her as these last few exhausting weeks of her pregnancy had been. But poor Hela, she was in such a state right now. And I really didn't know how to help her.

I pulled Leokadia's tickets out of my valise. "Would it cheer you up to get out of the house, hear some music with me this afternoon?"

"Oh for heaven's sakes no, Marya. For one thing, it's miserable outside." She gestured to the window, slick with raindrops. "And for another, look at me." She put both her hands on her belly, just as Klara finished her bread and ran out from the kitchen, hugging herself to my legs.

I picked her up, though she was almost getting too heavy for that, kissed the top of her head. She no longer smelled like a baby, but like a child, one who loved to explore and dig in the dirt when I allowed it. Her aunt's garden and the wetness today was her idea of perfection. "Oh my goodness, Klara, you are filthy," I said, noticing now the streaks of brown across her little forehead. She giggled in response. Clearly, that was her intent.

Hela's front door opened and shut; a man's voice called hello. "Jacques is home early," I remarked to Hela, who laughed, and shook her head.

"Not Jacques. That's Pierre." His voice was a strange echo of his brother's, but Hela, who was used to them both, was right. Pierre walked into the parlor not a moment later. I put Klara down so I could look at him. He kissed Hela on the cheek, asked her how she was feeling, then stepped back, stared at me, and smiled.

"Hello, Pierre," I said. "Nice to see you again." Though *nice* was not the right word. I felt something else, something warm and wanting and disquieting too.

"You too, Marya," he said. "And who's this?" He kneeled down to Klara's level, all without taking his eyes off my face. "Is this the one and only *princessa* Klara Zorawska I've heard so much about?"

Klara spent most of her time with women, and I'd never seen her warm up to any man, other than her father, and perhaps she was beginning to warm up to her uncle Jacques. But with Pierre she laughed and let him shake her little hand, seeming immediately at ease.

"Why don't you take Pierre to your concert," Hela said now, forcing herself into an awkward sitting position. "Pierre loves those sorts of cultural things. Don't you, Pierre?"

"A concert?" Pierre said, raising his eyebrows.

"Her friend from Poland, the pianist . . . What's her name?" Hela said.

"Leokadia," I said. "But really you don't have to, Pierre . . . And, Hela, Klara is a mess."

"I can clean Klara up," Hela said. "I haven't moved all day. It will be good for me to get up, practice mothering."

"But . . . it's raining," I protested.

"You don't go out in the rain in Poland?" Pierre asked. It was hard to tell whether he was teasing me or asking a serious question.

"Of course she does," Hela said. She waved us away with her hand, then patted the spot on the couch next to her. "Klara, do you want to sit down with me and hear a story about the rocks in my laboratory?" Klara, being the sweet and gentle and calm child she was, listened and sat down with her aunt. I bit my lip, knowing rocks could only get Hela so far before Klara began to squirm, but perhaps Hela was right. Perhaps she needed some practice at being motherly. Perhaps I was doing her a favor.

As Pierre and I walked down boulevard Kellerman to catch the carriage to Montmartre, he held his large black umbrella over both of us, and I told him a bit about Leokadia. About how I loved her, and how I hated her too. How I was in awe of her talent and also grateful that it had taken her somewhere away from me. I felt an openness with Pierre that led me to share honestly with him in a way I couldn't with Agata or my sisters. There was a comfort in how he listened to me speak and then continued on walking without making any harsh judgments about my marriage or my continued friendship with Kadi.

"But she is a good piano player, you say?" Pierre finally said, his only comment on my story.

"Yes," I said. "Wonderful, really."

"Ah, very nice then. We should be in for a treat this afternoon. I do not like to walk in the rain for nothing." I glanced at him, and a smile grazed his lips. He *was* making fun of me. As if he felt my eyes on his face, he turned too, so he was looking at me. We were both looking at each other as we walked. We didn't say anything more, just walked for a moment in the pouring rain, staring at each other.

I looked away first, and that's when I suddenly noticed Pierre stepping into the street to cross at just the wrong moment, inches away from an oncoming horse.

"Pierre!" I yelled his name, grabbed his jacket, and pulled him back toward me as hard as I could. He nearly lost his footing, and let go of his umbrella, which tumbled out in front of us and was promptly run over. His umbrella was trampled by the horse, crushed and flattened by the wheels of the carriage.

We both stood unmoving for a moment. My heart pounded furiously in my chest, my hands shook. The rain poured down upon us, drowning my bun and my face, but I could not feel the wetness.

Pierre spoke first: "Marya," he said. "You saved my life."

I shook my head. No. Surely he would've looked up at the last moment, stopped himself from walking in front of that horse even if I hadn't been here.

He walked ahead, retrieved his umbrella, tried to put it up again above our heads, but the spokes were broken and bent and the linen torn, providing no cover from the rain at all any longer. We both stared at the umbrella, and I wondered if Pierre was thinking what I was thinking, that this could've been him: broken, bent, torn. That life was delicate and fleeting, that we were all just one wrong step away from death, at any moment.

And here we both were, standing together in the pouring rain, alive and breathing.

MARIE

❧

Paris, 1906

I am walking with Pierre in the rain, holding on to him so tightly. *I love our life together,* he says, turning to me, smiling. *How did I ever get so lucky?*

There is no such thing as luck, I tell him, as he walks out into the street, one step ahead of me. His eyes, bright blue and filled with light, are still on my face. And then I see the horse, coming right at him. *Pierre, stop!* I cry out. I try to reach for him, to pull him back. But I can't grab ahold of him in time.

Why can't I just pull him back?

I sit up in bed, startled. Disoriented. I reach for Pierre next to me, but his side of the bed is empty. And I remember again, he is *dead, dead, dead.* Trampled and crushed. His beautiful brain broken. I am haunted by this cruel and recurring dream where I try to stop him, try to save him. But he's gone. I can't save him, can't help him, can't fix him as Hela once believed I would.

WE BURY PIERRE IN SCEAUX BY HIS MOTHER'S SIDE, ON April 21st, only two days after the accident. The press began clamoring immediately, and there were so many telegrams, and I just wanted them all to leave me alone; I just want quiet. We rush through everything, have a private family burial, in hopes the press will leave, and then in the days after, everything has happened so fast that I can't understand yet it's true. *He's gone. How can he really be gone?*

When I first tell Irène the news, she runs to her bedroom to weep. But then, only hours later, she comes to me, seeming completely untouched, asking if it is still all right if she goes and plays in the Perrins' garden with her friend. She is young, she does not understand the power this loss will hold over her for the rest of her life. And because of that, I forgive her insensitivity.

Yes, I tell her. *Go play next door. Be home for supper.*

Ève has no idea what she has lost. Fifteen months old, she toddles around the house, still pulling off her clothing at will and stealing Irène's toys. *She will never remember him. She will never know him.* I walk through days and days carrying that thought in my head, and that becomes my undoing. Pierre's loss is a great loss for the scientific community, a great personal and professional loss for me. But more than anything it is Ève's loss that breaks me. *She will never know her father.*

Jacques and Bronia both linger in Paris for weeks, hovering. Bronia looks after the children, stepping in for Dr. Curie in the evenings when normally I would. Jacques says he is straightening Pierre's affairs with the university and that he will go home when he is sure we are okay.

"We will never be okay," I tell him flatly, and he frowns, making his face look more angled, more like Pierre's.

"In time," Jacques says kindly, patting my shoulder. "In time."

But what does Jacques know? What does Bronia know? He will return soon to Montpellier to his own wife, Marie. Bronia will return to Zakopane and Mier and Lou. They will not work and live and breathe and raise their children alone.

I spend days in bed, not having the energy to get up, much less care for the children or tend the house. Bronia and Jacques do these things for me. Jeanne Langevin and Henriette Perrin stop by each afternoon with food, and Bronia thanks them on my behalf, feeds their delicious meals to my children, herself, and Jacques. I hear the noises of them downstairs. Normal noises, happy noises, laughter. I put a pillow over my head, drowning them out.

"*Siostra*," Bronia calls into the darkness of my bedroom. "Come, have dinner with us."

"I'm not hungry," I say back.

When I stay in bed, when I close my eyes and dream, Pierre is still here, still almost close enough to touch. I dream him here; I dream of ways to stop him, to save him. But every morning I wake up and remember again and again. He is gone.

EVEN THOUGH HIS BODY IS IN THE GROUND IN SCEAUX, I HAVE kept ahold of him in my own way. The shirt Pierre was wearing that last day, his bloody and torn and muddy shirt—I've folded it up and put it in a small brown paper package, wrapped it with string, and tied it to my stomach, wearing it with me underneath my clothing, holding the last pieces of him tight against my skin. It went with me to his burial in Sceaux, and it goes with me again when I go back with Jacques and Bronia and Dr. Curie to see his finished tombstone.

His name is on it. *Pierre Curie.*

It cannot be. It cannot be. His shirt is tied to me still. It has his blood, his life. They have made a mistake, engraved the wrong man's name.

"This isn't right," I say. "This can't be him."

"I'm sorry, but it is," Bronia whispers into my widow's veil. I don't want to listen. I want to go back to my bedroom, where I can be alone with my dreams and the last piece I have left of him.

How is it possible? *His name*, written on a tombstone, next to Sophie-Claire's, who has been gone from us nearly ten years. How can that be? *My Pierre.*

My sister-mother holds on to me. "You have to be strong now, for the children," she says softly. I think of them, Irène and little Ève. And then I tell Bronia about the piece of him I kept, that I have with me now.

Back at the house, she helps me untie it from my body. She lights a fire in my bedroom, and she says to me sternly, but kindly, "It is time to let go now. It is time to let go."

"I've spoken to the university," Jacques says, a week later, the beginning of May. Time has passed. I don't understand it. I clutch Pierre's watch still, feel it ticking on relentlessly beneath my fingers. "They will offer you a generous widow's pension for Pierre's position," he says.

"Widow's pension?" I laugh bitterly. "I am much too young for that."

Jacques nods, agreeing.

"And do they think I won't work any longer?" To be thirty-eight years old and to be *a widow*, to think that I should live the whole rest of my life and not be able to work. Pierre and I have left so much still undone in the lab, work with our radium unfinished. Who will finish, if not me? "I don't want a pension," I say. "I'll support myself. But I need the lab. They cannot take away the lab space from me." To lose Pierre *and* my work? It is too much; it is just too much.

Jacques pats my shoulder lightly, understanding. He is one of the kindest men I have ever known, aside from Pierre, and Papa, and his father. He will try and help me with anything I ask of him. "What do you want me to tell them, Marie? What will make you happy?" he asks gently.

Happy is a funny word. And as soon as Jacques says it, he must judge that it's the wrong one because he puts his hand to his mouth. There will be no *happy* going forward. There will be important work to do. There will be science. And now I will do it alone.

"I want his job," I tell Jacques. "I want them to give me his teaching position. His laboratory. I don't need the pension. Just the salary he was making so I can support my family. And I will earn it by doing the work he was doing, myself."

Jacques considers it for a moment. "You know they have never hired a woman to teach there before."

I nod. *Of course I know.* "But no woman ever won the Nobel Prize before I did either," I remind him.

BY THE MIDDLE OF THE MONTH IT IS SETTLED; JACQUES HAS convinced them. I will take Pierre's position at the Sorbonne, his lab space, and ten thousand francs a year of salary.

Jacques leaves to go home to his family in Montpellier, and Bronia takes the train back to Poland, her family. And then it is just me and Dr. Curie and the girls. Our house on boulevard Kellerman, where Pierre and I lived together for so many years, feels too big, too empty, too quiet.

"Shall I go too?" Dr. Curie says softly one night as we sit together in the parlor, after he has gotten the girls to go to sleep.

"Go?" I am shocked by his question. I have not considered it before.

"Jacques said there is room for me in Montpellier."

Of course. Dr. Curie was only here because of his son, and now his son is gone. And what am I to him but a Polish woman, unrelated by blood? He has another son, with a French wife, and two more grandchildren in Montpellier. "You want to go to Montpellier?" I ask him.

He frowns, puts his head in hands. Then rubs his eyes. He is tired, and he is sad, and it has never been so clear to me that he is an old man as it is in this very moment. "I want to do whatever you want me to do, Marie," he finally says.

I cannot imagine continuing on without him. Who will look after the children while I work? I can hire someone, of course, but it wouldn't be the same as their *grand-père*. "I want you to stay with us," I say. "The children need you. I need you."

Dr. Curie lifts his head, smiles now.

"But I want to move," I tell him. "I cannot live in this house any longer without him."

MARYA

❦

Hela's baby girl was born in the middle of the night on the third of May, two weeks after I arrived in Paris. The baby came out pink and screaming, aided in delivery by Hela's father-in-law, Dr. Curie, who still practiced medicine though he was getting up in years. He himself had tears in his eyes when he handed Hela her baby for the first time, and as Hela was already forty years old, and his Pierre was still unmarried, perhaps Dr. Curie had long believed that he might never have any grandchildren, up until that very moment when he held her in his hands.

I patted at Hela's forehead with a damp washcloth, staring down at my new niece in her arms. The baby had a tuft of pale blond hair, pink cheeks, and stunning blue eyes, like Jacques's and Pierre's. "She's beautiful," I said, and for a moment, I was transported back to Klara's birth, those overwhelming feelings of warmth and love and gratefulness rising through the haze of pain as I'd held her for the first time. Would I ever feel anything as wonderful as that again in my life?

Hela's labor had been long and painful, going on for nearly twenty hours. I was exhausted now just from being by her side, being awake all these many hours. And maybe that was what I was feeling now. *Exhaustion*, not nostalgia. Besides, I hadn't seen Klara for nearly two days. She was downstairs with her uncle Jacques and Pierre, who were both waiting somewhat impatiently for the baby's arrival. They had taken turns knocking on the bedroom door every two hours, asking if it was time yet. *Not yet!* I finally told Jacques around midnight last night. *I will come and get you as soon as it is, I promise.*

Oh, Jacques! I remembered again now, and I stood.

"Where are you going?" Hela moved her arm to reach for me, sounding desperate as the baby let out another cry, reminding me of the Nowaks' sheep. We would sometimes go to their farm on the outskirts of Loksow, where we could buy our milk and eggs cheaper than in the city. And Pani Nowak was so kind to Klara, always letting her pet the sheep. "Marya." Hela tugged on my sleeve. "Don't leave me."

"I promised to tell Jacques as soon as the baby is here," I reminded her. "He was checking in for hours, desperate for news. Let me go get him so he can meet his daughter."

She hesitated for a moment, then relaxed her grip and nodded. "But you will come back?" she said.

"I will," I told her.

"I don't know what to do with her." Hela's voice broke, sounding tired, worried. "I'm not sure how I'm supposed to take care of her."

Hela lived in an expansive house, in a beautiful and free city. She had money, a very kind French husband. And she had fulfilling work in a scientific laboratory that had even won her prizes. But when it came to having a baby, we were all the same. Hela's eyes welled with tears, of exhaustion or pain or fear.

"Hela, darling, none of us know what to do. You'll figure it out," I promised, leaning down to kiss her forehead. "I'll help you."

I SENT JACQUES UPSTAIRS TO MEET HIS DAUGHTER, AND I WAS so exhausted, I stretched out on the couch in Hela's parlor, allowing my eyes to close for just a moment.

"Mama!" Klara's small voice erupted in my ear, and I jolted awake, unsure how much time had passed since I'd lain down, minutes or hours.

"Good morning, *mój mały kurczak*," I said, though I was not sure whether it was still morning or not. She giggled, the way she always did when I referred to her as *my little chicken*, a nickname that had stuck since birth. And I grabbed her in a hug, pulled her onto my lap on the couch and buried my face in her hair to cover her with kisses. She smelled like honey and dirt, and I imagined her uncle and Pierre had let her play in the garden and also plied her with treats.

"Oh, there you are, *ma petite*." Pierre's voice floated into the parlor, followed by his footsteps. His suit was wrinkled, his hair disheveled, and I was reminded that he had been awake for hours, too. But here he was, so very pleasantly greeting my daughter.

"Thank you for watching her," I said.

"The pleasure was all mine. We had fun, didn't we, Klara?" Klara nodded, burrowing into my chest, shyly. "And we have just met the baby upstairs, Marya. She is very tiny. Much too tiny." Klara lifted her head to nod in agreement. Klara saw her older cousins in Zakopane at least once or twice a year, but this was the first cousin younger than she, her very first experience with a baby. I felt a little sad that I had slept through it.

"Her toes are too small, Mama," Klara said.

I laughed. "No, my love. She is a perfectly normal-size baby. She will grow, and before you know it she will be your size." I kissed Klara again on the forehead.

"Did Hela tell you they decided on a name?" Pierre asked. I shook my head. As of two days ago, before the labor hit, she and Jacques had not been able to agree. "Ah well, I will let Hela tell you then. Come, Klara, let's check on the sparrow's nest in the garden. There are eggs," he said to me. "We are counting on them to hatch before you return to Poland." He held out his hand for Klara, and she stood and took it willingly.

I watched the two of them go, yawned, and stretched before I stood. I walked back upstairs. Jacques sat in a chair by the bed, the baby asleep in his arms, and Hela sat up in bed, looking more like herself. Perhaps she had gotten some rest too, or at least she had combed her hair back into a neat bun, and her color was more regular.

She smiled at me, seeming more at ease than when I'd left her. "There you are," she said.

"Sorry, I was so tired. I sat down for a moment and fell asleep downstairs."

"Don't be sorry," she said. "It was a long, exhausting day and night, and you stayed with me through all of it. Thank you."

"Of course I did. You're my sister," I said. She smiled at me. "Pierre told me you decided on a name?"

"Yes." She clapped her hands together gently, so as not to wake the baby. "Marie Sophie Curie. We named her after you, Marya, with her middle name after Jacques's *maman*."

"Me?" I felt stunned. Why would Hela and Jacques do such a thing? Surely Bronia was more deserving, if they were to choose a family name, as *Bronislawa* had also been our mother's name.

And Bronia's daughter, who we all called Lou as a nickname, was given the name *Helena* at birth: Hela's name. "You are making a mistake," I insisted.

"Marya. Sweet, dear Marya." Hela reached for my hand. "So strong and so beautiful. Look at you, in our native country, raising your wonderful daughter while educating so many young women."

I blinked back tears at Hela's words, wondering if they were true. If that was really the way my sisters saw me. It wasn't the way I saw myself, saw my life, as it compared with the two of them, both of whom had doctoral degrees. Hela was making real contributions to science, and Bronia was healing sick people in Zakopane. And I was still poor, without an advanced degree, and living in a small apartment in Loksow. "I really don't think . . ." I stammered.

"You, my sister, are a revolutionary," Hela said. "And that is exactly who we want Marie Sophie to grow up to be."

A few weeks went by, and Klara got over the size of little Marie's toes. Or maybe her toes were already growing too fast, her life as a newborn slipping away quickly, as it had with Klara, too. I could barely remember those early days now, though they hadn't been all that long ago.

Hela had trouble nursing. Marie was losing weight, and Dr. Curie suggested a wet nurse, an idea which first made Hela sob uncontrollably, and then, once she was hired and Marie began growing, made Hela sigh with relief. In the beginning of June, Hela returned to the lab with Jacques, and I stayed with Klara during the day.

Only until we find an acceptable nanny, Hela insisted.

But I quite enjoyed her baby smells, and her baby toes, and her baby cuddles, and I did not feel in any rush for Hela to find someone else. Besides, Dr. Curie showed up many weekdays to spend time with his granddaughter and insisted I go out, enjoy the summer in France, the gardens and the sites with Klara.

When Kaz wrote me to ask when I might be coming home—I had already delayed my train ticket twice—I wrote back that Hela needed my help still. I consoled myself with the fact that it was only partially a lie. Kaz wrote that he missed me and Klara *desperately*, and I told him we missed him too. Klara missed him and asked about him often. But I was busy in Paris, surrounded by my family and by the beauty and culture of the city. And except for when his letters came, or when Klara asked, I didn't remember to miss Kaz very much at all.

ON SATURDAYS IN JUNE, I TOOK BICYCLE RIDES WITH PIERRE. He brought Jacques's old fixed-up bicycle to my sister's house on boulevard Kellerman, with the intent that I could use it to sightsee with him, to ride and learn the city firsthand from a native Parisian.

"Goodness," Hela exclaimed, eyeing the rusty old frame. "I can give you some francs to hire a carriage instead."

"Your sister enjoys this," Pierre insisted to Hela, who stared at me, eyebrows raised.

"I do," I acknowledged. "I don't even own a bicycle in Poland, and besides, the streets are too narrow to ride with all the carriages in Loksow, I'd be killed."

She shrugged, not at all understanding the appeal. She preferred riding a carriage, even over walking, because she claimed walking required too much of her attention to stay alive on the way to her destination. She preferred to think problems through in her head while someone else got her from place to place. But I quite enjoyed moving myself, pushing hard against the pedals until my legs ached and I felt the wind tangling my hair.

One Saturday near the end of June, Pierre offered to show me the Bois de Vincennes, a spectacular park in the middle of Paris. He pointed in the right direction, and I pedaled out ahead of him, my hair coming loose from my bun, blowing back behind my shoulders as the wind whipped around my face.

"Slow down," Pierre called from behind me. But he was laughing.

I was breathless and sweating, but I pedaled and I pedaled like fire. Past the gates of the park and the blossoming cherry trees. Until we neared the water, and I slowed down.

I hopped off, lay the bicycle on its side, and sat down by the edge of the lake, resting my sweaty face against the cool edge of my sleeve. Pierre was a moment behind me, and when he stopped, he pulled a bouquet of white daisies from his bicycle basket, then held them out to me, like a prize for reaching the lake first. I took the flowers and our fingertips touched, sending a current of warmth up my hand, my entire arm.

"Tell me more about your experiments," I said, lying back against the edge of the lake, half closing my eyes, holding the flowers to my chest.

Pierre had already regaled me last Saturday with a tale from his small corner of Jacques's and Hela's laboratory. He had become obsessed with Becquerel's rays this past year, and theorized that there was an undiscovered element inside the pitchblende Hela and Jacques were studying. He'd even gotten astonishing results after placing it in an ionization chamber he'd fashioned himself out of used grocery crates. But Jacques thought the readings must be wrong, that Pierre was a touch crazy, and Pierre did not have the funding to further the experimentation on his own.

"You should've seen the readings, Marya," he said now, his voice far away. "The radioactivity was higher than anything I've ever seen before." I nodded. "What would you do next if you were me?"

I liked feeling that he truly believed that I could wrap my mind around everything he was sharing with me, and that he was asking for my advice, that somehow we were equals, though I was only self-taught in physics and chemistry and had read up on the latest research only when Hela sent the papers to me. "Well," I said. "Is there a way for you to isolate this new element? People cannot deny what they can see and touch themselves, can they?"

"Not even Jacques," he said softly. Then he added, "I don't know. It would be a laborious undertaking. I only have a small space in the laboratory, and I'm not as young as I used to be, you know?"

I smiled. "None of us are, are we? But you have to try, Pierre. If you really believe you have happened upon a new discovery, this new . . . element. You have to try. For the sake of scientific advancement."

He stroked his beard with his fingers, lay back against his elbows, and stared out across the lake. Neither one of us spoke for a little while, and then suddenly out of nowhere, Pierre said, "Perhaps you could always stay in Paris?"

I laughed a little, held the flowers to my nose, inhaling their intoxicating scent.

PERHAPS I COULD ALWAYS STAY IN PARIS.

I imagined it in my head at night, lying in bed, in the moments before drifting off to sleep.

What would I do here? At thirty-eight, and having Klara, I was too old, too busy mothering, to get my degree at the Sorbonne now. Perhaps I could help Pierre in the lab, or, assist Hela and Jacques. When they spoke of their work at dinner, I could only truly understand the half of what they were doing, even though I nodded along as if I understood it all. They would have no need for me, untrained and unskilled for their experiments.

I could learn, though. I still loved to learn.

And how would Kaz fit in to my imagined life? He could work on publishing Hipolit's research here as easily as he could in Poland, but he did not speak French, and I did not think he could get a teaching job here without that. And we would not have money to live on, without him having a job.

But we did not need money, in this imagined life. My fantasy life was a life of flowers and sunshine and bicycle rides. A life with all the kindness of the Curies and no worry about food or money, or the revolution in the streets outside my Polish apartment.

IN THE BEGINNING OF JULY, A LETTER CAME IN THE POST FOR me from Agata.

The revolution was ongoing in Poland, yet things had changed in the past week. The school strike was finally over, and women were now legally allowed a higher education. After all this time, all these years. I could hardly believe it! The news made me so excited, I felt it deep inside of me, a lightness.

Hurry back, Agata wrote. *We can build our women's university out in the open now. There is so much to be done, Marya!*

And as quick as my Parisian fantasy had come to me, it disappeared. Hela had named her daughter after me, *a revolutionary,* whom she admired for educating women in Poland. I could not be that woman if I stayed here, if I daydreamed my life away in Hela's guestroom.

I hugged and kissed Hela and Jacques and baby Marie goodbye. Pierre and Dr. Curie were back in Sceaux, where Dr. Curie had come down with a summer cold and Pierre was looking after him. I thought about stopping there, on the way to the train, but it wasn't on the way at all. It was, in fact, quite out of the way, and besides I did not want Klara to catch a cold before our trip. "Tell Pierre and Dr. Curie we said goodbye," I told Hela instead, and she promised she would.

Then Klara and I took a carriage to the Gare du Nord, got on the train, and watched the city of Paris fade away into the summer morning, behind us.

MARIE

❦

Paris & Warsaw, 1906

The girls and Dr. Curie and I move into an unremarkable house on rue Chemin de Fer in Sceaux. It is not as nice or modern as our house on boulevard Kellerman was, but at least it is quieter here than in the city. And the backyard has a garden for the children to play and Irène to plant seeds. We are far from our neighbors, and perhaps in time I will miss having the Perrins and Langevins nearby, but now I am quite happy to be left alone.

I tell Dr. Curie I like the idea of bringing up the children in the very place Pierre was brought up, but the real reason I like our new house in Sceaux is because it is close to where Pierre rests now. When classes begin again in the fall, I will have a thirty-minute train ride into the city, rather than a short walk like on boulevard Kellerman, but I care less about that than about my distance from Pierre.

The first few days after we move, in the mornings, before the children wake, I take a walk and go and talk to Pierre's tombstone. I tell him how Ève is so small, I think about all the years and years it will take for her to grow, and how I don't know if I can continue to live for that many years on my own without him. How some people have been writing me to congratulate me on my new position at the Sorbonne. And how the very idea that someone might *rejoice* over me taking his position makes me impossibly angry.

Some mornings I linger too long, return to the house after breakfast, and Dr. Curie frowns at me. "It is not him. He is not there," Dr. Curie chides me gently.

As a scientist, I know he is right. But Pierre had always believed in séances, hiring a woman to conduct them to speak to his mother after her death. And though I did not enjoy them, or even believe in them the way he had, now I can understand his need for the otherworldly, for *something*. I cannot keep away from his grave. And I continue to go each morning just to talk to him there. And sometimes, I go in the evenings before bed, too.

PIERRE AND I HAD PLANNED ON SPENDING MOST OF THE summer in Saint-Rémy—classes will not begin again until November. But I cannot bear the thought of going back there again now. The last time we went, Easter, Pierre and I had ridden bikes and lain in the grass together holding hands, touching sunlight, reveling in our *luck*. It feels like a cruel joke now. Dr. Curie offers to go with the girls, and I decide to go to Warsaw and spend time with Hela instead.

"It'll be good for you to have a rest back in Poland," Dr. Curie says. But what he really means is that we both know I cannot take care of the children right now, that it is not good for them to see me like this, tired and listless and ill and drowning in grief. And it is not that I don't love them, or don't provide for them, but it is that I do not have the strength within my being to both grieve and be their mother.

"I'll write them letters," I tell Dr. Curie.

"I know," he says, offering me an acceptance, a condolence, in the form of a fatherly hug.

HELA'S HOUSE IN WARSAW IS SMALLER THAN I REMEMBER IN the years since I've seen it last. I estimate it at only a third of the size of our new unremarkable home in Sceaux. But she welcomes me to into it with the warmest hug and kisses on my cheeks, and an apology for not being able to make it to Paris in time for Pierre's funeral.

"Please," I beg of her. "Don't say his name." I close my eyes, bite back tears. I cannot bear to hear his name out loud, or even to speak it myself.

"Of course, I'm so sorry," she says, pulling me tighter in her hug.

"It's not your fault," I say, holding on to my sister-twin so fiercely, reveling in the way she still smells of lemons and corn poppies, as she always has. My entire world has grown and then imploded, and here is Hela, in Warsaw, exactly the same.

She offers me her daughter Hanna's bedroom for my stay, and Hanna stays in her parents' room. I unpack my valise, happy for the quiet here, for this space of my own. Happy that my children are half a continent away enjoying the summer in Saint-Rémy with their *grand-père*, and that I am not dragging them under with my grief.

Hela and Stan do not have much money, nor great acclaim in their work. Hela runs a small girls' school in Warsaw, and her husband, Stan, is a photographer. Their life is simple compared to mine in Paris. But in the evenings, at the dinner table, Stan reaches for Hela's hand, or catches her eye in a smile, and watching the way they love each other, so quietly, it almost tears me apart with wanting, jealousy.

I BEGIN TAKING VERY LONG WALKS EACH MORNING TO CLEAR my head, to try and satiate my sadness with fresh air and with exercise. I walk all around Warsaw, to the corners of my youth: the girls' gymnasium we all attended, and Papa's old home, and the homes where I attended Flying University classes with Bronia, which ignited in me that hunger for more, for a real university. I walk along the banks of the Vistula, as Bronia and Hela and I did as girls. And then I find myself each day for lunch inside the little café where Bronia and I used to go and study for our Flying University classes.

I order myself a *czarna kawa*. It is the color of night and nearly the consistency of mud, and it awakens my mind much more so than a Parisian coffee. I begin bringing my notebook along with me, and I start to think about work again. I jot down ideas for what I might say in my first lecture in November. What I might study when I return to my lab again. Coffee, and the thick summer air, and the ghosts of my youth remind me again how far I have come. How much I have left to do before I go. *Even without Pierre.* He would not want me to stop; he would never want me to stop.

One afternoon, I am concentrating very hard on my notes, my coffee, and then out of nowhere, a man's voice calls out: "Marya Sklodowska?"

I don't register at first that it is me he is speaking to. I have kept Sklodowska as part of my name, even since being married, so I am sometimes referred to as *Madame Sklodowska Curie* instead of *Madame Curie*. But no one, not even my sisters, has called me Marya in so many years. The sound of it shocks me now, and there is a moment of both dread and nostalgia, the memory of being so poor and desperate, so sad, so certain that my life would never take the path it has. And I think about what would I say to that girl now, if I could speak to her in this café. If I could tell her that she would someday have everything she ever dreamed and desired and more. And then, it would be pulled away from her, bloodied and trampled. And *crushed*. Just like that.

"Marya Sklodowska? Is that you?" I look up, and a vaguely familiar man stands in front of me. He is tall and brown-eyed, with a round face and a beard shorter and grayer than Pierre's was.

"I'm not Marya," I say. Marya was a poor, helpless Polish girl I have left behind forever.

"Oh." He casts his eyes down, disappointed. *That look.* I know that look. It is the same one he had on his face once when he came to me in Szczuki, when he turned me away and then he begged me for my forgiveness all at once. When he told me what his mother said, that I was penniless, that I would *amount to nothing*.

"Kazimierz Zorawski?" I say, disbelieving the words even as they escape my lips. He looks up again; he smiles. "I did not recognize you at first. No one has called me Marya in so long. I've been going by Marie for years."

"Ah yes," he says. "*Marie Curie*, world-famous scientist, winner of the 1903 Nobel Prize in physics." He speaks quickly, confidently, in a way that tells me he believes he knows everything there is to know about me. That he has followed my career.

I smile, remembering that once his mother believed him to

be much too good for me, and how much that hurt me at the time. And now I try to remember the last time I have even thought of him. Not for so many years, since Hela sent me the newspaper clipping about his marriage to that pianist. Her name escapes me now. "How have you been, Kazimierz?" I ask, to show him I have not done the same. I have not followed after him.

"I've been well," he says. "I've recently been named the dean of faculty at Jagiellonian in Krakow. We're back in Warsaw for the summer visiting my mother, who has been ill."

"I'm sorry to hear that," I murmur. All these many years later, I cannot bring myself to muster ill will for Pani Zorawska, who was perhaps only acting out of a simplistic protective instinct. Besides, she was very wrong about me, and that in itself is satisfying enough.

"Leokadia and I have three children." Kazimierz is still talking.

Leokadia, yes, that was her name. I remember again the clipping Hela had sent, that I had placed away in a textbook, so long ago. "And your wife . . . she is a pianist?"

He laughs. "Once, she played, yes. But now the children keep her very busy. She doesn't have time for piano any longer."

I feel a sudden sadness for her, this woman, *Leokadia*, this wife of Kazimierz's who I've never met. It is hard for me to understand a life where having children would force a woman to give up on her own work. "She can't do both?" I say, frowning. "Be a mother and a pianist?"

"She loves being a mother, looking after the children." He shrugs. "And I make a good living."

I nod and think about that morning so long ago at the train station, the last time I saw Kazimierz. What if I had not gotten on that train, but stayed here, married him instead? Would Leokadia's life be my life? I love my children, but I cannot imagine a life without my work. I cannot imagine who I would've become without it.

"You have children," Kazimierz says, more a statement than a question.

"Two daughters," I say. "Irène is almost nine and Ève is almost two. And I'll be starting as a full professor at the Sorbonne in the fall, and of course I have my work in the lab, too."

Kazimierz nods. Somehow he already knows this also. But my life has been detailed in the press for the past few years. Maybe it would not be so hard to keep up with me. "I was very sorry to hear about Pierre's accident," he says softly. At the mention of Pierre's name, I quickly look away from him.

"Please don't say his name," I say. It is warm inside the café; I'm sweating. I stand up quickly, too quickly, and my coffee begins to tip. Kazimierz and I both reach for it. He catches it just in time, and then catches onto my elbows.

"I'm so very sorry," he says softly. He holds onto my elbows for a moment, his eyes wide with sympathy, or maybe it is regret. I remember that he is a good man, a kind man. I am happy for him that his life has turned out well, that he has love and a family. But none of that belongs to me.

I gently pull out of his grasp. "I should get going," I say. "My sister will worry."

He nods, but keeps his eyes on my face for another moment. "It was so good to see you again, Marya."

"You too," I say. The air in here is stifling; being this close to him is stifling. I gather up my notebook and quickly walk out of the café, not turning back to see if he's still watching me.

Though somehow, I know he is. I can feel his eyes on my back.

ON THE LONG WALK BACK TO HELA'S, I THINK ABOUT KAZ-imierz and his three children, his wife who gave up her work to look after them. His mother, who lies in bed somewhere in Warsaw, dying. His prestigious job as the dean of Jagiellonian in Krakow. *None of that belongs to me*, but it could have.

What if I had not stepped on that train, but instead, stayed behind in Poland with him so many years ago? If I had married him, become a mother to his children, and given up on my own education altogether, I would not have my work now.

But then Pierre and I never would have met at the Kowalskis that night so long ago. We never would've shared a lab, fallen in love, gotten married. We never would've won a Nobel Prize. And Pierre never would have been walking in the rain on his way back from a science academy luncheon on April 19th.

What if I hadn't stepped on that train, but had turned around, chosen Kazimierz instead?

Then, right now, Pierre would still be in Paris somewhere, very much alive.

MARYA

Poland, 1907

I quickly forgot about my wayward fantasy of staying in Paris, as Pierre had suggested that lazy afternoon in the park. Because two momentous things happened to us in Poland in the beginning of 1907.

The first was that mine and Agata's school grew large enough so that we suddenly needed not just one room to hold classes, but three. And we had enough tuition money, enough regular students now, that we rented what had once been a girls' gymnasium on Aleja Wróbli. We liked it both for its size and the symbolic nature of the street name. Our Flying University was now housed out in the open, on an avenue named for sparrows.

We hung a large sign out front, designed by our art students, that proclaimed us to be the *Women's University of Loksow*. No longer hiding, no longer flying. In addition to my administrative duties that I carried out during the day with Agata, I also taught three courses, three nights a week: beginning chemistry and physics, and a new course this term, advanced physics, as we now had girls who'd been with us long enough to want more advanced knowledge.

The second thing that happened was Kaz finally finished writing up his and Hipolit's research. His paper was accepted for publication by the Polish Academy of Mathematics in March: *The Theory of Elasticity*. It was a very momentous and exciting moment in the mathematics field. As Hipolit was no longer alive, all the acclaim and accolades for the work fell squarely on Kazimierz. He received encouraging letters from as far away as America! And in May he was offered a guest lecture position at the University of Vienna to begin in the fall. It was a well-paying appointment, five times what Kaz would be paid in a year to teach at the boys' school here. As it would only be a one-year appointment, we decided it made the most sense for Klara and me to stay behind in Loksow, without him.

"For now," Kaz said, with a hopeful note to his voice, like he thought his appointment could be extended, and that I would be more than happy to join him. But what would I want from Austria? Poland was my home. Poland had always been my home. Now that my school was out in the open and thriving, I would not want to leave it.

"Maybe if this goes well," I told him. "You will get a good job back here?"

"Maybe, *kochanie*." He kissed the top of my head. "Finally the entire world might be opened to us. Just the way we always dreamed."

I thought about the sign we had recently erected on Aleja Wróbli, and it was not the *world* I wanted any longer. It was Poland, it was my own country. My own burgeoning part of it.

WE PLANNED TO GO TO ZAKOPANE FOR THE WHOLE MONTH OF July to stay with Bronia and Kazimierz, Lou and Jakub, and to spend some family time all together before Kaz left for Austria.

Agata and I put our school on summer break, just like the male universities, and I was so excited for this trip. My hands shook with glee as I packed for the three of us. It was the first vacation we had ever taken together, the first vacation Kaz and I had taken since that disastrous one with his family nearly ten years earlier.

Pani Zorawska was reportedly back in Warsaw these days and had taken ill. Kaz received monthly letters from his brother Stan, but he had not gone to seen his mother, not since that time many years earlier when she had offered to pay me to leave him. I still sometimes thought about that, even now. If I had taken her up on her offer, my life might have been completely different. But by the summer of 1907, I no longer desired a different life. The years had softened the blow of Kaz's betrayal, and since I had Klara, I could not imagine any sort of life that would be good for me, without her.

ON THE TRAIN RIDE TO ZAKOPANE, KAZ SEEMED MORE RE-laxed than I had seen him in so long, the features of his face softened. He had grown a beard in these last years, and it had gone half gray in the time he'd been working on compiling his research. There were wrinkles around his eyes that I couldn't re-member being there, even last year at this time, around when I returned from Paris. And I put my hand to my own face, won-dering if age had shown up the same way on me. If it did, did Kaz notice? Age looked handsome on him though, and sitting there with him, I remembered again how much I'd always de-sired him.

After a little while on the train, he put his arm around me, and I relaxed, too, and did something I hadn't in so long: I leaned in to him. I put my head on his shoulder and closed my eyes, enjoying the warmth of his body so close to mine, allowing myself to be lulled almost to sleep by the rocking of the train, the beating of his heart.

"Klara," I heard Kaz say, but I didn't open my eyes. "I heard your cousin Lou is going to teach you to climb mountains this summer and Jakub is going to teach you to swim." Bronia had written as much in a letter to me, which I had shared with Kaz. Our niece Lou was now almost fifteen and had taken up mountain climbing as her greatest hobby and passion, much to Bronia's chagrin, wishing for her to be more interested in science instead. And Jakub, now eleven, planned to spend his summer like *a fish in the lake.*

I heard Klara's beautiful giggle, resonating against the commotion of the train. "Mama, I'm too small to climb mountains, aren't I?"

I opened my eyes. She stared at me wide-eyed, serious. I smiled at her. "No, *mój mały kurczak.* You are not too small. You can do anything you want to do, you know. Anything you put your mind to. I am sure of it."

ZAKOPANE WAS BEAUTIFUL AND LUSH, GREEN AND SWEEPING, surrounded on all sides by the great green and brown hills of the Tatras. Bronia and her Kazimierz lived in a very large house on the rolling pasture behind their sanatorium. They had access to hiking and swimming, and though it seemed like a rare piece of paradise, Bronia spoke of how they hoped soon Warsaw would be free again, and they could move back there without her Kazimierz being in danger of arrest for the pro-Polish activities he'd taken part in as a young man.

I did not understand why anyone would choose the bustle and dirtiness of the city over the light and the peace here in Zakopane. "It must be like you are on vacation all year long," I exclaimed to Bronia, looking out the back window of her house, a wide view of the Tatras in the near distance, close enough that it almost felt I could reach my hand out and touch the mountains.

"Or purgatory," Bronia said, almost under her breath.

I turned and looked at her, surprised. I'd had no indication from her letters that she had anything but happiness in her life. But now that I thought about it, her letters recounted mostly day-to-day minutiae, the pursuits of the children, what they were doing and eating and learning, and how much they were growing.

"It's just," Bronia clarified, "in Paris there was so much going on all around us. Concerts, and lectures. Professors and doctors stopping by the house for a salon any night of the week. And there were so many opportunities to learn." She held her hands up in the air. "We have a wonderful tutor for the children here, but Helena finds her disagreeable, and all she wants to do is climb in the mountains all day. The truth is, there is not much else here to tempt her with."

We had called Bronia's Helena *Lou* since she was born, and hearing Bronia refer to her by her given name now only seemed to underscore her frustration. Suddenly, I had an idea. "What if she came back to Loksow with me for the fall term? She could take courses at my university. The women who teach are all wonderful, and we have everything, sciences and maths, piano and art. She could find an academic or artistic pursuit there perhaps?" Bronia wrinkled her forehead, considering it. "Kaz will be in Vienna, so I could use the help with Klara anyway."

Bronia nodded. "It's so kind of you to offer." She leaned in and kissed me on the forehead, sweeping a wayward hair out of my eyes. "I know she is fifteen, but still, I don't know if I can let my baby go, just like that."

"Well," I told her. "Papa let you go."

"I was much older," she said quickly.

"Think about it." I put my hand on her shoulder, gently. And for just a moment, I wondered which one of us was the sister-mother now.

Klara slept in Lou's bedroom, and Kaz and I had a room all our own—Bronia's house was large enough to accommodate all of us, even Hela and Jacques and Marie when they arrived in a few weeks.

"I told Bronia Lou should come back with us. Live with me while you're away. Attend my school," I whispered to Kaz that night in the darkness in our bed.

"That will be good, for both of you," Kaz said, approvingly.

Like we always did at home, we lay on opposite sides of the large bed, untouching. But when he spoke now, Kaz suddenly, unexpectedly, reached his hand across the empty space for mine. His fingers trailed against my palm, softly, slowly tracing a line. I hesitated for a moment, before taking his hand, interlacing his fingers with my own.

"Everything feels different here," Kaz said.

He was right. The past finally felt put away, the future felt spread out, wide and more hopeful before us. Kaz had made a mistake once, but I could remember again now that he was a good man, a kind man. He was my husband and Klara's devoted father. I squeezed his hand.

He moved across the bed, closer to me, closer still, and when he wrapped his arms around me, I reveled in his closeness, his warmth. "What will you do in Vienna all alone without us?" I whispered.

"I will miss you and Klara," he said. "I will write you every day. I will be desperately lonely." It sounded like a vow, a promise. He gently touched my face with his hands, and then he kissed me. For the first time in so long, I kissed him back, deeply, with feeling.

And I suddenly understood how lucky I was to be here this summer with him. To be lying here next to him now, sun-kissed and warm, his heart beating on next to mine.

MARIE

⚜

Paris, 1906–1907

Time moves forward on Pierre's pocket watch, and somehow, so do I.

I wake and I breathe and I eat, and I still cry at strange times, in the middle of the morning when no one is around to see me, when I wonder again about all the things I might have done differently in my life. And, if I had, would Pierre still be here? If I had stayed in Poland with Kazimierz . . . or, if I had turned down Pierre's endless marriage proposals . . . or if we had stayed in Saint-Rémy just a few days longer last April. Any of that might have changed the entire trajectory of our lives.

But time only moves forward on his pocket watch, not in reverse. There are no choices to be redone, nothing now that I can take back or change, no matter how much I might want to.

IN NOVEMBER, I BEGIN TEACHING AT THE SORBONNE, AND IT should be a happy moment in my life. Here I am, *the first woman* to have achieved this position. I am worthy and deserving of it in my own right, winner of a Nobel Prize in physics, after all. But instead all I can think is how it is supposed to be Pierre up here teaching this class; these are Pierre's students sitting before me, and it is very heard to breathe all throughout my lecture.

Still, somehow I do it, and then again and again. I take the train thirty minutes each morning into the city, then back at night. I leave most mornings before the children are awake, arrive home after they are in bed. Dr. Curie looks after them, and I hire a Polish governess to look after them too and work on their Polish. They are fed and clothed and well taken care of, and they want for nothing. As it goes, they are blessed and healthy. So long as they should not want for a mother who hovers over them, or smothers them with affection.

Grief is heavy and overbearing; it tugs me down. It fills my coat pockets with rocks and drags me to the bottom of the cold dark sea, holding me under so I can barely breathe. Days pass, seasons come and go. Time moves forward, but I feel heavier and heavier.

ONE WINTER EVENING, FAR TOO LATE, I GET HOME FROM THE city. It is cold inside the house and the fire is not lit properly—no one does it the way I do with exactly the right amount of paper and coal. It is simple science, the proper amounts of all things, kindling and accelerant, and why can no one understand fire but me? I add paper now, poke at the coals, stoking the flames. Smoke erupts, and tears suddenly burn my eyes.

And then I just find myself on the floor. The house is dark, but for the flames of the fire, and I lie down, unable to move, unable to get up, unable to do anything but lie on that floor and cry.

"Maman?" Ève's small voice calls out for me. "Are you all

right?" She must have heard something, gotten out of bed, and now she has found me here. More than anything I wish to stand up and carry her back to bed, rock her back to sleep, tell her that everything is okay and that she is a young sweet girl and should worry for nothing. I have made such an effort that no one, none of them should see me this way. Until now.

But I cannot move. I cannot do anything but lie here and cry. Ève comes and sits down next to me. Strokes at my hair, like she is the mother and I am her daughter.

"It's okay, Maman," she says. "You are crying because you're tired. I can help you go to bed."

"You have to get yourself together," Bronia says sharply. She has come for a visit in the beginning of the new year, not at my request, but she simply shows up late one evening at my front door. I suppose that Dr. Curie must have written her, told her I am worrying him. But he will never admit that to me if that is the case. And Bronia simply says she is overdue for a visit, which is also true.

"I am perfectly together," I say back, just as sharply.

She frowns; we both know I am lying. "It has been almost a *year*." She emphasizes *year*, like I am still her little sister-child, who can barely count.

I know. I know. I know.

It has been 302 days, 7,250 hours. I count them in my head each morning, keep track of them in a data chart in my mind, as if this life of mine were now an experiment. How long can I live without him? How many hours can I force myself to breathe? How many days can I continue to awake in my bed alone, forgetting in the first few seconds before opening my eyes, remembering all over again once I do open them that he's still gone? And I do not appreciate being shouted at like a toddler now, in my own home. "You don't know," I say, my voice shaking. "You don't know."

"Don't I?" Bronia's voice softens. She sits down in a parlor chair, rests her head in her hands.

I put my hands to my mouth, thinking about her sweet Jakub, seven years old and taken from her just like that.

"I'm sorry," I say, walking to her, putting my arms around her. "I didn't mean . . ."

She pushes me away gently. "After Jakub died, Mier almost went crazy. He started climbing, in the mountains. Him and Lou. The two of them still go, every morning. Lou tells me it is the way she breathes. Mountain climbing. Everyone needs something. You need something."

"And what did you do?" I ask her. I can't imagine Bronia climbing mountains. Physical exertion has always been one of her least favorite things. She never understood why I loved to bicycle so with Pierre. And perhaps if I could do that now, if I could pedal and pedal until my legs ache and I am too tired to breathe, then I would feel something again, other than the heaviness of my grief. But the bicycle is something I only ever did with Pierre, and the idea of riding it alone is too much to overcome.

"I worked," Bronia finally says. "I worked and I worked and I studied, and I sank myself into the latest research, became a better physician for my patients."

"Well, that is what I am doing," I say.

"No." She shakes her head. "You are taking the train into the city, teaching a class. What have you done in the lab?"

"How do you know what I do in my lab?" I snap at her.

But Bronia is right. I've read Pierre's journals over and over again, tracing my fingers over his script. But I have not done anything new, anything important. I haven't been able to bear it, the thought that I might discover something on my own, without him here beside me.

"Life is so very hard and tragic," Bronia says, matter-of-factly, and I hate her for the scientific way she bears it out to me. "But you have this brilliant mind, and more resources here in Paris than we ever dreamed as girls. You cannot waste that." She grabs my shoulders and holds on to them. "You cannot waste that."

EVERYONE NEEDS SOMETHING, BRONIA SAID.

I think of that as I sit down to help Irène with her studies, and when I pay attention, look at what she has been doing, what she has been learning here in Sceaux, I feel like I have been asleep for 302 days, and I have let my daughter's mind wither. She has not been learning anything! This will not do at all. The revelation that I have been so drowned in grief that I have let my daughter's education lapse shocks me.

What have I done, moving us out to Sceaux, where it is so very quiet? In our old house on boulevard Kellerman, we were surrounded by neighbors who were friends and academics, professors. There were always lively conversations and debates in our garden with the Perrins and the Langevins, and the children would play, and they would listen, and they would learn. Irène has nothing here.

"You are not going to attend this school any longer," I tell Irène. "I am going to start my own school."

Her eyes widen a little. I am either frightening her or exciting her, or both.

The next morning, back at the university, I tell Jean Perrin and Paul Langevin about my desire. "If we all enroll our children together, we can make a collective school among us. We can all take turns teaching them. They can learn from real academics."

Paul Langevin considers my idea, pulling on his mustache. Paul was Pierre's student, once, long ago, and now he is a brilliant academic in his own right. He was also a good friend to Pierre before he died. I want his approval, as if in some strange way it is akin to Pierre's approval. When he nods vigorously, I exhale. He is either as excited about this idea as I am, or excited that I have a new idea again. Any idea.

"The children will learn so much more from us. We will give them the best education," I say. I had participated in Flying University once in Poland, self-taught in Szczuki. Learned from the best professors in Paris and have become one here myself.

Everyone needs something, Bronia said.

Then I remember: I need now what I have always needed—education.

But organizing our collective school to teach the children isn't enough for me. I *need* science too. I begin making plans for the lab, *my* lab now. The lab was where I felt most happy, most at home, even before I met Pierre. And I know it can be my place again, after him, too.

There is a generous donation from Andrew Carnegie from America, and I use it to hire several research assistants, including my nephew, Maurice, Jacques's son. Jacques writes a very kind letter to thank me for my generosity, but he does not understand at all—Maurice, like Jacques, like Pierre, has a brilliant mind, and that is the reason why I hire him. He works hard, and he is very smart, and there is so much work to be done. We are attempting to purify radium chloride, isolating the radium metal. And we are trying again to determine the atomic weight of radium.

But when my assistants leave for the day, I stay in the lab often much too late, working on my own, too. I am developing a new method of measuring radium, a way to give weight to it. This excites me wildly, because if I can perfect it, it will allow radium to be used widely outside my laboratory, for the greater good of other scientists, or perhaps even doctors. And this, most of all, is what Pierre would've wanted.

The strangest thing is, when I am back in the lab again, back in the place Pierre and I fell in love and lived so many hours of our lives, that is the place where my mind can begin to carry on, where everything inside of me starts to lighten again. Late at night, all alone, the radium glows all around me, bright and beautiful and phosphorescent.

MARYA

❧

Loksow, Poland, 1908

Leokadia's mother died in the beginning of February—I
heard about it from her cousin, Zuzanna, who was a student in my introductory chemistry course. Leokadia and I still
exchanged the occasional letter, but I hadn't known her mother
was sick, and the news from Zuzanna hit me with a sadness I
did not expect.

Leokadia had done quite well for herself in the past few
years; her career as a concert pianist was blossoming as she was
traveling around Europe giving concerts to large, paying crowds.
According to her most recent letter, she had spent the last
months in Berlin, making a record. But no matter all that, I still
imagined her mother's death would hit her hard, and I felt for
her, remembering her kindness to me the week Papa had died.

Even knowing she would have to come back to Loksow for
the funeral, it was a shock when I nearly walked right into her,
as I was leaving my advanced physics class.

I had not seen her in almost two years—since I'd gone with
Pierre to hear her concert in Montmartre, and then we had

shared only a brief exchange and a quick hug just after her performance. Seeing her again now I was struck by how remarkably
she appeared not to have aged a single bit. Somehow time had
made her only more beautiful, more full of light in person.

"Marya!" She grabbed me in a hug before I could react to her
unexpected presence outside of my school. Klara clutched my
hand, pulled close to my leg. Leokadia pulled back from me and
noticed her. "And who is this?" She bent down to Klara's level,
and extended one of her petite hands for a shake. Klara hesitated
for a moment before accepting.

"Klara," I said. "This is Mama's friend who plays beautiful
music. Remember I have told you about her?"

Klara shook her head, confused, and I was caught inside
my lie. I had never mentioned Leokadia to Klara before. Not
because I wasn't proud and happy for what Leokadia had done
with her talent, what she had become these past few years. But
because talking about her out loud with Klara felt as if it would
be admitting other things that I would never want to admit to
her. We were a family, Kaz and Klara and I, and inside the bubble of our family there was a delicate balance. Move any wrong
way and the whole thing would burst.

"Yes." I wrapped myself tighter in my lie. "She used to teach
piano here with me, many years ago. Before you were born. I told
you, chicken, you just don't remember."

My sweet Klara nodded now.

She didn't have the capacity to believe I'd lie to her, and perhaps to make up for it, I kept on talking. "I bet Leokadia would
show you the piano while she's visiting. Teach you a song." I
stood back up and turned to her. "Only if you have time."

"Yes." Leokadia clapped her hands together. "I am here until the end of the week. I would love to see you both. Would tomorrow morning work?"

KLARA KNEW THE WOMEN I TAUGHT WITH, THE WOMEN IN MY classes, her aunts and her cousins, especially Lou, who had been living with us the past few months. But none of them played music, none of them sparkled with the radiance Leokadia had. And even at five years old, Klara had somehow picked up on this.

"Today we are learning piano with your very beautiful friend, aren't we, Mama?" We had gotten fresh eggs from the Nowaks' farm yesterday, and I boiled them for our breakfast now.

Lou sat across the table from Klara and looked up from her textbook. She had become quite interested in studying biology, and it amused me that it was only here, away from both her physician parents, that she had come to find a new scientific fascination with the body. "Piano?" Lou asked, her eyes lighting up a little.

"Yes," I told her. "My friend, she's a concert pianist. She's come to visit for the week. Would you like to come with us for a lesson this morning, too?" Lou nodded, looking delighted. She was sixteen, and looked every bit like a woman, the spitting image of Bronia at that age. But unlike sixteen-year-old Bronia she seemed not to have a mothering instinct in her entire body. Mostly, she acted like a little girl. And though I left her in charge of Klara from time to time, whenever I came home she was on the floor, playing whatever game Klara had commanded, a look of glee on her face. Sometimes I would stifle a laugh, thinking of how the whole scene would shock Bronia. In my letters to her, I told her only about how well Lou was doing in her biology courses.

And though there were no mountains in Loksow, Lou still went on very long daily walks, or else she said she got restless. I often sent her to the Nowaks' farm, and then we had fresh eggs for breakfast nearly every morning.

IT FELT STRANGE WALKING BACK INTO LEOKADIA'S OLD HOME, Kaz's old workspace, after all this time. The inside was exactly as I remembered, sprawling and filled with expensive-looking furniture and rugs, except now it was all covered in a fine coat of dust. Pani Jewniewicz had been dead only a week, but it seemed no one had cleaned her apartment in much longer than that. Her husband had gone years before her, her daughter all the way across Europe. I felt sad about the way she had died alone, her house oddly neglected, and I had the thought that no matter what else might happen in my life, I did not want it to end that way for me. I put one arm around Klara, one around Lou, and gave them each a half hug.

"Come in." Leokadia ushered us in to the back of the apartment, where the baby grand piano still sat in the same place it had years earlier when I'd watched her give lessons, taken a few lessons myself. It shone now, free of dust, and I imagined she had spent the morning cleaning it herself, though not a blond curl was out of place, nor was there a single wrinkle in her stunning blue velour dress.

I introduced Lou, and Leokadia quickly grabbed a chair for her from the dining room. Then she patted the piano bench, and Klara hopped up on it. Leokadia sat next to her and showed both girls the notes, running her fingers delicately across the keys. I sat on the sofa and watched, remembering myself here as I had been so many years earlier, so much younger. When I was deeply and blindly in love with my husband, and when Klara was nothing but a dream, a wish, I did not believe would ever be real.

I felt a strange sensation in the pit of my stomach, the memory of the beetroot stew that came back up in the street and the sting of deception that followed. And then, that desire of a young girl who wanted nothing more than to eventually make it to Paris. To study at the Sorbonne.

"Marya." Leokadia's voice interrupted my thoughts, and I shook my head, trying to push away the past.

I looked up and she stood before me. Lou and Klara both sat on the piano bench, together, and somehow they were already playing something that sounded pleasant, vaguely like the old Polish lullaby my mother used to sing us to sleep.

"Klara has perfect pitch," Leokadia said matter-of-factly.

"Perfect pitch?" I raised my eyebrows not understanding. "What does that mean?"

"That means your daughter is a musician," Leokadia said. I laughed. No one in our family was drawn to music, or even art. We were scientists, mathematicians, physicians. "I'm quite serious," Leokadia said. "You must start her on regular lessons now."

"But she's not quite five," I protested.

"Marya," Leokadia said seriously, "your daughter has a gift."

There was something that rubbed me the wrong way about Leokadia telling me what I *must* do, insisting she understood something about my daughter that had been hidden and previously unknown to me for nearly five years. Lou hugged us goodbye to go off on her daily walking, then to class, and Klara and I walked alone back to Złota Street. I asked her, as we walked, how she felt about the piano.

"It is the best thing I have ever touched, Mama. Do you think we could go back to Pani Kadi's house again and again?" Her voice was small and soft, but filled with an odd sort of desperation, a wanting I'd never heard from her before. Klara was so easygoing, content to simply go along with me to class and listen or play quietly in the back. Content to stay with her cousin any time I asked. Content to eat her supper and go to bed, then wake up and get dressed in the morning. She had never *asked* me for anything.

"Leokadia is only here for a short visit. She goes back to Berlin in a few days," I reminded her.

"Oh." Klara cast her eyes downward, her entire face sinking with disappointment

"But Pani Jankowska teaches piano at my school," I said. "And perhaps I could talk to her about special lessons, just for you."

She stopped walking, her eyes widened, and she nodded quickly. In the fall she would be old enough to attend the girl's gymnasium, but she had never had lessons in anything before, other than informal ones from me, working on basic reading and maths. It felt odd that I should start her formally on piano first, something I knew nothing, and cared very little, about. But her smile was so wide, and she grabbed my hand in excitement and began to skip toward home.

I loved her with my entire being; I wanted to give her everything I could not have afforded as a child. Everything she ever wanted.

KAZ RETURNED HOME FOR A FEW DAYS AROUND EASTER, HIS bag filled with Austrian chocolates for Klara, and for me, he brought a new copy of *Physikalische Zeitschrift*, one of the most respected physics journals in Europe, published quarterly in German. It might have been the nicest thing he ever gave me, and when he handed it to me I forgave him again for all the negative feelings our recent visit with Leokadia had reawakened in me. I stood on my toes, kissed him gently on the mouth. He tasted different than I remembered, like bitter coffee and a German tobacco he'd grown fond of in Austria.

"*Kochanie.*" He held on to my shoulders. "These past few months have been too hard. I've missed you and Klara too much."

"We've missed you too," I said, and it was true. Kaz and I had reconnected at Bronia's last summer, and then having him gone this year had ignited a feeling of emptiness inside of me. It felt too quiet at the dinner table, too empty in our bed sleeping in it all alone. I missed having someone to share Klara's daily pursuits with, and it wasn't the same to write them down and send them in a letter. And then there was Klara herself, who was constantly counting the number of days until she could see her father again. But it was not something we could change. Kaz needed to be in Vienna for his career, and his salary was so good, there was a relief now in not worrying about having money for food and clothing and coal.

"I have good news," he said. "I've been offered a position for the fall in Krakow."

Krakow was closer than Vienna, certainly, but it was not Loksow. Or even Warsaw, which would make it possible for him to come home every weekend. I sighed. "So you will be away, still."

"No, *kochanie*, you will come with me!" There was a certainty in his voice. In his mind, this was already a foregone conclusion. So many years ago we had wished for Krakow together, for more freedom, more opportunity outside of the Russian Empire. But now Loksow was my home. My life was here. My work was here. My school was here.

"I can't just leave my university," I said.

Kaz frowned. "But you could teach in Krakow, or take classes there. Whatever you want."

"I want to stay here," I said, though even as the words came out, I realized I sounded petulant and stubborn, like a child.

"Think about Klara," Kaz said. "She will get a better education in Krakow than in Loksow. So many more opportunities for her."

I opened my mouth, but did not say anything in response. Kaz wasn't wrong. Krakow was a bustling, cosmopolitan city, vibrant, cultural, and modern, and unoppressed by Russian rule. It was where we should've lived all along, if Kaz's parents hadn't disowned him after our marriage and he had been able to continue his education then.

In Loksow, we had a very nice two-bedroom apartment, but when we opened the windows and the wind blew just right, it smelled as though the red-and-white smokestacks that hovered at the edge of the city were in our very backyard. And the girls' gymnasium in Loksow would provide nothing but the most basic of educations for Klara.

And still, I pressed my lips tightly together. *My school.* Agata and I had worked so hard, so many years. I could not just move away, leave it. Just like that.

"*Kochanie.*" Kaz kissed my forehead softly. "I will finally be able to give you everything you want, everything you desire. You just have to let me."

I did not want Kaz to give me everything; I wanted to take everything I wanted for myself. And perhaps if it hadn't been for Klara, I would've told him that. I would've pulled away from his embrace, planted my feet firmly on the floor and refused to move from Loksow and everything I had built here.

But when I looked up, Klara stood in the doorway, watching us intently, hanging on our every word to each other.

MARIE

⌘

France, 1908–1909

We rent a place near the beach in the Normandy region of France for the summer of 1908, my family and the Langevins all staying together in one large house. It is perfect for Ève and Irène—Paul and Jeanne Langevin have four children now, so my girls have built-in summer playmates. And also, they have me for continued lessons in science and Paul for continued lessons in mathematics. Our collective school takes no breaks; learning is a year-round endeavor, after all.

I like Arromanches simply for the fact that it is not Saint-Rémy or Brittany. There are no old memories here, haunting me. Jeanne is just glad to be out of the city. And Dr. Curie enjoys the mornings by the water, the sea air. *Good for the lungs,* he tells me, and we both pretend not to notice the reoccurring bronchial spasm that has begun to rattle his chest at alarming intervals.

All six children love the sand and the water, and we send them outside to go and play and come back to us for supper, then lessons. They return dirty and exhausted and starving for a feast Dr. Curie prepares. During the days I catch up on my reading, and I write notes in my journal. My body is away from my lab; my mind never leaves it.

It is only Paul who seems unhappy here. He will disappear for the afternoon, and whenever I go to look for him to let him know supper is ready, I find him sitting alone in an empty corner of the beach, gazing off into the water with a steady frown on his face.

"Are you feeling ill?" I ask him one afternoon in early June. I put the back of my hand to his forehead, but his body temperature feels normal. I sit down next to him on the beach, gaze off into the water, but it is infinite and boring. I don't understand what he's doing out here.

He turns away from the water and offers me a wan smile. "I just need a break sometimes. You know how that is, Marie?"

"From work?" I ask him, not knowing how that is at all. Whenever I try to take time away from my work, I feel lost. Work is what nourishes me, keeps me alive.

He shakes his head. "It's just . . . do you ever feel that everything around you is crushing you? So much so that it is impossible to breathe."

It is strange the way he describes a feeling I've known well my whole life: when Mama died, when Kazimierz left me, and most recently when I lost my Pierre. "The dark fog," I say, resting my hand gently on his arm. "The heaviness."

He turns his eyes back to the water, but he moves his hand up to hold on to mine. "When I lose myself in the expanse of the sea," he says softly. "I can remember how to breathe again."

SINCE WE HAD LIVED NEXT TO THE LANGEVINS ON BOULEVARD Kellerman for years, I count both Paul and Jeanne among my *before* and *after* friends, along with the Perrins (who have decided to spend the summer in Brittany with family this summer, instead of with us). The Langevins were a part of my other, married life, and they have remarkably stayed my friends through the endless black tunnel of my grief and our move to Sceaux. It is both wonderful and terrible to have friends who have known you in both your best and darkest times.

Jeanne acts as though nothing has happened, nothing is different here in Arromanches than it ever was back on boulevard Kellerman when Pierre was alive. I find that to be her most remarkable quality; the way she just simply ignores my loss and the changes in my life. And mostly that is why I make a point to eat breakfast with her each and every morning during the month of June. We sip coffee, and Jeanne talks about herself, about her own marriage. "Paul is horrible to me," she confides one morning, about a week after Paul told me of his darkness on the beach. Jeanne's favorite topic of conversation is, and always has been, her marriage.

I sip my coffee, and nod and murmur softly. My friendship with Paul has always relied upon my balancing and ignoring Jeanne's badmouthing of him with what I know and see to be true with my own eyes. I have watched him teaching maths to our children these last months: He is soft-spoken, so unbelievably patient and kind, even with their painstakingly elementary grasp on the subject matter. And then I think about how lost he's been looking when I find him on the beach, the sweet sad sound of his voice when he told me how it is impossible for him to breathe. I can't imagine him intending to be *horrible* to anyone. But I have the feeling if I were to tell Jeanne all this, she would get angry with me. And it is nice to have a friend, another woman around me, for once. So I say nothing at all on the subject. I simply nod.

"He has a mean streak, you know," she tells me now, pouring thick cream into her cup, turning her coffee an unpalatable shade of tan. "He purposefully denies me money, Marie. Money I need to care for *his* children."

"If you ever need money," I say to her. "I could lend you some money."

"Oh no." She pushes my offer away with a flick of her wrist, then takes another sip of her coffee. "I'm not asking you for money. I'm just telling you, one woman to another, how hard it is for me. You understand?"

I nod, but the truth is, I don't understand at all. I have made my own money, relied on my own self, since I first left my home and moved to Paris so many years ago. I want to tell Jeanne, if she thinks her life is hard, she should imagine what it is like to grow up under Russian rule in Poland, to be so poor as a student in Paris that you faint from hunger. That she should imagine what it is like to fall in love and finally, *finally*, have everything, and then have your husband be crushed by a horse in the street.

But I don't say any of that to her, and Jeanne is already on to another topic, looking out the window, commenting on the clouds rolling in over the water. "I think it's going to storm tonight," she says.

I sip my coffee and look outside. The clouds are high and thin, nonthreatening. "I wouldn't worry," I say. "It doesn't look like anything serious."

IN THE MIDDLE OF THE NIGHT I AWAKE TO A LOUD CRASH above me. I remember what Jeanne said about a storm, and wonder if she was right after all, if the noise that awoke me was thunder. But the clouds had floated back out to sea in the afternoon as I'd suspected; the night sky had been black and starlit.

Above me now, I hear Jeanne's voice, saying words I can't quite make out. But her tone sounds frightened, or is it angry? *What was that noise?* My heart pounds furiously, and I get out of bed, find my robe. The Langevins have taken the upstairs bedrooms, the Curies downstairs. I tiptoe around downstairs, but Irène and Ève and Dr. Curie are all soundly asleep.

The entire house feels quiet and still, and I return to my room. Perhaps I dreamed the disturbance. But no matter now; I am wide awake.

I light a lamp and check Pierre's pocket watch, the last relic I have allowed myself to save of his, to keep with me always. It is nearly five in the morning, and I suppose there is no use going back to sleep. I take my notebook and quietly tiptoe down the hall and out onto the back porch. I will work by lamplight, then catch the sunrise across the water and enjoy the quiet until the children wake after the first light.

I am out here for only a few moments, when the door opens again, and I jump. Paul walks out, his head half-covered in a towel. I lift my lamp so I can get a better view. There is what appears to be blood running down his cheek, from just above his right eye.

"Paul!" I gasp. "Whatever happened to you?" The loud noise . . . Jeanne's voice. But I can't reconcile any of this with the blood on Paul's face.

"Jeanne got angry with me," he says softly, his voice resigned. Then he attempts a half smile. "The vase fared much worse than I did, I assure you."

I stand and go closer, holding the lamp to his forehead to examine the wound. I remove the towel gently—pieces of glass are stuck in his hair, and I pluck them out gingerly one by one with my fingers, then look at his wound again. "I have a needle and thread in my room. I can go get it, stitch this for you," I say.

"No." He gently moves my hand away, clasps my fingers in his own. I give his hand a small squeeze, before letting go. He reaches up to touch his wound, then winces. It's tender. "I'll be fine."

"Paul, you're bleeding."

"It's a superficial cut," he insists. "I'm telling you, I'll be fine."

He sighs and sits down on a chair beside me. He presses the towel to his wound until the bleeding seems to stop. I want to ask why Jeanne got so angry, and how exactly a vase came into contact with his forehead. And is she the reason for his crushing darkness, his need for afternoons alone gazing at the water? But I bite my tongue. Jeanne is my friend. Paul is my coworker, and also my friend. I shouldn't get in the middle of whatever is happening with them.

"What are you working on?" Paul asks, changing the subject, pointing to my journal.

"Polonium," I say, sighing. "So much work has been done with radium these last years. Good work. I, myself, have focused on it. But I named polonium after my homeland, and everyone's forgotten about it since. I'm dreaming up a study now to determine its alpha decay."

"That's what I always admire about you," he says quietly. "You don't ever give up, do you, Marie?"

"I suppose I don't. Or I . . . can't." The most important thing I have now is my work, and I can't imagine any sort of meaningful life without it.

"When Pierre died . . ." Paul starts, and then his voice trails off. Perhaps he remembers the way I got so upset when people spoke Pierre's name, shortly after he died.

Now that time has passed, I want to hear his name again, want to talk about him, remember that he was real and alive and beautiful and brilliant. And mine. But no one talks about him much anymore. "It's all right," I say gently. "You can say it, Paul. Please."

"When Pierre died," he begins again, his voice soft, wistful, "I just really admired your strength, that's all. There you were, all alone with two young girls, and you could've taken a widow's pension from the university and lived quite comfortably. But instead you took Pierre's job. You made it your own. You made the work your own. You're brave and amazing, Marie."

No other man scientist has ever seen me this way. Except Pierre. "Am I?" I say. "Or am I foolish and crazy?"

Paul smiles. "Don't we all have to be a little bit foolish and crazy to work long, thankless hours in a lab in pursuit of something no one else can quite see but us?" I smile back. It's true. "Will you tell me more, about polonium?" Paul asks. It's a simple request, one scientist to another, but his voice is soft and clear, and his question carries so much weight. It's as if Paul is truly asking about me, about my heart.

"Of course," I tell him. "What do you want to know?"

"Everything," he breathes, and for a second, I think of Pierre, that first night I met him in the Kowalskis' suite, when he was breathless in his fascination for my work. Paul sounds nearly the same way now. He wants to know and understand who I really am underneath everything else, and all at once, I feel lighter than I have in years.

I open my journal and show him the notes I've been writing

down all summer long. What fascinates me about polonium, I tell him, is the way it exists in the pitchblende with radium, but how its properties could not be more different. I suspect the alpha decay is drastically different as well. But I haven't had the time or space or money to prove it yet, and polonium has become something I think about only in my time off from radium. "Polonium should be just as revered as radium," I insist, my voice rising. "Or else I named them wrong in the first place. I wanted to honor my homeland, give it . . . something."

"You can take the scientist out of Poland," Paul says lightly. "But you can't take Poland out of the scientist, hmm?"

I shake my head and laugh just a little, delighted by how much Paul understands me. The sun has begun to come up, and now I close my journal. The sky is pink and orange, but the light is still dim enough for the lamp. I hold it closer to Paul's forehead, examine the wound again, and he's right. The bleeding has stopped. It does appear to be superficial.

I think about how Jeanne always tells me Paul is cruel, but I wonder if she has been the cruel one all along. It is strange the way you cannot really know what goes on in other people's lives, their marriages, even when we were neighbors on boulevard Kellerman for so many years, and friends for even longer. That even now, living here with them this summer, I don't really understand Jeanne or Paul or their marriage.

Paul turns back to me, smiles a little in a way that makes his handlebar mustache appear suddenly lopsided. I have the strangest desire to reach up and touch it with my fingers, but I restrain myself.

He moves first, puts his hand on my shoulder gently, pulling me toward him in a half hug, in a way we have never touched before. But I do not shift away. Instead I pull in closer to him and the two of sit there like that for a little while, staring out at the water glistening in the sunrise. Paul is right—this really is calming.

"When we are back in Paris," I finally say, "you should come to my lab and I'll show you more about my studies of polonium."

"I would like that," Paul agrees, his voice breaking a little. "I would very much like to visit your lab."

Six months later, in the spring term of 1909, we give up on our collective school. All of us are stretched too thin with our own work to continue teaching one another's children as well. And though I have a brief moment of sadness, I feel relief more—I am exhausted all the time, and I find a better school to enroll Irène in than the one she'd been in before. She will need official schooling to get into university later on, anyway. And without extra lessons to plan for the children, I can focus solely on teaching my classes at the Sorbonne and my work in the lab.

Though we are no longer schooling our children together, Jean Perrin and Paul Langevin and I often still take our lunches together near the university. But now instead of schedules and the children, we discuss our lectures and our lab work. Then Jean's lab becomes quite busy in the fall of 1909, as he is working hard to verify Albert Einstein's predictions on atomic theory, and he begins working right through lunch. So only Paul and I take a quiet table together by the window, lingering some days over our coffees and our conversation, long past the end of the lunch hour.

In the months since our summer in Arromanches, Paul has taken me up on my offer, come to visit my lab from time to time. And always, at our lunches, he asks me about my work, for updates on my progress, not just on polonium but radium too. Lately, I've been trying to achieve radium in a metallic state, and each day he asks about my results. All morning I look forward to talking things over with him during lunch, then pondering the questions he asks, after.

"Come work in my lab full-time," I implore him, one chilly afternoon in late November. I have assistants in my lab now, students, but I do not have a true partner. I desperately miss having a partner.

Paul smiles, shakes his head. "And who would complete my study on ultrasound waves then, Marie?"

Paul has his own work, of course, and maybe it is selfish of me to want him to work on my studies alongside me. But my studies could become his studies too, our studies. "Well, perhaps next year," I say. "When you are finished your current work."

He gets a strange look on his face, so I can't tell what he's thinking. Then he puts his hand on my mine, as he has been wont to do lately. It is familiar in a way, friendly enough that I don't think that I should pull away, or that it is in any way improper. Usually it is to emphasize a point, or to interrupt what I am telling him about the lab to ask a question. Now, his fingers linger on my wrist just a few seconds longer than they normally would, and then he gently strokes my palm with his thumb. "I can't work with you," he says softly.

"Why not?"

"It would be impossible to be that close to you all the time and not fall in love with you."

"Love?" I laugh a little. "I'm talking about science, Paul."

"So am I," he says, and his voice sounds completely serious.

A FEW WEEKS LATER, ONE EVENING IN MID-DECEMBER, I AM in my lab much too late. At lunch, Paul had given me an idea— why not use electrolysis to try and turn radium chloride metallic? And I spent the rest of the day planning out how this might work. But now my back aches from standing all day, and I can't suppress a rising yawn. Outside it is snowing, and I know the walk to the train will be long and slippery, bitterly cold. Pierre's watch tells me it is already after 8 p.m.

There's an unexpected knock on the door—perhaps one of my assistants has forgotten something or couldn't make it to the train in the snow. But when I open the door, there on the other side is Paul, his hat and thick wool coat covered in snowflakes. "I saw the lamplight through the window," he says apologetically.

"You came to work with me?" I cannot keep the glee from my voice, and I tug on his coat sleeve to pull him inside my lab, out of the snow. He shuts the door behind him, and for a moment I just look at him, not letting go of his coat.

"I don't know why I'm here," he admits. "I just . . . didn't want to go home," he says quietly.

I remember that morning in Arromanches, the tiny slivers of glass I plucked from his hair. None of us had ever spoken about that again, and the following morning Jeanne had been her usual self, chattering with me over coffee about the children. I'd wanted to ask her about what might drive her to smash a vase against her kind husband's head. But what went on between them really wasn't my business—I hadn't said a word.

The cut from Arromanches was superficial and has long healed, but I put my hand up to his face now, trace the lines of his forehead with my fingertips. His skin is cool and damp from the snow. He reaches his hand up to meet mine and holds it there. My fingers suddenly grow hot against his skin. I lean in closer, and it is chilly enough inside my lab tonight that his breath frosts the air.

I have not been with a man since Pierre; I have not wanted to until right this very moment. I remember what Paul said, that if he came to work in my lab, he would fall in love with me. And I wonder if love and science are, for me, one and the same.

Our faces are so close; I can feel his breath against my lips. I suddenly think of Jeanne, waiting up for him in their kitchen on boulevard Kellerman. "We shouldn't do this," I say softly, but I am shaking, my heart pounding in my chest. I run my fingers down his cheeks, trace his lips with my forefinger.

"One time," Paul whispers. "Just this once."

And then his lips are on mine, and my body is hot with wanting, and I can't pull away. I don't want to.

MARYA

❦

Kaz's treatise on elasticity posited the idea that materials were elastic if, and only if, they returned to their original form after all outside forces were pulled away. Our marriage, too, was *elastic* by this definition. The years and the things that had happened to us, the things we had done, had shaped and changed and molded us into something unrecognizable once in Loksow. But now, in a new city, a new life, away from everything and everyone, here we were again, simply a man and a woman who loved each other.

In Krakow, we rented a two-story brick house, walking distance to Jagiellonian University, where Kaz was teaching two mathematics courses each term and where he also had access to a lab to continue to further study elasticity. We had a small garden in the backyard where I began to cultivate lettuce and herbs. Enough money to enroll Klara in a private primary academy and weekly piano lessons. We could not yet afford our own piano for the house, but we were saving for it.

I made breakfast for everyone in the mornings, kissed Kaz

goodbye before he left for work. I walked Klara to school, and then, and only then, I understood my own elasticity. The worries about money, about the Russians' opposition to women learning—that was absent here in Krakow. And I was still the same old Marya, my mind restless and itching, wanting to learn, wanting more.

AT FIRST, I HOPED TO OPEN A BRANCH OF MY WOMEN'S UNIversity here in Krakow. Teaching young women was what I'd come to think of as my life's work in Loksow. But it was very hard to get started here. For one thing, it wasn't easy to meet like-minded people in a new city. Mostly, I got introduced to the wives of the men Kaz taught in the mathematics department with, and they were only interested talking about their houses, their children, and their husbands. When I tried to bring up the subject of advancing our own educations, they would laugh. Or look at me funny, like I made them uncomfortable. Suffice to say, I did not make any friends our first few months in Krakow.

But also the bigger problem was, there was not such a need for my school here, as there had been in Russian-controlled Poland. Women could enroll in Jagiellonian and had been allowed to since 1897. A few years ago, in 1906, the university had even hired their first woman professor. When I asked him, Kaz told me she was a part of the science faculty, but he had not met her yet. She felt to me like a mythical creature. And some mornings after I dropped Klara off at school, I would take a long path home, meandering by the science building on campus, hoping that, by chance, I might run into her. But it was silly, since I had no idea what she looked like. How would I even know if I walked right by her?

I wrote to Hela weekly and begged her to send me as much current reading material as she could, so that I could at least continue my scientific education on my own. But Hela was so busy with writing up her findings on elemental magnetism with Jacques that her letters to me, her packages of scientific papers and journals, came less frequently than they had when I'd lived in Loksow.

Our house in Krakow was on Golebia Street, and somehow it felt fitting that this street, too, was named for a bird. A pigeon, though, not a sparrow. And all the pigeons I saw in Krakow were never flying; they were prancing slowly on the street corners, pecking at wayward crumbs passersby had dropped in the street.

IN THE SPRINGTIME, WE BOUGHT A PIANO FOR OUR HOUSE, and Klara could not keep her hands off of it. She ran to practice the moment she woke up in the morning, and then again the moment she got home from her daily school lessons. I had to pester her to do her schoolwork in the evenings and tried to hide that stabbing feeling in my stomach when she would say, *Why, Mama? Why? Sciences and maths bore me. I want to play piano instead.*

"You can get back to the piano after your lessons are done. I'll help you with the maths and sciences," I would say. It pained me so that this was my favorite part of my day, and that she hated it.

But I could not deny that Leokadia had been right about her talent either. After only two years of lessons, her small six-year-old fingers could fly across the keys in a way that mesmerized me when I sat down and watched her play. And her teacher, an older woman who had come recommended to Kaz by one of the other professors whose daughter also took lessons, told us that perhaps we should look into something more for Klara, something better, a professional institute of music?

"Is there something like that here in Krakow?" I asked, genuinely curious. I had known of nothing of the sort in Loksow or Warsaw. And especially not something that would be open to young girls.

She nodded. "There is one institute that accepts girls: Chernikoff. But it is very hard to get in."

"Oh." I shrugged, and the truth was, as much as Klara loved piano, I still hoped for her to fall in love with science instead. And she was so young, only six years old. I was quite fine with her taking casual lessons with Pani Lebowska.

"But Klara is special," Pani Lebowska said matter-of-factly. "She'll practice a little more, and then I will secure her an audition."

"I HAVE A SURPRISE FOR YOU," KAZ ANNOUNCED ONE EVENING, coming in from work, the beginning of our second fall in Krakow. Klara was already practicing for her audition, the sweet melodic sounds of her piano overtaking the entire house.

Kaz had walked into the kitchen, where I was preparing dinner, put his hat on the table, and swooped in and kissed me. "Come, it's out front." He held out his hand, but I hesitated, not wanting our food to burn. "Come on, Marya. Come with me."

I wiped my hands on my apron before taking his hand, letting him lead me to the front steps of our house. And then when he opened the front door I saw it: a bright shiny red bicycle sitting out on our porch.

"What's this?" I asked him. I let go of his hand, stepped outside, and trailed my fingers along the handlebars. I hadn't ridden in years, not since that glorious summer in Paris when my niece, Marie, was born and I'd ridden all around with Pierre.

"I wrote your sisters, asked what I might be able to do to cheer you up." He paused, swallowed hard. "I know it has been hard for you here in Krakow this past year. You miss your friends and your work . . . and I want to make you happy again. Both Bronia and Hela suggested that you would like a bicycle."

It was a thoughtful gift, or, he had meant for it to be that way. But I felt a disquieting sensation curl inside my stomach. My sisters both believed all I needed to be happy was a bicycle? And Kaz truly believed that this would satiate my mind's desire to learn, my heart's desire to help people and improve the world? *A bicycle?*

Instead all I said was, "Kaz, this is much too expensive."

"But," he said, leaning in to kiss me on the forehead, "you are worth it, *kochanie.*"

MUCH TO KAZ'S DELIGHT I RODE MY BICYCLE ALL THROUGH-out Krakow while Klara was at school and he was at work the following week. I explored the historic buildings and museums, the Royal Castle, and Cloth Hall.

I rode and I rode, pushing my legs so hard that I could barely breathe, my entire body consumed with sweat. My life unfolded in front of me: Klara's schedule and audition, this bicycle, my garden, and cooking suppers for my family. It all stretched out, long and tedious and dull, and then I couldn't be sure whether it was sweat or tears on my cheeks. I pedaled and I pedaled, and I pushed myself, harder and harder, until it felt like my heart might explode in my chest.

What was I doing here? I was only forty-one years old, and I hungered for knowledge. How could Kaz or my sisters believe that a bicycle would solve any of that? Maybe it was that they couldn't know something I hadn't told them: it wasn't the bicycle I'd loved so much in Paris, but those beautiful scientific conversations with Pierre while we were riding together.

Pierre.

His letters had sounded defeated as of late. He'd given up on his pitchblende last year, as he'd said it was too hard, too much work to do alone. And then recently Henri Becquerel had discovered a new element, the one that Pierre had long suspected existed. Now it would forever be known as *becquerelium*, highly radioactive, even more than uranium. And Pierre wondered in his letters to me whether he should even carry on in science. *What have I done with my life?* he asked me.

I wrote him back, implored him not to give up on his scientific studies. Perhaps he could assist Hela and Jacques with their magnets until he figured out his next area of research. *Next time will be different*, I promised him.

Pierre wrote me back: *And what about you, Marya? What are you doing with your bright and beautiful mind in Krakow? There is more for you than gardening and bicycle riding, isn't there? I know there is.*

THE FOLLOWING DAY, I RODE MY BICYCLE TO THE TRADING shop, and I sold it.

My pockets full of crowns, I walked myself to the university and registered for my very first real university course. The registrar did not question my motives, nor ask why a woman my age would be interested in science. No, he simply took my money, asked me to fill out the registration card and to choose my classes.

I wrote *Marya Zorawska* at the top of the card, my hands shaking with disbelief and excitement.

"What course does the woman professor teach?" I asked the registrar. I did not have to walk through the university, hoping to seek her out. I could simply pay and enroll in her course. I could learn from her!

He sighed, like I was not the first woman to come in here and ask him that this week. "Introduction to chemistry," he said. "Professor Mazur."

It was likely I had self-taught past any *introductory* chemistry course. But I signed up for her course anyway, and, a physics course taught by a man. Both were given during hours while Klara would be at her own school. This would have no effect on her or Kaz's life or routine, but it would have a drastic effect on mine.

I put the remaining crowns back in my pocket and walked back toward Golebia Street. My legs were sore, quite tired now.

But it didn't matter. I had my wings again.

MARIE

Paris, 1910

By the beginning of 1910, I have crawled out of the long, dark tunnel of paralyzing grief and loneliness. And what is waiting for me on the other side? *Paul.*

Once, one time was a lie we told each other that first night we were together in December. But once is not enough. We spend more stolen nights together, late in my lab. But that is not enough, either. I want more; I need more.

So I rent us an apartment on the fifth floor at 5 rue Banquier, an inconspicuous sort of pied-à-terre. It is convenient to the university, easy to sneak away to during working hours.

From the outside, the building is quite plain looking, white plaster, with a small number 5 etched in front of the brown entrance door. The apartment itself is up five flights of stairs and has two bedrooms. I tell the landlord it is for me and my daughters, that I am needing a second home closer to my work now that my father-in-law has recently passed. *Our home is in Sceaux,* I say, nervously overexplaining, *but my work is always here.*

Most of that is true, except for the second bedroom, which

is not at all necessary. I will never once bring the girls here.
They are in Sceaux with their governess. We are all very sad
in the wake of Dr. Curie's death, but we take comfort in the fact
that he lived a good long life. And I have made an effort for the
girls' daily routines to remain unchanged. I take this apartment
because the location and price are good, despite the extra, un-
necessary bedroom. And I like that in order for anyone to stum-
ble upon this place, they must first undertake the inconvenience
of five flights of stairs.

Paul laughs when I tell him that, the first time we meet here
together in the winter of 1910, just weeks after the girls and I
have laid Dr. Curie to rest. Perhaps it is Pierre's father's death
that has finally, finally allowed me to admit the truth to myself:
I am falling in love with Paul. What we have together is more than
fleeting moments of pleasure. It is something with breadth and
longevity and *importance.* I am only forty-two years old, much
too young to be a widow for the rest of my life. Paul is the one I
want to be with. I want him as my partner at work, and in life.
I want everything with him that I had once with Pierre.

"But now *we* have to climb five flights of stairs before we
can be together," Paul says, laughing as I lead him up the stairs
into our very own space, our very own apartment together. But I
know he enjoys vigorous physical activity the way I do. And I can
practically feel the excitement coming off his body, an iridescent
glow that makes his cheeks ruddy and his blue eyes lighter.

Once we are inside the apartment, I shut the door and pull
him toward me. My heart pounds in a way it hasn't since I was so
very young, since I first stepped foot in Paris and the excitement
of this new world, this new life, overwhelmed me.

Paul kisses me, and I kiss him back, holding on to his face in my hands. His fingers trail down to the buttons on my lab dress, undoing them slowly, one by one, with the careful precision of a scientist. So by the time his cool hand finally touches my skin, it is hot with wanting.

WE BEGIN TO MEET IN OUR PIED-À-TERRE EVERY DAY THAT WE can get away. Whenever our schedules can allow. In between, we write each other love letters and send them to the apartment, so some afternoons I find myself there even if Paul can't make it, stretching out on the bed in quiet, reading his beautiful words to me.

I love your mind and your body equally, Paul writes, *the delicate curve of your neck is perhaps surpassed only by the elegant prose of your research. That paper you wrote on radium chloride! I want to devour your brilliance.*

"Maybe one day soon," I say to Paul one afternoon in late April as we are lying in bed, still unclothed, my head resting against his bare chest. "We can consider this apartment our home."

He leans down, kisses the top of my head. I feel the edge of his mustache against my forehead and it sends a tingle of warmth through my spine. He has already told me he wants to leave Jeanne, that we can get married soon, but that he needs time to get his affairs in order.

"We will need a bigger place, for all the children," he says now.

"Yes, of course. But the children can all live in our big house in Sceaux. We'll need a place closer to work, too. Just for us. For this."

"And a summer home in L'Arcouëst."

"L'Arcouëst? Where's that?" I say, sleepily, wondering if I

have time to take just a short nap here before walking back to the lab.

"In the cliffs, near Brittany. I wrote to you about it in my letter last week, remember? It's where half the department is going for holiday this summer."

I sit up, shake my head. I haven't received a letter from him in weeks, and in fact I had been beginning to think that he was tiring of writing love letters to me. "You didn't send me a letter last week," I say.

"I did," Paul insists. "I gave it to a house servant to mail and . . ." His voice trails off, and my skin grows prickly at the thought that Jeanne intercepted it. She has grown cold with me as of late. At a recent dinner at the Perrins' on boulevard Kellerman, we'd both been in attendance, but she had sat on the other side of the table, refusing to meet my eyes. But I had brushed it off as a manifestation of my own guilt. Perhaps the letter just got lost in the mail.

"Well," I finally say with a forced brightness I no longer feel. Outside it has begun to rain, and the window is wet, foggy, the street down below gray and blurry. "Your letter will turn up eventually, I suppose."

THREE DAYS LATER I AM LEAVING MY LAB SO LATE, I WALK outside into the moonlit darkness, and when someone is standing there, unexpectedly right outside the door, it scares me half to death and I let out a small scream. "Marie." My name in Jeanne's voice sounds sour.

"Jeanne! You scared me." I try and regain my composure, remembering we are still supposedly friends, but my hands are shaking. "It's so late. Is everything all right?"

She doesn't say anything at first. I make out her features in the glow of the streetlamp and they are calm and still. She reaches into her bag, then hands me an envelope. *Paul's letter.*

I swallow hard. "What's this?" I feign surprise, shake my head. *How bad is it?* He said he wrote about L'Arcouëst. But perhaps it was in general terms, talking about all the department going there together the way two friends, two colleagues, might correspond. Except I've read his other letters, and I know, this letter is bad.

"You must think I'm stupid," she finally says. Her tone is measured, her words matter-of-fact.

"Of course I don't think that, Jeanne," I say quietly.

"Maybe I am not a scientist like you and Paul. But you think I cannot understand what you are doing?"

I shake my head, as if to say there is nothing going on, nothing at all. But I think of what he wrote me once in another letter, about the curves of my body, about the way they excite something in him, a fire. A light. *Did you ever notice,* he wrote, *the way radiant and radium share a root word?* I close my eyes now, exhale once slowly.

"You are going to leave France," Jeanne says calmly.

I open my eyes. "What?" I laugh a little. "Why would I ever leave? France is my home now. My daughters are French. My work is right here."

"You are going to leave France, or I'm going to kill you," Jeanne says. Her voice is so calm, so quiet, her demeanor so still now, that her words wash over me with a slow and chilling clarity. Then, just like that, she walks away.

ONCE, I TOLD PIERRE THAT I WAS MARKED BY DEATH. MY ENtire life, it has hovered and held on to me. Whenever I believe I am well and life is good, there it comes again: my mother and my sister, my baby, my husband, my dear, sweet father-in-law. But I have not before ever been *threatened* so directly, considered my own fleeting mortality. I have never believed that my own life might be in danger before the very moment Jeanne Langevin stands before me outside my lab in the darkness, clutching Paul's letter.

After she leaves, I find it very hard to breathe. I wonder, for a fleeting moment, if I imagined the whole encounter. But I am still holding on to Paul's letter—the evidence is right here, in my very shaking hands. *You are going to leave France, or I'm going to kill you.* Jeanne said those very words to me.

What would happen to my work, my lab, if I were to die? And the children? They've lost their father and recently lost their *grand-père.* What would happen if they lost me too?

And then I don't know what to do. I can't just go home to Sceaux, forget this happened, can I? I can't go to the gendarmerie. I don't even know what I could possibly say. *This man I'm in love with ... his wife threatened to kill me. Can you help me?* Oh, how the press would love that if it got out.

I check Pierre's pocket watch, running my fingers over the smooth surfaces.

What am I supposed to do now, Pierre?

The watch ticks on in my palm, unknowing, uncaring. It is half past eleven, and despite the late hour I find myself walking toward boulevard Kellerman. The familiarity of my old neighborhood courses through me, filling me with regret, longing. Once, in what feels like another lifetime, Pierre and I sipped coffee in our garden here with the Perrins and the Langevins. Jeanne and I were friends; we talked about the children. She brought me lemons from her own garden.

You took her husband, mon amour, I hear Pierre's voice in my head. *What do you expect?*

But their marriage is already over. She doesn't even love him anymore. And he loves me!

I find myself standing on the Perrins' doorstep. Jean and his wife still live on boulevard Kellerman, and he remains a close friend to both me and to Paul and Jeanne. I put Pierre's pocket watch back in my pocket. It does me no good to wallow in a pretend conversation with a dead man. Instead, I ring the Perrins' bell.

Jean answers the door in his dressing grown, looking alarmed. And it is not until he says, "Marie, you're crying," that I realize I am. That my face is wet with tears.

"I can't die," I say to him. "I don't want to die."

"Calm down," he says to me gently, ushering me inside his house. "No one is about to die."

JEAN SPEAKS TO JEANNE AND HE NEGOTIATES AN AGREEMENT with her. She will leave me alone if I stay away from Paul. We will not speak, or write letters, or even work together in a professional capacity.

I agree, and so does he, and yet, for weeks, I go to our pied-à-terre and wait for him each afternoon during our lunch hour anyway. But he keeps his end of the bargain; he does not come to me, and I lie on the bed waiting for him, feeling cold and lost and empty.

Summer comes, and we leave the city for vacation. We go to L'Arcouëst after all, and Hela comes with Hanna and meets us there. I ache for Paul, and I write him a very long, very detailed letter and send it to our apartment. This agreement we have made is absurd, I tell him, and it must be temporary until we can figure out a better plan, a way to be together.

I don't know, he writes back, a week later. *I am too busy with work now for a detailed response. I will write more soon when I can.*

It is short and terse, but it is a response, and it is telling in and of itself. If he has received my letter, read my letter, he must've gone to our pied-à-terre in my absence. He is thinking of me, loving me still, wanting us to be together. And he is in the lab, working, not on vacation with Jeanne. When I return to Paris in the fall, we will find a way.

"What are you smiling about?" Hela asks, walking into the house, her cheeks aglow from spending the morning with Hanna and Irène and Ève by the water. In all these years, she has almost gotten over her fear of it, though I still have not seen her go in farther than her ankles.

"I'm working on writing up my findings on achieving radium in a metallic state," I answer her. Which I truly had been doing before Paul's letter arrived.

"Hmmm," she says. "Working, working, always busy working. Why don't you join us at the beach this afternoon? Your daughters tell me they hardly ever see you."

Hardly ever see me? But I am charting their growths in my notebooks in spectacular detail as I have done since they were born. Irène's body has begun to develop this summer, and Ève has grown two inches, started lessons in maths and sciences at my insistence, piano at hers. I tell Hela this now, and she laughs. "I'm not talking about their growth and development," she says. "They just want to spend time with you, enjoy your company," she says. "Come, sit by the water with us."

I don't understand the point of going to sit with them simply for the sake of sitting there, when I have ideas rolling through my mind I must jot down. "I can see the water from here." I point to the wide picture window behind me. "I need to get some more work done before dinner."

Hela frowns and puts her hand on my shoulder. "You work so much," she says, "and one day you will blink and your girls will be grown. And you will wonder how you missed it all."

But I tell Hela she is being silly; the girls have her and their Polish governess with them on the beach. They don't need me outside with them too. And besides, I'll see everyone later, at dinner.

MARYA

Krakow, 1910

Klara made it into the Chernikoff Institute of Music on her first try, and at only seven years old, she became their youngest female student ever. It was a rigorous course of study on piano—four to six hours of playing and piano studies daily, except for Sundays. And I worried it would be too much for my sweet young child. But Klara insisted that it was what she wanted, what she loved more than anything, *anything* in the whole entire world. And so Kaz agreed that the hefty tuition was worth it, and I agreed that she could give up her primary maths and sciences lessons, as long as she would allow me to continue to teach her those subjects at home at night.

"Do you really think we should let her do this?" I worried to Kaz in a whisper in our bed, the night before she was to begin her studies in the program in November. It was much warmer, more temperate in Krakow than it was in Loksow, but in only two years living here, I had adjusted to the climate so that now I was chilly during the mild falls and winters, and I needed an extra blanket even on temperate nights like tonight.

"Can you imagine?" Kaz whispered into my hair. "If your parents had the resources to help you reach your dreams?" His parents had; they had chosen not to after we got married. He had gotten here with his own hard work and determination. And if Papa had the money to send me to Paris right after I'd finished at the girls' gymnasium, I never would've become a governess, never would've met Kaz.

I reminded him of that now, and he pulled the blanket tighter around us, pulled me closer to him. "I don't know," he said. "I believe I still would've met you somewhere, somehow, *kochanie*."

And even after he fell asleep, after I heard him snoring softly next to me, I wondered if that was true. If no matter what choices we made, what we had and what we were given and what we took for ourselves or not, if there were certain people in our lives who we would find our way to, no matter what.

I COMPLETED MY FIRST TWO UNIVERSITY COURSES WITH PER-fect marks, scoring the highest of anyone in my classes on my exams in both chemistry and physics. But the remainder of the money from the sale of my bicycle went to Klara's Chernikoff tuition. And I didn't return in the fall.

Professor Mazur noticed my absence, and I was both astounded and pleased to find her knocking on my front door one morning, the week after Klara began at her new school. She was a small woman, smaller than me, and she wore her dark black hair in a bun so tight it almost appeared to raise the lines of her face into a permanent state of questioning.

"Marya," she said, when I answered the door. "Are you ill?"

"Ill? No. I am perfectly well, professor."

"Then why aren't you in school this term?" I was surprised she'd noticed, that she had come here looking for an explanation. But I had been the only woman in her chemistry course last term. The best performing and oldest student, too.

I invited her in. Offered her a coffee, which she declined, and then I sat with her in my parlor, and I explained to her about Klara's new piano school, both the expense and the time I would need to devote to teaching Klara other subjects in the evenings. And how I would no longer have the money nor time for my own studies this term.

She frowned. "But you showed so much promise, Marya. You can be a mother and a scientist. I promise you, you can. I am. I have two girls."

She said it like it was so easy, and that perhaps I was crazy for thinking that it wasn't. But I assumed, with her full teaching schedule, her time in the lab, either her girls were older than Klara or she was paying someone else to look after them. I had neither the money nor desire for that. Klara was my heart and my breath, and as much as I loved learning and science, I would always love Klara more. I did not want to pay someone else to raise her; not that I could afford it either.

But I smiled at her, genuinely flattered by her attention. "I hope to come back next fall, professor. Perhaps I could save up and manage by then."

She frowned again, looked down at her shiny black boots. I had the feeling she was not used to people saying no to her, and I felt bad that I was. Because truly, I wanted to continue at the university. Nothing made me feel happier and more content than when I was learning, studying, working. Nothing except for Klara.

She looked up again. "What if we could work out an arrangement? I need an assistant in my lab, but I do not have a stipend to pay for one. You could work in my lab for free, and I could ask the university to enroll you in classes as payment."

I opened my mouth to speak, but then didn't know what to say. No one had insisted upon my education like this, not since Bronia and Papa pushed me to go to Paris the summer I married Kaz instead. But that was so long ago now, it felt like a cloud in my head, hazy and blurry and ephemeral. A feeling more than a memory.

A new but familiar wanting bubbled up inside of me. The laboratory I'd always dreamed of being a part of now sat right here in Krakow, close enough to touch.

"Think it over. Discuss it with your husband," she said. She stood and patted me gently on the shoulder. "It would be a shame to let your mind go to waste."

And then as quick as she'd come into my house, she was gone.

PROFESSOR MAZUR'S LAB WAS WORKING TO STUDY COMBUS-tion and detonation theory, which I found so endlessly fascinating that I spent the rest of the afternoon daydreaming about the extent of the experiments I might be asked to work on as her research assistant. My thoughts still filled with blue-hot flames and fires as I walked to pick Klara up from school and then listened to her practice piano while I prepared dinner in the kitchen.

If I were to discuss this with Kaz, as Professor Mazur suggested, I felt sure he would take a practical tact. How would I have time to take care of Klara and him and the house *and* work in a lab? he might ask. But I could not stop thinking about what Professor Mazur had said: *it would be a shame to waste my mind.*

I sent an urgent telegram to Pierre, asking for his advice. He had spent most of his adult life in a lab, amid both his own recent failures and Hela's and Jacques's successes. I felt sure he would know what I should do.

Pierre responded right away.

Combustion! Marya, you must. Hela and Jacques are here and they agree. Hela says she met Ola Mazur at Solvay last year, and she is brilliant.

(Speaking of brilliant, your sister and my brother are having quite the success with their magnets. Do you find it hard to be the sibling to such brilliance? Or is it just me?)

All the Curies send their love, Pierre.

MARIE

Paris, 1910–1911

At the end of 1910, I put my name into the running for an open spot in the French Academy of Sciences. I do it almost on a whim—a spot has been vacated by a death. But it is not the first time, and it will not be the last time. The Academy is made up of older, dying men.

One of my research assistants says, *Madame Curie, you should try for it. They need someone like you.* Whether he means because I am younger, or the only Nobel Prize winner here, or a woman, he does not say.

He is quite young, still a student, tainted by the naïveté of youth, and perhaps in that moment I am blinded by his naïveté as well. *Why not?* Just like that, I put my name into the running.

And maybe also I am blinded by happiness. A new clarity about my future.

Paul and I have begun meeting at our pied-à-terre again this fall, but only once a week now. A stolen hour out of 168 during my entire week. It is not enough time with him, but it is also what I look forward to most. All week, I write down ideas to share with him, scientific questions to ask him, and when at last we finally see each other I am almost bubbling over with so much to say to him.

Paul is building a case that he can use against Jeanne, documenting the histories of abuse with his lawyer. And Jean Perrin has warned her if she threatens me again, or tries anything unsavory, she will be arrested, her children will be taken away from her. Paul will get everything. Whatever else I know about Jeanne, I also know she loves her children. She stays away from me, and I from her.

It unsettles me still, to think of her, though, to remember that we were friends once. She was very kind to me after Pierre died, bringing food to the house for the children. I cannot reconcile this with the woman who hates me now, with the woman who is keeping me from being with Paul. I try not to think of her at all. And then, when I remember again and again that she is *married* to the man I love, I feel something cold in my chest that makes it hard to breathe for a moment.

But when I am with Paul I think only of him, only about how I love him and he loves me. Once a week, we lie in our bed together in our pied-à-terre, and Paul kisses a trail of whispers down my bare arm. *"Je t'aime, ma lumière rayonnante,"* he says. That is what Paul always calls me: *his radiant light.*

I imagine what it would be like to have him all the time, and not just in our apartment, but in the lab with me, day in and day out.

"Bientôt," he promises me, when I tell him this. *Soon.*

I hold on to that word, a promise, and after our hour is up, I go back to the lab, my mind fresh and open with a new sort of clarity, a new and burning desire to work harder.

IT IS FOOLISH TO BELIEVE THAT I WILL BE ELECTED INTO THE Academy because my work is deserving of it. In the beginning of January, just before the vote, the papers begin to print the most terrible things about me. Lies about how I have accomplished nothing since Pierre's death, and how I only won the Nobel because of him to begin with.

"What about in the year after his death, when I established the atomic weight of radium *on my own?*" I say to Paul, wasting our one hour a week with complaints about the terrible press I am getting ahead of this vote.

He kisses my face, and I know he wants me to stop talking, to undress instead, but it is so hard to love someone for only an hour a week. It is hard to love someone and not be able to share your thoughts and your hopes and your dreams and your worries. I keep them inside of me all week long, and now that he is here, so close, it all comes pouring out of me. I can't help myself.

"They are all old men," Paul says. "They're worried about a woman who is smarter than them, upsetting their old ways of thinking. Ignore what's being said in the press. They're just trying to force you to drop out. Stay strong, and keep on with your brilliant work."

"Do you think it will really come down to my work?" I am skeptical now. I wish I'd never put my name in to begin with. It is hard to see so many negative and untrue things being printed about me in the papers now and hard to only have Paul to reassure me for just this one single hour.

"Marie," Paul says my name softly, kisses my other cheek. "We don't have much time. Come to bed."

In January of 1911, they take the vote, and I don't win the spot in the Academy. A man, with half the qualifications and more than twenty years my senior, is elected instead. It is not necessarily surprising, though I feel more disappointed than I would expect. My whole life I've been told no simply because I'm a woman. It was foolish to believe this time would be different.

Still, the next day I am back at it again in my lab. I will work even harder. Prove them all wrong, as I always have.

I am still trying to establish the decay of polonium and also planning for my new, bigger laboratory that the university has agreed to build. I am still working to achieve the international standard for radium, and we are so very close that I can almost taste the success of it.

I will show those men; I will show everyone.

Easter weekend, Paul manages to get away on Saturday afternoon, and I take the train to meet him at our apartment. I get there, and I find the door ajar. It is unlike Paul to forget to shut it, and I push it open a bit, alarmed. "Paul," I call out. "Paul?"

But the inside of the apartment is quiet, the drawer where we keep all our letters to each other in the living room wide open and shockingly empty. "Hello?" I call out into the apartment, my heart pounding wildly, but no one answers back. I walk through and the rooms are empty.

Paul opens the door a few moments later, walks in, takes one look at me and says, "What's wrong, *ma lumière rayonnante?*"

"The letters," I say. "Someone must've broken in and . . . stole all our letters."

Paul's face instantly becomes bloodless, and he hangs his head down between his knees as if he might vomit, or faint. I go to him, rub his back gently, until he stands up again. I put my hand to his face, trail my finger softly across the swirl of his mustache, his lips.

He leans down and kisses me gently. "I have to go," he says softly.

"But, Paul, you just got here."

"I'm sorry," he says. "Marie, I'm so, so sorry."

"SHE WANTS MONEY," PAUL SAYS TO ME THE FOLLOWING WEEK. He has come to my lab during lunch hour, and my research assistants stare at him now, curious. They haven't seen him in months, since Jeanne threatened me, and we agreed, through Jean Perrin, not to see each other. I take his hand and lead him outside to the street. The midday sun is hot, blinding, and I shield my eyes.

"How much?" I ask.

"Five thousand francs," he says, lowering his voice, looking at his feet.

I remember once how I had offered to help Jeanne if she needed money, but not like this. "And if I pay her . . . then she will let you end the marriage?" I ask.

He looks up at me, his eyes wide, and he shakes his head. "Then she will not release our letters to the press," he says softly.

The press. They've finally stopped printing lies about me now that the Academy vote has passed and I've lost the spot. I remember the poetry of Paul's words about my body in his letters. I shiver, even in the heat of the sun.

"They already tried to crucify you, a woman, daring to go up

for a spot in the Academy," Paul is saying now. "Imagine what they would do with these?"

I do not want to imagine. I lean against the wall of my lab, put my head in my hands. "Okay," I say. Five thousand francs is a lot of money, but it will not destroy me. "I'll give her five thousand francs."

"And we cannot meet anymore," he says softly. "I cannot risk what she will do to you now that she has those letters. She could ruin you. And I love you, *ma lumière rayonnante*. I would never forgive myself."

"No." I refuse to accept that. "Not being with you will ruin me. We will keep our distance for now. But I know we will be together, soon. I know it."

"Marie," he says my name so softly and so sadly, like he is singing a funeral song. "Marie, Marie, Marie."

I WAS WRONG. LOVE AND SCIENCE, THEY ARE NOT ONE AND the same. Love has come and gone in my life, permeating me with nothing but sadness in the end. Kazimierz. Pierre. And now Paul.

But science, it is always here. It never leaves me or abandons me or hurts me or stops needing me. My lab calls for me and waits for me. It is my life and my home, and the truest thing I have ever devoted myself to.

Jean Perrin reports that, in spite of my five thousand francs, Jeanne Langevin is still telling everyone on boulevard Kellerman she would like to kill me. "Perhaps you should leave for the summer?" he says gently. "Let her calm down."

"I already paid her to calm down," I say. "With the money I was going to use to rent a house in Brittany again this summer."

But I don't think Jean Perrin is wrong, and Bronia has been after me to bring the girls to Zakopane for the summer. She has room for us. We would only have to pay for the train, and Ève has never even been to Poland. I imagine both of my girls there, happy and carefree, picking berries and riding horses in the pastures and smelling the Polish country air of my youth. And I write Bronia to let her know that we are coming.

THE SUMMER AIR IN ZAKOPANE SMELLS SWEET AND FRA-grant, the city feeling a lifetime away. When we arrive, Bronia and Lou are in the kitchen together eating fresh-picked blackberries. My niece is now nineteen, a full-grown woman, an apparition of the Bronia I knew in Warsaw once long ago. She is more muscular, her cheeks more ruddy, but with Bronia's haunting eyes all the same.

Irène and Ève go to their room to unpack, and I sit down in the kitchen with Bronia and Lou, still unable to rid myself of the fog that hovered in the city—Jeanne's threats, and the ache of missing Paul. On the train I thought of so many things I wanted to share with him about my latest findings on polonium's decay, how excited he would be about my revelation, that the half-life must be much shorter than that of radium. And now I feel a residual emptiness, not being able to tell him.

"Here." Bronia holds her hand out across the table. "Have a blackberry. They are so sweet. I promise, they will fix what ails you."

I frown and shake my head, pushing the fruit away. I'm not hungry.

"You need to forget about him," Bronia says quietly. I've written to Bronia about Paul, but I have not told her about the death threats, or the five thousand francs I gave away. "He is married," she adds, her tone unforgiving, unyielding.

"Jeanne does not love him like I do," I say petulantly. I realize I sound like a child, but I don't care. "Their marriage is all but over."

Bronia frowns and chews on a blackberry. "But she is still his *wife*." Bronia emphasizes the word *wife*, like I do not understand its meaning. "No matter what happens between me and Mier, I would want to destroy any woman who believed she could have him. Who thought she could take him away from me."

Lou pops a blackberry in her mouth and chuckles, perhaps at how serious Bronia sounds, or perhaps at the ridiculousness of Bronia's statement. Bronia, the caretaker, the physician, could never *destroy* anyone.

"You would blackmail someone?" I say to her. "You would threaten to kill someone?"

"Her husband is being unfaithful to her," Bronia says, frowning. "Who is the villain in this story, hmm?" she adds softly.

My cheeks turn hot at the implication that I am *the villain*. Or is she saying that Paul is the villain? I open my mouth to lash out at her. What does she know? Her husband is still alive and working with her. They have their simple and beautiful life here in the mountains. But then I don't say anything at all because maybe she is also right. In another life, one where Pierre had not stepped in front of a horse on a rainy April afternoon, Jeanne might be the one I feel sympathy for now, not Paul. It is a hard thing to admit, even to myself, and I swallow, saying nothing else at all.

"I'm never getting married," Lou announces, standing. Bronia's frown creases deeper. But Lou ignores it, kisses Bronia on the head. "I'm going for a hike," she says, bored with our conversation. I remember what Bronia told me once about Lou and Mier and their fascination with hiking after Jakub died. Now, at nineteen, Lou is nearly a professional, she knows the Carpathians so well. Bronia, however, wishes she'd earn a degree in science instead.

"Take me with you," I implore her, in part because I want to go. I want to forget all about Jeanne and Paul and the fog that had hovered in Paris. But I also know my interest in Lou's hobby will annoy Bronia and will get her mind off my love life.

"You want to know the mountains, *ciotka*?" Lou asks, seeming surprised. "Mama says you are only comfortable inside a laboratory."

"Does she now?" I say, looking back at Bronia. She's still frowning. "Your mother might not remember that I used to ride my bicycle all throughout the French countryside. I am a big believer in the power of fresh air to help the brain and heal the body." And saying it out loud, I remind myself that it is also true.

I lace up my boots and follow Lou to the path. We climb and climb. For a long while there is only the conversation with my sweet niece about the beautiful nature that surrounds us, the fresh Polish summer air in my lungs, the big blue sky above us, my breath heavy in my chest, and the feeling of my heart bursting from exertion.

MARYA

Krakow & Zakopane, 1911

Leokadia came to Krakow to give a concert just before Easter, invited to perform as the special guest of the Krakow Philharmonic Orchestra. Her popularity had risen in Germany and Austria in the past few years, and as a native Pole, she was now highly sought after in Krakow, a city with both Polish and Austrian identities.

Kaz was away in Brussels at a conference, but I bought tickets for me and Klara to attend, and we made plans to have dinner with Leokadia afterward. Klara was so excited she could barely stand it, and she spent the day trying to teach herself to play the music from the Beethoven concerto Leokadia was set to play that night. It was, of course, still much too hard for her, but she wrinkled up her small forehead in concentration and taught herself the beginning portion, at a much slower speed.

"Do you think she remembers me?" Klara asked as we walked to the concert together that afternoon, arm in arm. The late day was warm, balmy. The pink amaryllis had just begun to bloom and they smelled divine. I inhaled, enjoying the contrast to what I smelled so often now in Professor Mazur's small lab as we worked side-by-side with combustibles: smoke and ash, everything burning. It was so hard to get the smell of *burning* out of one's nose, even after I went home for the night to Kaz and to Klara. I breathed deeply now, wanting the scent of amaryllis to stay with me forever. "Do you, Mama?" Klara prodded. "It was a very long time ago that I met her."

Perhaps in Klara's small life, it was a very long time ago. A time, for her, before piano. Before Krakow. I imagined it must be hard for her to even remember that other life of ours, our little apartment in Loksow on Złota Street with our view of the smokestacks. And all the hours and hours she spent with me at my school. "Of course she remembers you, *mój mały kurczak.*" I reached my hand up to smooth a stray hair back into her braid. "And I tell her about you in my letters whenever I write to her. She is very excited about your progress at Chernikoff."

Klara smiled and I relaxed into my half-lie. I had written to Leokadia about Klara attending Chernikoff, but only once. We did not write each other enough letters anymore for either one of us to keep up on anyone's *progress*.

I learned about Leokadia's progress as I read the concert program while we waited for the concert to begin. According to her biographical note, she had sold more records than any Polish woman pianist in history. And she was currently touring, performing with symphonies all across Europe and Asia.

When she walked out on stage, she was stunning, as always. She wore a shiny red dress, her blond curls swept back away from her face in a perfectly sculpted chignon. She sat down to play, and, after hearing Klara practice oh-so-many hours, I understood now just how divine, how precise and passionate Leokadia's piano playing really was.

"She's so famous, Mama," Klara said, her eyes wide, as we walked backstage to meet her for dinner after the concert. "That is going to be me up on that stage one day."

"You desire fame, chicken?" It was a hard thing for me to understand. I had my entire life craved learning, perfection, but I shied away from attention.

She shook her head. "No, Mama. I mean I want to play piano the way she plays. I want to be the best."

I smiled at her and kissed the top of her head. She was my daughter, after all, wasn't she?

Then Leokadia walked out, her face red and glowing, a sheen of perspiration across her petite forehead, and somehow her hair was still wrapped up inside that perfect chignon, not even one strand out of place.

"*Moi kochani!*" she exclaimed when she saw us, wrapping us both up in a hug. She stood back, stooped down a little to be eye to eye with Klara. "Oh, let me look at you, my little pianist friend." Klara beamed from the attention. "You have gotten so tall. So beautiful, just like your mama, huh?"

"Hi, Kadi," I said softly. She stood, smiled slowly at me, wrapped me again in another hug.

"Papa wanted to come," Klara blurted out, God knows why. "But he's at a conference in Brussels." There was no way Kaz would've come here with us, even if he were home.

Kadi averted her gaze and changed the subject by asking Klara what pieces she was studying now at Chernikoff. Then she told us to follow her to her hotel, where she had preordered us a dinner feast.

She was staying at a beautiful brick hotel on the Wisla river, and she had a huge suite there, complete with her own piano and a beautifully displayed fish dinner laid out on a dining table. The magnitude of her success did not quite hit me until that very moment, when we stepped inside her lavish suite. It was one thing to read it in the liner notes, and quite another to see the way she lived, to taste it.

FULL AND HAPPY AND EXHAUSTED, KLARA LAY DOWN ON Leokadia's parlor couch, closed her eyes, and fell asleep after we ate supper. And then Kadi poured two glasses of wine and told me to follow her out to her balcony so we could talk.

"I really should get Klara home," I protested. "It's late." But it was an idle protest. Kadi handed me the wine, and I took it. Klara had a few days off school for the holiday, and Kaz was in Brussels. There was nothing for the two of us to rush home for.

"How have you been, Marya?" she asked me, sipping her wine as she sat in a chair on the balcony. I sat down next to her. "Krakow seems to agree with you."

"Does it?" I said, taking my own sip of wine. It was a dry wine, dryer than I'd been expecting, and I puckered my lips as I swallowed. "I suppose it does. I've been working as a research assistant in a lab at the university. Working on combustion. Each day is explosive. Quite literally." I laughed at my own joke, and Leokadia smiled.

"And you are teaching still, like you were in Loksow?"

I shook my head. "No, but I'm learning so much now. I will teach again one day, and then I'll have more knowledge to give my students."

"Wonderful," she murmured. "Wonderful, wonderful. You were always the smartest one of all us, Marya."

I laughed a little, uneasy, thinking about how *stupid* I'd been when she had betrayed me once, and I had just let it happen, right before my very eyes. How Kaz was drawn to her because of her passion, because of her drive for her career, and how I had given up on that in my own life, once, all to be with him. "Well," I finally said. "Look at you. World-famous pianist."

"Hmmm." She frowned, took another sip of her wine, and stared out across the night sky, the river, and then, the heart of Krakow sparkling in front of us.

"Are you not happy?" I asked her. "You have everything you ever wanted."

"What is happiness, really?" she said. "You can love your work or you can love your family, but it is impossible as a woman to have both, to have it all, isn't it?" I thought about how Professor Mazur promised me you could have both work and family, but I wasn't so sure. As her assistant, I left the lab when it was time to pick Klara up each afternoon, but she would often work through dinner; sometimes, she would tell me, until almost midnight. How did her daughters feel, without their mother at home at night? "I have had great success in my work," Leokadia was saying now. "But it is lonely sometimes. This great big room, it can be very, very lonely."

"Still . . . you have sold more records than any Polish woman in history," I said, repeating what I'd read in the liner notes on the program.

"Any European woman," she corrected me gently. "Not just Poland." Then she grimaced a little. "But record sales cannot hold your hand or kiss you goodnight, can they?"

"No," I said, finishing off the last drop of my wine. "I suppose they can't."

TWO MONTHS LATER, IN THE SUMMER QUIET OF ZAKOPANE, I felt restless. I had the whole summer ahead with Klara and my sisters and my nieces and nephew. But I thought about what

Leokadia had said: that you could have your work, or you could have your family, but you could not have both. I missed the burnt smell of Professor Mazur's lab, missed having my hands and my mind busy with combustion all day long. Kaz had stayed behind in Krakow this summer to work, and so had Professor Mazur— she had sent her own daughters off to Berlin to stay with their grandparents, and she planned to continue in the lab. She'd asked if I'd wanted to stay this summer too, but I had chosen Zakopane, Klara, my family.

I was grateful for the sun-kissed air, and the feel of Klara's warm red skin lying close to me in bed each evening. In the dark we would whisper our favorite parts of our summer days. Mine was always the time I spent with Klara each morning after break- fast, trying to catch her up on her maths and science studies. Hers were the hours she got to swim in the lake with her cousin Jakub. At fifteen now, Jakub was tall, looking startlingly like Papa, and I knew it was good for Klara to play with her cousin in the fresh air, so after the first weeks, when she begged me to skip her maths and science lessons in favor of time outdoors, I acquiesced.

Then I read all the latest research on flame theory that Professor Mazur had given me before I left, the paper Henri Becquerel had published on his findings about *becquerelium* that Pierre had sent to me, somewhat in despair that he himself had not been able to publish it first.

It felt silly but I wished I had a bicycle again; I needed ex- ertion and exhaustion to clear my mind and my heart. When Lou arrived from Paris with Hela, Jacques, Marie, and Pierre, I asked her to take me hiking, thinking perhaps I could climb my way out of this strange empty feeling that had settled in my stomach.

"Aunt Marya." She laughed. "I don't hike anymore. I need to study to get ahead for my courses next term." After falling in love with biology at my school in Loksow, Lou was now studying to become a doctor in Paris. "And I promised Klara and Jakub I would teach them how to dissect the dead frogs they found yesterday," she said.

Bronia smiled, nodded her head approvingly, and I could not argue with the fact that she was about to inject some love of science into Klara's summer, even if it would be taking the shape of dead frogs.

"I will hike with you," Pierre offered. He walked in from the kitchen, where he had been eating breakfast, and I hadn't realized he'd even been listening to our conversation.

"Do you know the Carpathians well?" I asked, skeptical. Yes, my body longed to climb and ache and soar. But I did not want to die in the mountains either.

He pulled out his pocket watch to show me that it also had a compass. "I enjoy exploring, and we won't go too far," he said. "Anyone else want to come?" he offered to Bronia, Hela, Jacques, but no one else took him up on it.

"TELL ME," PIERRE SAID, BREATHING HARD AS WE BEGAN TO climb. We had not gotten too far, but already Bronia's home and sanatorium looked like toys in the distance below us. "Where is your husband this summer?"

"He has too much work to do, back in Krakow," I said. I felt a strange sort of jealousy that, as a man, Kaz could simply stay behind, allow his work the utmost importance in his life and be revered for it. But also, I felt sorry for him. He was missing these beautiful light-filled days with our family, missing watching our daughter swim and play with her cousins, and dissect frogs. And this—Pierre and I reached the top of the peak, and we were both breathing so hard that we had to stop talking, catch our breath, inhale this view. I stood at the edge, looked out at the great lustrous verdant valley below us.

Pierre walked up next to me, looked out, too. "I have felt very lost this past year, Marya," he admitted. "I had a séance to talk to my father again, to ask him what I am supposed to do." Hela had written me when her father-in-law passed away last year, and I know that Pierre now occupied that great big house in Sceaux all by himself. I thought about Leokadia, complaining about large empty lonely rooms. But at least she had her record sales. For Pierre, those empty rooms must only compound the failures he also had felt with his work these past years.

But I didn't know anything about a *séance*, nor did I believe in anything like that. "And was this . . . *séance* successful?" I asked him, humoring him.

Pierre shrugged. "He wants me to marry, to have a child still." I bit my lip. From what I knew of Dr. Curie, he would've made that fairly clear while he was still alive. "I am fifty-two years old." Pierre was still talking. "I have become an old man. But how can that be? I still feel like a young man. And I don't know that I will ever find my place in this world. Perhaps it is too late for me."

He had climbed this mountain with a fierceness I'd had trouble keeping up with. His beard was grayer than it once was perhaps, but nothing about him seemed *old*. He was vibrant, brimming with vigor.

"It is not too late for you," I reassured him. "It is only too late when you are dead. And you're standing here with me, very much alive, Pierre."

He reached out his hand for mine. I took it, held on to him. His skin was warm; his grip firm. And we stood there for just a little while before we turned to climb back down, holding on to each other, feeling, both of us, on top of the world.

Marie

⚜

Brussels & Paris, 1911

I have not seen Paul in months when I leave for Brussels for the Solvay Conference in the beginning of November. I am quite excited about the conference: physicists from all around Europe will convene and present our latest work. But Paul and Jean and I are to ride the train together, and as I get onto the train, I feel a nervous sort of anticipation building in my stomach at the thought of being close to Paul again.

Paul wrote me exactly one letter this summer when I was in Poland visiting Bronia. He and Jeanne had a terrible fight. She threw a plate at his head, and he left early with their two oldest boys for a vacation in Brittany. Then, she tried to file an abandonment claim, despite the fact he had planned the trip with the boys for months in advance.

Now, when I first see him again as he boards the train to Brussels after me, I notice how tired he looks. How he seems to have aged years since last spring when he begged me for five thousand francs in the street in front of my lab. I put my hand to my cheek, wondering if the same has happened to me.

I stare at him, but he turns away, refusing to meet my eyes, and he sits as far away from me as he can, at the back of the train.

I keep glancing up from my reading on the journey to see what he is doing, but never once does he look up, toward me. Jean Perrin has taken the seat next to me, and he's chattering away about what he believes to be the highlights of the upcoming conference—he is quite looking forward to talking with Albert Einstein, whose recent paper on quantum theory he found quite exciting. And he continues talking even as we all arrive at the hotel together and check into our separate rooms, while Paul and I say nothing.

It is only once I am in my own room, alone, in the quiet, that I close my eyes, lean against the door and allow myself a few tears. Paul and I are here, so close, and I want nothing more than to talk to him, to touch him. To hold on to him again.

There is a gentle knock on my door; I feel the vibration of it against my back, and I jump. I open the door slowly, and there Paul stands on the other side, his face reflecting the same sadness, the same longing, that I feel.

He walks into my room, quickly shuts the door behind him. And we are holding on to each other so fast, so tightly. I cling to the familiar feel of his tall body, the clover smell of his pipe on his neck. "*Ma lumière rayonnante*," he whispers into my hair. "I have missed you so."

We go to my bed, and we lie down together. But we keep our clothes on. We simply lie there, holding on to each other, staring at each other, whispering about our work, about the life we still long to have together. Next week it is my birthday—I will turn forty-four, and he says by the time I am forty-five we will figure out a way to have our future.

He promises me, kissing my face.

THE WEEK IN BRUSSELS IS GLORIOUS. PAUL AND I TALK ABOUT physics with our peers during the days and spend our nights inside my room together. There is nothing but science, no one else but us.

Paul stays an extra two days in Brussels for another meeting, and the morning Jean and I are to take the train back, Paul kisses me softly on the lips, one last kiss before I go.

"I don't want to leave you," I say, clinging to him. "Can't we just stay here like this forever?"

"I promise you," he says. "*Bientôt.*"

But *soon* is an intangible promise, and I already feel it—the happiness we found together this week is a bubble. Delicate and ephemeral and about to burst.

I hold on to him for just another moment, then take my valise and walk to the door. Before leaving, I turn back again, look at him one last time, my stomach feeling uneasy. I'm not sure now if the ache I'm feeling is desire or dread. Or hope.

WHEN JEAN AND I ARRIVE BACK IN PARIS, WE ARE GREETED BY a strange storm of press at the train station. They are shouting at me as we step off the train: "Madame Curie! Madame Curie!"

"No one cares this much about Solvay," Jean says to me, puzzled.

"Madame Curie!" they shout. "When did the love affair begin? Is it true, you and Monsieur Langevin tried to run away together?"

At the sound of Paul's name I grow suddenly cold and then

begin to sweat. "What is going on?" I whisper to Jean, who shrugs in confusion.

We keep on walking, pushing our way through the crowd without saying a word to the press. I push forward, my heart thrumming too fast in my chest. My stomachache deepens. And then I see it: a stack of papers on the newsstand outside the station. I am the front-page headline. *We* are the front-page headline, Paul and I.

A Story of Love: Madame Curie and Professor Langevin.

And then another: *A Romance in a Laboratory: The Affair of Mme. Curie and M. Langevin.*

I buy copies to read before Jean manages to get us in a carriage. And inside, once I am sitting, the shouting of the press muted, I read through the articles, my hands shaking. Not only has Jeanne told the papers about me and Paul, but she has shown them all our letters. And then she lied and said we had both run off together this past week, our whereabouts *unknown*.

I can't believe it. We had an agreement. I gave her five thousand francs. Then I think guiltily of the way I left Paul, just this morning, in Brussels with a kiss. But Jeanne had no way of knowing that. And we had been there to attend a conference with our peers; we were not running away together.

I throw the papers down, my hands shaking. Jean picks them up and reads for himself; his face turns bloodless.

"The entire department knows we were at Solvay for the conference," I say. But my stomach clenches, and suddenly I know I am going to be sick. "Stop the carriage," I say. The driver doesn't listen. "Stop the carriage," I yell.

We come to a sudden halt. I throw open the door, step out, and vomit right there. The little bit of breakfast I'd eaten in Brussels with Paul swims liquefied and putrid in the street.

"We'll set the press straight," Jean says quietly, when I get back inside the carriage. "And everything will be fine."

BUT IT IS NOT FINE. I DO NOT KNOW IF IT WILL EVER BE FINE again.

The press gather around my house in Sceaux, an angry mob demanding answers at all hours of the day and night. I try to ignore them; they throw stones at my windows. But I refuse to go out there, and we become trapped in our home like prisoners. I cannot leave; I cannot go to work.

I type up a statement and mail it to the papers, explaining about the conference in Solvay, and how we were there with twenty other physicists who can account for both our whereabouts. But no one seems to care about that part. They continue to print terrible story after terrible story, crucifying me for carrying on an affair with a married man, for *ruining* Jeanne's life and the lives of her children.

I think of what Bronia said to me last summer, *Who is the villain?* All of France believes it to be me. I love Paul, and he is still technically married to Jeanne. But their marriage was over long before Paul and I got together. It's not Jeanne's life that is being ruined now, it's mine. Every day, the papers print worse and worse things about me:

She is not really a scientist at all.

She clings to her dead husband's fame, having done nothing in her own right.

She is a hack and homewrecker.

She was already rejected from the Academy, and rightly so. They will never accept her now!

And what is it that they are really saying? Because I am woman who desires to be loved, I cannot also be a respected scientist? As a woman, you cannot win. You cannot have it all. The press will simply not allow it. And what of Paul? There is no mention of his scientific career being over in any paper.

I throw all the papers in the fire, lies upon lies upon lies. And I stand there watching the flames grow higher and higher, watching the lies burn hot and blue and orange.

A FEW DAYS LATER, AN UNEXPECTED TELEGRAM COMES FOR ME.

Irène is huddled in the corner of the parlor, reading the latest papers, in tears. Ève plays a song on her piano, indifferent, or uncaring, or simply too young still to understand—it is hard to tell which. My stomach aches and aches; I have barely been able to keep down a thing since returning from Brussels.

"Madame Curie." The house servant brings me the telegram, her own face drawn, her hands shaking, as if she thinks I might blame her for whatever terrible news it must contain.

But none of this is her fault. I thank her and take the telegram, and then I notice it has come from *Sweden*. Suddenly a memory hits me like a punch and I inhale sharply: Pierre running into our lab once, so many years ago, when I was drowning in loss and sorrow and grief over my dead baby, my dead nephew. *A telegram from Sweden, mon amour! They are giving us half of the Nobel Prize for our work on radium. You and I. Half the Nobel Prize!*

Pierre is so far away from me now, it is hard to remember the sound of his voice, or the feel of his hands, but all at once, my senses flood with him, and I cannot breathe.

Here it is again, right in front of me, typed across the telegram from Sweden. I am being awarded the 1911 Nobel Prize. In Chemistry this time, to recognize the advancements I have made *by discovering radium and polonium, the isolation of radium, and the study of the nature and the compounds of this remarkable element.*

I read the words, and then I read them again, disbelieving them, my eyes stinging with tears. I want to run and tell Pierre. *Look, look what we have done, my love!* But I can't even leave my house, much less go to his grave now. Not with all the reporters outside. And it's not as if it matters anyway. Pierre is dead.

Then, I long for Paul, but he has returned from Brussels and is hiding out somewhere in France—Jean Perrin has not told me where, and even if I were to know, it would be impossible to go to him without making everything worse.

"What is it, Maman?" Irène stands close to me, her worried eyes peering over my shoulder, trying to make sense of what news I've just received.

I turn to look at my eldest daughter. She is tall and slender and serious, more a woman now than a girl. The intensity of her eyes reminds me of her father's. But she is not him, and she is not Paul. She is an apparition of my younger self. And just like me, she has a propensity for science. I hand her the telegram, let her read the news for herself.

"Another Nobel! Maman, this is wonderful." Her face alights with joy, and it is strange how just moments ago she had been crying. It is strange how life has a way of being terrible and wonderful all at once.

I RECEIVE A SECOND TELEGRAM FROM SWEDEN A WEEK LATER, this one asking me not to come to Stockholm for the ceremony in December to accept my prize. Jeanne has now given all our letters to the press and copies of them run in the papers for all of France to read. It seems everyone in the country, all of Europe maybe, knows every detail of mine and Paul's innermost thoughts. And no one even seems to care or notice that I am being awarded a second Nobel Prize. I am not simply the only woman to achieve this honor now, but the only one to do it *twice*.

But the Swedish Academy writes that they are worried about all this embarrassing press. Their concern is that it might follow me all the way to Sweden, distract from the ceremonies. *We think it might be better if you don't attend,* they write.

Better for whom?

I write back and tell them that my personal life has nothing to do with my scientific endeavors. They have awarded me a prize, a prize that I deserve for my work, and I plan to come to Stockholm to accept it.

"Do you think they will be angry with you?" Irène asks, when I show her the telegram exchange. Within the space of two weeks trapped inside our house, in hiding from the press, isolated from my lab and the world, and Paul, Irène has become more than my daughter. Now she is also my confidante.

"I am a woman, Irène," I tell her. "And I have now won two Nobels, two more than almost any man scientist ever receives in the course of his career. And you see what they're doing to me in the papers now, don't you? They will continue to viciously attack me. They will do anything, *anything* they can to bring me down. To try and ruin me. I cannot worry about people being angry with me. I deserve this prize."

Irène bites her lip, trying not to cry, but we are not going to be sad about people trying to ruin me. We are going to choose to be happy about what I have accomplished. We are going to celebrate my accomplishment.

"No tears," I say to her, more gently. "Go pack your things. I'm taking you to Sweden with me. Aunt Bronia will meet us there and you can both watch me accept my Nobel Prize."

MARYA

❦

Krakow & Stockholm, 1911

In November, I received the most wonderful news in a letter from Hela. She and Jacques had been awarded the Nobel Prize in chemistry for their work with elemental magnetism. They would accept the prize in Stockholm in December, and she invited me and Bronia both to come to Sweden and watch her, wanting us to attend so badly that she sent money for our train tickets along with her letters.

I was thrilled for her, but I felt something else too. It was a little bit of jealousy, or, maybe it was wanting. What if I had been the one to go to Paris all those many years ago, instead? Could I have accomplished all that Hela had by now? And if I had, would I feel happier, be more fulfilled? I loved my life with Klara, working in Professor Mazur's lab, but could there have been more for me?

I told Professor Mazur about Hela and Jacques's prize, the day after I received her letter. We were in the lab, working on trying to condense hydrogen to liquid in a vacuum flask. Professor Mazur had recently gotten the funds from the university to acquire the materials in Brussels when she'd gone to the Solvay Conference there, a few weeks earlier.

"Marya," Professor Mazur said my name sharply, instructing me to hold on to the flask just the way she'd showed me earlier to keep it still for her now. We wore masks today, in addition to our glasses, so her voice came through more muffled than usual. And we had rid the lab of any fire today, as liquefied hydrogen, should we succeed in our task, was highly flammable.

I followed her instructions, precisely, as always, then helped her seal the flask. She put it into the cooling chamber we'd constructed last week, and then removed her mask, wiping at the sweat on her brow with the back of her arm. That's when I told her about Hela.

"The Nobel?" Professor Mazur said, her voice thick with disbelief. But then she smiled warmly. "How wonderful for Hela. She was so kind when I saw her at Solvay. Especially when I told her what a great help you are to me in the lab. It is so very rare for someone to be both kind and brilliant. It must run in your family."

I felt my face reddening a bit at the unusual compliment. Professor Mazur was intense, always focused on the work, with little time for chatter or compliments. "Hela really wants me to go to Stockholm next month, but it will be too hard to get away from Klara. And from the lab," I added. After the long summer away, we had settled into our routine again: Klara at school, me working in lab, Kaz teaching his fall courses. I devoted all my time out of the lab to Klara, helping her with her studies, listening to her piano music.

"Marya Zorawska! Your sister is going to be the first woman to receive the Nobel. I command you to go to Stockholm and report back every detail to me when you return. I want to know all of it. In case I should ever win someday." She chuckled a little, but I doubted she was kidding. "And my governess can help you out with Klara for a few weeks," she offered. "So there, now you have no excuses."

Later that night I talked to Klara about it, asked her if she would mind being looked after by Professor Mazur's governess while I was gone. Her eyes lit up, repeating what I'd told her back very slowly. "Aunt Hela has won the biggest scientific prize in the world. The first woman?"

I nodded and bit my lip a little. I was so deeply proud of my sister-twin. But I couldn't help but think of what Pierre had written to me once, about how it was hard to be the sibling to brilliance. I was so deeply proud. But I was still that something else too. The feeling sank in my stomach, aching just a little.

"Mama, you have to go," Klara insisted. "I'm almost eight. I can take care of myself."

I smiled and leaned over to kiss her forehead. "I know you can, *mój mały kurczak.*"

THE TRAIN RIDES TO STOCKHOLM WERE VERY LONG, AND after nearly twenty-four hours alone in a cold and bumpy train car, I wondered whether going all alone to Sweden, leaving Klara and my life in the beginning of winter, had been a mistake. But then I finally made it, and Hela hugged me so tightly. Her face glowed pink; I had never seen her so beautiful, so happy.

Hela and Jacques had splurged for the occasion—the Nobel came with a handsome amount of prize money—and got us lovely large hotel rooms. Bronia and I shared a room, and Pierre stayed next to us in his own room. It felt very strange, all of us here without our children, without our adult responsibilities. We went out to eat dinner and stayed out very late, talking and talking and drinking brännvin.

Bronia and Jacques got into a heated discussion about the potential uses of his and Hela's magnets in the field of medicine—Jacques believing they could be helpful, Bronia arguing they could not be. She told Jacques he should stick to the lab and let her understand medicine. Hela tried to mediate, posing her own arguments on both sides. And me? I just sipped my brännvin slowly, careful not to have too much. Pierre caught my eye across the table, shrugged a little, smiled at me, and raised his glass in my direction. "Do you want to go back?" he mouthed to me.

I nodded, and we excused ourselves. Bronia and Hela and Jacques were still arguing back and forth and barely seemed to notice us.

"Tell me about your work with combustion," Pierre said as we walked slowly back toward the hotel. The night air was crisp, quite chilly. I shivered a little. "Are you warm enough? Would you like my coat?" Pierre asked.

"I'm fine," I lied, not wanting to take his coat. I had this strange feeling if I put it on, if I wrapped myself up in the warmth and the smell and the feel of him, I would never be able to take it off.

Hela had asked about my combustion work at dinner, but just as I'd begun to speak about it, Bronia had interrupted with a question for Jacques about his speech tomorrow. "There's not too much to tell," I said to Pierre now. "It is Ola Mazur's work, really. I'm helping her. We're trying to liquefy gas right now, to see how it works as a detonator."

"That sounds . . . dangerous," Pierre said.

I shrugged. "We take all the proper precautions. Neither of us has exploded yet." I was making a joke, but Pierre didn't laugh. I was used to the fires and smoke and the explosions in the lab now. It didn't feel dangerous. It simply felt like my job. "What have you been working on Pierre?"

"Becquerelium," he said with a sigh. Then he added, "Sort of." I slowed down my pace and turned to look at him, wanting to know more. "I think there's a second element with radioactive properties in the pitchblende. My readings can't be explained by becquerelium alone. I believe there is another element with an entirely different chemical composition, too."

"That's fascinating," I said.

"Yes." He rubbed his beard. "But I haven't the space in the lab or the strength as one man to try to chemically wash the ore on my own."

"Perhaps you could publish a paper explaining your theory?" I suggested.

He laughed, bitterly. "Yes, I have tried that. The French Academy refuses to publish it without results or the backing of an established scientist. And Jacques is busy with his own work."

"Well, you can't give up," I implored him. "You will find a way."

"Perhaps," he said, his voice trailing off, as if he didn't believe me. "Perhaps."

THE NEXT MORNING, A FEW HOURS BEFORE JACQUES AND Hela were to present their acceptance speech, Pierre knocked on our door and asked if we would like to take a walk, explore the city with him.

"Go ahead," Bronia implored me. "I'm feeling tired. I'm going to rest a bit, and I'll meet you both at the ceremony later." She'd come in late last night, and I wondered just how much brännvin she'd allowed herself so far away from her husband, children, home, and patients.

I was wearing my nicest dress, a blue chiffon that had been made just for me in Paris many years earlier for Hela's wedding. And I had been overjoyed to find it still fit before I left. It was a little tight around the middle, not the most comfortable for walking around, exploring a city, but I took a breath, kissed Bronia goodbye, and left to walk with Pierre.

We walked slowly, not saying much of anything at first, as we had already exhausted our talk of work the night before. We took in the sights and sounds and smells of this new and beautiful city. All around us there was the bluest water and quaintest red roofs, and now that we were here today, walking in the daylight, it felt strangely like we were on a holiday. Together.

We walked along the river path in the beautiful, flowering Djurgården, and I wondered out loud about the various species of flowers, different than the ones I knew so well, native to Poland.

"I have been thinking so much of you, Marya," Pierre said suddenly, out of nowhere. "Ever since I returned to Paris, I have been greatly missing our hikes." He had written that to me in a recent letter, too.

"Yes," I agreed now. "The Carpathians were so beautiful last summer, weren't they?"

"The mountains, yes," he said. "But I mean I've been missing this. Your company. Our talks."

We had talked about everything on our hikes, science and family and love and loss. About getting older and failing and happiness. And the truth was, I missed our talks too. Back in Krakow I talked to Klara and to Professor Mazur. Kaz and I gave each other an obligatory peck on the lips in the mornings, and exchanged quick pleasantries, but I was focused on Klara, and then my work in the lab. He had his own work, and in the evenings, we were both much too tired to truly talk as we once had when we were younger.

"Look," Pierre said, tugging gently on my hand. "Look across the water, Marya. Swans."

I did as he asked, and there they were, swimming toward us, an entire splendid family of swans in tandem, their beautiful white long necks bobbing across the water.

The male and female pecked each other playfully, and then Pierre took my other hand, pulled me close enough to him that I could feel his chest against mine, his breath against my face. "Marya," he said my name, his voice raspier than usual.

I had the strangest feeling that he wanted to kiss me, and that if I let him, if I kissed him back, everything would change.

"I can't," I whispered, our faces close enough that my breath became his breath, my words became his words. I felt the frown that stretched across his face in my own self, a heaviness that coursed through my entire body, all the way down to my toes.

"What if you and I were destined to be together?" he said softly.

It sounded so logical in his quiet voice. But I did not believe in destiny. I believed in science, in making our own choices. And if I kissed him now, if I let myself get even an inch closer to him, I would be making a choice I could never take back, the way Kaz had, many years ago.

I pulled away from him, took a step back. "I almost moved to Paris once," I said. "But then I got married instead. And now I have a life in Krakow, a beautiful daughter."

"And what if we had met in Paris, so many years ago? Everything might have been different," he said quietly.

We stood there for a little while longer, staring at the water, watching the swans, not touching, not saying anything else at all. And perhaps we were both imagining it, what could've happened, what might've happened, if once, so many years earlier, I had stepped on that train.

BACK IN KRAKOW, I THOUGHT ABOUT THAT MOMENT IN THE Djurgården with Pierre a lot. At night, when Kaz was working late in his lab and I was lying all alone in bed in the darkness, I reimagined it over and over again. I moved in just a little closer, put my lips on his. Felt the thrilling scratch of his beard against my chin. I held on to him, inhaled him. He did not smell like the pine cones and peppermint of my husband, but of the fire of my lab, the flowers of Sceaux.

There was a choice. There was always a choice. Had I made the wrong one? Could there be a happiness for me with Pierre that I would never have with Kaz? Or was it wrong to believe that my happiness, in and of itself, was inherently connected to any man at all? Maybe my true happiness was in the sound of Klara's piano notes, in the smell of Professor Mazur's smoke-filled lab.

"Mama," Klara's small voice called out for me in the darkness one night, interrupting my thoughts. I pushed Pierre away again, to the deepest back corner of my mind.

"What is it, *mój mały kurczak?*"

"I had a bad dream." Her voice quivered, thick with tears. I remembered what she told me before I'd left. She was eight, old enough to take care of herself. But I felt a warmth coursing through my body now, knowing that she still needed me. She was my happiness, my heart.

"Come, lie in bed with me." I patted Kaz's empty side of the bed, and Klara ran up, got in. I held her close, smoothed back her tangled hair with my hands. "Do you want to tell me about your dream?" I asked her, kissing her head softly, reveling in the soft flower-petal feel of her hair. She shook her head vigorously. "Sometimes it helps to talk about it."

"You went on the train again to Sweden," she finally said a few moments later, her voice very quiet, very small. "And then something happened. You never came back."

"Shhh." I held her body tighter against mine. "It was only a bad dream, chicken. Mama is here. She's not going anywhere."

"Papa is here too." I had not heard Kaz come in, but I looked up at the sound of his voice, and he stood in the doorway. I wondered how long he'd been standing there, listening.

He walked over to the bed, leaned in and kissed Klara gently on the forehead. Then he leaned across her and kissed my forehead too. His lips were cold, and he smelled like pipe smoke, the German tobacco he loved.

"There is room for me?" he asked. His voice rose and broke, a question.

Klara rolled in closer to me, and there was room. I patted the empty space with my hand, and Kaz took off his shoes, got into bed with us. After only a few minutes, Klara snored softly, back to sleep. "I did not know if you would ever come back to me either," Kaz whispered into the darkness, a confession. He reached his hand across Klara for mine, grabbed my fingers and squeezed softly.

"I chose you," I said squeezing his hand, after a few moments. "I will always come back."

MARIE

❦

Paris, 1912–1914

Paul becomes a never-ending ache in my stomach, and after I return from Sweden it hurts worse and worse, and then one afternoon at the Sorbonne, I feel myself falling down, the ground collapsing beneath my feet. I'm unable to bear the pain any longer, unable to stand.

"We have to get her to the hospital," I hear one of my students say. His voice cuts through a fog, a haze of pain.

And then, I am being carried, falling in and out of light and darkness. Jeanne will not have to kill me; the press will not have to crucify me. Here I am, dying, all on my own.

Paul is far away and blurry, out of my reach. I imagine him again, that snowy night in my lab when he came to me, held on to me, promised me, *just this once. One time.*

If I could go back to that moment now, I would pull away, say no. There is no man worth this pain, worth my career. Worth my life. If I could go back again, I would not choose him. I would choose myself.

But Paul is not the true cause of my ache; there is a scientific reason behind it. At the hospital, I am diagnosed with severe kidney problems, caused by lesions on my uterus. In the spring of 1912, I require surgery to remove the lesions.

It is meant to make me feel better. But instead, after the surgery, I feel profoundly worse. I am in so much pain, I can barely move. I lie in my bed, unable to work, unable to move or see the children. If I were to believe in any sort of penance, any sort of punishment for all those wonderful afternoons with Paul, then maybe this is it?

I spend weeks in bed, trying to organize my affairs. I write to Jacques in Montpellier and beg of him to see that all the radium I have in my possession stays safe if I die.

He writes back, saying that he will always help me with anything I want, of course. He will always be my brother. The girls' uncle.

But you are not dying, Marie, he writes. *You are much too young to die.*

The truth is, in the spring of 1912, I am forty-four. This is two years older already than my mother was when she died. Only two years *younger* than Pierre was when he died. Over six times the age of Bronia's Jakub, and five of my sister Zosia.

I have won two Nobel prizes, had so much success in my work. But I am empty and alone, and, even if I get well, I'm unsure I'll ever be able to work again. The papers still report terrible things about me. One even reports that I am pregnant with Paul's child, and that is why I have been out of view for so long.

It is a ridiculous fabrication, when I am in so much pain that I can barely move, barely breathe, hardly walk or get out of bed. When I haven't even seen Paul in so many months.

Death is a shadow. It follows me and hovers over me. *I am marked by death.* Perhaps it is surprising that I have even made it to forty-four years of age. Perhaps I should just give in to it, let it take me now. If I were dead, I would no longer be in such pain.

WHAT IS IT PAUL SAID TO ME ONCE, IN THE HALF-LIGHT OF Arromanches?

That what he admires most about me is my strength. I don't give up, I can never give up. I am brave and amazing. Or am I foolish and crazy?

For months and months, I am not feeling any better, and yet, I can't stop trying a rest cure. I leave the girls with their nanny and tutor and check into a sanatorium in the Alps as Bronia, so the press can't find me: *Madame Dluska.* Then in the summer, I take a boat to England, traveling as *Madame Sklodowska.*

I read the latest journals in bed, and so much work is being done in radium without me. I feel jealous of all the work carrying on in my absence. I must get better, so I can contribute to it again. There is so much more to be done, and there is ongoing construction in Paris on a new, wonderful lab that will be mine if I can get well enough to work there.

And then I wonder if death, like anything else, is a choice, and if maybe I am not ready to choose it yet.

IN THE SUMMER OF 1914, I AM WELL ENOUGH FINALLY TO RE-turn to Paris on a ticket in my own name. The press have, at long last, forgotten about me, and there is no fanfare, no one waiting for me at the station upon my return. All the papers are reporting about the recent assassination of the heir to the Austrian throne and speculation of a *war*. Who has time to worry about one woman scientist in Paris now?

It is a relief to walk through the streets of Paris, of my own volition, unwatched and unnoticed, and free of the pain and the press that have haunted me for so very long.

Ève and Irène are already in L'Arcouëst with the Perrins for the summer—I will join them in a few weeks after I get my affairs back in order in Paris. My house is empty, dark, and dusty, quiet. When I step inside it again, I feel like a stranger in my own home.

Even the yellow flowers that are blooming in a pot out front are unfamiliar to me, planted here by someone else, in my absence.

Work on my new lab is almost completed: *Institut du Radium*. Now it stands, a large three-story brick building on rue Pierre Curie—we could fit ten of our sheds where we first discovered radium inside. And it is only a few streets away. So close. *So far.*

I go there straightaway after dropping my things at home, and I stand out front, taking in its near completion, its three stories of grandeur and splendor. I am hit with a sudden sense of overwhelm.

Oh, Pierre. If you could see what they have built for us.

I am very much alive, and there is more work to be done here, so much more to be done.

A FEW DAYS AFTER MY RETURN TO PARIS, JEAN PERRIN writes me from L'Arcouëst. Ève has made new friends and loves to play all day, and Irène studies and continues to work on her maths. I have not seen the children in many months. But they are well and happy, and they want for nothing.

And I thought you should know, Jean writes at the very end of his letter, a postscript, *Jeanne and Paul have reconciled now.*

Reconciled?

Once that word might have hurt me, but I am surprised I do not feel anything when I read it. Everything I had with Paul is far away and feels unimportant after I have struggled so long to regain my health. I want Paul to be happy, and I do not believe he will ever be happy with Jeanne. But their marriage feels out of my reach. I no longer desire a life with him. I simply want a life of my own. I want to work and I want to learn and I want to run my new *Institut* and make more advancements in the field of radium.

Or perhaps I am just like Pavlov's dog. And now at the ripe age of forty-six, nearly forty-seven, finally, finally I am learning. Every man I have ever loved has brought me pain in the end. What is the point of loving another man, of longing again for that kind of relationship in my life?

I have a tenuous grasp on my health. I have my mind and my work.

Good for Paul and Jeanne, I write back to Jean Perrin. *But it is no longer any of my concern. I have more important things to worry about.*

I DO HAVE MORE IMPORTANT THINGS TO WORRY ABOUT. FOR one thing, I cannot make it to L'Arcouëst the following week as I've planned, because France begins mobilizing troops, trains suddenly stop carrying civilians. A *war* really is building, and not just in Austria-Hungary, but in France, too. Within a week, all the men of age are conscripted, including my nephew, my former lab assistant, Maurice. Jacques writes from Montpellier with the news, and now it is my turn to reassure him.

Maurice is very smart, very quick on his feet, I write, *he will be just fine*. But my worry for him brings a new ache in my chest. Maurice is a scientist, not a soldier.

I walk to the post to mail my letter, and planes buzz overhead. Suddenly the ground shakes beneath my feet. There is a rumble, an explosion. I run into an alleyway, and when I peek out again, my ears are ringing, my hands shaking. In the distance, there is the rise of smoke plumes, the sounds of screams.

A German bomb has already fallen in Paris, on rue des Récollets, not even six kilometers away from my new lab.

A SINGLE GRAM OF RADIUM SITS INSIDE MY NEW LAB, DESIGnated for research purposes. It is the only bit of radium in all of France, and irreplaceable, as we have neither the money nor the resources to obtain more.

After the first bomb, there are two more in quick succession. Irène writes me, begging me to find a way to L'Arcouëst, as she is worried for my safety in Paris. But I write her that I am fine, and I feel this strange safety in the fact that I have already touched death these past years and come through it, made it to the other side. *It is the radium I worry for now*, I write Irène. *Not myself.*

Perhaps in another life, one where my gentle and persuasive Pierre were still alive, I would find my way to L'Arcouëst to huddle in safety with my family. But in this life, where I am finally well again, my work is everything I have, everything I am. And I am deeply worried for my radium.

It is so expensive, I will never be able to replace it if something happens. And what will happen to my research if it is destroyed? I write letters, send urgent telegrams, until I finally convince the government of the importance of ensuring my radium's safety. In the beginning of September they agree and let me accompany my radium, packed inside a heavy lead-lined box, on a train to Bordeaux.

Two soldiers accompany me to a bank, where I rent a safe deposit box to store it, and it is only once it is safely inside, locked away, and I clutch the key, that I allow myself to exhale.

"You must really have something valuable inside that box," one of the soldiers says, frowning. His annoyance at being sent on this mission with me is clear. Perhaps he feels he could be doing more, fighting Germans on the front lines. I am dressed modestly in the same black dress I always wear to the lab, but perhaps he is mistaking me for a wealthy French woman, worrying about her silly diamonds.

"You want to know what is in the box?" I say to him, sharply. "One gram of radium. Only the entire scientific and medical future of France."

The other soldier cocks his head and looks at me. "Radium. I know you . . . Madame Curie," he says. "I remember reading all about you and your love affair in the papers."

"You can't believe everything you read," I say, gritting my teeth.

"Yes . . ." The other soldier recognizes me now too. "You're that *fille* who ruined that poor woman's life."

This story, this one choice, it will follow me around forever, no matter what else I do. It will continue to sicken and ruin and destroy me.

Only if you let it, mon amour, I hear Pierre say.

"I am nobody's *fille*," I say, firmly, petulantly. "I am a scientist."

MARYA

Krakow and L'Arcouëst, 1915

I did not believe that the war would touch us in Krakow at first. Fighting hovered around us—we read the news of the battles and invasions across Europe. But not in our city, our country. Life felt strangely normal, even as Hela sent a letter that they were evacuating Paris, leaving their lab for the safety of L'Arcouëst. After a scare with a German bomb falling too close, they grabbed Marie and Lou, who was still living with them, finishing her medical degree, and escaped to their home in the cliffs of Brittany.

Join us, Marya, Hela implored me. *We have plenty of room.*

She tried to convince Bronia too, but to no avail, as Bronia said she felt quite safe in Zakopane, and there might be a war raging but there were still sick people who needed to be treated. And she could not just abandon them. I resisted at first too, writing her that everything was perfectly safe in Krakow.

Our first sign in Krakow that the war would change us was when Chernikoff announced they were canceling the rest of the term and closing for the remainder of the war. It came just after a night of looting by Russian soldiers, outside the city, but still close enough to make people afraid. Jagiellonian also drastically cut down its staff for the spring term. Luckily Kaz had enough seniority in the math department that he was still kept on to teach, as was Professor Mazur. But there were no funds for her lab, or for me to assist. The irony was, in the last four years, I'd been helping her perfect a liquid-gas detonation device. Professor Mazur said she tried to explain that if we were allowed to finish, it could be helpful to the war effort, but the men in the university's administration said there was no money for her women's lab now.

"Our funding has been completely canceled," she said, frustration wrinkling across her small forehead. "But we will be back at work, after the war. We will not give up, Marya. I promise you, we will not."

I nodded, but I swallowed back my own uncertainty. It already felt impossible to imagine a time *after* this war when life would be normal again.

Klara was bereft without her intense schedule of piano. At home she moped and lay on the parlor couch like she was dying.

"Why don't you go and practice, chicken?" I implored her. "You have to keep up your skills in spite of the war."

"What's the point?" she complained. "There's nowhere for me to perform now anyway."

At twelve years old, Klara was looking more and more like a woman and sounding more and more like a piano virtuoso, both when she performed and in her entitled attitude. Her teacher had spoken to me about a program in Berlin he'd wanted us to consider for the summer, and I'd liked the idea for nurturing her talent. I'd disliked it for what it might do to her already inflated ego. But that was all before the war. Klara was not wrong. There was no more music in the city now. Nowhere for her to perform. Even the Philharmonic had stopped giving concerts.

By the summer of 1915, Klara and I were trapped in the house. Looting outside the city grew worse and worse, and when two houses a few blocks from us were stormed by Russian soldiers one night in June, Kaz suddenly agreed with Hela, that Klara and I would both be much safer in L'Arcouëst.

L'ARCOUËST WAS A CITY TUCKED AMONG THE CLIFFS AND THE seashore in the northwest corner of France. A summer playground for the faculty of the Sorbonne, many of them owned summer homes here, including Hela and Jacques, who had built theirs after collecting their Nobel Prize money a few years earlier. Though Bronia had complained to me that she worried about them spending their prize on the extravagance of a second home, a vacation home, now it felt the most practical decision they had ever made, as there was strange protection from the war here. Even though the occasional warplane would buzz overhead, it was only a wayward and distant reminder.

Hela and Jacques had a full house: Marie and Lou, Pierre, me and Klara, and their neighbor from Paris, who had recently been abandoned by her *good-for-nothing* husband, as she told me the first morning over breakfast, Jeanne Langevin.

I had not seen Pierre in person for the past few years, though we had continued with the occasional letter, mostly to share our advancements in our respective labs. Pierre had finally gotten Jacques to take interest in his research and to help him explore the possibility of the second radioactive element he believed to be in the pitchblende. But everything was left behind in Paris when they fled, and their favorite topic of conversation each morning in L'Arcouëst was fretting over the lab's current status and safety.

Now, seeing him again, he really had aged. His beard was completely gray, he walked a little slower, his shoulders stooped. But what I noticed most of all was his relationship with Jeanne Langevin. The two of them strolled along the beach together each morning, arm in arm. Pierre would stop to bend down and collect seashells or other treasures, until his suit pockets were filled or until Jeanne would seem to lose interest and start to walk on, without him. He would run to catch up to her, catch her hand in his own. I watched them from the window enough mornings that finally Hela said, "Marya what is so interesting out there on the beach that has you staring and staring? Is it the water, hmmm?" This was my first time being so near such a large body of water, and it frightened me too much to go in, though Klara swam in it with no fear, a strong swimmer from all her summers at the lake with Jakub.

Hela peered over my shoulder, saw Pierre and Jeanne walking together, and frowned. "Leave it be, Marya," she said softly. "Poor Pierre has been lonely for so many years, and he's finally found a companion in Jeanne."

"I'm confused," I said. "Is she still married or not?"

"It's complicated," Hela said. "Her husband, Paul, ran off with a house servant and their two youngest children last year, leaving her with nothing. Their marriage was quite difficult. She always told me how terribly he treated her, but I'm afraid I never really paid enough attention, until he left. I suppose she and Paul are still legally married, for all the good it does her now. She's had a rough year. And Pierre makes her happy."

"A house servant?" I repeated, stuck on that part, softening toward Jeanne. I felt sad that not only had her husband betrayed her, but also that he had abandoned her, taken her children. How awful. That poor woman.

Hela shrugged. "It's not unusual in Paris these days for a man to take a mistress of that standing. But he certainly doesn't *run off* with her." She said it like it was so commonplace, nothing. And I turned to her, raised my eyebrows, wondering if Jacques had ever taken a mistress. "I'm a scientist first. Jacques's partner in the lab. His wife second," she said, addressing the question I hadn't even asked out loud. "What Jacques does on his own is his own business. But, he would never *leave me*." She said it so matter-of-factly, like his indiscretions were of no consequence to her.

I remembered Hela as a girl, my sister-twin who smelled of lemon and corn poppies, always filled with light and hope, and now, here she was before me, a famous scientist, but was she made of stone?

"I still think about how desperate Kazimierz was to get you back that morning he came to our apartment in Warsaw. You were already at the train station and you almost left for Paris without him." Hela was still talking, and now her voice sounded far away. "I've always envied you, Marya, for having a love like that."

"Oh, Hela," I said, putting my hand on her shoulder. "Kazimierz is no saint, believe me."

Still, all these years later, the thought of him and Leokadia together hurt, a physical pain deep in my gut. But it was so long ago, I barely thought of it. Kaz would not leave me, and I would not leave him. We had built a life together, a family. But I didn't think we had the kind of life Hela should envy. Not when she had a Nobel Prize, a lab in Paris, and a vacation home in Brittany.

"Do you ever wonder how different our lives might be now if I had gotten on that train to Paris?" I asked her.

On the beach, Pierre grabbed onto Jeanne's hand. She smiled at something he said to her, and they continued walking down the shore, hand in hand. Perhaps Hela was right, that they were good for each other, that Jeanne deserved happiness with Pierre, whether she was still legally married or not.

Hela laughed a little. "But then you wouldn't have Klara, and I might not have a Nobel Prize," she said.

"Or Marie," I added.

"Right. Or Marie," she repeated softly. "And then . . . who knows where we'd both be standing right now, in the midst of this god-awful war."

How hard it was to imagine our lives without our beautiful daughters, and perhaps everything we had done, every choice we had made had led us to them, to our safety here together during this war. And then none of it felt like it could be wrong.

Hela took my hand and pulled me away from the window. "Come, let's leave these two lovebirds be, and I'll show you the paper I've been writing up on electromagnetism. I think you'll find it fascinating."

I WOKE UP EARLY IN L'ARCOUËST, BEFORE THE FIRST LIGHT, MY stomach aching with worries about the war and the world, and the safety of my house and husband back in Krakow. And while Klara remained snoring, I would tiptoe into the kitchen to make myself a coffee and read by lamplight the scientific papers Hela left out for me. I learned so much about Hela's research and began to wonder if her theory on electromagnetic charges and atoms could possibly work hand in hand with Professor Mazur's research on detonation. I wrote Professor Mazur a rambling letter, filled with ideas, and then I was quite disappointed when for weeks and weeks I received nothing from her in return.

Kaz and I wrote letters to each other every few days. He told me about the courses he was teaching, the students he still had left. About the terrible state of the produce at the local market and how dreadful his soup tasted, how he remembered my clear potato broth back in Loskow when we lived together in our one-room apartment, and how he longed for something that delicious now. How he longed for me, for the way everything about our life had been *close* then. *There was no place in that apartment I could stand without touching you*, he wrote.

Oh, you are in a sorry state if you remember that soup being delicious, I wrote him back. But I chuckled as I put the words to the page, marveling at the way, with this distance, this space between us, this war, Kaz somehow felt closer to me than he had in years.

KAZ ARRIVED FOR AN UNEXPECTED VISIT AT THE END OF HIS fall term, showing up unannounced one night while we were all in the middle of dinner. He walked in, and Klara was so delighted to see him, she jumped up from the table, squealing, "Papa!" forgetting for a moment that she was a teenager, and in company no less. She jumped into his arms like she had as a toddler.

"*Kurczak!* How you've grown!" He kissed the top of her head but looked over her, toward me. I could tell there was something wrong, in the way his cheeks were hollow and his eyes were dark.

I stood and kissed his unshaven cheek, closed my eyes for a second and inhaled the familiar scent of him, pine trees and pipe smoke. "Kaz . . . what is it?" I asked. "What happened?"

"We should talk in private," he said, his eyes looking around the table, landing on Jeanne, the only one here he'd never met.

I turned and caught Hela's eye. She frowned. "Kazimierz—" She stood, taking charge. "Take a seat and have some stew, and tell us what is going on. We are all family here."

Kaz looked at me, and I nodded. Hela was right. Whatever was wrong, he could say it in front of my family. He took the seat Hela offered him next to her, and I sat back down in my seat next to Jeanne. "I'm so sorry, *kochanie*." The words tumbled out of him as Hela placed a bowl of stew in front of him. "But Ola Mazur was killed."

"Killed?" The word felt foreign on my tongue, unfamiliar and unexpected and unlike a word that belonged to me. I could not understand it nor absorb it. That such a word could be used in a sentence with *Ola Mazur*. My mentor and my savior. There was so much to be done with her in the lab still after the war. She had promised me that! She could not be *killed*.

"It was a terrible accident." Kaz was still talking. "There was looting on her block, and she tried to intervene, help the old woman who lived next door to her. The old woman didn't want to lose her things, you see, and Ola stepped in, and the looters pushed her into the street. She fell and she was run over by an automobile."

I imagined Professor Mazur's tiny body flying through the air into the street, crushed by an automobile, her beautiful mind bleeding out into the road. I covered my mouth, swallowing back the taste of bile in my throat. She was just a few years older than me. Her girls, just a few years older than Klara. *Oh, her girls.*

"Your research," Pierre said, and at the same time I said, "Her children!"

Jeanne looked at him, then at me, and she put her hand on mine. "I'm so sorry for your loss, Marya," she said patting my hand. "This war," she said, "This great big terrible war."

"I wish there was something I could've done," I whispered.

Kaz met my eyes across the table. "But what can we do? What can any of us do? I just thank God that you and Klara came here when you did, that you are safe, *kochanie*."

Later that night, in bed, Kaz's arms were wrapped around me for the first time in months, but I couldn't sleep. All I could see behind my lidded eyes was Professor Mazur, bleeding and dying in the street.

I watched her fall, again and again, powerless to stop her, powerless to save her. And the feeling of helplessness curled up inside of me, making it hard to breathe.

MARIE

❧

Western Front, 1914–1916

After I secure my radium in Bordeaux, I ignore the Perrins' continued pleas to come to L'Arcouëst. So many men are dying in this terrible war, and I insist that if I stay in Paris, I can use my lab, use science to help. I cannot simply while away the war in the safety of the rocky cliffs of Brittany, not when there is something I can *do* here in Paris.

I get the idea that if I can make X-ray units mobile, fit them into cars, I can drive them out into the field to diagnose soldiers and save their lives. It seems like a daunting task at first, since I don't even know how to drive, and I must lobby to secure the funding. But then I bring Irène back to Paris to help me, and suddenly there we are, working on my idea together, side by side in the lab. A team.

WE HAVE OUR FIRST RADIOLOGICAL CAR UP AND RUNNING BY 1914, and Irène and I do our first test run. I drive us right up to the Battle of the Marne, much to the consternation of a general who shouts at me, no, *demands* that I stop my car and return to

Paris, *at once*. "The front lines is no place for a woman!" he yells to be heard over the noise of the Renault's engine.

I gun it a little in response.

"I'm serious, lady," the general shouts at me.

"They told me that about the laboratory too," I shout right back. "And two Nobel prizes later, I quite disagree. Now, step aside so we can help your soldiers." He stands perfectly still, crosses his arms in front of his chest. "Step aside," I shout again. "Or else I will be forced to drive right over you."

I gun the engine of the Renault again, and finally he moves, perhaps thinking me crazy, thinking I might run him over if he were to stay there standing in front of me. "It's not my problem if you're both killed," he shouts. I ignore him, steer the car past him, parking it by the medical tent. I kill the engine, and my hands are shaking. I ball them into fists so Irène won't notice.

"Were you really going to run him over, Maman?" Irène asks. Her eyes are wide, and her face is a strange shade of green.

"No, of course not, *ma chérie*. The thing you must learn about men is that they might try and put up a fight, but then they will always, always move out of your way. There is nothing that frightens them more than an intelligent woman." She nods slowly. "Now, come. We have made it here, let us put our X-ray machine to good use."

By 1916, we have twenty radiological cars in the field, *Petites Curies*, as we have come to call them. All of them equipped with mobile X-ray units and their own dynamo, an electric generator, which I have designed myself and had built into all the cars so that we have electric power for the units.

Irène and I divide our time between driving to the front

ourselves and training other women to drive the cars and use the radiological equipment back in Paris at the lab. (Irène all the while keeps up her studies at the Sorbonne and has achieved her certificates in maths and almost nearly in physics and chemistry.) All in all now, we have nearly 150 capable women, with the ability to drive, x-ray, and diagnose. I keep one car for myself, the Renault, and I drive into the field when I can and when I'm needed. I receive regular telegrams and telephone calls, letting me know where to go, and I dispatch the cars from Paris.

The laboratory has been, nearly my entire adult life, the place where I have felt most free, most at home. But now, driving my Renault from post to post out in the field, changing flat tires and cleaning carburetors, diagnosing wounded men, saving lives, I have never felt such excitement, such a thrill. Such a comfort and surety in my work.

By September 1916, Irène is at her own post in Hoogstade, Belgium, sleeping for weeks out in the medical tent with the nurses. She reports in her letters of the bullet fragments she finds in bones, of a man whose life she saves by diagnosing his wounded lung.

I get a dispatch that another unit is needed, and all my women are off elsewhere, so I take my Renault, drive to Hoogstade myself to assist.

"Maman," Irène says, her tired face erupting in glee when I get out of the car. Her face no longer belongs to a girl, or even a teenager, but now it is the worn face of a woman. A woman who has seen things and done things and learned things. She embraces me tightly, and as she is a bit taller than me, she lowers her lips to kiss the top of my head. "How wonderful you came!"

"Of course I came," I said. "I got a dispatch that there were too many injuries for just one car."

"Oh." Irène's face fell. "It was silly of me . . . but I thought . . . it was my birthday that brought you." She shrugs, sheepishly.

Her birthday. Is it really? It has been weeks, or maybe it has been months since we've last seen each other. It's hard to keep track of time in the war, in the field. I measure my days in miles, in radiographs of broken bones and bullet-ridden chests. In number of men saved, and transported for treatment, and lost despite my greatest efforts.

"Happy birthday, darling," I say to her, giving her another quick hug. If I were not standing in the middle of a war, perhaps I would take a moment to remember it, that precipitous joy that erupted from me on the morning of her birth. The way Pierre had cried out that she was *so small, too small.* Perhaps I would ruminate on the fact that Pierre has been gone so long, he would not even recognize our baby who stands before me now, a woman, a scientist.

But there is no time to be nostalgic. I kiss her cheek and pull out of the embrace. "Let's be happy you and I are both alive. So many men are injured, dying. They need us. There will be other birthdays. Come, let's drive to the field. You lead the way. I'll follow behind you in my car."

She nods, and I can tell she feels the same excitement about going back out into the field that I do. Her blue eyes light up the way her father's did once in our laboratory shed, watching our radium glow and glow and glow upon the table.

MARYA

❧

Krakow, 1918–1919

Krakow became liberated from Austrian rule first, on October 31, 1918, a few weeks before the end of the war. And then after the signing of the Treaty of Versailles, Warsaw was liberated from Russian rule, and for the first time in my lifetime and more, over 100 years, Poland was *Poland* again. No more Austrian Poland, Russian Poland. Out of the horribleness and death and destruction of the war, my country had at long last regained her sovereignty. I wished my father were alive to see it.

Klara and I returned to Krakow once things stabilized, near the end of the war. And with Chernikoff still closed, Klara practiced piano on her own at the house for hours each day, but now without the sour attitude. She had been without a piano for so long at Hela's that she was grateful just to be able to play again. And I was grateful to be able to taste the end of the war, to revel in the feeling of my Poland being Poland, and to hear the sounds of Klara's beautiful music, filling our house with light and joy and wonder again.

ONE OF THE FIRST THINGS I DID WHEN WE GOT BACK TO KRA-
kow was go to Professor Mazur's home to check on her daughters. She and I had been together only in the lab, teacher and
student, researcher and assistant. We had not been friends—I
did not know her daughters. I had met Nadia and Emilia only
once before. And I didn't even know the exact location of the
Mazurs' home because I had never been there. But Klara remembered where it was from that time I went to Sweden and
she had spent time with the Mazur girls and their governess.
When I asked her for help, she stepped away from her piano and
said, "Mama, I'll go with you to see them."

The Mazurs' house was only five blocks away from ours, in
a location I'd walked by a few times before on Nadzieja Street.
Klara and I walked there together, our arms linked. At fifteen,
she was lithe and beautiful, and she wore her pale blond hair in
curls. She was a few inches taller than me, and when we walked
together now I got the distinct feeling she believed she was holding me up. When I looked at her though, I still saw my little girl.

Nadia, the Mazurs' older daughter, nearly eighteen, answered the door when we rang the bell. She had blossomed in
the years since I'd met her, and here she was before me now,
a ghost of her mother, small and pale with shining black hair.
She looked at me, uncertain. Then her eyes caught on Klara
and recognition glimmered on her face. She smiled. "Oh, Klara!
Marya?" She greeted us, opening the door wider.

I handed her the loaf of bread I'd baked last night with what
I could scrape together at the market. Yeast and flour were scarce;
my loaf had barely risen and more resembled a misshapen cracker.

Klara gave Nadia a hug. "Come in," Nadia said to both of us. "I have been hoping you would return to Krakow."

"I was so very sorry to hear what happened to your mother. How have you and your sister been?" I asked, as we walked inside. Boxes were stacked in the corner of the foyer, and the parlor room was mostly empty. "Are you moving?" I asked.

Nadia nodded. "Papa was offered a job at a university in Chicago, and Emilia and I can study there."

"America," Klara said, her eyes wide, with surprise, or was it jealousy? I had never met Professor Mazur's husband, but I knew he was also a professor, literature, or . . . history?

"It's been hard," Nadia said. "Everything has been hard. The war . . . Mama's passing." She blinked back tears. I held on tightly to Klara's hand. I wished there was something I could've done to save Professor Mazur, but I was also so grateful that Klara and I had found safety during the war, that my family had come through it intact. "It will be good to start over somewhere new. For all of us," Nadia was saying now.

I nodded. "Your mother meant a lot to me," I said. "I still can't believe she's gone. We were supposed to go back into her lab together, once the war was over. There was so much more work to be done." I sighed.

"She had told us." Nadia nodded vigorously. "Oh! Hold on, I have something for you."

Nadia disappeared into the other room, then returned a few moments later with a stack of notebooks. I recognized them immediately: Professor Mazur's research journals. She had never been without one in the lab, and she was always scribbling down notes. Nadia put the pile of them into my arms now, and I had no choice but to accept or let them drop to the floor.

"What am I supposed to do with these?" I asked, stunned.

Nadia shrugged and smiled at me. "We didn't want to get rid of them, but we don't want to move them either."

"But I don't . . ." I stammered.

"I'm sure you will take good care of them," Nadia said. Then she turned to Klara to ask about her piano schooling. I heard Klara telling her about Chernikoff still being closed, and Nadia saying that in America she hoped to study biology, maybe become a doctor.

In my arms, Professor Mazur's life's work felt so heavy that I suddenly wondered if I might collapse under its weight.

IN THE SPRING OF 1919, WE HOPED THAT CHERNIKOFF WOULD reopen, and that Klara could continue her musical education. But Max Chernikoff's son had also been killed in the war, and Max, consumed by grief, announced his permanent retirement. His school would never reopen. Klara had been without a professional piano education for nearly four years, and now there was nothing in Krakow for her. I wasn't sure what to do for her, and I wrote Leokadia a letter to ask for her advice. She had gotten Klara, and me, into this life consumed by piano, I reasoned. It was only fair to ask for her help now. Besides, maybe she still owed me. Maybe she would always owe me.

I had not seen Kadi in years, not since her concert in Krakow, but we did still exchange letters occasionally. She had relocated to America during the war, and was, by her own account, becoming the darling of the New York orchestra scene. She was seeing an older man, an heir to an American shipping company, but she'd repeated the sentiment she had told me once, when we were so young and living in Loksow, that she would never marry. Her piano career was her entire life, her world. Still, I was happy for her that perhaps she was not quite as lonely as she once had been.

Leokadia's reply came a few weeks later, and just like that, a spot opened up for Klara at the top piano conservatory in Paris. *I know you will feel good to have her near your sister,* Leokadia wrote, *and her education will be top-notch in Paris. Better than anything she could ever get in Poland.*

I stared at the word, *Paris,* in Leokadia's neat script. All of a sudden, I saw everything I'd lost within Klara's reach. If I could send her to Paris, I could give my Klara what I once denied myself: opportunity.

In August of 1919, I bought two train tickets so that I could accompany Klara for her move to Paris. She insisted that, at almost sixteen, she was old enough to take the train there alone, and besides, Hela would meet her at the Gare du Nord. She would live at Hela's house while she was studying, so she would not be alone. And all that was true, but I could not bear the thought of the worry I'd hold at her going all that distance without me, and so I insisted that I would take her, and that it would give me a nice visit with Hela and Jacques and Marie anyway.

The night before we were to leave, Kaz reached for me in bed, pulling me close toward him. He kissed the back of my neck, and I felt a familiar warmth travel down my spine, toward my legs. "*Kochanie,* our baby is a grown woman, isn't she?" he whispered into my hair, his voice thick with pride, or regret, or was it longing?

It felt as though her entire childhood had vanished while we weren't paying attention, and now Klara was no longer our child. It felt impossible that tonight would be the last night she would sleep in our house, in the room right next to mine, and I felt a sudden wetness on my cheeks.

"What will I do without her?" I choked out into the darkness, in between tears.

He pulled me closer to him and whispered for me to *breathe*. I could suddenly remember him holding on to me in just this way in our very tiny apartment in Loksow so many years ago, after my baby Zosia had died and I did not know how I would ever get out of that bed again. He had held me close and held me up. *Steady*.

"Who am I, if I am not her mother?" I whispered into the darkness. My life for so many years had been about Klara: putting Klara first, getting Klara fed and educated and keeping her safe. And now what?

"I think the answer is right over there, on your dresser," Kaz said. He reached out his arm and pointed to Professor Mazur's large stack of journals. I'd put them down there months ago after Nadia gave them to me and hadn't touched them since.

I shook my head. I had no idea what to do with them. I had only been Professor Mazur's assistant. I did not have the education she had, nor the clout she had at the university.

"Remember what you said to me after Hipolit died?" In the dark Kaz's voice was brimming with quiet excitement. "*You have all the research*," he said. "You're going to finish it . . . publish it. And you are going to be fine. We are both going to be just fine."

But Kaz's words were hard to believe or understand, and I lay there for a long time in the dark feeling deeply unsettled, wondering if it would even be possible for me to live the life of a scientist, after all this time.

MARIE

Paris, 1920

The smell of cherry blossoms permeates the air, as I walk to my lab one May morning. And though the war is now behind us and the day is pleasant, I feel quite unsettled on my walk to work.

I have agreed to an interview today with an American reporter, and I am already dreading it. As a general rule, I do not ever meet with reporters or talk to the press. My entire career the press has chased me and vilified me, and once, it nearly killed me. Usually requests for interviews, numerous which they may be since the end of the war, are thrown away by me or by my assistants in the lab.

But perhaps it is that Missy Meloney is American, not French. That she has written *so many* times claiming she wants to help me, it felt a cruelty to continue to ignore her. And she wrote something in her last letter that I feel a sort of connection to: *It is impossible to exaggerate the unimportance of people,* she wrote. *But you have been important to me for twenty years.*

Yes, exactly! I had thought when I read that. It is not I who am important, it is my work. And in those words, it seemed that Missy had understood that too.

Still, when I walk inside my lab now and see a strange woman sitting there, pale and small and timid, I'm annoyed with myself that I've agreed to this particular meeting, in spite of the fact that she actually looks quite harmless.

"Madame Curie!" Missy stands and calls out for me.

I sigh and invite her inside my sparsely furnished office. She walks with an unassuming limp, and I pull up two chairs close together, offer her one and sit in the other. I've been having trouble with my hearing lately, but I don't want to tell her that is why I'm sitting so close. She must assume it is because I feel a kinship with her, and she reaches out and pats my hand. "I have but ten minutes before I will have to get back to my work," I tell her brusquely, pulling my hand back.

"Of course, you must be very busy," she says apologetically. "So tell me." Missy turns to look at me, her coal eyes wide, trained on me, intensely. I wonder if she is judging me, sizing me up: my worn black lab dress and my gray hair and the wrinkles on my face. I put my hand up to smooth back my bun. "This great big beautiful laboratory of yours. Is it filled completely with radium?"

I laugh. "Oh goodness, no. I wish you were correct. We have but one gram housed here in my lab, and that is all we have in all of France. Not like you have in America. Fifty grams of radium!" My voices rises. "Four in Baltimore, six in Denver, seven in New York . . . shall I go on?" I know the location of every single gram of radium in the world.

She shakes her head. "Surely you can acquire more?"

"For a hundred thousand American dollars, yes. Then we would be able to acquire one more gram for testing. Right now, I can't even use the gram we have in my research. It's reserved for medical treatments in France."

"A hundred thousand dollars," she muses. "Well, certainly you must have the money, from all your patents and royalties?"

"I have no patents," I say. "Radium is for everyone. For the good of science. It's not mine to profit from. I never patented it."

Missy frowns, like she believes I made a grave mistake. And maybe I did. My intention was to share radium with the world, but I never imagined it would become so expensive once others started extracting it, that I would not be able to afford to continue my own research.

Missy chews on the end of her pen, considering what I've just told her. "So you are saying that you, *Madame Marie Curie*, discoverer of radium, that you do not now have in your possession enough radium to continue your experiments? Nor do you have enough money to acquire more radium?"

I nod. It is a terrible position I'm in, not to be able to afford to continue my own work. I put the prize money from my second Nobel into war bonds, which have since disappeared. I am living more than fine with my 12,000 francs a year teaching salary, and the sale of a book I've recently completed. But the university doesn't even have enough money for equipment and materials to continue the work I want to do in the lab, much less for more radium.

Missy chuckles, and now I worry she is mocking me. That she will write an awful and distasteful article about me for all of America to read. "Don't write this in your article," I say.

Her face grows serious again. "Well . . . why not?" she finally asks. "In fact, what if I were to write *exactly* that. What if I could help you?"

"I don't see how you could possibly help."

"What if I were to raise the 100,000 dollars you need to buy more radium, from the American women who read my magazine?"

Now I chuckle. "That sounds preposterous," I say. "Raise the money, from your readers?"

"You underestimate American women, Marie. May I call you Marie?" I nod. The fact that she seems to care about my situation, that she offers a solution, albeit it a ridiculous one, makes me like her just a little bit, in spite of her profession. "I'll make you a deal," Missy is saying now. "You let me try and raise the money, and when I do, you'll come visit me in America to pick up your gram of radium in person."

The truth is, I can think of nothing I'd hate more than a long, tiring journey across the ocean, taking me so very far away from my lab and my work. But I agree to her deal. What's the harm in being polite? There's no way she will ever be able to raise the money to get me another gram of radium.

IT IS NOT JUST MY EARS THAT GIVE ME TROUBLE NOW, BUT MY eyes too. Day by day, the world grows darker, softer. Everything becomes cloudy, then murky, and my ears buzz and hum.

At first I pretend this means nothing, no bother to me at all. I move chairs closer together, talk close to people's heads. I use a magnifier for everything. But it grows harder and harder to work each day, to teach, and to read. Irène and Ève notice, and they become my eyes and ears. Irène at work. Ève at home. Each night, Ève opens my letters, and reads them aloud to me at dinner, speaking loudly and slowly so I can keep up.

I dictate my replies, and Ève pens them for me, and then she excuses herself afterward to go practice her piano. I beg of her to take on more studies in science. She tells me that she plans to become, of all things, *a concert pianist.*

"Maman," she insists petulantly. "I am never going to be a scientist like you and Irène."

"But you have to," I implore her. "You can always have piano as a hobby but what good will it do you in world? And further, what good will your piano playing do the world?"

She gets up and leaves rather than argue with me, and I hear her music in the distance, coming through the dull buzz in my ears. Talking to her is like shouting into a void. It makes me feel sad and empty and restless.

ONE EVENING A TELEGRAM ARRIVES, AND EVEN WITH THE buzzing in my ears, I can hear the sound of Ève's sobbing with a startling clarity. I know whatever news it brings, it is not good. We have recently lost Hela's husband Stanislaw back in Poland, and now what else can it be? Bronia or Mier? I just left Irène at the lab and nothing was amiss there. In the foyer, Ève sits on the floor and howls.

"What?" I demand, my heart clenching in my chest. I'm remembering that terrible summer so many years ago when my baby died and Jakub died, and my dear sweet Pierre rescued me from my ocean of grief. I am too tired now to be pulled under by such a tide. I cannot survive it again.

"Cousin Lou has had a hiking accident," Ève says between sobs. "Aunt Bronia says she is completely paralyzed. They don't know if she will ever walk again."

I close my eyes, put my hands to my ears to try and stop the buzzing. Bronia and I have achieved so much since we were girls.

The war is over and Poland is free, and Bronia and Mier are finally talking about moving back home, to Warsaw.

And then this great tragedy befalls them. It is too much. It is just too much.

Oh, sweet Lou. I remember hiking with her that long-ago summer, ascending from my terrible fog, breathing in the air of her beautiful Carpathians. Bronia wished for her to go into science and she would not listen, she refused to listen. If only she had listened.

I open my eyes again. Ève's tear-streaked face is but a shadow. "This never would've happened if she just would've undertaken a course of scientific study like Bronia wanted her to," I say.

"Maman, are you serious?" Ève snaps at me. "Not everything is about science."

She drops the telegram on the table, and runs out of the room. I close my eyes and wait for it. Not even a minute later there is the sound of her piano, far away, dark, like a growing storm.

MARYA

∽

I fell ill with a terrible case of grippe on my return to Krakow after moving Klara to Paris, and Kaz was so worried he summoned our niece, Lou, a physician herself now. After I had introduced her to biology in Loksow, she had gone on to study medicine in Paris, then returned to Poland to work alongside her parents in their medical clinic. She moved into Klara's empty bedroom for a few weeks to watch over my health day and night.

I was so very ill and so very lonely without Klara. It was hard to breathe, I was delirious with fever, and I truly wondered if the grippe might kill me. I desperately missed the comforts of Klara's noise, her piano that I'd grown so used to after so many years listening to it.

Play all the concert halls you dream of, my beautiful girl, I'd told her when I'd left her in Paris, feeling it was my last real chance to be her mother, to give her advice. *And if you fall in love, make sure it is with a man who sees you as his equal, and that you love each other and that he does not hold you back.*

Like you and Papa, Klara had said with a smile.

But was it, really? I had wondered, the whole way back on the train. If I had taken my own advice to Klara, perhaps I would've said no to Kaz, gotten on my own train to Paris so many years earlier.

But Kaz was still here with me now, somewhere, all these years later. My sickness held on and dragged me into darkness. And Kaz's voice came in and out of my fever dreams, distant and hazy, calling for me as he had once at the train station so long ago: *You can't go . . . Wherever it is you are going, you . . . you can't. Stay here. Stay with me.*

Then I didn't step on a train to Paris, or, maybe I did? In my feverish haze, I came out of the Gare du Nord, sunlight so bright I couldn't see, all of Paris before me and yellow and blinding, melting. And burning up into the blue-hot fire in Professor Mazur's lab. Everything was too hot to touch.

ONE MORNING, QUITE SUDDENLY, MY FEVER BROKE, AND I SAT up in bed, sweating and breathless. The December sun shone in through my bedroom window, illuminating Professor Mazur's stack of journals on my dresser. "Lou!" I called out. "Lou!"

She came running into my room, her face drawn. Lou was a woman now, and barely anyone still called her by her childhood nickname but me. She was *Dr. Helena Dluska*, tall and serious, stern and motherly, just like Bronia. It was hard to find even a glimmer of that girl who once traipsed through the Carpathians. My chest rattled with a cough, and I struggled to catch my breath as she walked over to my bed. "Can I get you something, *ciotka?*" she asked, her voice thick with concern.

I nodded and pointed to the journals on my dresser. "Yes, bring me those." Klara was in Paris; my head felt clear for the first time in months. I could not ignore science any longer. I could not ignore the legacy that Professor Mazur had left for me.

LOU RETURNED TO WARSAW A FEW DAYS AFTER MY FEVER broke, but I was still too weak to get out of bed and do much for weeks. I spent the time with Professor Mazur's journals, carefully reading all of her notes, combing through her calculations, and then making notes of my own in the margins.

"She was so close," I said to Kaz, one night after he'd come home from work, sat down on the farthest edge of the bed, the only spot free of scattered journals and papers. "It's just . . . I would need to get back into her lab. These calculations aren't quite right. I'd need more testing, and I have a theory that incorporates Hela's electromagnetic research with my—"

"*Kochanie,*" Kaz cut me off. He loosened his tie and leaned across all the papers to kiss me softly on the forehead. "I think I can help, with the lab."

"What?" His words didn't make sense.

"I've spoken to the dean, and Ola's old lab space has been empty since the war. They plan to hire a new chemistry professor next year, but until then, he said you can use her lab. On the condition that you also clean it out, get it ready for the next professor."

"Kaz!" I moved the notes aside and jumped across the bed to hug him. "Thank you. This is wonderful news!" The idea of a lab, all my own, even if temporarily, bubbled up inside of me, filled me with new possibility and hope.

IT WAS A STRANGE THING AT FIRST TO BE BACK IN PROFESSOR Mazur's lab, all alone. There was no one to instruct me, no one to decide what to do. No one at all, but me. Whatever happened here next would be of my doing and mine alone. That was both a glorious and terrifying thought.

The air in the lab smelled stale and somehow smoky even after being closed up all this time. It was windowless, dark, and hot inside, but still, standing here, I could breathe deeply again for the first time in months. My heart thudded wildly in my chest as I unpacked the equipment that had been stored away for years, cleaned off the canisters and combustion and cooling chambers.

I had only a few months to finish Professor Mazur's lifetime of work, but I had already spent weeks in bed charting out what I would do. If I considered Hela's theory about electromagnetic energy and applied this to the gas rather than trying to liquefy it, as we had been doing before the war, I theorized I could create an electrically charged detonator.

I wrote both Hela and Pierre for advice, and Hela encouraged me; she was excited by my idea. Pierre wondered if it would be too hard to do it alone. What if I came to Paris, worked on it at the Curie Institute with him and Jacques and Hela and our niece, Marie, a budding scientist? But I was Polish. I belonged here. Any discovery I might make belonged to Poland and to Ola Mazur.

And besides, I like working alone, I wrote back to Pierre. *I like making my own choices, being entirely responsible for my own results.*

I ROSE FROM BED EACH MORNING AT DAWN, AND THOUGH MY body was exhausted, my mind was utterly alive and buzzing with thoughts and ideas. I spent every waking hour inside my new lab. Sometimes, I did not even come home at night until after Kaz was in bed, already asleep.

One night in April when I made it home in time for dinner, Kaz greeted me at the door with a gentle kiss. Then he picked up my hands, stroked my fingers and frowned. "*Kochanie*, your fingertips are black."

I shrugged and wiped sweat from my brow with my free hand. My face was still warm, burning from the heat I'd created in my combustion chamber, and my entire body ached from standing all day. But my mind felt so wonderfully alive that I barely noticed the physical toll the lab was taking on me or the blackness of my fingers.

"You have been working so hard, *kochanie*," Kaz was saying now. "Maybe we should take a vacation?"

"I can't leave," I told him. "Not now. I don't have much time left with the lab. I need to seize every moment I can there."

He nodded. "Well . . . then, maybe I could buy you another bicycle?" he said kindly. "Oh! I could buy two and we could ride them together."

I smiled at him, grateful for his concern. "That sounds nice," I lied. In truth, bicycle riding sounded utterly exhausting. And he'd said it on such a whim, I figured he would forget all about it.

But he did not forget. A few weeks later when I got home from the lab, two shiny red bicycles were waiting outside on our front porch. Kaz sat in his rocking chair, smoking his pipe, reading by lamplight in the dusk. He had been waiting for me; he watched for my reaction.

"Oh, Kaz." I laughed and ran my fingers across the handlebars, noticing the black streaks I left behind on the metal.

"Come, *kochanie*, take a ride with me." He stood, putting his book and pipe down.

"Now? It's late. It's almost dark out." Besides that, I was exhausted from standing in the lab all day.

He walked to me and gave me a hug. "So, it is late?" he said into my hair, his breath tickling my neck. "Why not? We are still young."

I laughed at the absurdity of him believing us to be *young*, but then I felt a sudden surge of energy, and I wanted to ride. I wanted to *feel* young and free and light again. I got on the bicycle, and I began to pedal down our street.

"*Kochanie*, wait. Slow down! You are too fast," he called after me, laughing, sounding like the young man he once was in Szczuki. Both of us like the young people we once were.

I pedaled and pedaled, Kaz and the wind behind me, meandering through the streets of Krakow, through the gates of the university, not stopping until I was back at my lab. Kaz pedaled in behind me, breathing hard but smiling. "Did you forget something?" Kaz asked, motioning toward my lab.

I shook my head. It was true what I told Pierre, that I liked working alone, liked being in charge of my own results. But I had accomplished something earlier that I wanted to share with someone else now. "I want to show you what I have been working on," I told Kaz, putting my bicycle down on the grass.

"Now? But it is too dark to see."

I held out my hand for him. He hesitated for only a moment before he took it, and we walked into the science building. We climbed the stairs, walked inside my tiny lab. It was very dark, and he reached for the lamp. "Don't," I said, gently pulling back his hand.

"But I can't see what you're doing in the dark," he insisted.

"No, Kaz, look."

I gently turned his shoulders so he was facing the combustion chamber, where, a little while ago, I'd left mercury in an electrically charged tube. I'd finally gotten the electric charge right, lighting the mercury into fire. In the absolute blackness of this night, the mercury fire glowed, making my dark, small lab alive with an ethereal silvery-blue firelight. Here it was, right in front of our eyes: the key to Ola Mazur's detonation device. Blue and alive. Otherworldly. The last sliver of dusk.

"Oh, *kochanie*," he said, staring at my mercury flames. "Look what you have done!" He stepped closer to the combustion chamber, and his face illuminated blue and gold. "It's the most beautiful thing I've ever seen." And it was.

MARIE

❧

America & Paris, 1921–1922

Our voyage across the Atlantic feels painstakingly long, and I spend most of my time aboard the RMS *Olympic* in my suite, feeling dizzy. Ève and Irène leave me, to enjoy the extravagant meals and the views with Missy, who traveled to Paris to accompany us to New York. Then they come back periodically to check on me. They cluck likes hens, worried I haven't been eating enough, getting enough exercise, haven't been *having fun*.

"This is not vacation," I tell them, more sharply than I mean to. "This is work."

After all, a deal is a deal. In less than a year's time, Missy has raised her 100,000 dollars, the women of America coming through with their donations just as she believed they would. I suppose I underestimated her, the way people have been underestimating me my entire life. And the fact that she pulled this off makes me actually admire Missy. I am thrilled that I will soon have another gram of radium for France. But I hate the fact that I have to undertake such a journey: this transatlantic voyage, to be followed by a *seven-week* speaking tour of America, stopping at women's colleges, accepting honorary degrees. We will end in Washington, DC, at the White House, with the presentation of my new gram of radium by President Harding. I tell Irène and Ève this is *work*, but what it truly feels like is a distraction from my real work in the lab. I'd give anything to be back there instead.

The truth is, I can barely see now, and I'd confided as much to Missy in a letter last month as a way to perhaps get me out of this journey, after all. But then instead she wrote me back to tell me she set up an appointment for me with a specialist in New York. And now that feels more than half the reason for taking this voyage in the first place. I want my radium. Yes, I do. But more, I need my eyes back. I need to be able to see again in the lab, or the radium itself will be useless to me. And all the doctors I've seen in Paris have told me nothing useful but that perhaps I should retire. They say it is the radium and the X-ray exposure during the war that is causing me such problems in the first place. But I am still much too young to retire from the lab. My lab is my life; my work is my entire world. What do I have left if I am forced to leave it?

"Marie," Missy says to me, trying to cheer me up on the journey. "So many women in America, they adore you. You inspire them. They are so excited to meet you. How wonderful this will be for you to get so much attention!"

What is it she wrote me once, about *the unimportance of people*? Why do they care about me? They should care about the science, the radium.

"They do!" Missy promises me. "How do you think I managed to raise all this money in just a few months' time?"

But Missy doesn't understand the way this trip looms ahead of me in darkness, the way I dread all the talking and the social interaction and the press. *Oh dear God, the press.* Missy has promised me there will be no mentions of my *scandal* with the Langevins, saying no one in America cares about that sort of thing. But once I am halfway across the Atlantic, the ocean surrounds me, the rocking of the boat across the water makes me dizzy and ill, and I wonder how I have gotten myself into this. What I wouldn't give now for my eyesight and a simple anonymous existence, toiling away my days in the lab.

WHEN AT LAST WE DOCK IN NEW YORK CITY, I DRESS IN MY old comfortable black dress, but I adorn myself with a new and modern taffeta hat that Ève picked out for me before we left Paris. I feel ridiculous in it, but before I can change my mind and take it off, the press is already waiting, swarming, shouting for me: *Madame Curie. Madame Curie!*

I hear them over the buzz in my ears, see a horde of them gathering through the fog and film of my eyes. And suddenly I am getting off that train from Brussels again, my stomach filled with that never-ending pain and loss.

It is hard for me to breathe, and I let Missy and Irène and Ève do most of the talking. I sit in a chair in between them, trying not to cry. Answering only a few questions about radium.

The next morning the *New York Times* prints the most egregious front-page headline: MME. CURIE PLANS TO END ALL CANCERS.

"This is not at all what we told them." I wave the paper around at the dining table in Missy's elegant Greenwich Village apartment, nearly knocking over my china coffee cup.

Ève steadies my cup, takes the paper, reads the article, and looks up. "They call me the 'girl with the radium eyes.'" She laughs, delighted.

"That's preposterous," I snap at her. "If you had radium in your eyes, it would blind you." Though even as I am saying it, I understand how apt it is. How beautiful, how phosphorescent my youngest daughter is. I should tell her that, but I don't. That's not the point.

I try to remember now my exact words about radium and cancer at the dock, but it wasn't this. I'd only said that I planned to use my new gram of radium to experiment with new cures for cancers, never promising I can *cure them all*. "I'm here one day and already the press is lying about me. I need to go back to France. Irène, buy us tickets for the next boat!"

Irène sits perfectly still, frozen, like she is trying to decide what to do, how to temper her own joy of experiencing New York City and my anger. She opens her mouth to speak, then closes it again saying nothing at all.

"Marie." Missy stands, walks to me, puts her hand calmly on my shoulder. "I'll call them and we'll get them to print a retraction, all right? It is not done with malice, simply excitement. America adores you, that's all. And people are excited about a cure for cancer! You did this. You're saving so many people's lives."

I soften at her compliment, and agree, that yes, a retraction might do.

The following day, they do indeed print one: RADIUM NOT A CURE FOR EVERY CANCER. But Missy and I have to flip through to page sixteen to find it.

THERE ARE SO MANY SPEECHES AND COMMITMENTS OVER THE next weeks, and I tire so easily, feel so dizzy, that Irène and Ève stand in for me more and more as we travel across the country, from east to west, New York City, and upstate, and then on to Pittsburgh. We stop in Chicago and the festivities are larger than in New York. Missy says it's because many Poles live here, and they all come out, cheering for me. But what they are cheering for exactly, I don't know.

I feel like an exhibit, a commodity, and I am itching to flee, back to Paris, my lab, back to the science. I am doing what I must to get my radium—smiling, waving, speaking when I can. But it is harrowing and painful. I despise every minute of it. It is not what I want, never what I wanted.

Lou is in a facility in Chicago, trying to regain sensation in her legs, and we schedule a visit with her into all the busyness. It is a shock to see her in her wheelchair, crippled and despondent, staring out her window at the steely Chicago sky.

"Your color is so good," Ève lies, kissing her cousin on the head. Irène nods eagerly in agreement.

Lou turns to look at me, and I go in close to her face so I can see her, really see her. Her eyes are round and large and vacant. I hold on to her shoulders in an awkward hug. "It is too hard to live this way, *ciotka*," she says softly to me.

Her voice sounds flat, and it is hard to remember that girl who took me up in the Carpathians, once. But she is in here somewhere, I know she is. "You are a strong woman," I tell her. "Like me. Like your mother. We have all endured so much. You will get through this."

She pulls away from me, frowns, and turns her gaze back out the window.

She worries me, and I hate to leave her like this. But she cannot walk; I cannot bring her with us westward. And Missy has us scheduled for two weeks more.

THE FOLLOWING YEAR, BACK IN FRANCE, EVERYTHING IS looking brighter.

I have my new gram of radium, new work underway. I've had surgery for my cataracts in both eyes, after the doctor Missy set me up with in America diagnosed that as my problem. And I can see again now, with the help of my magnifying lens.

When the urgent telegram arrives from Bronia, I pull it from Ève's hands this time, wanting to read it myself.

Lou is dead.

I read the words, and they sink inside my body, a weight.

"What is it, Maman?" Ève asks, alarmed. "Is it Lou?"

I am surprised by Ève's perceptiveness, but perhaps I shouldn't be. She had been cheerful in Chicago, but she had been there. She had seen Lou's vacant stare and terrible crippled legs. "She took her own life," I say, reading through the rest of the telegram, breathless.

Ève puts her hand to her mouth, and her eyes well up with tears, and she runs out of the room. I don't realize my own hands are shaking until Irène pulls the telegram from them, places it down on the table, and sits down on the floor with me, putting her arms around my shoulders.

This can't be right. This can't be true. My chest aches for my sister-mother, both her children gone too soon. Why must death hover around my family? I try to breathe and my lungs burn, as if I've run and run for days. So many people gone; so much loss surrounds us.

What if I had done things differently in my life—could I have stopped this all from happening? Perhaps I could've talked to Lou that summer in the Carpathians, tried to convince her to give up hiking for science. Or I could have gotten a doctor to heal Jakub if I'd convinced Bronia to stay in Paris just one summer longer. And Pierre. What if I had stopped him from going out that one afternoon into the rain? In all these years, I have changed the entire course of science; why have I not been able to save my family?

"It is all my fault," I say. "Everything is my fault."

Irène clings to me. "Maman, how could this be your fault? What could you have possibly done?"

"I could've stopped them; I could've done things differently."

"Maman," Irène whispers and strokes back my hair, like I am the child and she is the mother. "Lou was in terrible shape when we saw her in Chicago. There was nothing to be done."

I hold on tightly to Irène, breathing in the scent of her: flowers and sunshine and the lab. "You will never leave me," I say. "My darling girl, promise me that."

"I promise," Irène says.

MARYA

❦

L'Arcouëst, 1922

I spent the summer of 1922 at Hela and Jacques's house in L'Arcouëst, and even Bronia agreed to come for a few weeks so all of us sisters and our children could be together again. Our husbands mostly stayed behind to work, except for a few weekends here and there. But the three of us and all our children were together for the first time in so many years. It was glorious.

I'd spent the past year writing up Professor Mazur's research and my results into a paper. I no longer had use of the lab at Jagiellonian, as the dean had hired a new chemistry professor for Professor Mazur's job, an older man who had no interest in continuing with me on my mercury research, in spite of all the arguments Kaz tried to make to him on my behalf. Still, I had months of results, a paper to prove it now. I brought my paper with me to L'Arcouëst for Hela to look through, and I hoped that she would agree that applying her electromagnetic theory to mercury was highly exciting. That she might even want to endorse my findings about using mercury to ignite an electrical switch, and that she might help me get it published in a scientific journal.

"Marya," she said, after she was finished reading my words. Her cheeks were pink, her voice effusive. "This is brilliant. Your research could be revolutionary. If ever there were another Great War, imagine how this device could help with precision in bombs, and . . . aircraft."

I smiled, but Hela was getting ahead of herself. I'd gotten mercury to ignite in an electrically charged tube, and theorized the rest, that this could work as a detonation device, or in a switch. That seemed far off still from controlling bombs, and another war? *God forbid.* I said all that to Hela, and she laughed.

"Well, every large idea is a small idea, first." She paused for a moment, as if to think, and I remembered a Latin phrase I'd learned once at my Flying University in Loksow: *omnium rerum principia parva sunt.* The beginnings of all things are small. "Why don't you come to Brussels with me in October, Marya, and we can present this paper at the Solvay Conference, together? Perhaps someone there would want to undertake more of this research with us."

"Solvay?" I remembered how Professor Mazur had attended, how she had met Hela there once, just before Hela had won her Nobel Prize. I was almost entirely self-taught. I could not imagine I would fit in with scientists like Hela who had advanced degrees from top schools. "I don't know," I said.

"I will pay for your ticket," Hela said. "You have no reason not to go."

"Oh, you two." Bronia rolled her eyes. "Can we stop talking about science for five minutes and go enjoy this beautiful view, hmmm?"

"You should talk, Bron," Hela retorted. "You are always working."

"I have taken this entire month off," Bronia retorted back, sounding uncertain, like she could barely believe her own words. "Lou and I both have."

"I'll stop talking about science, if Marya will agree to come to Brussels with me," Hela said. Both her eyes and Bronia's fell squarely on my face, staring at me, waiting for me.

"Yes," I finally said, feeling both excited and terrified. "I'll go to Brussels with you."

THEN I SAT OUT ON THE BEACH IN BETWEEN MY SISTER-mother and my sister-twin, and all of us, with our wrinkled faces and graying buns now, we forgot about science for a little while. We watched our grown children swimming, racing each other in the water, laughing and teasing one another, cousins and comrades. Lou was the fastest one, with Jakub coming in second. (*Of course* Bronia's children were the best and fastest, just like their mother.) Marie beat Klara—my beautiful, musically inclined child always came in last, the least athletic of all her cousins.

Out on the beach, Hela reached for my hand, and I reached for Bronia's hand, and we all sat there like that together, three old women, forever connected to one another by blood and by love. And yes, by science, too.

"Look at all we have become, all we have done," Hela said, a smile in her voice as we stared out at our children and onto the great expanse of water. I'd grown used to its size, so I no longer feared it. I still didn't like to go in, but I enjoyed taking in its enormous beauty. Bronia squeezed my hand in response, and I squeezed back.

My sister-twin had won science's biggest prize, and she and

Jacques had patented their discovery, making them flush now with royalties and allowing them to construct a three-story lab of their own in Paris where they were continuing with their work. Marie was finishing up her degree in chemistry to work alongside them.

My sister-mother and her Kazimierz had run a successful sanatorium in Zakopane for years and were making plans to move back to Warsaw and open their own hospital there, where Lou planned to work too. Jakub was studying medicine at Jagiellonian, and one day no doubt, there would be an entire hospital staffed with a full line of Dluski doctors.

And me? I had raised my beautiful and talented daughter, given her life and music and opportunity. And I had taken Professor Mazur's research and turned it into something of my own, a theory, a paper. A small thing that maybe would become a big thing. After I went to Solvay with Hela, if I managed to get my paper published, perhaps one day when I was no longer here on this beach to watch my Klara swim, or listen to her give a concert, a little piece of me, a little piece of my idea, would still be left behind in this great big world.

PIERRE HAD STAYED IN PARIS ALL SUMMER, WORKING WITH Jacques, finally, on his pitchblende. Hela said the real reason he stayed behind was for Jeanne, who refused to be in a room with Hela any longer (much less spend the summer in the same house) since Hela had hired Paul to work with her and Jacques last year. *He's a highly qualified scientist,* Hela had said to me with a shrug.

I felt annoyed with her on Jeanne's behalf. *Oh, Hela,* I said, *was there no one else?* But anyway, I didn't believe what Hela said to be true. Pierre had wanted to test his theory on the pitch-blende for so many years. That meant more to him than any woman, any love. That's why he stayed in Paris.

But then Pierre showed up in L'Arcouëst late one afternoon in August, just a few days before we were all set to go home. His beard was a shocking snowy white, and his hairline had receded enough so it almost disappeared, leaving him nearly completely bald. But when I caught his eyes, they were still as deep and blue as the water surrounding Stockholm.

"Is everything all right with the lab?" Hela asked, alarmed to see him. She and Jacques were working on using their electro-magnetic research for medical imaging, and her new lab was now her most important child.

"Yes, quite," Pierre said. "I just needed a few days out of the city. Jacques is still working, not to worry."

"Hmmm." Bronia folded her hands in front of her chest and stared at Pierre with the same look of disdain she'd given him once so many years earlier when we'd returned to her house in La Villete after watching the bicycle race. I smiled a little at the memory.

"If you must know," Pierre said, looking at the three of us a little like all together we were a force that frightened him. "Jeanne and Paul have decided to reconcile."

"Oh, Pierre," Hela said, offering him a quick hug. "I'm so sorry." Pierre shrugged, but he kept his eyes on me. I offered him a small smile, a shrug of my own in return, surprised that maybe Hela had been right about why he'd stayed in Paris this summer all along. Love, not science.

"There's vodka in the icebox," Bronia said, walking toward the kitchen. "Pierre, you look like you could use it."

LATER, AFTER EVERYONE HAD GONE TO BED, PIERRE AND I SAT out on the back deck, still nursing our vodkas. A lamp sat on the table between us, and in the flicker of the flame, I could sometimes see the waves in the distance as I heard them crashing against the rocks.

"I don't know that I ever really truly loved her," Pierre said softly.

"You must've. To have stayed with her for years," I said.

"Hmmm," Pierre said. "But maybe there is a difference between a great love and companionship, *mon amie.*"

I thought about Kaz, all our many years together, and I didn't know if I agreed with Pierre. What was a *great love* if it did not fill in the spaces of loneliness over so much time? If all a person needed to survive was her studies, her work, her lab, then I would've stepped on that train to Paris so many years ago and left Kaz at the station. But that was not all there was. What was the point of work at all, if you had no one to share it with? "How is your pitchblende?" I asked him, changing the subject.

He smiled wanly. "Jacques and I may have finally isolated what I've been looking for all along. An entirely different element than becquerelium, with different chemical properties."

"Pierre! That's wonderful!"

He nodded, took a large sip of his vodka. "Yes, I suppose I should feel happy. But . . . what does it matter now? Who else will care but me? And, I'm old and barely a real scientist."

"For one thing, you are very much a real scientist. And for another, you're not that old," I said to him.

He sighed and swished the vodka around in his glass. "Anyway, my legs are quite tired," he said. "It is hard to get out of bed in the mornings, much less undertake the strenuous work of scientific study. I think I'll retire to Sceaux and spend my remaining days in the gardens of my childhood."

"Nonsense. You're in good health. You must continue your work," I insisted. I thought about how much Hela's support of my paper meant to me, and I wanted to give the same to Pierre. "I'll make you a deal," I said. "Hela wants me to come present my research in Brussels at Solvay this fall. I'll go present my research if you also come present yours."

He laughed, like he thought I was joking, and then his face turned when he noticed my serious expression.

"Well, why not?" I said. "What if generations of future scientists can use these things we discovered? What if our small discoveries make the entirety of our lives and all our choices matter?"

Pierre finished off his drink and stared into the flicker of the flame. "What if, indeed," he finally said.

MARIE

Paris, 1925–1926

Irène completes her doctoral thesis on the alpha decay of polonium in the spring of 1925, and I'm thrilled that this daughter of mine and Pierre's is continuing on with our work. Polonium has still been largely ignored since we discovered it, and that has continually been my greatest regret as a scientist.

But my darling Irène takes a special interest in polonium, and I love her even more than I ever have. She finishes her thesis and achieves her degree from the Sorbonne.

We work side by side together in my lab, day in and day out. We have everything. Satisfying work, good salaries, a beautiful home in Paris and also the one we are building now in L'Arcouëst for summers. We take our meals together each day and walk to the lab together. She is my eyes and my ears and sometimes my mind. Why would we ever need anything else aside from each other?

But then I assign her to train a new, young chemical engineer in the lab, Frédéric Joliot, on how to use precise laboratory techniques in radiochemistry. And suddenly, she is staying late to help him, arriving early to help him. Abandoning me to help him.

I must walk to the lab alone some mornings, because she has already eaten, left ahead of me to get there early. And the walk down rue Pierre Curie to our lab suddenly feels very long and very lonely indeed.

In June, Missy writes me a letter about an American girl who'd been working for the US Radium Corporation in their plant in New Jersey. She was a dial painter, painting watches with radium, and now she is suing the company, claiming that her work, which required her to use her lips to prepare her radium brush, has caused damage to her health.

Ève reads me the letter over supper, as my eyes are giving me quite a bit of trouble again and Irène is not yet home from the lab. I'd left her there hours earlier, working with Frédéric.

"Missy wonders about the effects of radium on your health, Maman," Ève says, as she continues reading down the letter, discussing nine factory women who have supposedly died. "I worry, too, about you and Irène working with radium all the time like you do. And didn't those other two men just die in France?"

Marcel Demalander and Maurice Demenitroux were young men who had worked in my lab once, and more recently were preparing thorium X for medical uses in a factory outside of Paris. They had recently died a few days apart of different illnesses, causing the press to try and blame radium.

"Don't be silly," I say, pushing her concerns away with a flick of my hand. "My lab is very safe. I've always taken every precaution. We vacation away from the city every summer, get plenty of fresh air and outdoor activities to clear our lungs."

"But these girls, and . . . your health." She puts the letter down and frowns.

Ève does not understand what we do. In spite of all my protests, she has decided to pursue piano professionally, and she will give her first concert in Paris soon. I do not understand her attraction to the piano as a career, or how she believes it will sustain her mind and her body for the entirety of her life. But no matter what I say to her, how much I've tried to engage her with science, she has gone back to her piano again and again.

"There is nothing wrong with my health," I say now. "I am a perfectly fit fifty-seven-year-old woman."

"Who can barely see or hear," Ève says. "And you're exhausted all the time."

"You have no idea what you're talking about," I say, my voice shaking.

"Don't be angry." Her voice softens. "I just worry about you, that is all, Maman."

"I don't need you to worry about me. Perhaps if you undertook a scientific course of study like your sister you would understand," I say.

Her face falls, like I have slapped her, though I have not moved at all. And she stands up, walks out of the room.

A few moments later I hear the sounds of her piano drifting across the house. She is playing something soft and high and sad, and it reminds of the sound of the raindrops on the metal roof of my laboratory the afternoon Pierre was killed.

I bite back tears, and I think, *I should go to her. I should tell her that.* I love Ève, but I never know how to understand her, how to talk to her. I am always saying the wrong thing to her.

But Ève is also right, I am exhausted. I sit there listening to her play, and I close my eyes, thinking of those raindrops, that last day I saw Pierre alive. And I fall asleep right there in my chair, dreaming of that other life, that other time.

ÈVE WANTS ME TO ATTEND HER FIRST PIANO PERFORMANCE A
few weeks later, and I plan to go. But I am much too tired when
the night arrives, and I stay home and go to bed early. Irène goes
in my place, accompanied, Ève reports the following morning at
breakfast, by *Frédéric Joliot*.

"You are getting too attached to him," I tell Irène. "I want
you to work with another student in the lab, starting today."

Irène blushes, makes a face at Ève, then sips on her coffee.
"Fred is sweet, Maman. And funny."

Fred? "Hmmm," I say. "What use does a Curie woman have
for *sweet* and *funny?*"

"I could think of a few," Ève jokes.

"He is a brilliant scientist, too," Irène shoots back, both of
us ignoring Ève.

"You are the brilliant scientist," I say to Irène. "And Fred is
nothing but a distraction."

"Maman." Irène shakes her head, closes her eyes, and frowns
deeply. For a second I remember that once Pani Zorawska had
believed of me what I am now saying of Fred. But this is different.
This is completely different. Irène is too good to be distracted
by any man.

"I'm serious," I say. "I want you to stay away from him."

Irène sighs, stands up, clears away her breakfast dishes. "I
need to get to the lab," she says abruptly, kissing me on top of my
head before she walks out.

I'm still watching her go, considering if I should go after her,
when Ève says, "If you were wondering, Maman, my concert last
night went very well. I'm going to play another one in Brussels in
the summer. I hope you'll be able to come?"

I am tired of arguing with her. Tired of begging her to choose me, to choose science, and my mind is with Irène, imagining her walking into the lab without me, talking to *Fred*.

"Maman?" Ève asks.

"I will try, darling," I say, distractedly. "I really will try."

"I have something to tell you," Irène says, a few weeks later at supper.

"Hmmm?" I am not very hungry tonight, and I have been looking over a paper, leaving my food barely touched. Irène has been quiet these last few weeks, tiptoeing around me, ever since I told her to stay away from Fred. I'm relieved she wants to tell me something now, and I put the paper down and look up.

"Fred and I are going to be married," she says abruptly.

Her words reverberate and shock me, and I blink, thinking I misheard her. "What?"

She repeats it again, *married*, and I hear her, watch her lips move and her mouth turn up into a smile. But it is as if she's speaking another language or playing one of Ève's songs on the piano. Something I cannot possibly understand.

"No," I say. "I will not allow it."

Her smile turns to a frown, a look I have barely seen on her face, one that is more similar to Ève's favorite expression. "Maman," she says gently. "I am twenty-nine years old. Fred and I are in love." She pauses. "We have everything you and Papa once had, a shared love of each other and our work. How can you not understand that?"

My eyes sting with tears, thinking of Pierre. *A shared love of each other and our work.* But that is what I have with Irène now. She is my partner; she is my confidante. What will I do without her?

And what would Pierre say, if he could be sitting here in this moment? *We want her to be happy,* mon amour. *We want for her a good and easy life.*

But she is happy already, with me.

Mon amour, *she is a twenty-nine-year-old woman. She is in love.*

But what does she know?

"Maman," she tries gently again, bringing me back to her. "I'm not asking for your permission. I'm telling you what is going to happen. Fred and I love each other. We are getting married."

What can I do? What can I say? I have lost so much, so many people. As worried as I am for her, giving herself over to a man, I cannot stop her. She is a grown woman, a brilliant scientist. But I cannot lose her either. And most importantly, she cannot lose her herself.

"I will insist upon a prenuptial agreement," I finally say. "Stating that the lab and all the radium belongs to you and only you."

"Fine," she says. "Fred doesn't care about any of that. He loves me, and I love him."

"Perhaps you love him now." I want her to understand, I only want what's best for her. I do not want her to be hurt by love the way I have been. "But love is fleeting," I tell her. "Science will never leave you."

MARYA

Warsaw, 1926–1932

After Klara graduated from the conservatory, she got a job with a symphony in London. And once she was supporting herself, I told Kaz what I desired more than anything was to move back to Warsaw, my childhood home. Agata had relocated to Warsaw after the war and had expanded our university there, renaming it *Women's University of Poland*. I wanted to teach with her once more.

Kaz said that he, too, was ready for a change, and most of all, he wanted me to be happy. He retired from his position at Jagiellonian, and we moved into an apartment in Praga Połnoc, Warsaw, with a very nice view of the Vistula River from our bedroom. I returned to teaching with Agata just a few days after we moved in.

Our children were grown, and our lives were completely different than they once were—Agata's husband had passed away three years ago, and her son Piotr was studying art in Krakow, but our friendship returned immediately, with all the ease we'd once had working together in the Kaminski house in Loksow.

"Oh, Marya," Agata said. "How good it is to be with you again." And I agreed completely, feeling the same about her. "The school was never the same without you."

I smiled, relieved and happy, thanking her for welcoming me back after all this time and after all the work she had done to build it without me, from the small university it once was in Loksow.

But Agata said that she was the lucky one. "The students have so much to learn from you now, after what you have accomplished, Marya." She beamed at me with pride.

After I went to Solvay with Hela a few years ago, she helped me patent my device, which I called the *Mazur-Zorawksa detonator*. But I did not desire money, or fame, and I'd handed the patent over to the Polish government in hopes they could explore ways to use it to help my beautiful country stay beautiful and free and Polish for many generations to come.

I had my experience in the lab and the Mazur-Zorawska detonator to teach a new generation of Polish women about. I taught chemistry and physics classes at Women's University, as I once had, so many years ago. But now I had a very nice classroom, inside a very nice building, and no fear to walk inside of it.

I reveled in the comforts of teaching, of sitting inside a room with windows and walking to a café for lunch, breathing the fresh Warsaw air again. I loved the sounds of the free Polish language as I walked on the streets each evening toward home, the same paths I'd walked as a girl. Perhaps most of all I enjoyed watching my young students' faces and eyes light up when I told them stories about Hela and Jacques accepting their Nobel, and me completing Ola Mazur's research using Hela's theory, and even Pierre discovering his new element after so many years of wanting.

"You must never give up," I told these young women, as their bright eyes trained steadily on my face. "You cannot let circumstances or misfortune or age stop you. You must make a choice to keep going. You always have a choice," I told them.

KAZ'S RETIREMENT DIDN'T LAST VERY LONG, AS HE MISSED the daily interaction with students and conversation about maths. After a few months in Warsaw, he returned to teaching two mornings a week at the University of Warsaw. And then at night, over supper, Kaz and I took pleasure in discussing our students, what we taught and also what we learned each day.

Bronia lived nearby in the suburb of Anin, where she and her Kazimierz and Lou ran a medical clinic, helping patients recover from tuberculosis. Kaz and I saw all three of them at least once a week, for suppers on Sundays.

Hela was still in Paris with Jacques and Marie, all three of them working at the Curie Institute, where they had made great advancements in using magnets for medical imaging. But mainly Marie stayed there to run the lab while Hela and Jacques traveled to give speeches about their work and raise money for their continued research. They went all around Europe, even to America twice, but Hela did not enjoy the travel and wrote to tell me how the older she got, the more she missed Poland, and me, and Bronia.

There is very little science in fame, Hela wrote me, *and very little joy for me and Jacques when we are not working in the lab together.*

I urged her to move back to Warsaw, to be near me and Bronia, to come and teach with me, and share her knowledge with other young women. *Jacques would never leave France,* she wrote. And I wondered if, in spite of her complaints, a part of her secretly loved the fame, or if she felt bound to it, some wayward duty? I felt sad that she might never be able to leave it behind, to have a quiet and beautiful life like Bronia and I were enjoying in Warsaw now.

Pierre wrote to me that some days he made it into the lab to assist Marie, but most days he rode his bike through his gardens in Sceaux and was content to let Marie carry on his work. I imagined him riding, his completely white hair and beard fluttering in the wind while he reveled in the scent of flowers. Kaz and I had brought our own bicycles to Warsaw, and on the weekends, we still rode them together, too, sometimes bringing a picnic lunch to enjoy along the banks of the Vistula.

In 1929, Marie sent me a scientific study she published so I could share her results with my students. She was studying the alpha decay of Pierre's element, and she had determined its half-life to be just 138 days. Which was especially noteworthy compared with that of becquerelium, which was thought to be 1,600 years.

Imagine two such radioactive elements, side by side in the pitchblende, so similar and yet with such a different half-life, she wrote.

Half-life, I thought. *What a funny word. So unscientific.*

To me it sounded more like the way I might describe how I had lived my entire adult life. One foot inside my reality with Kaz, one foot inside the fantasy of what might have been, what I might have become, had I gone to Paris as a young woman to study at the Sorbonne.

As principal pianist with the London symphony, Klara gave concerts all around Europe, and Kaz and I traveled to see her whenever we could manage the cost and the distance, especially in the summers, when neither one of us were teaching. In the summer of 1932, we went to Belgium to hear her play at the Ancienne Belgique in Brussels, then on to Paris, where she played at the Salle Pleyel, and Hela, Jacques, Pierre, and Marie attended with us.

How beautiful she was up on stage, dressed in taffeta as blue as her eyes! And sitting in the audience, I was mesmerized by the way her fingers moved across the keys, fast and furious and delicate all at once. Somehow we had made her, Kaz and I. But she had worked hard and practiced and practiced. She had gone after her dream; she had made herself, too.

Kaz squeezed my hand, and when she finished performing and stood up to take her bow, he turned and kissed my cheek. "You're crying, *kochanie*," he whispered to me, reaching up to wipe away my tears. "Don't be sad."

"I'm not sad," I said back to him. "Watching her, now I know we have done everything right. Made all the right choices in our lives, haven't we?"

"Yes, *kochanie*," he agreed with me. "We have."

"TAKE A WALK WITH ME," PIERRE SAID THE MORNING AFTER the concert. He'd come to Hela and Jacques's house, where we were all staying for a few days for a visit, all of us laughing around the breakfast table this morning: Kaz and Klara, Hela and Marie and Jacques. Pierre whispered the request close enough to my ear, and no one else seemed to hear or notice him.

I stood. "I'll be right back," I said to Klara, who was sitting next to me. She smiled and dove back into conversation and laughter with her cousin, Marie.

"Come," Pierre said. He held out his hand for me to take it, and I did, finding a comfort in his familiarity. He moved slower than he used to. His shoulders were a bit stooped, his hair gone, his beard thinned and pure white. "The delphinium are all in bloom in the Parc Monceau," he said. "And I swear it, they are all the color of your mercury flame. Every time I've walked by them, I've thought, *How Marya will love these flowers.*"

I didn't have a garden in Warsaw like I'd had in Krakow, and besides, I felt too old to tend to one now. It was harder to breathe than it once was, and as Pierre and I walked, I had to slow down. I began to cough.

"Marya?" Pierre stopped and turned to me. "Are you ill?"

"No, no," I said. "Just a little cough, that's all." But inside my chest, my lungs constricted, pushing against my ribs, so that the words came out of me in a wheeze. Pierre's face fell with concern. "Don't worry," I told him. "I will have Lou examine me when I get back to Warsaw, hmm? But I'm sure it's nothing. Come, show me your delphinium."

I DID NOT EXACTLY LIE TO PIERRE, BUT I DID NOT LET LOU examine me for six months after I returned to Warsaw. And maybe it was because deep down, I knew. I was a scientist and a teacher; I knew the body, my own body, well enough to understand it was failing me. But still, I could not push past my own denial, my own stupid hope that if I simply ignored it, it would go away. I would improve.

A little bit of the grippe coming back to haunt me, that is all, I reassured a worried Kaz for months and months as I coughed.

But by the winter my cough had become unbearable, my breathing more labored, and I could not ignore it any longer. I took the train out to Anin one Thursday when Kaz was teaching a class, wanting to go alone.

"Oh, *ciotka,*" Lou said, examining my chest X-ray. Three

months earlier, she had married a writer she'd cured of tuberculosis in their clinic, and up until this very moment, her face had been pink with joy.

"Just tell me the truth," I told her. "Don't soften it."

She handed me the X-ray so I could examine it myself. The large black spots on my lungs confirmed what I already knew deep down. There was a cancer growing inside of me. And perhaps it was not at all surprising, after all the smoke that had filled my lungs day in and day out in the lab in Krakow.

And still, I felt shocked by it. That it was happening *to me*. My hands shook with disbelief. "Are you sure this is my X-ray, Lou?" I asked, handing it back to her. Perhaps it had fallen from the machine, belonging to someone else, another patient.

Lou put her arms around my shoulders, holding on to me. She stroked my hair with her hands. "It is too much to operate," she said quietly after a few moments. "And we have no treatments for cancer other than surgery, you know."

I nodded, I did know. There was nothing to be done for cancer, no curative therapy to treat it. "How much time do you think I have?" I asked her.

She didn't say anything for another moment; she just held on to me. And then finally she said, "If you're lucky and the cancer isn't too aggressive . . . Maybe a year?"

MARIE

❧

Warsaw, 1932

There is a great big Radium Institute opening in Warsaw, entirely devoted to Curietherapy, using my radium for the curative treatment of cancer. I travel to Poland by myself for its grand opening at the end of May; neither of my daughters can make it.

Irène has recently given birth to a baby boy she named Pierre, a tribute to her father, and she and Fred are back in Paris looking after him, and my lab. I've had to admit I was wrong about Fred. Irène is right; he is kind and he is funny; he is a good scientist and now a good father, too. Everything my Pierre would've wanted for Irène. I have not lost Irène to Fred at all, but I have, instead, gained another scientist and a son-in-law. Irène is better than me; perhaps for her, love and science really can be one and the same.

I've spent most of the last years traveling, raising money for my institutes, giving speeches, and accepting honors, and it has been good to have Irène and Fred back in Paris. I'd much rather be in the lab with them, but who else will do these things, raise the money to keep my work going, if not me?

When she is not otherwise engaged with her piano perfor-
mances, Ève accompanies me in my travels. She is nothing like
me, or Irène—she is a dreamer, her head in the clouds, like her
father. I am wont to remind her to pay attention every time she
crosses the street. But it is silly, because she is the one looking out
for me as I walk, as my eyes have failed me so. I wish she could've
come to Warsaw with me, but she is busy, and she does not understand how important this particular journey is to me either.
It is not just another speech, another honor—I have finally given
something to my homeland.

Still, the train ride to Warsaw is very, very long, and very
lonely to undertake by myself. I'm exhausted by the time I arrive,
and it is hard to remember why I've been looking forward to this
trip so. My entire body aches.

But then my sister-mother and my sister-twin are both waiting for me at the train station, and seeing them again, holding on
to them again, I feel a glimmer of happiness.

THE CITY IS QUITE EXCITED TO RECEIVE ME, BESTOWING UPON
me honorary degrees and so many kind words. It is a strange
thing to reconcile this with the city I knew as a poor young girl,
with the country who refused to hire me, to want me, to love me
and Pierre, once. Now, I stand here in front of my new institute,
hearing a crowd cheering, *for me?* There is even a special brick in
the building inscribed with an homage to me.

Hela and Bronia both attend the ribbon-cutting ceremony,
and how wonderful it is to be here with both of them. They each
hold on to one of my hands, and the three of us stand here and
stare up at my great big beautiful institute, long after the ribbon
has been cut and the crowd has dissipated.

"Look what you have done," Hela says, softly, squeezing my hand. "Papa would be so proud."

I have lost so much, so many people. I am old and ailing and often quite lonely. Sometimes I wonder what my life would be like now if Pierre were still here. I think about that last sun-drenched morning in Saint-Rémy, when love and light and our little family all glowed there around me—*luck*, as Pierre called it.

But that was so long ago, so far away. In all the years since, amid all the loss, I have never lost sight of my work. My radiation therapy will help cure so many Polish people of cancer, right here, in this very institute. And staring up at this great big beautiful Polish building, for a second, I believe every choice I've made was the right one.

Bronia nods and murmurs in agreement with Hela. "Very proud," she says. "And I am very proud to be the medical director here." Though today is the official opening, we have been admitting patients, curing them already for a few months, under Bronia's direction.

I get up close to examine my sister-mother, to be able to see her face through the clouds of my eyes. She is too pale and too thin. I worry for her, living alone in Warsaw, with no family left, but Hela. Mier passed away two years ago, and in the time since, Bronia has thrown herself into overseeing the building of this institute, raising the funds to get it finished, and now running it as the medical director.

Still, she appears frail before me, her wrinkled skin sagging from her bones. But I ask her to tell me about the people she's treating here, and her face lights up a little. Even after all this time, my sister-mother wants to be needed, needs to be needed.

It is the people of Poland who need her now, to treat them with my cancer cure.

"I'm tired," Bronia says, finished speaking about her patients now. "It is time to go home."

But I am not ready to let her—or my time with my sisters—go yet. I grab her hand and beg of her to walk along the Vistula with me. To examine the bright blue water, to let it calm us and carry us as it did when we were girls. She protests that it is getting late, but Hela agrees with me, insists.

"Life is so strange and too short," Hela says. "What if we are never all together again?" And now it is true, that all three Sklodowska sisters have outlived their husbands, and that Bronia has also outlived her children. Bronia and Hela do hold each other close here in Warsaw, but my life is still in Paris, my lab in Paris. The very long trip here has exhausted me more than I have ever felt before, and I do not know if I will ever make it home again.

But I will not admit that out loud to my sisters. Instead I say, "Who knows when we sisters will be together again, hmm?"

Finally Bronia relents, and the three of us walk toward the river.

We are older now, and we all move slowly. My eyes give me so much trouble that I am holding on tightly to my sisters, counting on them to lead the way, to guide me.

"Do you remember when we walked here after Mama died?" Hela says. "What you told us about the river, Bron?"

"It was so long ago," Bronia says. "I don't know."

But I remember. We were so young then, so sad. So lost. We knew nothing of the world outside of Warsaw or all the things the future would hold for us. We knew nothing of men or love, of science or of war. We had lost our mother; we thought we had lost everything. We did not know that we could lose so much more, that we could survive so much more, too. We did not know what we were capable of, what we would become, how we would change the course of science.

Bronia had insisted then that the fresh air, the water, it would do us some good. She had grabbed on to mine and Hela's hands and practically dragged us here, and then we had stood by the banks of the big blue river and Bronia had said, *Look, my sisters! Look at the way the water moves, on and on and on. It never stops. It can't stop.*

Once we reach the river again now, it is just as blue, just as beautiful and striking as I remember it being when we were girls.

"Look," I say to Bronia. "It is still moving. Always moving. It never stops. It can't stop."

MARYA

~

Warsaw, 1934

I am sixty-six years old and I convalesce, my lungs no longer able to carry the weight of my breath. Nearly all day I sleep, but still I dream, comforted by the sounds of Klara's concertos in my mind. In waking moments, Bronia and Lou and Kaz tend to me, bringing me soup and flowers and sitting by my bedside, talking to me softly. Outside my window I can catch a glimpse of the palest summer Polish sky, or, on days when I am well enough to sit up, the sparkling blue waters of the Vistula in the distance.

Klara comes from London, and that is when I know, it is truly the end, that the cancer has grown larger than my will to breathe. Kaz must've called her and told her to come as fast as she could.

Mama, is there anything you need?

I can see the shape of her when I open my eyes again, more a shadow than my beautiful daughter. *Play for me,* I tell her. *Play me a song.*

Her sweet music floods my ears, a balm, a memory. A dream-scape.

Promise me something, I say to her. *You never stop playing that music. And if you fall in love, you make sure he is your equal. That he will not hold you back in your career. You never stop, Klara. You reach for everything you want, and, you never stop.*

From the other room, the sound of her piano goes and goes and goes, and I close my eyes listening to it, smiling.

MAMA. KLARA'S VOICE AGAIN.

Hours have passed, or maybe just minutes? Or has it been days? My beautiful daughter, *mój mały kurczak,* she is a shadow, hovering again. No, there are two shadows now.

Someone came to see you, Klara says. *He came all the way from Paris!*

His shape becomes a memory, and my sense of smell has not left me yet. I inhale: the flower gardens in Sceaux. The cherry blossoms as we rode bicycles through the streets of Paris, pedaling too hard, the sun on our faces.

Slow down, mon amie. *You are much too fast.*

Marya, he says my name. *Oh, Marya.* I remember the way his face fell in Sweden, standing by the river, wanting to kiss me. The way he looked when he swirled his vodka glass by the sea, finally understanding that his work mattered. That his life meant something. *Means* something. He is here now, and he is alive and breathing, and he will continue on, even after I am gone.

He must've sat down in a chair by my bed, because when I open my eyes again, his shadow is smaller, closer to me. I am young again, riding a bicycle through the cobblestone streets of La Vilette, climbing through the Carpathians on the bluest-sky day of July. We are standing on top of the world together, staring out at the valley below us.

You came all this way? I think I say. Or maybe I don't say anything at all.

Imagine, Pierre says. *If we had met when we were younger. If we had married. Imagine what our life could've been, Marya.*

I close my eyes again, and somewhere between sleep and waking, somewhere between life and death, between breathing still and taking my very last breath, I imagine it.

MARIE

France, 1934

The end seems to come upon me fast, even though it has been coming upon me for so very long. I have been ill and tired, having trouble with my eyes and with my ears and with my legs for so long, that it seems I will exist and exist and exist this way forever.

I continue in my lab until I cannot stand any longer. I am struck by a terrible grippe, and then I cannot move from my bed for days. Ève sends in doctor after doctor to examine me.

"I will find someone to make you better, Maman," she insists, squeezing my hand too hard in the darkness of my bedroom.

Ève is not a scientist. She does not know, does not understand the body the way I do. "It is time," I tell her, and now I know that it truly is. "It is time to let go."

But I am very weak, very tired. Maybe I do not tell her this at all?

Then, one morning, I awake in a sanatorium in Sancellemoz, and Ève sits by my bedside, crying, and I know. She understands now.

I AM SIXTY-SIX YEARS OLD AND I CONVALESCE, MY BONES NO longer able to carry the weight of me out of this bed. Nearly all day I sleep, but still I dream. Pierre comes back to me most of all, and the pain of losing him catches again in my chest, and I stop breathing for a moment. Then I awaken, and I start again. I am not dead just yet.

Ève does not leave me. She calls my name out in the darkness. *Maman, is there anything you need?*

I can see the shape of her when I open my eyes again, more a shadow than my youngest daughter. *The girl with the radium eyes.* I wish I'd learned to understand her piano music more when I'd had the chance. I wish I'd held her closer to me, loved her better, enjoyed her talent. *Maybe there is more than science for you,* I want to tell her now. *Play all the concert halls you dream of, find a man who is your equal and love each other.* But the words don't quite come out.

Of course, I will play you a song, she says.

So maybe that is what I have asked of her instead. Because then, there it is, the tinkling of piano keys, like raindrops on the metal roof of our laboratory the last morning I ever saw Pierre.

MAMAN. ÈVE'S VOICE AGAIN.

Hours have passed, or maybe just minutes? Or has it been days? My beautiful daughter, she is a shadow, hovering again. No, there are two shadows now. I wish for the second one to be Irène, my eldest daughter, my heart, my companion, my confidante. But it is not she. The shadow is much too large, much taller than Ève.

Someone came to see you, Ève says. *He says you were friends long ago, back in Poland.*

He?

The shape becomes a memory, and my sense of smell has not left me yet. I inhale: peppermint and pipe smoke. And then the icy river in Szczuki; the pine cones and fir trees lining the road where we last walked together.

Why is he here? He has lived his entire life without me, married Leokadia and became a well-respected mathematician in Poland, just as his mother dreamed he would.

Marya, he says. He must've sat down in a chair by my bed, because when I open my eyes again, his shadow is smaller, closer to me. I feel the weight of a hand on mine, and I know. I just know. It is *his* hand, and it still feels the same after all these years, all this time. I am twenty-two again, skating on the river, dizzy and laughing. Which is ridiculous, scientifically impossible. My bones are nearly dust. I cannot move out of this bed.

Why are you here? I think I say. Or maybe I don't say anything at all.

The biggest mistake of my life, Kazimierz says, *was ever letting you go. I should've married you.*

I close my eyes, and I imagine it: the different choices I might have made, the ways I could have saved my family. I might've lived so much differently: an anonymous life, a happier life, a Polish life. A life without science.

I OPEN MY EYES AGAIN, BUT EVERYTHING IS STILL BLACK.

"Maman." Irène's voice is very far away, like it is coming for me through a deep, dark tunnel. I feel her hand on my hand, Ève's hand on my other.

Kazimierz is gone, or maybe he was never here at all. Pierre is so close, I can almost feel his hand on my cheek, almost hear his voice calling out for me: Mon amour, *slow down, you are pedaling much too fast.*

I love our life together. How did I ever get so lucky?

But there is no such thing as luck. Only the choices we make. Only the work we undertake. Only the legacy we leave behind.

"My life might have been so much different," I say.

"Sssh, Maman," Irène says, not understanding. "I'm here now. Don't try and talk. Just rest. The lab is safe, I promise you. Fred and I will take good care of it."

When I close my eyes again, the blackness turns brighter, yellow and gold and ethereal, just the way the radium looked that night in our lab so many years earlier, as if Pierre had reached up into the sky, grabbed starlight, and put it in glass for me.

"Oh, Pierre," I say. "Look what you have done!"

He climbs up onto our worktable to sit within the glow. His face illuminates green and gold. "No, look what you have done, *mon amour.* All these years, all your brilliant work. Look what you will leave behind."

Radium has a half-life of 1,600 years, so it will exist on and on and on, long after I take my last breath.

Pierre disappears, and Irène and Ève have faded into the darkness. My radium glows before me now, bright and beautiful, powerful and healing. In the end, it is everything, the only thing.

Look what I have done.

AUTHOR'S NOTE

Marya Zorawska was not a real person, but she might have been.

The real Marie Curie was born Marya Sklodowska in Poland in 1867, the youngest of five children. She worked as a governess for the Zorawski family in Szczuki in the late 1880s, trying to earn enough money to move to Paris to study at the Sorbonne and also to help her sister Bronia get through medical school there. (Bronia, in turn, would help support Marya when she eventually moved to Paris.) But while working as a governess, Marya fell in love with the family's oldest son, Kazimierz Zorawski. They got engaged, but Kazimierz broke the engagement off due to the disapproval of his mother, who said Marya was just a poor governess who would never amount to anything. Shortly after, Marya moved to Paris to live with Bronia, changed her name to the more French *Marie*, and began her studies at the Sorbonne.

Kazimierz Zorawski eventually did marry Leokadia Jewniewicz, a budding concert pianist and daughter of a prominent mathematician, Hipolit. They had three children together, and Kazimierz became a prominent mathematician himself, teaching at Jagiellonian University in Krakow and the University of Warsaw, after World War I. (Separately, his father in law, Hipolit, was working on the theory of elasticity before his death, and his work was published posthumously in 1910.)

I don't know if the real Marie ever had any lingering regret over what happened with Kazimierz, and from everything I read, I believe Pierre Curie was her greatest love, her scientific equal and partner in every way. But Kazimierz reportedly spent the last years of his life sitting outside the Radium Institute in Warsaw, staring at the statue of Marie that had been erected out front after her death in 1934. It was reading that tidbit that first gave me the idea for this story.

The Marya chapters in this book are all completely fictional, a what-if, my own imagining of how Marya Sklodowska might have lived her life differently and become someone else, if she'd made one different choice. But the Marie chapters are all based on the real Marie Curie's life. The tragic deaths and ups and downs and scandals of her personal life as well as the highs and lows of her scientific career are all based on historical facts. I have taken a few fictional liberties for my story. Namely, I don't know whether Marie and Kazimierz ever saw each other again after 1891. Or what they might have said to each other if they did. And in that vein, the scene in the novel where he tries to stop her from getting on the train to Paris is completely fictional. As is the one where they meet again in a café in Warsaw in the summer of 1906.

I have also followed historical fact for the people surrounding Marie in her storyline: Bronia and Hela's lives, Pierre, Irène and Ève, and even Jean Perrin and Jeanne and Paul Langevin (who did reconcile in 1914, though later Paul would go on to have another affair). The Curies and the Langevins did vacation together in the summer of 1908, and there was also an incident where Jeanne struck Paul over the head, though to my knowledge it did not happen during their summer vacation and I took some liberties with that timing. The details of the length and breadth of Marie and Paul's affair are somewhat hazy and unknown now, though they did reportedly have a pied-à-terre in Paris by 1910, and the details about their letters, Jeanne's threats and blackmail, and the fallout in the press are all reportedly true. Marie did use electrolysis to turn radium chloride into its metallic state around the time she was with Paul, but I fictionalized that it was Paul who gave her the idea.

Bronia did tragically lose both her children much too young, as described here, and also outlived her husband and Marie. She was medical director of the Radium Institute in Poland when it first opened. Irène worked with her mother in the field during World War I and afterward at her Institute in Paris. She married Frédéric Joliot (against Marie's wishes—Marie did make him sign a prenuptial agreement), but he did grow on Marie after they married. Irène and Frédéric went on to win their own Nobel Prize in 1935, a year after Marie's death, for their work on artificial radioactivity. Ève became a concert pianist, then a writer (penning her mother's biography after Marie's death), and a war reporter during World War II. She married an American diplomat and later worked for UNICEF. She was the only member of her family *not* to win a Nobel Prize, though her husband, Henry Labouisse, did—he won a Nobel Peace Prize for his work with UNICEF. She also lived to be 102, untouched by the high amounts of radiation that would kill her mother and her sister at much younger ages.

I made one notable omission to Marie's family. In real life, there was one more living Sklodowski sibling in these years, a brother, Józef, a doctor, who lived in Warsaw and was a part of Marie's, Bronia's, and Hela's lives. I left him out of this story for my own novelistic purposes.

The city of Loksow is fictional, though all the other places in the book are real, from Zakopane (where Bronia did have a sanatorium) to Saint-Rémy, where Marie and Pierre did spend one last wonderful Easter weekend before his death, to L'Arcouëst, which was a summer playground for the faculty of the Sorbonne. Marya's women's university is fictional, but the Flying University was a real thing in Warsaw. And the real Marie did attend with Bronia before they both moved to Paris. In real life, the school became legal around 1905–1906 and later became known as the Society of Science Courses. After World War I, it became Free Polish University. Agata and the other women at the school with Marya are all fictional, with the exception of Leokadia Jewniewicz, who, in real life, was the concert pianist who married Kazimerz Zorawski in the years after he broke up with Marya. I wondered how her life would've been different too if Marya had married Kazimierz instead, and if she'd continued with her piano career instead of marrying and having children.

For further reading about the real Marie Curie's life, I suggest *Marie Curie* by Susan Quinn, *Madame Curie* by Ève Curie, and *Marie Curie and Her Daughters* by Shelley Emling. These books were enormously helpful to me for establishing the timeline of both Marie's and Marya's lives, and any errors or omissions here, intentional or otherwise, are all my own.

ACKNOWLEDGMENTS

SOME BOOKS come to me easily, their plots fully formed. But with *Half Life* I struggled for months with how I wanted to tell the story, where and when to set it, and who the main characters would be. Over the course of a year I began (and scrapped) two different novels called *Half Life*, each connected in a different way to Marie Curie and each set in a different time, with different characters than the ones in this final book. It wasn't until I was eighty pages in the second time that I realized that Marya Zorawska needed a voice, and that the real story I longed to tell was this one.

I am always enormously indebted to my brilliant agent, Jessica Regel, and even more so this time that she not only trusted me to figure this out, but also that she didn't think I was crazy when I called her and told her I was starting this book over, for the third time. I'm also so grateful that she read and encouraged me through the false starts to the final version, and that she never lost enthusiasm for me writing a novel about Marie Curie. Thank you also to the amazing team at Foundry who work so hard on my subsidiary rights and contracts, especially

Claire Harris, Richie Kern, Sarah Lewis, Sara DeNobrega, Marin Takikawa, and Natalie Todoroff.

Thank you to my wonderful editor at Harper, Sarah Stein, who was amazingly unfazed by me changing my mind early on, and whose wise advice and careful edits helped me make Marya's and Marie's stories shine. Thank you also to assistant editor Alicia Tan for helping with so many details throughout the process. I'm very grateful to the entire sales, marketing, and publicity teams at Harper for getting my books into the hands of readers. A huge thank-you to Doug Jones and Amy Baker for their continued enthusiasm and support for my work

I'm grateful to have so many supportive writer friends who are always there to listen and read early drafts. Huge thank-you to T. Greenwood, Maureen Leurck, and Brenda Janowitz who kept me sane with text and email support and offered early feedback. I always call my friend Eileen Connell when I get stuck on a plot point and she talks me through it—this time, she helped me figure out what the final two chapters should be. An enormous thank-you also to Jean Kwok and Marie Benedict, who read and offered their endorsements and support (even during a pandemic). And to Andrea Katz, who is an amazing champion of my books, but I'm also lucky to count her as a friend. To my friends on the homefront, thank you for the mahj and the mimosas and the Facetimes and the endless love and support.

Thank you to my family who always believe in my writing even when I'm struggling to figure it out myself. To Gregg for still being my best friend after all these years, and for always offering to be my first and most enthusiastic reader. And to my kids, who are amazingly wonderful teenagers and readers.

ACKNOWLEDGMENTS

Thank you to all the incredible booksellers and librarians who support my books and get them into the hands of readers. And last but not least, to my readers around the world who keep reading and discussing my books in their book clubs—an enormous thank-you for choosing to read my books and allowing me to keep doing what I love.

ABOUT THE AUTHOR

JILLIAN CANTOR has a BA in English from Penn State University and an MFA from the University of Arizona. She is the author of award-winning and bestselling novels for teens and adults, including *The Hours Count*, *Margot*, and *The Lost Letter*, which was a *USA Today* bestseller. *In Another Time*, her latest historical novel, was an Indie Next pick. Born and raised in a suburb of Philadelphia, Cantor lives in Arizona with her husband and two sons.

About the author

About the book

Read on

Insights,
Interviews
& More . . .

Q & A with Jillian Cantor

Why did you choose to write a novel about Marie Curie set in two timelines, a real and an alternate one?

I knew I wanted to write a novel about Marie Curie and call it *Half Life* for a year before I figured out exactly what story I wanted to tell. After two false starts, I kept coming back to one detail about Marie's life that fascinated me most of all: the fact that she had been engaged to Kazimierz Zorawski as a young woman in Poland, and that the only reason she didn't marry him was because his mother thought she wasn't good enough for him. So much about this intrigued me! There was the fact that this amazing, brilliant woman, who would later go on to change the course of science and win two Nobel Prizes, was deemed not good enough as a young poor woman in Poland. And then I read that in his later years, Kazimierz would sit in Warsaw and stare at a statue of her, erected after her death. All those years later, did he still regret not marrying her? But what if he had married her? Her life would've turned out totally differently if she'd never moved to Paris to get her education or met Pierre.

One of my favorite movies is *Sliding Doors*, and I've always been fascinated by that concept. How would life have turned out differently with one different choice? The train we missed, the job we didn't take, the person we didn't date or marry. I imagined that but on an even larger scale for Marie Curie. What if Marie Curie hadn't ever become . . . Marie Curie? I was fascinated by the way one choice would not only affect her and her family on a small personal scale but also how it would affect the course of science and history and the world in ways both good and bad.

But the real Marie Curie also had an amazing life filled with personal triumphs and tragedies, and I wanted to delve into that too. So I decided to set her real story side by side with the fictional Marya's.

What was the most challenging part of telling a story in two timelines, one real and one fictional?

There were so many challenging things! One big one was keeping the two timelines straight and remembering which characters lived (or died) in each. But also it was a challenge to remember how each character was slightly different in each timeline depending on the circumstances. For instance, Pierre Curie in Marie's timeline is never the same man as Pierre Curie in Marya's, so I always needed to remember those nuances and keep them straight as I wrote.

Marie's real life was so fascinating, and filled with so many highs and lows, that it was a challenge as well to stay true to and capture that while also trying to pace the story and make this work as a novel.

But it was Marya's storyline—the fictional story—that was my biggest challenge of all. I struggled awhile with the right ending for her and with figuring out a way to ultimately make science important in her story, even if it was on a smaller scale. ▶

Q & A with Jillian Cantor *(continued)*

What was your favorite part of writing this novel? Least favorite?

My favorite part of writing this book was figuring out the ways scenes could echo in both women's lives but could mean entirely different things. I loved putting Marya and Marie in the same places (in Sweden, for instance, with Pierre and the swans) but deciding how those exact scenes would play out differently due to the differing circumstances. It felt like a really fun puzzle that I was constantly solving and re-solving as I wrote the first draft.

I also loved thinking about all the things Marie might have wanted to change in her own life and giving her the power to do that in Marya's storyline. She manages to alter the course of her niece's and nephew's lives and she stops Pierre from walking in front of a carriage, and her fictional relationship with her musical daughter is much different than the one based on her real-life relationship.

My least favorite part was working on the scenes based on Marie's life that were marred by tragedy, and there were a lot of them—Pierre's death and the fallout from her affair and the death of her nephew and niece. I came to have a real fondness and respect for Marie and all the many obstacles she overcame to achieve what she did. So it was emotionally draining to keep reimagining and writing these terrible things that actually happened to her. But then it was inspiring, too, to reimagine the ways she always managed to persevere.

You're not a scientist, so what was it like to write about a woman whose entire life was science?

I still get a knot in my stomach when I think about my high school chemistry class, so it was admittedly a little daunting when I first considered writing about a woman who won a Nobel Prize in chemistry. But even though this novel is about a scientist, I think, at its heart, it's really about a woman struggling and pushing to be the very best in a man's world. I don't see *Half Life* as being about science as much as I see it being about gender and class and what it means to achieve as a woman when everything is stacked against you. These things are very relatable to me! That said, I really tried to do a lot of research on the science aspects of the story and hopefully got them right.

What's something that surprised you while writing this novel?

The most surprising things were details I learned about Marie Curie's life before I decided to write the novel. I knew that she and Pierre won a Nobel Prize for discovering radium. But the details of her personal life really astounded me. The idea that she almost married Kazimierz in Poland, of course, was surprising. But I had no idea that Pierre died fairly young and so tragically or how that would go on to shape the course of the rest of her life. I was also captivated and surprised by her sisters, and her daughters, and the amazing things they also achieved.

Which character do you relate to most?

I relate to Marya more than Marie on a personal level. Her life is quieter and ▶

focused on her family. And even though she has this burning desire to learn and make the world better, she also has this overwhelming connection to her daughter.

But my favorite character in the novel is Pierre Curie, the brilliant dreamer with his head in the clouds. I loved writing him in both timelines, and I was so sad when he died in Marie's story. I loved that I got to keep him alive in Marya's story and write him becoming an old man.

This novel is a departure from your last two World War II–era novels. Why did you take that leap?

In all of my novels I'm always drawn to writing stories about strong women who do extraordinary things, and so writing about Marie Curie didn't feel at all like a departure for me in that regard. I also have a penchant for telling stories that ask "What if?" And *Half Life* fits with that theme too. The backdrop and setting for this novel are very much different from my previous ones, but I found myself exploring the themes I come back to time and again: motherhood and sisterhood and what it means to be a woman and face adversity.

What are you working on next?

My next novel is called *Beautiful Little Fools* and will be out in 2022. It's a reimagining of *The Great Gatsby* from the women's points of view. It takes place before, during, and after the original novel and centers on the lives of the women and a detective investigating Jay Gatsby's death.

Reading Group Guide

You have a choice. There is always a choice. This refrain is echoed throughout the book, both by Marya and Marie. Do you agree or disagree with this sentiment? Do you believe Marya and Marie both truly have choices? Why or why not?

Marya's life splits into two versions in 1891 when she makes one simple choice: She decides to get on the train to Paris to further her education. Or she stays in Poland and marries Kaz. What do you believe is the greatest impact of this one choice on Marya's life? On Marie's? What about on the world as a whole? On science?

Compare and contrast the circumstances and opportunity for Marya in Poland and Marie in Paris. How much do you think environment and opportunity for the women shapes each one of their lives? Which one do you believe ultimately lives a better life?

Marya and Marie are technically the same person, and yet many of their choices and actions diverge in different ways throughout the novel. Discuss the ways in which their characters are ultimately similar. Different?

Both Marie and Marya have an important relationship with Pierre Curie. How does the scope of Pierre's life, and work, change in each woman's story? What is the importance of Pierre as a character throughout the novel? What is most important in Marie's life: love or science? ▶

Reading Group Guide (*continued*)

What about in Marya's? Which woman has the better love story? Which woman made the greatest contribution to science?

Both Marie and Marya say, "My body was not built to carry a baby." But how is pregnancy ultimately different for each of them, based upon their circumstances? Who becomes a better mother, Marya or Marie? How and why does Klara turn out differently than Irene and Ève?

In Marie's storyline, Leokadia marries Kaz but gives up her piano career. In Marya's, Leokadia pursues piano professionally and never marries, but she is still drawn to Kaz. Which life is a better life for her? Why do you think she still finds her way to Kaz in both storylines?

Near the end, Marya clings to her sisters' hands and says they are "three old women, forever connected to one another by blood and by love. And yes, by science, too." Marie is similarly connected to her sisters at the end of her life. But Bronia's and Hela's lives turn out drastically different in the two storylines. Compare and contrast their lives in both stories. Which storyline is better for Bronia? For Hela? How do Marya's actions irrevocably change her sisters' lives, in ways both good and bad?

From Poland to Paris to the rocky cliffs of Brittany to the front lines of World War I—what role does setting play in the novel? How does the setting help inform and shape Marya's life differently from Marie's?

In the very end, Ève plays piano for Marie and Klara plays it for Marya. What role does music play both here and throughout the book? How is the piano both different and the same for Marie and for Marya?

The book opens and closes with Marie on her deathbed, examining the choices she made in her personal life: love, marriage, education, motherhood. But in the very end she thinks that radium is *everything, the only thing*. What do you think she means by this? What is the importance of radium in both Marie's life and her death? How is this different in Marya's story?

Marya thinks that *half-life* is such a funny term, *so unscientific*. While Marie thinks in the end that the half-life of radium is 1,600 years, that her radium will long outlive her. Why is the novel called *Half Life*? Discuss both the scientific and personal significance of that term for Marya and for Marie. ∾

Excerpt from
In Another Time

PROLOGUE
Hanna, 1958

I haven't told Stuart the whole truth about where I came from. Because for one thing, he wouldn't understand. How could he, when I don't really understand it for myself? And for another, even if I did tell him, he wouldn't believe it. He would frown, and his blue eyes would soften, crinkle just around the edges, illuminating both his age and his kindness. *Oh, my dear*, he might say, as Sister Louisa once did, after I'd stumbled into the last-standing church in Gutenstat, freezing cold and sick with thirst and hunger.

Sometimes, even now, I wonder if I made it all up. If Max, too, was just a dream, a figment of my imagination. Impossible, like all the rest of it.

You have been through a trauma, Sister Louisa reminded me, after I first saw the doctor in Berlin. *Your mind plays tricks to protect you.*

And it was a strange thing, but when Sister said it, I almost believed her. How could she be wrong, after all? This nun with her wrinkly face, pale as snow, and light gray eyes, with her habit and her soft smile. She wouldn't lie. Then she pointed to my violin in my hand. *Can I hear you play, my dear?*

She touched my Stradivari. I'd had it since my sixteenth birthday, an extravagant present from Zayde Moritz, just before he passed. I was holding it when I came to in the field. I'd held it playing for Max, in the bookshop once, too. And sometimes the only thing to me that still feels real, even now, is my violin.

I have played the violin since I was six years old, and it has always felt a part of me, another limb, one that is necessary and vital to my daily survival. My violin connects my present and my past, my dreams and my reality. My fingers move nimbly over the strings, my mind forgetting all I've lost or forgotten. There is only the music that is my constant companion. Nothing but the music. Not Stuart. Not Max. Not now. Not the past, either.

"Hanna," Stuart interrupts me today. I've etched the date, November 6, 1958, in pencil at the top of my music, so I know it is real, so I don't forget. I do this every single day and have since I was living in London with Julia. While I sometimes still forget how old I am now, my fingers do not move as they used to. Some days my knuckles swell, and I must cover them in bags of ice when I get home after practice. I hide this from Stuart, too, like so much else.

Today, I'm practicing at the conservatory, as I do every day after the group rehearsal. The orchestra will tour again in the spring. We'll go around Europe this time, playing Bach and Vivaldi and Holst. London, Paris, *Berlin*. As first chair violinist, I must play everything right, everything perfect. Though I already know all the music well, it is not enough. I have to breathe it, too. It has to sink into my skin, into my memory, so I will never ever forget it, a sweet perfume that lingers on and overtakes all my senses.

When Stuart walks in, I rest my violin ▶

on my knee and smile at him. Dear, sweet Stuart who brought me into the orchestra's fold five years ago. He's ten years older than I am and would like nothing more than to marry me. Which he has told me on more than one occasion. But I laugh and pretend as though I believe him to be joking, though we both know he's not. *You're an old soul,* he told me once, as if trying to explain away our age difference. It was only then that I'd thought: *Maybe Stuart really does know me?*

"Hanna," he says now. "You have a friend here to see you."

My world in New York City is a bubble. Rehearsal and practice. I live alone in a one-bedroom apartment in Greenwich Village, and though I am friendly with nearly everyone in the orchestra, I wouldn't call any of them dear friends. Only Stuart. And it's only because he thinks he loves me, thinks he understands me. "It must be some mistake," I tell him, bringing the violin back to my chin.

"No mistake," Stuart says. "He asked for Hanna. He said the 'girl who plays violin like fire.'" Stuart laughs. His eyes crinkle. He is both amused and stricken by the accuracy of the description.

Once, so many years ago, when I was insisting I would have to give it all up, that I had ruined everything, Max had told me that I would have other auditions. Other orchestras. *And you can't give up,* he'd told me. *You play the violin like fire, Hanna. You can't give up on your fire.* ❧